PRETENDER'S GAME

The Hearts of Rebellion Series

Book One

Louise Clark

Cover and Book design by eBook Prep
www.ebookprep.com

November, 1999, 2015
ISBN: 978-1-61417-772-2

ePublishing Works!
www.epublishingworks.com

REVIEWS & ACCOLADES

"A thoroughly entertaining and sensual romance."
~*RT Book Reviews*

"…a story that will make you laugh, make you cry, and leave you satisfied long after the last page."
~Kayla Perrin,
USA Today bestselling author

DEDICATION

To Muriel Whitlock Gillespie Allen
Great Aunt Boots

CHAPTER 1

Edinburgh, Scotland,
February 1750

There was an air of impatient hurry in the Tilton household on this late winter evening. Sir Frederick Tilton, his wife Arabella, and their two daughters, Theadora and Isabelle, were invited to the home of Judge Malcolm Denholm, for a soiree he was giving. Invitations to the judge's parties were eagerly sought after, for Denholm was an influential member of Scottish society, and the Tilton ladies were pleased to be amongst those attending.

Sir Frederick, the general commanding the English garrison in Scotland, paced the scarlet, blue, and gold Wilton carpet that covered the floor of the drawing room. His hands were clasped behind his back, the knuckles of one slapping the palm of the other with each measured step.

An ormolu clock on the mantelpiece ticked away the passing minutes with relentless regularity. Sir Frederick didn't want to be late, thereby insulting his host, nor did he wish to be early and appear overeager. An hour ago, when he had finished donning his suit of rich chocolate-brown velvet with a contrasting gold waistcoat, he might have worried about the latter happening. Now, however, he felt there was real danger that the Tilton family would reach Judge Denholm's far later than would be fashionably acceptable.

The cause, he fumed, his speed quickening, was his eldest daughter, Thea.

For all her intelligence and charm, Thea couldn't grasp the concept of being on time. Earlier, he'd told her he wanted to reach Denholm's by nine o'clock. She had opened her large brown eyes wide and promised faithfully she would be ready. Then she had smiled a mischievous smile and told him he worried too much.

Tilton reached the end of the carpet, executed a snappy, parade-ground about-face and marched back the way he'd come. Here it was, eight and thirty, and Thea still wasn't ready. His wife, Arabella, was with her now, trying to speed the girl up. Gloomily, he wondered how much good that would do. Thea was a stubborn creature when she set her mind to something. The trait had already caused her to refuse several offers for her hand. In her obstinate way, she had decided she wouldn't marry until she found a man she could respect and like. Being a far too lenient father, Tilton had never pressed her to accept a suitor not to her taste. That was why, at the age of two and twenty, his lovely daughter was still unwed.

Tilton sighed. Suitable matches were not exactly thick on the ground here in Edinburgh. If he didn't find Thea a gentleman of rank soon, she would most likely remain a spinster all her life. With her vital, loving personality that would be a shame.

The clock rang the quarter hour and Tilton felt affectionate irritation rise again. Devil take the girl, would she never be ready?

Upstairs, seated in front of a dressing table and still wearing her loose powdering robe over her shift and petticoats, Thea critically inspected her reflection in the gilt-framed mirror above the table. Meticulously, she added a black satin patch to a point just below the corner of her wide, generous mouth. The task completed, she sat back, smiling with satisfaction.

"Thea," her mother said for the tenth time since she had

swept into her daughter's small, airy bedroom, "you look lovely, you know you do. But dearest, can you hurry? Just a trifle?"

Thea laughed, leaning forward to dust a little rice powder over her too-healthy complexion. "In a few more moments, Mama, I shall be ready."

Somehow Arabella doubted that. Though Thea's burnished golden locks had already been powdered, she still had to don her elegant satin damask gown, not an easy task over panniers, the wide oblong hoops that were currently fashionable. Hurrying Thea when she didn't wish to be hurried was like making water flow uphill—virtually impossible. Arabella refused to say totally impossible, because miracles did happen. Unfortunately, they happened very rarely.

"I want to be certain I look my best," Thea was saying. Her lips, the upper bowed, the lower full and passionate, curved in a mischievous smile, enhanced by the provocative placement of the black patch. Above a short, patrician-straight nose, her large, almond-shaped brown eyes danced with naughty amusement.

Arabella sighed. Few people could resist Thea's charm when she had a mind to use it, and her mother was not one of those hardy souls. "Your father will be wearing holes in the carpet from his pacing."

Serenely darkening her fair eyebrows, Thea commented absently, "Papa worries over trivial things. I'll talk to him when we go downstairs. I can always rouse him from whatever ails him."

This was the simple truth. Sir Frederick was no more immune to Thea's particular charm than her mother was.

At that moment, Thea stood up, an engaging twinkle in her eyes. "See, Mama. I shall be ready in no time at all. Jenny, my gown, please."

Arabella waited until the cream-colored gown was over Thea's head and being twitched into place by the maid, before she hurried off to warn her younger daughter, Isabelle, that her sister was finally ready.

Isabelle, who had been reading a stirring tale of haunted castles and runaway heiresses while she waited, reluctantly put the book aside to don her own peach-colored satin gown over a pale blue petticoat. While Arabella, already dressed in rose silk, was fussing over the final preparations to Isabelle's toilette, Thea appeared in the doorway of her younger sister's room.

"Oh! Thea, you look magnificent!" Isabelle breathed.

Thea smiled and glided into the room. "Thank you, dearest." Four years separated the sisters, and their natures were quite dissimilar. Where Isabelle had a penchant for light subjects and housewifely duties, Thea was of a more serious turn of mind. Not that anyone would dare to call her a bluestocking. Her beauty and wicked sense of humor precluded that. However, she enjoyed heated intellectual and political discussions, stating her opinions in a decidedly unfeminine way.

Though Sir Frederick bewailed this to his wife in private, he'd never been able to bring himself to remonstrate with his outspoken daughter. In English society such conduct would not have been condoned. The Scots, however, seemed to like opinionated ladies. Thea was one of the belles of Edinburgh society.

Now she was scrutinizing Isabelle with the critical eyes of an older and more experienced sister. Coming forward, she twitched a curl into place so it lay coquettishly over the younger girl's shoulder. "You look lovely, Isabelle. You'll dazzle all the interesting people at Judge Denholm's soiree tonight."

"Not if we don't hurry up," Arabella interjected practically. She smiled at her younger daughter. "Thea is right, my dear. You do look pretty tonight. I'm proud of having two such handsome daughters."

Isabelle blushed, not used to compliments yet. She had only just entered the society Thea had graced for the last three years, and lacked her sister's polish. There was no doubt she was lovely, though. Her skin was rose-petal soft and her features perfect. The expression in her round blue eyes was warm and gentle. Arabella had hopes of giving Isabelle a London season, and she thought a little experience in Edinburgh society would do her no harm.

When they reached the top of the wide, heavy staircase, Thea's mischievous dimple appeared and she raised a finger to her lips. "Shh! I want to surprise Papa!"

Arabella sighed, shook her head, then smiled as she followed her two daughters quietly down the worn steps to the spacious entry hall. As one of the footmen draped Thea's cloak over her shoulders, she winked at her mother. "I wonder what is keeping Papa," she announced in clear tones. Her silken skirts rustled as she swept toward the open door of the drawing room. There, Sir Frederick, still deep in his somber thoughts, could be seen pacing across the thick carpet.

"Papa!" she said, halting in the doorway. "Are you not ready to leave? Mama and Isabelle and I have been waiting for you in the hall for simply ages! If you do not wish to be late, you really must hurry!"

Her brown eyes glowed with naughty amusement. Tilton, without hesitation, forgot the irritation he'd been feeling at Thea's tardiness. It was always this way. Whenever he was faced with the vivid warmth of Thea's personality, her faults dwindled into unimportant flaws not worth bothering about.

A smile twitched at his thin lips. "Thea, I'll have you know, I've been waiting patiently for you ladies for some considerable time. I am quite ready to leave."

"Then, Papa, should we not be on our way?" Thea's eyes twinkled. "I would not wish to be late for one of Judge Denholm's parties. He is such a nice man and I know how you value his assistance."

"Wretch," Tilton said fondly. "I don't know why I put up with your teasing."

Thea laughed. "Because I make you happy, Papa, and everyone likes to be happy."

As they left the house, Sir Frederick reflected that as usual Thea had burrowed straight to the truth of the matter.

* * *

James MacLonan didn't care if he was late or not to Judge Denholm's soiree. In fact, if he had his way he wouldn't be going at all. He'd had enough of fashionable social gatherings during his travels on the Continent.

His reluctance was evident in the casualness of his dress as he stood leaning against the mantel in his father's drawing room, staring into a crackling blaze and sipping a glass of good French claret. His shirt was fine lawn, with deep falls of lace at the wrists and neck, as fashion dictated. At that moment, the soft material was only covered by a sleeveless white waistcoat, laced with silver. Later, he would don the sapphire blue coat that matched the velvet breeches he wore above white knee-stockings. For now he allowed himself to be comfortable in the overheated room.

He raised the glass of claret and sipped. As he watched the firelight flicker in the rich red of the wine, he remembered another night some two years before when he had been sitting before a fire, drinking wine and brooding about the future. That night he had been without hope. Tonight hope was there, but so was reluctance. He sighed, tossed down the claret, and crossed to a gleaming walnut table to refill his glass from the crystal decanter that rested on it.

Cynically, he surveyed the room he was in. It was a far cry from the crude cottage on the border of France where he had been billeted on that cold, wet spring night when his present and future had merged into a bleak, grim failure.

There, Henri Joubert's cottage had been no more than three rooms and a cramped attic. The rough wooden furniture was all of Joubert's making, sturdy, but lacking artistry and polish. In his father's elegantly furnished Edinburgh residence the ceilings were high, the windows large, and there were more than a dozen spacious chambers. Despite this, he was as dispirited in this luxurious residence as he had been in Henri Joubert's tiny cottage.

He could still remember the smells that permeated that little cottage. There was the pervasive odor of the onions and garlic that Madam Joubert used constantly in her cooking, the rank smell of unwashed bodies, the reek of cheap tallow candles, and the smoky scent of a wood fire. These smells were so common that James had hardly noticed them. He did remember that on that night he *had* noticed the rich, pungent scent of the dark burgundy wine in his glass as he savored it. Little pleasures were all he had left in those days. Perhaps, if he did not fulfill the terms of his pardon, they would once again become all that remained to him.

Impatiently, he flung himself away from the table, over to the fireplace, where he used the excuse of a sputtering log to kick away some of his anger, frustration, and yes, fear. He could never forget the despair that had enveloped him that night, as he stared into his wine and catalogued all he had lost. He was an exile, a Scot who had fled to France for his part in the failed rising of Bonnie Prince Charlie. He had become a mercenary soldier in another nation's army, an outsider in a foreign land.

As long as he lived he would remember those feelings, and he admitted now to himself that he would do anything to avoid being in that position again. He had returned to Scotland and this time he intended to stay.

And yet, a part of him was reluctant to make the concessions that he knew he must in order to fulfill the terms of his pardon. That was why he was standing in this handsome room, brooding about the past instead of dressing in his elegantly furnished bedchamber for the evening ahead.

At that moment the sound of a cane tapping slowly along the oaken floors announced the arrival of Grant MacLonan, James's aged and infirm father.

Grant MacLonan was a big man of over six feet. Once straight and hale, he was now slightly bent and the flesh seemed to have wasted from his large frame. He continued to dress with care, however. In fact, as he entered the room it was clear that he was far more formally attired than his errant son. His coat, with its wide cuffs turned back almost to the elbow to expose the cascade of lace at his wrists, was plum-colored silk, the waistcoat cream-colored and laced with opulent gold. At his knees and on his black shoes were buckles set with diamonds. The garments proclaimed him for what he was—a man of wealth and position.

He stopped when he saw his son standing by the hearth. "Jamie! Have you changed your mind, laddie? Are you not going to Denholm's this evening?"

James swirled the wine in his glass and fought resentment. "No, sir, I am going."

"Then you'd best dress a shade more formally! What damn fool notions did you pick up while you were gallivanting about on the Continent?"

Damn fool notions. James drank deeply, once again remembering that night two years ago when his bleak reflections had been interrupted by the noisy clank of metal and the snort of a horse.

France, 1748

James stiffened warily, his mind suggesting, then discarding reasons for the sound. On a night like this one, storming and cold, only those with urgent business would be out. Something was afoot, but what?

The answer came surprisingly quickly. A fist hammered on the cottage door, demanding entry. James rose lithely to his feet and grabbed for the sword he always kept within reach of his hand, as Henri Joubert hastened to answer the knock, scuttling from the small bedroom where he cowered with his family. By the time the Frenchman had the door ajar, James's blade was out of the sheath and at the ready. Firelight glinted on the naked steel.

"That's a fine welcome for an old friend!" mocked a lazy, English-accented voice.

James peered through the dim light. He hadn't bothered with candles this night, for the fire that warmed the cottage was all he needed while he drank wine and let himself be eaten by regret. But now he wished he had a dozen candelabra to illuminate the room. He thought he must be dreaming, for he could not believe he'd identified the voice correctly.

Still holding his sword at the ready, he edged over to the

fireplace, now smoking from the draft caused by the open door. Grabbing a spill, he thrust it into the flames, then used the burning reed to ignite a tallow candle standing in a crude pottery holder on the mantle. This he raised so he could better see his visitor's face.

"By God! Staverton, it is you!" He tossed the sword on the table, then clapped his friend on the shoulder in wordless delight. The viscount responded in kind and for a moment there was silence. Then James stepped back, eyeing the sodden cloak his friend was wearing over a plain, dark coat, breeches, and riding boots.

"You must be frozen, Staverton. Here, come before the fire. I'll have Joubert help your coachman stable your horses."

"Horse," Lord Staverton corrected softly. "I rode, MacLonan. A man can evade patrols better that way."

James sucked in his breath at this information, but he didn't ask for reasons or details, not yet. "Hey, Joubert! I want you to look after my visitor's horse. And be quick about it!"

The little Frenchman mumbled an abject agreement, bobbing his head in an unamusing parody of a bow, his eyes downcast. An expression of contempt crossed James's patrician features. In Scotland, where he had been raised, the Highland clans were closely knit units and even the poorest man felt he had the right to stand up to his chief and speak his mind. James had been taught to treat people with respect, but in the France of Louis the fifteenth, the lower classes had few rights and even fewer expectations of decent treatment. He despised his own role in this country.

While they waited for Joubert to return, James offered Lord Staverton wine. Wordlessly, as he tossed his wet cloak on the back of a chair, the viscount nodded agreement. Then he stood before the fire rubbing life back into his cold fingers. James pulled up a second chair for him and they sat.

"How long are you quartered here?" Staverton asked conversationally.

"Until campaigning begins again. A few weeks, no more."

"How do you stand it?" the viscount murmured, withdrawing an enameled snuffbox from one pocket and flicking it open with a practiced turn of his wrist. He offered it first to his friend.

James shook his head, then laughed shortly. "I've lived in worse places."

"That hardly seems possible." As he looked around at the simple furnishings and bare plank walls, Staverton absently took a pinch of snuff and inhaled. "You could be in Vienna or Madrid, James. Why here?"

Pent-up anger flashed in MacLonan's hard blue eyes. "You know why!"

Staverton contemplated his wine glass. "You found yourself in exile because you fought in the rebellion. Your brother was killed and your aging, chronically ill father was imprisoned. That does not explain why you took service with the French."

"Damn you, Staverton!" James crashed his glass on the table. Wine sloshed over the edge on to the scarred tabletop. "You know what went on in Scotland after the rebellion. You know about the slaughter at Culloden and reprisals through the Highlands that followed!"

"Yes, I know!" The lazy, indolent manner fell from Staverton as easily as he'd shed his wet cloak. Beneath lay a hard, determined man, far colder and much more calculating than James MacLonan. "I know because I was there! I fought at Culloden, James. I was on the Prince's staff and I saw the clansmen fall. I fled the field with our inglorious leader, but before I did I watched our men die. I've no love for King George or the Whigs who support him, but I am well aware that they are not the English people."

At his words, James stiffened. "I meant no disrespect, Staverton. I know there were Englishmen who supported the Prince as faithfully as the clans did."

Staverton accepted that with a brief nod. He eyed his friend shrewdly. "I think you feel guilty that you were not with the Prince at the end."

James toyed with the wine glass. "I would have been at

Culloden if I could."

"Then you would have died beside your brother."

"It was not my decision to leave Scotland!"

"No, it was mine and Neil's and your father's." Staverton's voice softened and his expression warmed. "You were grievous wounded, James, when we put you on board that ship bound for France. We all knew by then that the Prince was not capable of leading us to victory. Neil and your father...they knew the future would be uncertain. If the Whigs won, exile would be the only way for those Jacobites who fought for the Prince to survive. You were in no state to be able to move quickly. They wanted you safe, MacLonan. So we smuggled you on board a ship sailing to France when you were too weak to protest. It was for the best."

"It has cursed me," James muttered.

They were interrupted by Joubert, who crept into the hovel, bringing with him a gust of cold, damp wind.

"Shut the door, you fool!" James snarled. Since taking up his commission he'd found it expedient to slip into the prevailing manners of his brother officers, even though he knew they were wrong.

Joubert made haste to obey. "The horse is stabled, milord," he whined, slinking along the wall toward the little back room.

"Good. Then get upstairs and take your family with you," James ordered. "And shut the trap behind you. I don't want you eavesdropping on my conversation!"

"Of course, milord. I wouldn't think of it, milord." He bowed low, almost scraping the floor. Guilt gnawed at James. The little attic room had no heat and damn little space for two adults and three children. To force his French hosts up into that tiny enclosure was a cruelty he disliked, but what Staverton had to say to him was private. Although they were speaking English, he would take no chances that Joubert might overhear and understand what was being said tonight.

Staverton waited in silence until Joubert and his family were safely locked away. Then he reached into one pocket and pulled out a letter. "Your father asked me to deliver this."

James considered the sealed parchment. Mail from England was slow, but it did get through. It was read by both governments, of course, to be sure no state secrets were being communicated, but James and his father were not in the habit of exchanging bits of political news.

"Are you mad, Staverton? You were only pardoned a few months ago! Why jeopardize your freedom now?" His face twisted as he turned the paper in his hand. "Or did you so enjoy those months you spent wandering about Europe acting the fop and proving to the Whigs how very unthreatening you could be, that you are prepared to do it again?"

A little smile twitched the viscount's hard mouth. "You are closer than you know, MacLonan."

"You were given a pardon, Staverton. Your exile was lifted. You were able to go home. Because I was serving in the French army, I was exempted from the general pardon. France and England are at war and to English minds, I am twice a traitor, first for joining the Pretender's rebellion, then by throwing in my lot with France. But you! Why risk your freedom for,"—he held up the thin parchment—"for this!"

"Read it," suggested the viscount gently. "Then we can talk."

James scrutinized his friend's face, but Staverton was a past master at masking his expression. Finding no answer there, MacLonan broke open the seal. It took him some minutes to grasp the contents of the letter because he had to read the shaking scrawl several times before he'd believe what he saw on the paper. He looked up, his thick, dark brows drawn tight in a frown. "You know what is written here?"

Staverton nodded. "Not the actual words, of course. But your father and I discussed the subject before he composed the letter."

"He thinks he can arrange a special pardon for me. He wants me to resign my commission."

The viscount nodded again.

"How," James demanded, "does he expect to acquire this special pardon? Why would the Whigs agree to a pardon for me now? I'm still fighting for France. To them I remain the traitor I was a few months ago."

"Money." Staverton laughed. "He'll buy you a pardon."

"From whom?" James retorted incredulously. The Whigs in Whitehall were no more—and no less—corrupt than any other government of their day, but the rebellion had frightened them badly. For some Scottish rebels, no amount of money could buy them a pardon.

Staverton leaned forward, his hazel eyes compelling. "Listen to me, MacLonan! The Prince of Wales and the King are feuding again and the Prince is short of funds. If you will but make an appearance of repentance, the pardon is yours! Rumor has it that peace talks to end this damnable war will begin in weeks. Resign your commission now, before that occurs, and people will assume you've come to your senses and refuse to fight on the side of England's enemies."

"So simple," James mocked. "And what am I to do until the pardon is bought?"

Staverton hesitated, then grinned. "Come with me on a Grand Tour of Europe."

MacLonan shot him a sardonic look. "What you mean is, we must grace the salons of every fashionable idiot on the Continent!"

"And see the sights. Visit museums. MacLonan, the Grand Tour is a perfectly respectable way for a man of your education and breeding to pass a year or more without an eyebrow raised or a question asked."

James downed his wine, then restlessly moved to refill his glass. The bottle was empty. He banged it down onto the scarred surface of the crude table and rose. Surefooted in the dim light, he crossed the room to retrieve another bottle. Staverton waited silently, allowing James to mull over the situation before he made a decision.

When he returned with the open bottle, James filled his glass and the viscount's before sitting heavily on the wooden chair. "I hear Glenmuir was burned by the English after Culloden."

"The Whigs wanted to ensure that another rebellion did not occur. We frightened them, MacLonan, with our march into England." Staverton's voice grew wistful. "We came so close..." He shook himself and became brisk once more. "The reprisals were brutal. No one can deny that. Innocent clansmen transported or hung, women raped, homes and lands burned. The laws now forbid the speaking of Gaelic, wearing the tartan, or bearing arms. The Whigs are determined that a Jacobite host will never again march out of Scotland toward London."

"Forbidding men to wear the tartan will not stop them from hating the English. Nor will a law prevent them from keeping their arms. They'll just bury them the way they did before." James moved restlessly. "The estate needs a master, someone to take the rebuilding in hand to bring prosperity back to it. The clan also needs a leader."

"Your father cannot do it. When he was freed from prison he gave his parole that he would not go to Glenmuir. The terms of his freedom have not changed. He's now allowed to stay in Edinburgh, rather than in London, but..."

"Will this pardon give me any more freedom than my father's has? Will it allow me to live in the Highlands?"

"I don't know," Staverton said honestly. "Your father wants to see you back in Scotland. He feels the lack of a master at Glenmuir keenly. The steward there, Gregor MacLonan, does his best to manage the lands and the people, but he's not the clan chief. Or his son."

"I know that!" James retorted impatiently. "But to return, only to be an exile in England—"

"Is being an exile in France any better?" the viscount countered.

"Damn you, Staverton, you've always had a smooth way with words, especially when it suits your own ends." The comment was a bitter one, but there was a soft shading of amusement in MacLonan's voice.

"This is your chance, James, take it! If you do not, you will remain an exile for the rest of your life. Your father's estates will be forfeited on his death and, I'm sure, so will his fortune. Listen to me. To return is no crime. Others have already done so. The terms of the pardon may force you to live in London for a few years to prove your reliability, but they may not. Think, MacLonan. You are needed at home, not wasting your life as a mercenary for France!"

James stared bleakly into the fire, considering possibilities and probabilities. Finally, he looked over at his friend. A smile lightened the grim planes of his face. "A year or so of gawking at bad paintings and playing the fool at society parties. If Whitehall only knew the sacrifices I am willing to make for this damned pardon, they'd allow me to return to Glenmuir immediately!"

Staverton laughed and raised his wine glass. "To the future."

James looked at the wine in his glass, then slowly followed suit. "To the future."

CHAPTER 2

Edinburgh, Scotland,
February 1750

Grant MacLonan thumped his cane. He was sitting in one of the solid wing chairs that filled the drawing room. He had no use for the delicate furnishings in the style made popular by Louis the fifteenth of France. Grant labeled them spindly and not made for a man to sit in. He preferred comfort to fashion.

"Jamie! Will you do me the honor of paying attention to me when I talk?"

James returned to the present with a start. "I'm sorry, sir. I was thinking of other things. You were saying?"

Grant shot his son a shrewd look from beneath bushy white brows. "I was speaking of Judge Denholm and advising you that he was a useful man to know."

James drank wine and considered the form of Judge Denholm's power. "He attracts the best of Whig society, does he?"

"Aye, he does, Jamie, and there is no reason for you to be contemptuous of it. Denholm believes in Scotland, but he's no fool. He's not about to cast in his lot with a quick-talking weakling."

James looked at his father. The expression in his blue eyes had hardened perceptibly. "I will not deny there were many who followed Charles Edward Stuart because of his charm and his way with words, but there were those of us who chose to support him because of what he stood for." James tossed off the claret in the glass in one smooth, angry movement.

Grant sighed. "Jamie, do you still adhere to the Pretender?"

James pushed away from the mantel. He crossed impatiently over to the table holding the decanter of wine. "No," he said curtly, concentrating on pouring himself another glass. It was a suitable excuse not to look at his father.

"I'm glad," Grant said simply. "The Stuarts have claimed enough MacLonan blood."

James's hand tightened around the neck of the crystal bottle. A sharp, angry retort hovered on his lips. For the thirty years prior to the Rebellion, a wily Grant MacLonan had kept his clan free from the constant political struggle between Jacobite and Whig that had torn Scotland apart. It had taken his son Neil, hotheaded and stubborn, to embroil the MacLonan clan in war. The decision by Neil and James to support Bonnie Prince Charlie had driven a wedge between father and sons and created a rift that had taken death and exile to mend.

The arrival of the Viscount Staverton saved James from uttering words that he would later have regretted. As usual, Staverton was able to assess the situation quickly and accurately. He interjected smoothly, "Since the Prince was exiled from France and decided to travel incognito about Europe, he has lost the respect of most of the Jacobites who were long-time supporters of the Stuart cause. I doubt that he would be able to raise another army if he returned to Britain again."

James carefully put the decanter back on the table. His knuckles were white, he noticed. Slowly, as he released his stranglehold on the container, the skin started to return to a more normal color. "Any man who clings to a belief the Stuarts would make better kings of Britain than German George is blind, or a fool."

"Alas, too true," Staverton murmured.

Grant shifted in his padded chair. "Aye. Bonnie Prince Charlie never fulfilled the promise he once showed."

James snorted. "I sometimes think the fellow became deranged during his months on the run in the Highlands." He moved to a chair opposite his father's and flung himself into it. "Since Louis of France threw him out, he's been acting as if the English have a price on his head."

"They do," Grant observed mildly. "Thirty thousand pounds, I believe."

James scowled at the glass in his hand, then suddenly grinned. "And what would they do if they caught him? Hang him? That would do the Stuart cause more good than leaving the Prince alive and free to make sane men more scornful with every one of his mad acts."

Staverton stirred restlessly in his comfortable chair. "Let us hope that no one in the government has the opportunity to put the idea to the test. Let the Prince continue his games. He is having a wonderful time using disguises, calling himself by aliases, and deliberately obscuring his movements. While we were in Europe one could never be certain whether or not he might turn up at a party or in a museum. It became very wearing."

"It was damned annoying," James growled. "It is all very well for the Pretender to call himself Chevalier Douglas or Mr. Smith, or some such nonsense, and indulge in a game of hide-and-seek to assuage his pride, but it does his cause no good. No, King George and the Whigs don't want to capture him. They're too shrewd not to realize the Prince is his own worst enemy."

"I'm sure they would like to know exactly where he is, however," Grant said tartly.

Staverton said musingly, "Europe certainly buzzed with the Prince's diverting antics. I understand that there has been much correspondence speculating on exactly where he is and what he might be doing."

"As long as he is harmlessly racketing about Europe, hatching one fantastic plot after another, there's no need to worry." James's mouth tightened into a thin line. "And I pray he remains in Europe! If he is fool enough to return to Scotland..." He didn't finish the thought. There was no need to. They all knew Scotland could not sustain another war like that of '45. This time England's reprisals would be even bloodier than before.

James downed the claret and stood up, his movements abrupt, decisive.

"You're going to Denholm's?" Grant asked.

James raised one dark eyebrow. "Was that ever in doubt, sir?"

Slowly, Grant shook his head. His gaze ran over his son's careless dress and he said briskly, "When you've donned your coat and a proper wig, come down and fetch me here. Lord Staverton will keep me company while I wait."

James frowned. Grant rarely stirred from his comfortable residence these days, and almost never for a mere social evening. James hadn't expected him to be going to Denholm's soiree. "Surely, sir, that is not necessary—"

"Not necessary?" Grant bellowed, thumping his cane for emphasis. "Indeed, sir, it is! Do you think I would not bestir myself to see my son properly launched in Edinburgh society?"

James grinned. He was not the only stubborn MacLonan.

The rooms in which Judge Denholm held his soiree were large, lofty, and despite the frosty temperature out of doors, overly warm. Dozens of beeswax candles provided a soft, mellow light, but added to the heat generated by a hundred silk-and-velvet-clad bodies. The atmosphere was redolent of fragrant perfumes, smoky beeswax, and earthy human sweat.

Neither the heat of the room nor the pungent aroma detracted from the enjoyment of Denholm's many guests. Conversation was animated and voices were raised in laughter or to emphasize one point or another. In the background, often drowned out, a violin quartet played a pleasant harmony. Good French wine flowed freely, and set apart in one of the elegantly decorated rooms, a buffet table was loaded with the exquisite concoctions the judge's French cook had labored over for days.

Theadora Tilton was thoroughly enjoying herself. At the moment she was standing in the largest room, energetically fanning her cheeks to dispel at least a measure of the heat. Beside her, her sister Isabelle's stiff posture indicated that she was more than a little intimidated by the august company.

Thea's admirers that evening had included Judge Denholm himself, who stopped to give Thea all of the details of the history of Scotland he was writing; the Duke of Argyll, a powerful Whig politician who had ruled Scotland in England's name in the years prior to the rebellion; and Mr. Brendon Ramsey, a member of the wealthy merchant class known as Tobacco Lords. Each was a mature man, well into or, past middle age, and so certain of his position and power that he felt no threat in conversing with an intelligent, opinionated woman.

Though Judge Denholm was a widower, the other two were long married, and their flattering attendance on Theadora Tilton did not stem from a desire to court her. Denholm, too, was not a suitor or likely to be one—he was reputed to be enamored of a plump widow near to him in age and endowed with a substantial fortune by her first husband.

Not that Thea cared if the intelligent gentlemen who buzzed around her had marriage on their minds. Over the past three years she had met most of the members of polite Edinburgh society, and there was not a single gentleman who combined the qualities she sought in a husband. Never one to allow herself to be daunted by what she could not change, she accepted this and got what enjoyment she could from her busy life.

As Brendon Ramsey was drawn away, ending the animated discussion he'd been having with Thea, Isabelle drew an exhausted breath.

"Thea!" she whispered. "How do you do it?"

Thea turned lively brown eyes in her sister's direction. "Do what, love?"

"Know what to say to all these…these important gentlemen!"

Thea laughed at the awestruck note in Isabelle's voice. Several heads turned at the liquid sound. Thea smiled in acknowledgment as she replied. "It isn't hard. I listen carefully to what they are saying and think before I speak. That way I don't babble the first thought that comes into my head."

"I shall never be able to cope in society!"

Tender amusement danced in Thea's eyes and enlivened her delicate features. "Of course you will, Isabelle! You are young and green. When you have a little polish, you will get on as well as I." She tapped her sister's wrist lightly with her closed fan. "Remember, I have been out in society for nearly three years. I know most of the people…"

Her voice died off. She certainly did not know the gentleman who had just entered the room. His face was narrow, his cheekbones high. A sharp beak of a nose jutted over a wide, mobile mouth and a square, determined chin. But it was his eyes, intense, deep-set, and very blue, placed beneath thick brown brows, that made her completely forget what she'd intended to say.

He was watching her. Even across the room she could feel the heat of his gaze. It set delicious little butterflies fluttering in her stomach, a sensation she hadn't felt for many long months.

Her breath caught as the stranger's gaze left her face to rake down her body. Daringly, she allowed herself to do the same to him. Tall and lean, he had an appealingly muscular build. A sapphire blue coat lay perfectly over his broad shoulders, and was elegantly combined with a white waistcoat, richly laced with silver. Long, muscular legs were snugly encased in matching sapphire breeches. She found herself hoping he was as impressed by her figure as she was by his. Her wanton thought made her blush, and all of her cool, social poise deserted her in a rush.

His narrowed gaze returned to her face. Taking note of her heightened color, he smiled. Thea's heart began to pound. Every nerve in her body seemed to tremble. With embarrassment? Or excitement? Thea didn't know, nor did she have the leisure to reason out her extreme physical reactions to this man. She was too busy concentrating on holding on to what poise she had left.

After a moment, he looked away, saying something to the younger of the two men beside him. His action released Thea from her trance. She lifted her fan and waved it to cool her heated features.

"Isabelle!" she hissed.

Her sister, who was watching her with an expression of considerable surprise on her sweet face, demanded, "Thea! What's the matter? Why did you suddenly stop speaking? And you're blushing! Heavens, I haven't seen you blush since—"

Thea ignored her sister's questions. "Isabelle, do you see that man?"

Isabelle gawked around. "I'm not certain. Oh, do you mean one of the two gentlemen who seem to be coming this way?"

Thea, who had deliberately avoided looking in the unknown man's direction once she had been able to tear her eyes away from him, uttered a small, suppressed shriek. "What!"

"Miss Tilton," said a light tenor voice. It sounded familiar. Thea looked up quickly, surprised the stranger would have a voice that flickered in her memory.

He didn't. The voice belonged to the Viscount Staverton, a young Englishman whom she had recently met. Thea hardly noticed him, though, for the intense blue eyes of the stranger were smiling at her in a way that made her body shiver. Making a heroic effort, she managed to cover her scattered wits with a cloak of social polish. She smiled as she extended her hand. "Lord Staverton, is it not? How delightful to see you again."

The viscount bowed. He was a handsome young man, with regular features and a well-muscled body. At that moment, however, Thea could have been staring at a ghost for all she was aware of what she was seeing.

"I have come at the behest of my friend," Lord Staverton

said, "who was so bowled over by your beauty, Miss Tilton, that he positively demanded an introduction! I do hope you will forgive a besotted man's impetuosity."

The speech, spoken in a tone of world-weary mockery, was too much for Isabelle. She giggled. Lord Staverton looked over at her, his expression perfectly grave, his hazel eyes dancing with sympathetic amusement.

Neither Thea nor his friend noticed. From the moment Staverton began to introduce him, Thea's eyes had turned to his. Now she was caught in a stranger's gaze, aware of nothing else.

Vaguely, from a long distance away, she heard Staverton finish the introductions. As she lifted her hand, she savored the stranger's name. James MacLonan. The words had a musical ring. James MacLonan, she repeated in her befogged mind. The name suited him.

He caught her hand and raised it to his lips with an elegant little bow that spoke of France. His mouth brushed her skin. The caress broke through the trance that held Thea. Suddenly, she felt more vibrantly alive. When he smiled at her, everything seemed so simple. Instinctively she knew he was intelligent, and in the hard bones of his face she could read integrity.

They were well matched. Was this the elusive man she had sought for so many years?

Involuntarily, her heart said yes.

CHAPTER 3

She was beautiful, just as Staverton had pointed out when he'd offered to introduce them. Her smile was wonderful, suggesting wit, good temper, and a genuine happiness. James liked the combination. A woman blessed with such a smile would be easy to live with, a good candidate for marriage, in fact. Moreover, as he looked at her, his body was warming in ways he didn't want to contemplate in a public place.

He discovered that her hand still rested in his and that he was unwilling to let it go. Her skin was warm, throbbing with vitality. A bringer of life. A wife. With a little mental shake, he released her hand: slowly, reluctantly.

Staverton said smoothly, "Miss Tilton, may I inquire the name of your lovely companion?"

James heard the laughter in his friend's voice, but he shrugged it off. He thought perhaps he deserved to be the butt of the viscount's amusement, for he was responding to Miss Tilton more like a boy in the throws of calf love than a man with too much experience of life.

Theadora Tilton dragged her beautiful dark eyes away from his to focus on Staverton. A sudden surge of jealousy shocked James with its intensity.

"Your companion," Staverton was prompting gently.

His manners were perfect. Not for a moment did his expression expose what James knew was a very lively interest in this meeting. They had known each other for years, since they had both attended Oxford University, and they had been friends and allies ever since. It was to Staverton that he had vented his rage over the clause in the pardon that forced him to marry, and it was Staverton who had briefed him on the suitable women who might be at the party tonight. When he had mentioned Miss Tilton, Staverton had paused, then laughed very softly. Alerted, James had demanded to know what was wrong with the lady. The viscount had replied that James should experience Miss Tilton's charms for himself.

Staverton, as usual, was right. A man might try to describe Theadora Tilton's beauty, but he would fail to capture the glowing warmth that gave it life. And he was about to leave the field clear for James by taking away the pretty young woman standing beside her.

Thea laughed gaily. "Of course. How remiss of me! Lord Staverton, Mr..." Her voice shook slightly. "Mr. MacLonan. My sister, Miss Isabelle Tilton."

James murmured a polite "How do you do," while Lord Staverton bowed extravagantly over Isabelle's hand and said something ridiculous about the color of her eyes reminding him of the Mediterranean Sea on a clear day.

Isabelle gasped, blushed, and lowered her lashes demurely. She murmured disjointedly, "Lord Staverton! Oh, you are too kind!"

"I speak only the truth," he returned, apparently quite serious.

Isabelle blushed harder, but she was smiling in a way that said how pleased she was. James thought admiringly that Staverton had always had the knack of charming women. If the viscount had been the one with the wretched marriage requirement, he'd have been wed by now.

"My sister has only been out in society a few weeks, Lord Staverton," Thea announced frostily, shooting a cautionary glare in the viscount's direction.

Staverton smiled in a reassuring way. "I find Miss Isabelle's freshness quite charming. Miss Isabelle, would you care for some refreshments? I believe Judge Denholm's chef has outdone himself this evening."

Isabelle didn't hesitate. "I should be delighted, sir."

Staverton promptly transferred her hand onto his arm and patted it reassuringly. Isabelle smiled guilelessly up at him.

"Isabelle! Pray do not impose upon Lord Staverton's good nature!"

"I shall not, Thea," her sister replied innocently as she allowed the viscount to lead her away.

Thea's concern for her younger sister touched James. She was trying hard not to make a scene, but a little of her disquiet had slipped through. An urge to comfort her made James say gently, "She is quite safe with him, Miss Tilton."

She had been watching the couple stroll away, a tiny frown marring her smooth forehead, but at James's words she looked directly at him. Once again he was captured by her eyes. They were brown, dark and warm, endlessly exciting. He continued, a hint of rueful amusement in his words. "I believe Staverton was simply doing me a kindness by allowing me to be alone with you."

Thea dimpled at that, and a little of the anxiety in her eyes eased. "You know Lord Staverton well, sir?"

James smiled, but he chose his words with great care. "We traveled together in Europe, ma'am."

He deliberately kept the explanation simple. He wanted to soothe her, not frighten her with the reality of why he had been on the Continent. Thea's dimple showed again, and James relaxed. It had worked. She was reassured. He could now concentrate on finding out something of Miss Tilton without the lady worrying about her sister's fate in one of Judge Denholm's crowded party rooms.

She lifted her fan in a coquettish way, hiding her mobile mouth as she languidly waved the fragile creation. Above the fan, her eyes glowed with vibrant enjoyment of the moment. "You were saying, Mr. MacLonan, that you were in Europe recently?"

"I returned to Scotland only last week, ma'am."

Her fan moved, allowing James a glimpse of the

mischievous smile on her mouth. "You will find Scotland dull after the excitements and pleasures of the Continent."

"That, Miss Tilton," James replied fervently, "is exactly what I am hoping for!"

Thea's wonderful rippling laugh rang out. Forgetting pretense, she lowered the fan. James felt the full impact of her lovely features animated with pleasure.

She was, he thought, more charming than any of the jaded court ladies he had met on his travels. True, she knew all the sophisticated manners, the flirting looks and movements, the teasing notes that added to her beautifully modulated voice, but beneath the surface he sensed true depth and integrity, not the shallowness he had come to associate with society women.

"Indeed, sir! You must not admit to such an emotion or your reputation will be in tatters!" She tapped him playfully on the wrist and managed to arrange her delightful features into a serious mask. Her expressive, almond-shaped eyes still danced with amusement. "Instead, you must affect a languid air and...do you take snuff, sir?"

Smiling faintly, playing along with her game, James admitted he did occasionally indulge in the habit.

"Very good! Then, Mr. MacLonan, you must take your snuffbox—one of French manufacture, of course!—and hold it in your hand, thus!" She posed lazily, her head thrown back, one slim hand, palm upward, extended. "Then, sir, you must flick open the box, survey the company—in your most haughty manner, mind!—and as you indulge in a pinch of snuff,"—she made the motion suit the words—"remark upon what a charming little village Edinburgh is and,"—her voice dwindled to a slow, disparaging drawl and the expression on her vivid features mimicked the utterly bored one of a court dandy—"that you cannot imagine living anywhere else."

James was lost in admiration. Theadora Tilton was beautiful, she was confident, and she was intelligent. She would make a very good wife for a man, for the right man—for him.

The terms of pardon that had allowed him to return to

Scotland were constantly in his mind. The hateful requirements, and the unnerving possibility that he would not be able to fulfill them, would leap into his thoughts at unexpected moments, bringing a grim frown to his brow and a dark bitterness to his spirit. But tonight, in the company of the charming and very beautiful Miss Tilton, the familiar regret didn't wash over him. Instead, he joined in her playful teasing and knew only the pleasure of being with her.

Although he was chuckling at her outrageous sally, James pretended to look surprised. "Why, Miss Tilton! Is that not exactly what I told you?"

Laughing, Thea agreed it was. "But," she added with mock severity, "you did not quite have the correct manner, Mr. MacLonan. You must drawl and contrive to look—"

"As if I'd rather be somewhere else," James finished ruefully. "I am a simple Scot, Miss Tilton. I love my hills and heather. I would prefer to be here rather than anywhere else in the world."

Something he'd said made her blush and wave her fan a little too energetically for propriety. Exaltation surged through James. He'd touched her. He'd affected her emotions the way she had his. Perfect.

"Yet you went to Europe," she murmured, hiding her expression behind the fan.

Briefly, James hesitated. Then he shrugged. "A gentleman is expected to do the Grand Tour."

"So you and Lord Staverton roamed about the Continent, visiting moldy old museums and overgrown ruins." She laughed. "I cannot imagine either of you in such a situation!"

"We did participate in fashionable society where possible," James retorted distastefully, remembering the fevered, occasionally almost demented, search for pleasure he'd encountered amongst the titled class of Europe.

"And you hated it," Thea observed shrewdly. He started, looking down at her with a frown. She smiled gently, reassuringly. "I would, too, I think. I am a woman who likes to speak her mind and indulge in intelligent conversation. Heedless frivolity would become exceedingly tiresome."

Smiling, James caught her hand and once more raised it to his lips. "Miss Tilton, may I compliment you on being a lady whose personality sparkles with as many facets as a diamond, but who is far, far more beautiful?"

Thea's charming laugh rang out once more. "I see, sir, that you have learned your lessons well on your Continental travels. You flatter superbly! Tell me about the dusty old museums you visited and the wonderful ruins of ancient Rome! I am all agog to hear of your travels."

James raised a dark brow. "You truly wish me to describe the places I toured?"

Thea nodded. "I am fascinated by the culture of the ancient world, though I have never had the opportunity to journey to Europe." Her tone lightened, the teasing note audible once more. "So I must ask you, Mr. MacLonan, to indulge my curiosity and describe what you saw on your travels."

In the months James racketed about Europe with Staverton, he had visited, it seemed, hundreds of museums and dozens of crumbling ruins. They'd had no program, no purpose to their travels, except to avoid the appearance of fraternizing with other known Jacobites. The Pretender had begun his frenetic game of hide-and-seek with the Hanoverian government, so James and Staverton had simply gone where they knew the Prince was not.

Those months were bleak, desolate ones for James, yet to satisfy Thea's eager interest, he found himself trying to paint word pictures of what he had seen and done. He became more expansive under her interested questions, and was even able to describe in an amusing way incidents he certainly hadn't considered funny at the time. As she listened, her eyes lit with laughter and her appreciative chuckle expressed her pleasure.

Gradually, James felt a sense of rightness, of being exactly where he wanted to be, that he remembered, but hadn't felt since before his flight from Scotland, four years ago. He was home, home to stay. There were still obstacles to be overcome, but as his gaze caressed Theadora Tilton's animated features, he was certain he would have no problem fulfilling the terms under which his pardon had been granted.

From one corner of the large room Sir Frederick Tilton watched his daughter as she talked with James MacLonan. The conversation was obviously a lively one, for she smiled and laughed and flirted with the fellow in, to her father's critical eye, an outrageous way.

Clearly, she was enjoying herself. The general could only see MacLonan's face in profile, but from the way the man stood, his head bent, leaning toward her so he would be closer, and from the descriptive way he moved his hands as he spoke, he was as involved with Thea as she was with him.

Curse it! Tilton thought irritably. The chit could charm almost every man in this room. Why did she have to choose a newly returned Jacobite rebel to practice her talents on?

A Jacobite, moreover, who had more reason than most to be susceptible to pretty ladies whose political affiliations were the opposite extreme from his own.

A footman, dressed in rich blue-velvet livery, stopped in front of the general and bowing, offered him a glass of brandy from the silver tray he carried. Absently, Tilton picked up a fresh goblet, replacing it with his empty one. Downing a large swallow, he wondered if he should go over there and rescue his daughter from the Scot.

Might cause a scandal, he thought. The fellow was doing Thea no harm. If he deliberately detached her from the man for no obvious reason, these prickly Scots might feel the honor of their nation had been besmirched by England. Better to do nothing.

As commander of the English garrison in Scotland, General Tilton knew of the anger that simmered beneath the peaceful surface of Scottish life. Charles Edward Stuart's defeat on Culloden Moor had probably ended forever an effective Jacobite presence in Scotland, but the violence of the English retribution had created a sullen resistance that permeated every level of society.

As he was privy to many secret reports, the general knew for a fact that claymores and pikes had been buried in bogs and on the moors, not handed over to the authorities to be disposed of as was required. They were there, slowly rusting, waiting until the spark of bitterness flamed into open rebellion once more.

James MacLonan, Sir Frederick noted grimly, was a man of those wild Scottish hills. Even as he stood quietly talking to Thea, there seemed to be an aura of dangerous power about him, emotions leashed to conform to the strictures of society, but never quite suppressed and only roughly tamed.

Sir Frederick swallowed more brandy, studying the couple over the rim of the glass. At that moment, James threw back his head and laughed. Handsome devil, Tilton acknowledged reluctantly, with those strong, lean features and tall, muscular body.

Beside him there was the tap of a cane and a rather slow, dragging step. Sir Frederick abandoned his scrutiny of his daughter and her admirer and looked around. He immediately stiffened.

"They make a handsome couple, do they not, Sir Frederick?"

Tilton's brown eyes, so like his daughter's, but colder and much harder, narrowed. He bowed politely. "Mr. Grant MacLonan, I believe?"

Grant contented himself with a nod. It was well known that his infirmities didn't allow him to attempt the graceful bow usually expected in polite society. "At your service, General. It is so rarely my health allows me to go out into the world that I find myself meeting people I have only known through correspondence before now."

Tilton suppressed the urge to say something cutting. He knew Grant MacLonan to be as stubborn, independent, and intractable as the rest of his race, and on some levels he rather admired the Scot's gritty courage. MacLonan stood slightly bent, but barely leaning on his cane, giving no indication either on his face or in his manner of the ailment that plagued him or the pain he was rumored to suffer.

Grimly, Sir Frederick reminded himself that Grant MacLonan had been polished by age and infirmity into appearing to be a civilized, sophisticated gentleman. But the Scots were also men like his son, James MacLonan, dangerous, half-tamed barbarians who would never completely bend to society's dictates.

And that barbarian was presently charming his unwary daughter into a blind submission.

At that though, Tilton's first inclination was to inform Grant MacLonan to keep his son away from Thea. On the heels of this impetuous idea, he remembered Grant's wealth and his powerful connections, both here in Scotland and in London. Shrewdly, the man had cultivated politicians of every persuasion. His freedom and his son's presence in Scotland proved it. This conversation would have to be handled delicately.

Taking a sip of brandy to fortify himself, Tilton said blandly, "Your son seems happy to be back in Scotland."

"My son will not long remain in Scotland if he does not fulfill the terms of his pardon."

So much for subtlety, Tilton thought, a sneaking amusement twitching his lips into a faint smile. "I am aware of the requirement," he admitted cautiously. If the conversation was heading in the direction it seemed to be, he couldn't fault MacLonan's boldness, but he had no intention of being caught off guard.

"I bought my son the pardon," Grant said musingly. "I am a wealthy man, Sir Frederick, and James is my sole remaining child. If he cannot live in Scotland, what need have I for money? I do not mind using my funds to ensure he remains here."

Tilton looked at Grant MacLonan, a sudden fierce anger blazing in his eyes. "Let us speak plainly, sir! As you know, I am not a man who would lower himself to allow the prospect of a payment of gold to affect his judgment in matters of importance!"

Grant didn't flinch under the caustic lash of Tilton's tongue. "Then you are a better man than the Prince of Wales," he murmured quite truthfully, but somewhat wickedly.

As MacLonan's jibe was unerringly accurate, Sir Frederick wrestled with the urge to laugh and the knowledge he should, as a King's officer, give this irreverent Scot a sharp reprimand. He settled on the short bark of laughter he couldn't quite contain.

His red-hot fury having cooled, he glanced at his daughter again. MacLonan was right, they did make a handsome couple. And Thea, flirting and laughing with young James MacLonan, appeared to be quite taken with the fellow. "My daughter likes Scotland," he remarked at last, promising nothing, but offering the opportunity to begin anew.

Grant permitted a small smile to cross his weathered features. "May I compliment you, sir, on your daughter's good taste? Obviously, in this case, rumor does not lie. A truly intelligent young woman, as well as a beautiful one."

With true disdain, Colonel George Harris watched the bright flirtation between Thea and James MacLonan. A stocky, florid-faced man in early middle age, Harris wore a midnight-blue coat, of good-quality silk, which had seen much wear, as had his white waistcoat. The trim on his garments was braid, not lace, and hidden beneath the waistcoat, his shirt was not the fine lawn a wealthy gentleman would wear, but a coarse hemp. The buckles at the knees of his yellow breeches were simple silver, unadorned with glittering jewels. In Colonel George Harris's opinion, it was not wise to dress too richly when attending a party where one of the main guests was your commanding officer.

Harris was colonel of the regiment of dragoons stationed in Edinburgh. As the officer directly below General Tilton in the hierarchy of command, his position was quite a powerful one. However, he had neither the fortune nor the political connections to ever aspire to a higher rank. Here in Edinburgh he was able to mix with men of wealth and status, and he was content with his life, in most ways.

The colonel was a single man, a bachelor who had never, until recently, cared to subjugate his official duties to private ones. He'd reached the age of forty without finding a woman who had the passionate spirit to invade and capture his cold military heart.

Until he met Theadora Tilton, that is.

The first time he'd seen her, he had been on duty. There had been some sort of official presentation in the esplanade before Edinburgh Castle. A reviewing stand had been erected against the gray stone wall, and there the prominent Edinburgh dignitaries were seated. Harris's dragoons, in full-dress uniform, had been the guard of honor.

It was windy that day, he remembered, and the horses, well trained though they were, tended to prance and shake their heads. He'd been nervous. He had only recently been assigned to the Edinburgh garrison, and he had badly wanted to impress his new, rather formidable commanding officer. In the midst of trying to control his troops and his agitated horse, he'd looked over at the reviewing stand and lost himself in the mischievous brown eyes of the most beautiful woman he'd ever seen.

His lapse had been only momentary. His sense of duty was too deeply ingrained for him to be overwhelmed for long. However, when he was finally off duty he'd searched for, and found, the golden-haired vixen who had so enchanted him.

At first, the knowledge that she was Sir Frederick Tilton's daughter had daunted his ardor. As the general was connected to some of the most powerful Whig families in England, his daughter could have the pick of the young beaux in London. Gradually, though, he'd realized Sir Frederick was not a rich man. Indeed, like Harris, he was a serving officer who lived mainly on his pay.

The knowledge bridged the social gap between plain George Harris, whose family were sturdy gentry, and the aristocratic Sir Frederick Tilton, who was the cousin of an earl and the grandson of a duke. Suddenly Miss Theadora Tilton was within his reach, and Harris grabbed.

Not literally, of course. He did move to fix his interest with the lovely Thea, though. In the small, open society of

Edinburgh, Harris and his commander moved in the same circles, so he was able to see Thea with great regularity. He talked to her, he danced with her, he all but worshipped at her feet! Thea, however, never displayed more than the warm friendliness she'd shown him from their first meeting.

He had convinced himself she was one of those women who did not feel passionately, and he'd gone to her father to ask for her hand. Tilton, the arrogant devil, had turned him down, claiming Thea did not feel her affections could be engaged by Colonel Harris. Yet the very next time he'd seen her, Theadora had been as warm and friendly as before. Harris simply could not believe her father had ever spoken to her on the subject of his proposal. He would wait, he'd decided, and try again after a suitable time had elapsed.

Now, as he watched Thea's animated face, his dreams crumbled under the ruthless glare of reality. She was looking at a stranger—a man she'd only known a matter of minutes—with the passionate intensity Harris had always coveted for himself. Suddenly, the vengeful anger he had harbored against her father settled itself on Thea's delicately boned shoulders. The flighty wench was enjoying herself mightily, flirting with the Scottish rebel. How would she feel when she learned who he was and why he smiled so engagingly at her?

Harris bided his time, waiting until James MacLonan had been drawn away by Judge Denholm before moving over to Thea. She greeted him with her usual candid warmth, as a friend.

A pox on all fickle women, Harris thought savagely.

"Miss Tilton, you are alone at last!" Colonel Harris said heartily.

Thea smiled gently. "As you see, Colonel."

"You must be quite parched. Come, I will take you to the dining room where Judge Denholm has laid out a collection of delicacies to tempt the most jaded palate. You can refresh yourself there."

With James gone, Thea's bedazzled intellect was slowly

returning to its usual quick shrewdness. She heard the jealousy just below the surface of Colonel Harris's voice, and knew he'd seen her flirting with James MacLonan. Feeling a little sorry for him, she thought it might soothe his hurt pride if she allowed him to take her to sample the lavish refreshments.

Moreover, her conscience was bothering her. She wanted to find Isabelle and make sure the polished Lord Staverton hadn't overwhelmed her. And the last time she had seen the pair, they had been on their way to the refreshment room.

So she said in a friendly way, "Why, thank you, Colonel Harris. Yes, I would be delighted to join you."

He led her to the dining room, elegantly decorated in shades of pale blue and soft pink. A huge mahogany table was loaded with concoctions ranging from slices of spit-roasted beef and fresh oysters on the half shell, through rich fricassees served with sweet patties, and braised pigeon from the judge's own dovecote. A selection of fruit creams, meringues, and macaroons were provided for those with a sweet tooth, as well as cheeses to complete the meal.

Harris found Thea a chair set apart from those already filled, and went off to collect her a sampling from the heavily laden buffet table. While he was gone she scanned the room, mentally cursing Harris for tucking her away in this obscure corner. Isabelle was nowhere about. Ah, yes, there she was! Relief and a little guilt surged through Thea, for their mama was seated at the table with Isabelle. Lord Staverton was nowhere to be seen.

Thea was speculating whether Staverton had left Isabelle before Arabella Tilton had arrived, or because Lady Tilton had indicated he was not welcome, when Colonel Harris returned with a plate of delicacies. After thanking him somewhat distractedly, Thea made an effort to concentrate on what he was saying.

"Are you enjoying yourself, Miss Tilton?"

Conversations with Colonel Harris were always like this. He asked a perfectly ordinary question and Thea answered in a perfectly ordinary way. "Yes indeed, Colonel. Judge

Denholm has gathered a most interesting group of people for his soiree this evening. I always—"

Uncharacteristically, Harris interrupted. "I noticed a few new faces tonight."

Thea blushed. She couldn't help it. One of those new faces was James MacLonan's and she had just spent the best part of an hour in intimate conversation with him. "Quite," she managed to say, her voice strangled.

Harris's bass tones hardened. "Yes, James MacLonan. Fresh from Europe."

The way he'd said James's name was an insult. Thea's hackles immediately rose. "He mentioned that," she said. "He was on the Grand Tour. We had an exceedingly enjoyable conversation about the sights he'd seen."

Harris snorted derisively. "I doubt Mr. MacLonan went to the Continent in order to broaden his education!"

Thea reminded herself that Colonel Harris was a disappointed suitor, and counseled herself to be patient when she really would have preferred to snap his head off. "Colonel Harris, I think we should speak on other subjects. I do not like gossiping about people behind their backs."

Harris blundered on. "In fact, the fellow only went to France when Scotland became too hot for him!"

At first Thea wondered if James had committed some kind of crime. Then understanding dawned. "You mean James MacLonan is a Jacobite?"

"He didn't tell you?" Harris grinned nastily.

Thea's cheeks flamed and her eyes snapped dangerously. "You overstep your bounds, Colonel Harris!"

His mouth shaped itself into a feral smile, frighteningly close to a snarl. "Not only is the man a damned rebel, but he fought for France against us, once he'd escaped from the clutches of our Duke of Cumberland!"

She didn't want to know that James MacLonan was a rebel. Or that he had fought for France. She didn't want to think of him firing a musket at her father or her brother, who was also an officer in the army. She didn't want to imagine him in hand-to-hand combat, slicing and stabbing with a sword, trying to kill one of those she loved best. At that moment she hated Colonel George Harris with a passion. She wanted to strike out at him. Instead, she kept her voice cool and calm. "Then why is he here now, Colonel Harris?"

"He acquired a pardon, Miss Tilton." Harris made it sound as if James had gotten the pardon through nefarious means. "It is a most interesting document, my dear. The terms would fascinate you, I know."

Chills were running up and down Thea's spine. "Terms?"

"By which he is allowed to remain in Scotland. Would you like to hear them?"

The plate full of delicacies she was holding with one hand wavered dangerously. Carefully, Thea set it down on the empty seat beside her. She was afraid to look at Harris, to see the venomous glint in his eyes. She felt helpless, unable to move, unable to say the words that would halt his vicious tirade. "N-no…"

He paid no more attention to her protest than he had before. "Your father and his senior officers have been made aware of the requirements of his pardon, of course. MacLonan is a dangerous man! He claims to be reformed and no longer a supporter of the Stuarts, but…who can tell if a rebel is ever truly honest in his political assertions? That is why, Miss Tilton…" Harris leaned forward, his eyes now boring into Thea's. "That is why James MacLonan is required to marry a woman whose family has strong ties with the Whig party and are loyal supporters of King George and the Hanoverian dynasty!"

Thea felt the blood drain from her face. Harris laughed. "Why, Miss Tilton, you are quite pale. Do you feel faint?"

CHAPTER 4

"My dear, you must have another one of these scones. My cook is quite famous for them, you know." Olivia Ramsey held the plate of scones invitingly until Thea took one. Olivia rattled on, hiding a very real intellect underneath a pleasant social manner. "And don't forget to have some butter and jam with it. The berries used in the jam are from our estate outside Edinburgh. They have the most wonderful flavor! One of the reasons I just adore going there in the summer is for the fruit. Cook makes the most delightful concoctions. Lovely! Of course, that is not the only reason I enjoy going. Edinburgh becomes so unpleasant during the summer, don't you think?"

As the Tilton family did not have a Scottish country estate to adjourn to during the hot summer months, Thea just smiled and ladled some of the wonderful jam onto her scone. Arabella murmured something appropriate and the conversation turned.

The Tilton ladies, Arabella, Theadora, and Isabelle, were taking tea with Olivia Ramsey and one of her daughters. Olivia was the wife of Brendon Ramsey, the Tobacco Lord, and money was of no concern to her. She was a plump lady, good-natured, although she tended to ignore the sensitivities of others, and very proud of her husband's success in life. She had two daughters who had absorbed their mother's pride of position, but lacked her mellow temperament.

Indeed, they could both be exceedingly unpleasant when they chose.

With their father's fortune behind them, each of the Ramsey girls had married well and now spent little time in Edinburgh, much to their mother's dismay. When her daughters were away, Olivia found pleasure and companionship in other young people, particularly Theadora and Isabelle Tilton. As Brendon Ramsey was a member of the Scottish Parliament and so worked closely with General Tilton, there were many visits between the families. Usually, Olivia was on her own when the Tilton ladies stopped by. Today her younger daughter, Joan, was there. She was deep in conversation with Isabelle, leaving Thea and Arabella to talk to Olivia. That suited Thea just fine.

Olivia was beaming at Thea, pleased at her consumption of the scone and jam. "I do like a girl who has a good appetite. You must be feeling better today."

Thea paused, the scone halfway to her mouth. "I feel fine, Mrs. Ramsey."

"Good, good. Last night you were quite pale, and I did wonder if you were ailing."

Heat began to steal up Thea's neck. "Last night?"

"At Judge Denholm's soiree. I was in the supper room when you came in with Colonel Harris. He does seem to be a nice man, not encroaching at all, as you might expect from one of his sort. But I digress! I noticed that you became quite pale after he had brought you a plate of the judge's delicious refreshments, and I did wonder if you had eaten something that disagreed with you."

Thea put the scone back on the plate. Very carefully, she placed the plate on the table beside her chair. "I was quite fine, Mrs. Ramsey."

"Excellent, excellent! Such a relief to hear. But you were so pale, Thea. Was there a problem of some kind?"

Thea's stomach was decidedly upset right now. "No, no problem."

"My dear! Why, you are doing it again! What is the matter?" Olivia leaned forward and put her hand on Thea's in a friendly way. "Have I said something—oh!" Her eyes grew round. "It's Colonel Harris! Has he proposed to you again?"

The first scone felt as if it had taken up residence just below her breastbone and grown to triple its original size. Thea said weakly, "Colonel Harris did not propose to me last evening, Mrs. Ramsey. I doubt even he would be so thoughtless as to choose such a place for a proposal of marriage."

"Perhaps." Olivia looked as if she wanted to pursue this interesting topic, but Arabella jumped in with a question about the Ramseys' estate and successfully diverted Olivia's attention.

Unfortunately, Joan had noticed Thea's discomfort. She suggested rather smugly, "Perhaps Thea paled because Colonel Harris told her that James MacLonan was a rebel."

Thea lost what little color she still had, and Joan chortled with delight. "Why, I'm right! That is the reason Thea was so upset last night! Who would imagine it? A general's daughter, an *English* general's daughter, bowled over by a Jacobite rebel. Why, that's rich!"

"Joan, do be quiet!" her mother snapped. "If Thea did find Mr. MacLonan to be an interesting man, well, why should she not? Your father has a great deal of respect for the MacLonan family. He has done business with Mr. Grant MacLonan for nigh on thirty years and found him to be the most honorable of gentlemen. That is why he arranged to have him released from prison as soon as he heard—"

"James's father was in jail?" Thea asked.

Olivia waved a dismissive hand. "It is nothing to worry about, my dear! Nothing at all! They all were imprisoned after Culloden, all the clan leaders, I mean. Mr. MacLonan did nothing wrong, after all. It was very unjust to have put him in jail."

Thea sat up straighter. "He rebelled against King George, Mrs. Ramsey! How can you say he did nothing wrong?"

Olivia smiled and shook her head. "His sons rebelled, my dear. Mr. MacLonan did not. He is a canny man, the MacLonan. He made sure that it was well known that he did not adhere to the Pretender, even if his two wild sons did. The ploy worked very well in the end, for it got him out of prison and allowed him to do what was necessary to get James back from Europe."

"Ploy? Then it was true? He did follow the Pretender?"

"The MacLonans are a close-knit family, my dear. The two boys worshiped Grant, and James...well, James worshipped his older brother too. You should have seen them together, both so tall and dark, striding along, their kilts swirling about their fine straight legs. Two handsome men, my dear. James was the soldier, he led the clansmen, while Neil was the courtier. He was a member of the Prince's staff, you know."

"No, I didn't," Thea murmured. She wasn't sure if she wanted to hear all the details that Olivia was prattling on about, but it was helping her recover her color and allowing the odious Joan to forget her indiscretion.

"Yes," Olivia was continuing, rather misty-eyed. "The Prince took Edinburgh at the beginning of the rebellion, you know, and he gathered his army here. We saw them all; the young men so eager and brave; the chiefs, fierce, angry, determined; and the clansmen, just ordinary folk, here because their chiefs demanded it of them. The MacLonan brothers were at the center of it all. Fine young men, who believed in the Prince and everything he promised. I do believe they truly thought that they could defeat the English. And that it would be for the best! Yes, for the best! I truly believe that."

She looked at the polite expressions on the faces of the Tilton ladies, and for once showed some sensitivity to someone else's feelings. "But you don't want to hear about that, I'm sure."

Arabella murmured disastrously, "Not at all, Olivia. Your recollections are most affecting."

Olivia beamed and started talking about the Prince's army again. "I remember one time when James MacLonan's quick thinking saved a little girl from injury."

Thea's interest quickened.

"The Prince took the city of Edinburgh quite early in the

rebellion, in September it was, although he never did capture the Castle. That meant the guns could be turned upon us at any time, although for the most part one would hardly credit it. Most of the time, having the Prince here was like being part of a giant, never-ending fair. There were parades and reviews, with the Highlanders marching about, the pipes skirling and their kilts swinging about their brawny legs." She waved her hand. "Though that is neither here nor there. I was going to tell you about James MacLonan and the little girl, wasn't I?"

Arabella shot Thea a long-suffering look. "Yes, you were."

Thea caught herself smiling. Olivia Ramsey was a good soul, but she could be trying at times.

"Yes, well. The English commander—not your dear husband, Lady Tilton!—but a truly old and feeble man named Lieutenant General Guest, would occasionally shell the men as they drilled outside the city walls." She hesitated, looking dubiously at Arabella and Thea. When neither appeared disturbed she continued. "The bombardment rarely did much harm, but where the cannonballs hit, there could be damage from flying debris. James was one of the most energetic commanders, drilling his men nearly every day, to prepare them for the dangers of battle, I suppose." She frowned. "How dreadful! I never thought of it that way before. You know—"

"What was a little girl doing close to where men were drilling?" Arabella, the general's wife, demanded.

"Ah, yes, the little girl. Well, she had crept from her family's home to follow the MacLonans as they marched. She was, oh, all of twelve years old, I suppose, and quite besotted with the pageantry of it all. Well, the cannonballs were hitting the ground with great thumping noises, and for the most part no damage was done. The clansmen continued to drill, despite the bits of earth that flew about. Occasionally a ball would hit something more substantial, such as a stone wall, and cause a shower of chips that would injure a man, but the clansmen continued. That was war, James said, and they'd best get used to it."

"Very sensible," Arabella said. "Apparently Mr.

MacLonan was a capable commander."

"Yes, I think he must have been. Well, he also must have known this girl was nearby because suddenly, when another cannonball hit a tree and huge slivers from the trunk started to fly about, he bellowed something like 'take cover' and instead of doing just that, he dove for the girl. He knocked her to the ground and covered her with his body. That saved her life."

Unwillingly, Thea allowed her imagination to come into play at Olivia's words. She could picture James at the head of his men, tall and straight, his eyes gleaming with the fierce passion of an idealist intent on his cause, yet still the careful commander, training his men so that they would be ready for anything. And a thoughtful man, aware of what was going on around him, willing to do whatever he must to save another. "You say he saved her life," Thea said. "How?"

"Why, his quick action kept a huge sliver of wood from piercing her skin! He was wounded, not as badly as the second time, of course, but it was enough to put his arm into a sling for most of the weeks he was in Edinburgh, although he could not be kept from the fight at Preston Pans." She sighed. "It was a most romantic sight, the tall Scot marching at the head of his men, wounded, yet carrying on."

It was clear that to Olivia the war had been little more than a bright pageant for her pleasure. Yet Thea could not forget that the marching and drilling were preludes to a much darker occupation. Nor could she forget that less than a year later the clansmen who'd provided the pretty entertainment met the English army on the field of Culloden, and at the end of the day most were dead, while many more, like James MacLonan, took ship for France and exile.

And now James MacLonan was back. Until that moment Thea been deluding herself with the happy fiction that Colonel Harris had been suffering an excess of jealousy when he told her of James MacLonan's history. Unfortunately, everything he'd said was true. James might have saved a little girl, but he was a Jacobite, a rebel, and worst of all, a traitor.

If the rest of Harris's accusations against James MacLonan were true, what about the last, most horrible one?

There was one thing Thea was certain of. No matter how much she liked James MacLonan, she would not allow herself to become embroiled in his desperate schemes to remain in his homeland. The next time she saw him she would have to snub him. It was her only defense.

The musicians struck up a lively jig, for those energetic couples more interested in dancing than in conversation or cards. James MacLonan, having dutifully squired the pretty cousin of the Duke of Argyll onto the floor for the last country dance, deposited the insipid lady with her gushing mother and sidled away as quickly as he could.

He had just taken a glass of wine from a tray carried by a passing servant, when he noticed Lord Staverton standing in the doorway. With relief, he decided he could abandon his duty for a few minutes and converse with his friend, instead of leading yet another marriageable lady out onto the dance floor.

"So," Staverton said, his eyes amused. "How goes the campaign?"

"Wonderfully," James replied, taking a substantial swallow of wine. "I have danced with every unmarried lady here tonight and I cannot remember a thing about any one of them."

"Deliberately, James?" Staverton drawled. He waved to the servant and acquired his own glass.

James scanned the ballroom and considered Staverton's suggestion. Was it possible that he was trying to avoid the inevitable? That would not be a sensible thing to do, given that he must marry and soon. Besides, there was Miss Tilton. "I have very vivid memories of Miss Theadora Tilton. She is a very charming lady."

The amusement in Staverton's eyes deepened. "She is a Whig, James."

"Isn't that one of my most important requirements in a wife, at least according to the pardon?"

"It is," Staverton retorted mildly. "I was just reminding you, James, so that you would be prepared."

"Why? Do you think Miss Tilton would accept an offer of marriage from me?"

Staverton shrugged. "Perhaps. She is two and twenty and has been out in society for three years or more. Yet she is still unwed."

James found he didn't like the implication that Thea might be getting desperate to find a husband. He couldn't imagine any man not being enchanted by the lively, intelligent Miss Tilton. "God's teeth! I hate this cold-blooded business of taking a wife to ensure my freedom! Damn the English!"

"The Whigs, James, not the English. Don't tar all of us with the actions of a few politicians."

James sipped his wine. "When I mentioned Miss Tilton to my father, he spoke of her very appreciatively. He'd discovered that her family background met all the requirements of the pardon."

"Did he say anything else?"

James's mouth hardened. "No, I wouldn't let him. I didn't want to listen to the recitation of a pedigree." The jig ended and couples began to leave the floor. James scanned the room looking for Thea. He noticed the handsome woman whom Staverton had identified as Arabella Tilton, Thea's mother. He watched her, waiting for her daughter to return from the dance floor.

Distasteful as it was, he had no other choice than to comply with the pardon. He'd had enough of exile, enough of fighting another nation's wars, enough of wandering about Europe with no destination and no fixed point to return to. He was home now, and he planned to stay in Scotland for the rest of his life. If that meant taking a wife he didn't care for, so be it.

But he did like Theadora Tilton. The thought ran through his mind at the precise moment she glided up to join her mother. A portly man was with her. Theadora was laughing, and the heavyset fellow was panting as he bowed over her hand. Evidently he had just brought her from the dance floor.

James studied her for a moment as he swirled the brandy in the glass with an absent gesture. Her eyes were large, almost almond-shaped, set beneath thin, arched brows. Her nose was small, her chin rounded, the bones of her face strongly marked, but delicately made. Surprisingly, her mouth was wide and generous. She smiled easily, with great warmth and considerable mischief. At those times a dimple would appear in her cheek, an utterly charming feature that added life to an already animated expression.

The gown she was wearing, a pale blue satin, emphasized her fair complexion, just as the square-cut, boned bodice and fashionable hoops accentuated the natural curves of her figure. A disturbingly sensual image of the lovely Theadora dressed with much less formality rose in his mind. Sternly, he repressed it, but a small smile twitched his mouth. He'd wager his pardon that the lady would be a passionate joy to bed. Both fiery and playful, she would delight the man who earned the right to be her partner.

"She really is a beautiful creature," Staverton murmured beside him.

James had to agree.

The portly man moved regretfully away, and for a moment the laughter died on Thea's expressive features. She looked tired, somehow sad. James felt an immediate desire to chase the melancholy from her expression and bring the mischievous vitality back into her eyes.

The strains of violins, starting a minuet, gave him an opportunity. "Excuse me, Staverton. I think this dance with Miss Tilton is mine."

Behind him, Staverton laughed, but James didn't bother to look back. As he approached the Tilton ladies, he heard Arabella say, "Colonel Harris has become marked in his attentions, Thea. It is not wise, or kind, to trifle with him if you do not return his feelings."

Thea's head shot up, her expression surprised. "I have not done so, Mama! Colonel Harris presumes on the merest smile! I do not even like the—"

She broke off when she saw James. He smiled at her. His

smile deepened when she blushed and swallowed. "Miss
Tilton, how enchanting you look this evening."

Thea flicked her fan back and forth in short, hasty
movements. "Mr. MacLonan, I believe," she drawled in a
faintly scornful way.

Arabella raised her brows. Her surprise at her daughter's
reaction was evident.

James continued to smile, but his eyes had become
watchful. "I am delighted you remember me. Our previous
conversation has lingered in my memory as one of the
highlights of my return to Edinburgh."

Thea quickly looked down, but there had been a snap of
anger in her eyes that she couldn't quite hide.

"Allow me to introduce my companion to you," she said,
only the husky quality to her voice giving away the intensity
of her hidden emotions. "My mother, Lady Tilton. Mr. James
MacLonan."

James bowed over Arabella's hand with the elegant style
he'd perfected in France. "It is easy to see where Miss Tilton
derives her beauty."

Arabella smiled, and a dimple much like her daughter's
came into existence.

"I hear the musicians beginning a new set," he said. "Miss
Tilton, would you join me in the dance?"

The fan in Thea's hand once more waved in an agitated
way. "I fear, sir—" she began in a frosty tone.

Her mother didn't allow her to finish. "You must be quite
recovered from the last dance, Thea. I believe this is to be a
minuet. Do go ahead. I am sure you will enjoy yourself with
Mr. MacLonan."

Surrendering with a polite smile, Thea laid her hand on
James's extended arm and allowed him to lead her into the
ballroom to join the set just now forming. Through the rich
green silk of his coat, James could feel her hand trembling.
He wondered what it was that was shaking her composure,
but before he could inquire into what disturbed her, the
dance began. He thought he would have to wait until after it

was over to find out more. He was wrong.

"Dissembler!" she hissed as the steps of the dance brought them closely together.

James frowned. Evidently, she was not one of those women who hid their feelings behind a wall of patrician coolness. "Kindly explain that accusation, ma'am."

"Are you not a supporter of the Stuarts, Mr. MacLonan?" she retorted in haughty fury.

So that was the cause of the anger he'd seen in her eyes and the shaking fury she couldn't quite hide. Since their meeting she had heard gossip about his past. "I was," he replied carefully. "But I am no longer."

The movement of the dance separated them. When they met once more, Thea immediately picked up their conversation where it had ended. "You told me you had just returned from the Continent," she said bitterly, while smiling brilliantly so no one would know of the anger building between them.

He raised his brows. "Quite true. I was exiled for my part in the rebellion."

"You admit this?" she hissed incredulously.

"I am not ashamed of my actions," he replied evenly.

Once again, the dance separated them. The moment they met again she attacked. "You fought for France!"

An anger he'd sternly suppressed surged into life. His activities in Europe were not generally known here in Edinburgh. Only the military, Lord Staverton, and a few close confidants of his father's were in on the secret. James was certain neither Staverton nor his father's cronies were sources of Thea's information. That left the military. Damn the English!

"You are again correct, Miss Tilton. After I left Scotland I took service in the army of France. I was," he added dryly, "a Captain of Grenadiers." The Grenadiers were a crack unit. To be their captain was a position of respect and trust. James didn't think Miss Tilton would know that, and he discovered he was rather glad, for it would probably only add to her fury.

The outrage that blazed from her dark eyes very nearly overpowered the brilliance of her artificial smile. "Traitor!"

Evidently, she knew more than he'd expected. A thunderous scowl settled on his face. "Not to my own beliefs, Miss Tilton!"

She looked away, hiding her expression from him. "A traitor to everything I hold dear, sir! You have met my mother. Have you, perchance, met my father—Sir Frederick Tilton?"

The dance was reaching its climax. The measured strains forced them to move apart. James found himself smiling emptily at a young lady he'd met at some point over the last few days. She was making play with vacuous blue eyes. He had no idea who she was. Nor did he care. All he could think about was the last disdainful remark Thea had made.

Sir Frederick Tilton. General Sir Frederick Tilton! How could he have been such a fool? He'd been captured by a pair of fine brown eyes and a mischievous smile and hadn't bothered to look any deeper. A good Whig family indeed!

The dance drew to a majestic close, bringing partners together once more. James and Thea did battle with their eyes while their mouths curled in unnatural smiles. She curtsied and he bowed; then she placed her hand on his arm to allow him to lead her from the room, all as custom demanded. When they touched, James felt a thrill of physical pleasure. Desperately, he tried to deny it.

"You are English!" he complained as he strode impatiently from the floor.

"Indeed, sir. How astute of you to realize!"

"I want nothing to do with an Englishwoman!" he growled, staring straight ahead.

Thea shot him a contemptuous look. Her voice shook with emotion. "Nor I with a traitorous Jacobite, sir! Kindly do not approach me in the future!"

They had reached the spot where Lady Tilton was standing, conversing with Olivia Ramsey. James bowed over Thea's hand with mocking grace. "With pleasure, ma'am!"

As he turned on his heel and marched away, he was fighting the desolation of passionate emotions gone wrong.

"What a pleasant evening," Arabella Tilton remarked later.

It had been hours since Thea's argument with James MacLonan, and her cheeks ached with the effort of continually smiling when she felt as if her world had crashed about her feet.

"Yes, indeed," Sir Frederick agreed heartily, heading for the drawing room, where he knew he would find a warm fire and a decanter of brandy. The night air was still sharp with winter cold, and he felt a need to thaw himself out.

Isabelle yawned. "It was a wonderful ball. I danced with dozens of different gentlemen. I am quite exhausted. I think I must bid you all a good night and seek my bedchamber."

Thea murmured, "Sleep well," then asked quickly, "Papa, may I speak to you privately?"

Sir Frederick's austere features showed nothing of his thoughts. "Of course, my dear."

"I'll come up with you, Isabelle," Lady Tilton said, tactfully leaving Thea alone with her father.

Reaching the drawing room, Sir Frederick poured himself a brandy and took up a strategic position before the hearth. Thea, he noted thoughtfully, prowled like a wild creature infuriated at being caught in a cage. Since she showed no inclination to come out with whatever was on her mind, he gave her a not-so-gentle prod. "Now, my dear, what is it you wished to discuss with me?"

She wrung her hands, distress in her every movement. "Papa, I met a gentleman at Judge Denholm's soiree, one Mr. James MacLonan. Do you know him?"

Tilton's brows rose. He said cautiously, "I am aware of who the gentleman is. However, I have not had the pleasure of being introduced to him."

"Then you know he is a disloyal Jacobite!" Thea burst out passionately.

Sir Frederick felt the same empty hollowness he'd once

experienced when the regiment he commanded had been forced to retreat from a superior enemy. Then he had cheered himself with the knowledge that war was simply a game of strategy and tactics. A defeat could be righted with a victory in the next battle. He reminded himself of that now. Finding a suitable husband for a beautiful, but intelligent—and damnably independent!—daughter was as difficult as a major military campaign.

"Thea," he said placatingly, "while it is true Mr. MacLonan fought the '45—"

She tossed her head. "I could overlook such an indiscretion! He is a Scot, a Highlander, I believe. His support of the Pretender stemmed from a traditional loyalty to the Stuart cause."

"Well then, what's your problem, daughter?" Tilton demanded, somewhat impatiently.

"He fought for France in the late war!"

Sir Frederick didn't immediately reply to his daughter's outraged cry. He had also had difficulty accepting this particular part of James MacLonan's past. However, after his first tentative conversation with Grant MacLonan there had been another. The reservations he'd felt were slowly dwindling away. He had come to believe James MacLonan was indeed an honorable man.

"France is a traditional ally of Scotland, Thea. Remember, too, MacLonan was an exile. He believed he would never return. Why should he not fight the very people who forced him from his homeland?"

"You are remarkably tolerant for the commander of the English garrison in Scotland, Papa!"

Sir Frederick sighed. He looked down at the fire. When he spoke his voice was tired. "The rebellion began five years ago, Thea. Culloden and the reprisals which followed occurred almost four years ago. The time for bitter hatred is past. Scotland needs men like James MacLonan—"

"Men who will stir the Highlands to rebellion again?" Thea interjected scornfully.

"Men who have seen the error of their ways and who wish

to rebuild a shattered society," Sir Frederick corrected firmly. "It can only be to England's benefit to have a strong, contented nation on her northern border. Men like James MacLonan, men of honor and strong principles, can forge a new, abiding bond between our two nations."

Thea had stopped her agitated pacing, but her hands were clenched into fists at her side. "A new bond," she repeated softly. "A bond such as Jacobite and Whig, Papa? English and Scot? Is that why James MacLonan is required to marry within four months of his return? To forge that new bond?"

"Who the devil told you about that?" Tilton burst out angrily, striding away from the fireplace. He halted inches from her.

"It does not matter, Papa! That is not the point—"

"It does indeed, daughter! The information is confidential. There are damn few people who…Harris!" Thea's gaze faltered, confirming his guess. Tilton stepped away. He downed the brandy, then carefully placed the glass on a nearby table. "'Has the fellow been making bad blood between you and MacLonan?"

Astounded, Thea gasped, "Bad—Papa there can be nothing *but* bad blood between James MacLonan and me!"

"You seemed pretty taken with him at Denholm's soiree the other night," Sir Frederick reminded her pointedly.

"I did not know who he was, then. He…he was simply a charming stranger who entertained me with interesting stories of his travels on the Continent."

Her father eyed her thoughtfully. "He still is that man, Thea."

"He lied to me!"

Smiling humorlessly, Tilton demanded, "How?"

"Why, he told me he'd done the Grand Tour! When all the time he'd been a serving officer in King Louis's army!"

Gently, her father said, "Will you believe me, Thea? I've made a point to look into MacLonan's background and I promise you, he resigned his commission over two years ago and since that time he has been, as he told you, traveling in Europe."

Learning James hadn't lied to her brought a smile to Thea's face. "Is that really true, Papa?"

Relief coursed through Sir Frederick. "Indeed, it is, Thea. His father, Grant MacLonan, assures—"

Bringing Grant MacLonan into the conversation was a mistake.

The smile died on Thea's lips and her eyes flashed dangerously. "Have you and Mr. Grant MacLonan been discussing the possibility of a union between James and me, Papa? Because I regret to inform you that I will not, under any circumstances, consent to *bond* my life with his son's!"

She whirled, her chin held disdainfully high as she swept from the room.

Sir Frederick thoughtfully poured himself another brandy and went back to the comfort of the fire. A defeat, he admitted, ruefully. His thin lips curved in a grim smile. But the war was not yet over, not by any means.

CHAPTER 5

"Thea, look at the beautiful print on this muslin! Don't you think it would be perfect for a summer gown?"

Thea and Isabelle were on a shopping expedition, supposedly to purchase new clothes, but mainly to draw Thea out of the dismals she had fallen into in the week following her angry flare-up with James MacLonan. Their first stop was the seamstress patronized by most of the ladies of fashionable Edinburgh.

In one corner of the spacious showroom, Thea had been contemplating a display of fashion dolls newly arrived from France. Now she wandered over to where her sister stood.

"It is lovely," Thea agreed. She fingered the soft cloth. It spoke of green grass, open spaces, and coolness in the midst of summer warmth. She thought of Edinburgh in the summer, hot and sultry, with the noxious odors from the lake below the Castle often forcing people to stay indoors. Her mischievous dimple peeped out. "This would be perfect for a stay at Olivia Ramsey's wonderful estate in the country. Perhaps she will invite us and you could wear a gown made of this fabric."

Isabelle laughed. "Then we could eat the wonderful berries that make such superb jam and we would all be perfectly happy."

Laughing, Thea said, "We would be if Mrs. Ramsey had her way. I have never met a woman who so wants to bring order to everyone's life."

"Whether they like it or not!"

"We should not belittle Mrs. Ramsey. She means well."

The dressmaker bustled over at that moment, and the Tilton ladies abandoned themselves to the pleasure of ordering new gowns for the summer. As they were leaving the shop, Thea said, "Mama asked me to stop by the linen drapers. She needs some cloth for new shirts for Papa." They turned down High Street, away from the looming presence of the Castle.

Although this was the broadest street in Edinburgh, it was still narrow by comparison to streets in other large cities. Thus, it was impossible to ignore people on the other side, and there were many greetings exchanged back and forth. So it was not surprising that when Thea and Isabelle saw James MacLonan and Lord Staverton opposite, Isabelle should respond to Lord Staverton's greeting with a curtsy and a broad smile. Thea contented herself with a small, curt nod.

"You should not be so friendly with Lord Staverton, Isabelle."

Isabelle looked at her in surprise. "Why not?"

Thea colored. "He is a friend of Mr. MacLonan."

"Yes." Isabelle said, her bewilderment deepening. "What has that to do with my being pleasant to Lord Staverton?"

"He is probably a Jacobite like Mr. MacLonan."

"He was," Isabelle said casually. "He gave up all thoughts of following the Pretender after the rebellion. He had to flee to France and he hated it."

Frowning, Thea demanded, "Doesn't that bother you, Isabelle?"

"No, why should it? I like Lord Staverton. He pays me outrageous compliments that make me laugh and he talks to me as if he takes pleasure in my company and wants my opinion. I enjoy being with him. He has told me that he regrets having followed a man who is quite obviously unstable and who would have made a poor king, and I believe him."

"How can you accept so easily, Isabelle? When I

discovered that Mr. MacLonan was a returned Jacobite, I refused to speak to him again."

A dimple much like her mother's and sister's peeked into life in Isabelle's cheek. "It is very simple, Thea. My feelings are not involved."

Thea halted abruptly in front of a shop window and dragged Isabelle to a stop beside her. "Repeat that, if you will."

Isabelle laughed. "Thea, when you met Mr. MacLonan you were very clearly much struck by him. Oh, you hid it cleverly, but you lit up in a way I've never seen before. Then something happened. I'm not sure what, but you have been quiet and subdued ever since."

Thea stared at the display of men's suiting as if her life depended upon it. "The change in weather has made me gloomy, that is all." While it was true the late winter sunshine had been replaced by cold dreary rain, her excuse rang hollow, even to Thea.

Isabelle patted her on the hand. "Everyone finds the rain difficult." She giggled. "Perhaps we should continue on. Our interest in men's clothing seems to be creating something of a stir."

Thea shot a quick, horrified look over her shoulder, and did exactly as her sister suggested. "Isabelle, by the terms of his pardon, James MacLonan must marry by the end of April. It is now almost the end of February. He is looking for a wife, and quickly."

Isabelle nodded and smiled at an acquaintance. "Do you know, Thea, I cannot blame Mr. MacLonan," she said at last. "His life in France was probably a very lonely one. He must have been desperate to come back to Scotland."

They reached the linen draper's shop and turned inside. Thea didn't want to think of James MacLonan as a tormented man willing to do anything to find a way to return home. She wanted to hang on to her image of a cool, manipulative man who could not be deeply touched by anything or anyone.

A lonely, desperate man who fought his fears and kept his dignity intact was a vulnerable man, one she could respect as well as feel compassion for, and she was already too intensely aware of James MacLonan for comfort. Despite her imperious pronouncement to her father that she would never consider marriage to James MacLonan, she could not deny to herself that he fulfilled most of the requirements she looked for in a husband.

Blindly, she picked up a bolt of cloth. "Do you think Mama would consider this fine enough for Papa's shirts?"

Isabelle fingered the material. "No. The thread is too coarse. This one would be much better."

After testing it herself, even Thea could tell the difference. She was glad that Isabelle had always loved fabric and had a knack of picking the finest quality after a quick look or touch, for it meant that her sister would not notice that Thea had hardly been aware of what she was doing when she picked up the bolt of cloth. After purchasing the required number of yards, Thea ordered the package delivered to their residence and they left the shop.

"Isabelle," she said with a sigh. "What shall I do? You are right, I am attracted to Mr. MacLonan, but I cannot forget that he is a Jacobite."

"Was a Jacobite," Isabelle said gently. "Thea, have you discussed his political leanings with him?"

Thea thought of the heated exchange in the midst of the minuet and her sense of humor sprang into life. "In a way. I told him I did not want to speak to him again and he said he had no interest in having anything to do with an Englishwoman."

"Oh." The scope of Thea's disagreement with James MacLonan was beyond Isabelle's experience.

"The trouble is," Thea continued. "Since that evening I find myself watching him. I notice who he is dancing with or talking to and I wish that I was the woman he was with. I know I should not. I know he is a Jacobite, reformed or not. I know he is lost to me, through my own actions and because of my own beliefs. But...I cannot stop, Isabelle. James MacLonan lurks in my mind and I can find no way to chase him out."

"Mama would know what to do. Have you spoken to her?"

"No!" At Isabelle's surprised look, Thea said more moderately, "I can't talk to our parents about this."

"Why not?"

Thea hesitated, then said miserably, "Papa thinks I should learn more of James MacLonan. He thinks a marriage between us would be a good alliance for me."

"Well, then! Thea, if Papa approves of Mr. MacLonan, why are you being so stubborn?"

Thea frowned at her sister. "I'm not being stubborn!"

"Of course you are," Isabelle said comfortably, nodding at another of her new acquaintances. "Think, Thea! Papa is the commander of the garrison here. If anyone had a good reason to loathe Jacobites, it would be him. He's the one in the military, not you! He is the one who would be forced to deal with a new uprising, not you! If he thinks that James MacLonan is a good match for you, then it is because he respects James MacLonan, the man, and believes it when James MacLonan says he is a Jacobite no more."

They stopped for a moment to talk to an acquaintance who had hailed them. Thea couldn't remember afterward what had been said, but she hoped she had not blurted out something stupid. Her thoughts had been all of James MacLonan. She was beginning to believe that she had acted too hastily. She said as much to Isabelle. Then she sighed. "But it doesn't matter. Mr. MacLonan would never forgive my insults."

"How do you know?" Isabelle chided gently. "If you want to change the way things are, Thea you must try. Isn't that what you have always told me?"

"But how, when I am not speaking to Mr. MacLonan and he is not speaking to me?"

"We must find a way for you to approach him. Or for him to approach you. We're almost home. Let's discuss it with Manna. She will know how it is to be done."

Hope fluttered into nervous life in Thea's breast. "Do you really think she would be able to sort this out?"

Isabelle laughed. "Of course. She always does, doesn't she?"

* * *

They held a family conference that evening over which Sir Frederick presided, but which Arabella directed. As was usual in the Tilton household, everyone had the opportunity to voice an opinion. This was followed by considerable discussion, until Sir Frederick called closure and made the final decision. In this case he bowed to his wife's suggestion that they should hold a party and invite everyone who was anyone to it. Sir Frederick would talk to Grant MacLonan to ensure that his son James would attend. Then it would be up to Thea to win James over.

As the party was to be held within a sennight, there had to be a good reason for it, for it was unusual for parties to be given at such short notice. This too was simply managed. Sir Frederick had recently been promoted to the rank of lieutenant general, so it was decided that this would be used as the excuse for a celebration.

With only a week to organize the party, Thea threw herself into the details and pushed thoughts of James MacLonan to the back of her mind. This was difficult, for she saw him often. He was always polite, but very formal, and Thea followed his lead. By the evening of her own family's party she was quite certain that it was a wasted effort. She would never be able to rekindle the interest James MacLonan had once shown her.

James MacLonan was extremely reluctant to grace the Tiltons' party.

He stood in front of the blazing fire in Grant MacLonan's salon with his hand on the mantel, watching the flames leap and dance. "I will not go," he growled for the fourth time.

His father thumped his cane. "Do you want to stay in Scotland, Jamie?"

"Yes," James said to the fireplace.

"Then you will go! Think laddie. This is an opening, an olive branch from the Tilton family. Sir Frederick as much as told me so."

"Did he? And what exactly did he say?"

Grant waved his son's question away. "He made no promises, if that is what you mean, but he personally brought the invitation to me and added his own request that you attend. Go to the party, Jamie. Talk to Miss Tilton. She has all the necessary qualifications you need to meet the terms of your pardon." He stopped for a moment. When James didn't speak, he added, "You like her, do you not?"

James stared into the dancing flames and thought about Theadora Tilton's mischievous humor as she mimicked perfectly the bored drawl of a society dandy and pretended to take snuff. Or the fire that leapt from her eyes when she was outraged. Slowly, he said, "She is intriguing, sir, but she would not make a comfortable wife."

Grant snorted. "Comfortable! What sane man wants a wife who is merely *comfortable*?"

James had to laugh. His father was right. He'd be bored within the week with a wife who waited for him to tell her what to do and then went out and did it. MacLonan women were spirited, fierce, demanding, and independent. He looked for nothing less in a marriage.

He sighed and turned around. "Sir, Miss Tilton is English—"

"Aye, that she is, laddie. That is why she fits the terms of your pardon. That's the point of the clause that demands you wed a woman with a suitably Whiggish background. They don't want you to marry a Highland girl and beget more Jacobite sons."

"—and she would not be prepared for life in the Highlands."

"According to her father she spent most of her life on his estate in Kent. She's not unused to country life, Jamie."

"Kent is not Glenmuir."

"True enough, but neither here nor there. You can't assume the girl would refuse to live at Glenmuir until you talk to her."

James bent to throw another log on the fire. He knew that he was making difficulties where none were required. Why was he doing that? He liked Theadora Tilton. Physically, he found her attractive. Of all the women he had met since returning to Edinburgh, she was the only one he could envision himself happily spending the rest of his life with. So why was he finding excuses not to go to this wretched party?

"She is English," he said at last. "Her father is a general in the English army. This party is to celebrate his promotion! How can I overlook that?"

"When all is said and done, Jamie, she is just a woman and this party is just an excuse to allow you and Miss Tilton to find out if you can overcome your differences. Go, Jamie. At least talk to her. What harm will it do?"

"He's not coming." Thea waved her fan far too quickly and pretended to smile. "Isabelle, he's almost two hours late. He's not coming."

"Lord Staverton is here," Isabelle said, smiling and nodding in that gentleman's direction.

"What does that matter?"

"Well, they are great friends, you know. I should think that if Lord Staverton is attending a party, Mr. MacLonan is also likely to."

Thea laughed and shot her sister a knowing look. "Isabelle, Lord Staverton is here because of you. Now don't blush! I know he finds you quite charming."

"Nonsense, Thea," Isabelle said, sounding very much like their mother. She opened her fan to hide her hot cheeks.

Thea laughed again, but the sound withered on her lips as a familiar male voice said, "Miss Tilton, what a pleasure it is to see you again."

She held out her hand numbly. Now that the moment was here, she was not in the least sure what she should do. "Mr. MacLonan. We are delighted you are able to attend our celebration this evening."

He lifted her hand to his lips with an elegant French flare.

"It is my pleasure, Miss Tilton. The invitation is, I believe, something of an olive branch?"

Thea snatched her hand out of his grasp. James MacLonan might have learned elegant mannerisms in France, but underneath he remained a forthright Scottish Highlander. She heard Isabelle murmur some excuse as she slipped away, but Thea was focused on James MacLonan. Her eyes snapped with annoyance at his bluntness, but she was duty bound to try to make amends, even though she had concluded that this evening was very likely a mistake. "Perhaps, sir, we should start afresh. I believe you were as surprised about my background as I was about yours. I said some words that were perhaps rather strong..."

He pulled a delicately carved snuffbox out of one pocket, held his palm out, and flicked the box open with a practiced motion. Then he took a small pinch of snuff between two fingers. He paused and said in a bored voice, "Why, Miss Tilton, do you really think calling a man a traitor is likely to cause him offense?"

Thea had to laugh. "As I recollect, you responded by stating you wanted nothing to do with an Englishwoman."

"Then we are even, madam." James dropped the box back in his pocket and dusted off his fingers without taking the snuff.

Thea observed that thoughtfully. James MacLonan, it seemed, was willing to make an effort to begin again, just as she was. "Mr. MacLonan, what we are we will always be. You are a Scot and a follower of the Stuarts. I am the daughter of an English general and the sister of a captain. By birth and belief I am loyal to King George."

He caught her hand again. This time he gently rubbed his thumb along the soft skin on her knuckles. Pleasant sensations rippled through Thea.

"I have nothing against the English," he remarked. "I have been friends with the Viscount Staverton for years."

He paused. Thea found herself holding her breath, and had to deliberately remember to let it go. Finally he continued. "It is the politics that divides us, is it not?"

"King George and his enemy, the Young Pretender. You are right, Mr. MacLonan, it is the politics that places the true barrier between us."

After one final silken stroke, he released her hand. Thea wanted to sigh with disappointment. His very public caress had given her sensual pleasure, but even more, it had given her hope.

"And yet, what place does politics have between a man and a woman?" He watched her through hooded eyes, waiting for her reaction.

The common answer would be none. Women had been used to solidify alliances between people of different political beliefs for time immemorial.

Thea, however, was far from the marriageable pawn of tradition.

"Beliefs, strongly held, are the essence of men and women. Since meeting you, sir, I have heard stories of your conduct during the rebellion." Her lips curled into a rueful smile and her impish dimple peeped out. "I know I should not be listening to gossip, but...alas, I could not resist. I wanted to know what kind of man you were."

He raised his brows, somewhat cynically. "And common gossip gave you the answer?"

She should have been offended. Instead she laughed. "Mr. MacLonan, you are not kind! Did I not hint to you that I was deeply ashamed of myself?" She tapped his wrist gently with her closed fan, her dimple very much in evidence. "You should not force a lady to admit outright that she has erred in listening to gossip. It just is not done!"

He laughed, a deep appreciative chuckle that caused Thea's spirits to soar in a mercurial way.

"Miss Tilton, I beg your forgiveness."

"It is gladly given, sir."

James looked down at her, a faint smile still curling his lips. "I am intrigued, Miss Tilton, how the daughter of a good Whig general overcame her perfectly natural distaste for a man who was a traitor to England through listening to gossip. I think you were about to explain that deep dark mystery to me."

"You are a most determined man, Mr. MacLonan." She pouted, glancing up at him from beneath her lashes. "You refuse to allow me to divert the subject away from my transgression."

"Others have made the same complaint, madam," he said rather ruefully.

Thea sighed in an exaggerated way. "Alas, I fear I must confess all." She looked up at him again, her head cocked, and her eyes twinkling. "The truth be known, there is not much to tell. I was persuaded to listen to the history of the rebellion from the point of view of the other side. I began to see that you were an honorable man, acting according to your beliefs. In truth, I do not think you could have done other than to pledge your sword to Charles James Stuart when he raised the clans. You were only doing what your honor demanded."

Complete silence followed her words. Thea found herself searching his face, far too anxiously for her peace of mind.

Finally, after what seemed an eternity, he said very slowly, "Miss Tilton, I do not know how to reply."

She turned her head away. Gently he caught her chin, uncaring who might be watching them, then turned it so that she had to look up into his eyes. Briefly, his thumb stroked lightly, temptingly, along her skin.

"I did not mean to hurt you," he said softly, "but your words left me mute. It is rarely that a man receives a confession and a compliment phrased so gracefully. I only wish that my own explanation could be as elegant."

He caught her hands and squeezed them gently. Thea's fingers tightened in his and something flared in his eyes, deepening the blue. Her heart pounded in response and she took a deep breath. Being near to James MacLonan was causing her body to react very strangely, in ways that she decided she liked very much.

"Your own explanation, sir? I do not understand."

"Why I agreed to come to your party, Miss Tilton," he said gently. "Why I borrowed Staverton's snuff box so I would have a way of approaching you that ensured that you would be willing to speak to me."

"Oh," Thea said, feeling quite silly, but wonderfully

flattered. Her voice sounded breathy to her own ears. She wondered if James MacLonan had noticed her lack of composure. "Why did you do those things, Mr. MacLonan?"

His eyes caressed her face. Slowly, he turned her hands so that the palms lay upward. "I could not get you out of my mind," he said simply. Then he bent and kissed first one palm and then the other with a graceful flourish that spoke of the Continent.

Thea's breath caught as her heart began to pound, and a strange longing made her want to drift forever in the pleasure of his touch. "James," she whispered.

He looked up at her and smiled, then dropped her hands. Some of the tension that had kept Thea tight with anticipation eased, but not all. Her whole body continued to tingle with awareness of him.

"I think, Miss Tilton, that we should join the dancing, or people will accuse me of monopolizing your company."

Thea's lovely rippling laugh rang out. "One of the prerogatives of holding your own party, sir, is that you may bend, and even break, the rules. No one will condemn either of us for talking overlong tonight."

"Then I will not hesitate to monopolize you." He took her hand and placed it on his arm. "Is there a place where we can be more private than this? Do you have any suggestions?"

"My father's study," she said a little breathlessly, knowing that after the intensity of their conversation, she was not just breaking, but shattering, all of the rules. "We did not open it for the party tonight. We can be alone there."

Briefly, he hesitated. Then he smiled down at her in a way that was almost possessive. "An excellent suggestion, Theadora. I am yours to command."

She swallowed, then whispered, "Thea. I am Thea to my family."

His smile only deepened.

* * *

"A bit early to be in the country, I know," Olivia Ramsey said as she and the Tilton ladies wandered down a gravel path in the manicured gardens at Ramsey House. She waved her hand somewhat dismissively at the soft earth edging the well-groomed path. "But the weather has been so warm for this time of year that I could not resist planning a quiet little weekend with some of my favorite people for company!" She beamed at Arabella, then at Thea and Isabelle. They all smiled back. Olivia Ramsey was as unstoppable as the winter snows, but she meant well.

The Ramsey estate was located some distance from Edinburgh, beyond the thickly wooded wilderness of the Forest of Drumselch. Brendon Ramsey was town bred and had had no connection with the land when he bought the property from a Lowland laird whose addiction to spirituous liquor and gambling had destroyed his fortune. Brendon had torn down the small, two-hundred-year-old house and built himself a palace in the graceful Classical style that was so very popular in Europe and England. Though he had hired the best architect in Britain, imported marble from Italy, brought precious woods from the Indies, used only the finest local stone for the walls, and cut down most of the thick woodlands that edged the property, his very Classical house looked out of place amongst the rolling hills of Scotland. That did not matter to Olivia or Brendon Ramsey, however. In their eyes the house spoke of their wealth, the importance it bestowed upon them, and the triumph of civilization over the wild barbarism of the Highland Scots.

"The Duchess of Argyll will be here for a day and night," Olivia was saying with considerable zest. "She cannot remain longer, unfortunately, but I am delighted she was able to make space in her very busy schedule to attend my house party. She is bringing her young cousin. A charming girl." Olivia shot Thea an amused look. "The duchess was not invited to your party the other evening, was she, Lady Tilton?"

Thea blushed while her mother murmured a polite response. For the past week people had been making sly comments about her disappearance with James MacLonan. Speculation raged on how they had spent the hour they had been together alone in her father's study. It was evident to Thea that few believed her protestations that she and James had sat before the fire and talked.

She didn't mention that James had held her hand throughout. Or that toward the end of their hour together he had kissed the sensitive underside of her wrist enticingly, then tempted her further as he continued the caress along her arm to the place where the expensive lace that adorned the sleeve of her gown fell in thick profusion. By the time he brushed the lace away for one final kiss Thea's heart had been pounding and her cheeks were flushed with excitement. Then the kiss ended and he straightened, sitting back in his corner of the settee as if nothing had happened, until he smiled at her with tender intimacy.

Though she would never regret slipping away with James, she had hoped that in accepting Olivia Ramsey's invitation to her country estate she would escape the constant prying. It seemed that she was wrong. Olivia Ramsey was no more able to ignore the opportunity to meddle than anyone else.

Olivia was saying airily, "George Drummond, our Lord Provost, will be here, of course, such a fine man! And the Honorable Mrs. Forrest will arrive today. Mr. Forrest will be joining her on Friday and will stay through Sunday. They have a daughter who will be entering society in the fall, did you know that, Lady Tilton?" Another amused glance at Thea. "A delightful girl, just eighteen and very beautiful. She will rival your lovely Theadora and Isabelle for the men's affections, I wager!"

At that Thea laughed while Isabelle colored. "I hardly think my sister and I have any special hold over the men of Edinburgh society, Mrs. Ramsey, but thank you for the compliment."

Olivia shook her head. "You must not be so modest, Theadora."

They were almost at the house. A broad terrace rimmed by a stone balustrade adorned the side that faced the expansive gardens. A man stood on the terrace, his hands placed squarely on the top of the balustrade as he surveyed the sculpted grounds. A tall man whose clothes bore the unmistakable stamp of the Continent in their fashionable tailoring.

"Did I mention that Mr. MacLonan has consented to be one of my guests?"

On the terrace, James straightened as he scanned the group. Then he made his way down the broad stone steps to the path where Olivia and her guests waited.

He walked with the straight back and crisp step of a soldier. Having spent her life in close proximity to the military, Thea knew that the gait could be drilled into any man, but in James MacLonan there was also the faint swagger of the officer in that swinging stride, mixed with an assurance that spoke of a born leader. An odd sensation, curiously close to pride, washed over her as he approached.

"What a fine-looking gentleman," Olivia murmured, carefully keeping her voice low so that it would not carry to MacLonan's ears. She tapped Thea on the wrist. "Now remember, my dear, you must not be naughty the way you were the other night. Mr. MacLonan is a very eligible gentleman...for a Highlander."

Unfurling the fan that dangled from her wrist, Thea waved it with considerable force. "Mr. MacLonan would be considered a gentleman in any country. As to eligible, I suppose any one of the young women you have invited this weekend would not scorn his handsome features, gentlemanly manners, and honorable character."

"Thea!" her mother said reprovingly.

Isabelle gawked at her.

Thea flushed. She wasn't sure why she had defended him, because no matter how good-looking he was, or how much money his father had, he was still a pardoned rebel who had to fulfill the terms of that pardon. Yes, he was eligible, but not for all. But for some reason, defending him had been something she had to do, even at the risk of offending her hostess, Olivia Ramsey.

Then James MacLonan was standing before them, greeting his hostess, bowing over Arabella's hand, smiling at Isabelle, then finally, dropping a lingering kiss on Thea's hand. Thea's color deepened with pleasure and a tremulous smile crept onto her lips.

"Well," said Olivia, noting this exchange with interest. "Will you walk with us, Mr. MacLonan?" She set off back up the path with a brisk step, one arm tucked into Arabella's, the other into Isabelle's, leaving Thea no option but to walk alongside James MacLonan.

"It seems, sir, that Mrs. Ramsey has arranged this on purpose to leave us together."

"I do believe you are correct, Thea." His lips twitched. "Mrs. Ramsey is walking so rapidly that she is almost dragging your mother and sister along with her." A teasing gleam entered his eyes. "All is not lost, however. I am capable of walking much more quickly. If you wished we could catch up with them."

Thea laughed up at him. "By no means, James. I would much prefer to wander with you along these meandering paths. Besides, I would not like to disappoint Mrs. Ramsey when she has been kind enough to arrange for us to be alone together in a way that will not cause any comment."

He stared ahead, his expression set. When he looked down at her and spoke, his tone was serious. "Have you received much criticism for spending time alone with me that night?"

Thea looked up at him and laughed. "James, our tryst has been the primary focus for Edinburgh's gossips this past week. We are to be congratulated for providing them with a most interesting subject for discussion!"

For a moment he grinned at her sally, but then he was serious once more. "I hope I have not ruined your reputation."

Thea was touched. "I think it will survive," she said huskily. "Undoubtedly, I will be teased and criticized for a time, but soon the gossips will be bored with my transgression and will find another impropriety to condemn. I can manage until then."

"I would not have you harmed because of me," he said grimly.

Shaking her head, Thea smiled sweetly and said, "I appreciate your concern, James, but it is misplaced. I chose to take you to my father's study, you did not drag me there. I wanted to talk to you, to see if we could begin again and this time learn more of each other, and I was not disappointed. I am not sorry we slipped away together." Her mischievous dimple appeared. "And I would do it again, without a second thought."

He reached down to capture her hand and put it on his arm. Then he placed his hand over hers. Their pace slowed to a gentle meander. Ahead of them, Olivia Ramsey and Thea's mother and sister disappeared around a bend in the path. To all intents and purposes, they were alone. James drew her to a stop.

He asked huskily, "Would you consider spending the afternoon with me, Miss Tilton, so that we could continue to learn about each other? I would like to know how Theadora Tilton thinks and what is important to her. In return, I promise to be as open and forthcoming about myself as possible."

Thea didn't care if others remarked on the amount of time she was spending with James MacLonan. Her response came without hesitation. "Yes, James, I would like that very much."

They talked idly that day on subjects that expressed a great deal of themselves, but dealt little with the overriding political issues between them. Thea already knew she liked James very much, but at some point during that relaxed and delightful afternoon, she decided that she could also respect him for his values, his code of honor, the way he treated people. Should he care to ask, she knew she would be willing to spend her life with him.

That evening, when the company met for a light supper, Thea was keyed up. Waiting for James to make the next move was far more difficult than making the decision to accept his proposal, should he offer one.

After a fine meal created by the French chef Brendon Ramsey had coaxed from Paris, the men remained in the long dining room, drinking French brandy and discussing the events of the day, as was the custom, while the ladies retired to one of the many drawing rooms. It was not long, however, before the gentlemen tired of their debate and joined the ladies.

The Ramseys' very modern mansion possessed every conceivable luxury skilled craftsmen were capable of creating. The furnishings had been made specifically for the house and none of the fireplaces smoked, almost unheard of in this region where keeping warm from the damp and cold was a constant battle. After a day of warm spring sunshine, a dinner of fine food and wine, and the comfort of deeply padded chairs, the guests were well content. Olivia Ramsey was delighted and did not hesitate to show it. She made it no secret that she liked to entertain and to show off her fine house.

"A wonderful party," the Duchess of Argyll was saying in her nasal tones, carefully modulated to keep the Scottish burr from intruding. "You are to be commended, Mrs. Ramsey. It is a pity that my young cousin and I must leave on the morrow, we have enjoyed ourselves so."

"You are always welcome, Duchess."

"Alas, it is not possible to stay. We are committed to travel down to London to attend the duke. As it is, I have pushed the limit of our time. If we do not leave in the morning we cannot be sure of reaching London in less than a sennight, even with good weather and satisfactory road conditions."

"But the roads are excellent to London!" Olivia paused in her needlework, surprised.

"Compared to what?" the duchess asked humorously, one eyebrow raised in polite query.

Olivia frowned. "Why, some of the roads into the Highlands, I expect."

"Oh, the Highlands." The duchess waved a disdainful hand. "I was talking of roads, my dear Mrs. Ramsey, not animal tracks."

There was a moment of profound, uncomfortable silence. Then James sauntered over from where he had been standing by the fire talking to Lady Tilton. He looked down at the duchess, his features showing no emotion, the expression in his eyes hidden by lowered lids. "Do you have some objection to the Highlands, Duchess?"

"None at all, provided I am not expected to live there!" She sniffed. "Fortunately, my dear husband, the duke, has never required me to spend time in any of his more barbaric castles."

"Truly a profound loss," James murmured.

Seated to one side, Thea was able to watch both James and the duchess. Even though his expression was polite, she thought she could detect a gleam of annoyance in his eyes and she sympathized with him. The duchess was a condescending, self-absorbed woman who insulted everyone she met.

"Quite so. These wild Highlanders would benefit from the civilizing forces the duke and I could bring," the duchess was saying complacently, apparently under the belief that James was in agreement with her.

"I must differ, Duchess, unless you can show me a civilization that has left barbarity behind." The whiplash contempt in James's voice made even the self-centered duchess stare. He shrugged, aware that the conversation was entering dangerous ground. "If you will excuse me, Duchess." He spun around, almost blindly seeking an escape. Thea smiled up at him. Gratefully, he held out his hand. "Miss Tilton, would you consider taking air on the terrace with me?"

"I would be delighted, sir." As she took his hand and rose from her chair, Thea was keenly aware that all eyes were upon them. James draped her shawl over her shoulders to keep off the night chills. In accepting his hand she had somehow passed through a door and closed it firmly behind her. Where she had gone, where she would end up, she wasn't sure, but she had put the Duchess of Argyll and people like her on notice. Where James MacLonan was concerned, Thea was firmly on his side.

CHAPTER 6

The moonlight bathed the terrace and the grounds beyond in a soft, pale light. Thea leaned against the balustrade. The stone was chilly beneath her skin and she shivered.

"Are you cold?" James asked, his voice husky.

She looked over at him and smiled. "Perhaps a little."

He took off his coat and draped it over her shoulders. "Thank you."

She snuggled into the velvet, which was still warm from his body. James stood very close, leaning against the stone railing, his back to the gardens. He was watching her, his expression impossible to read.

"I went to Oxford University some years back," he said. "That was where I met Staverton. Did I tell you that?"

Thea shook her head.

He continued in a meditative way, "People knew I was a Scot, of course, for my accent was stronger in those days. At first I was accepted as any other, until they discovered I was from the Highlands. Then the jokes would begin, the cruel comments that were based on nothing but blind prejudice. I ignored them for the most part. I still do, until I meet a smug woman like the Duchess of Argyll, who should know better." He straightened and took Thea by the shoulders, turning her so that she was facing him. "You will have to endure that, Thea, if you marry me. I hate it, I would not have you subjected to it, but there is nothing I can do to stop it. Do you think you could bear it?"

Thea began to laugh. "James, is this a proposal?"

His fingers flexed, tightening on her shoulders. "I guess it is. It isn't quite what I'd planned, but—"

Thea lifted her hands to cup his face. "Then begin again, James, and ask me as you'd planned to ask me."

"I had thought to do it in the sunshine," he said softly, "out of doors, amongst the trees and plants where I feel most comfortable. Or perhaps in your parents' drawing room where you would feel most comfortable. I would talk to you then, and ask you about your hopes and dreams. If I was satisfied that you would be happy with me, I was going to go down on one knee, thus,"—he suited action to words—"and beg you to consider spending the rest of your life with me."

Thea sank down until their eyes were level. The stone was cold and hard beneath her knees. "James, beg me to consider. Let me answer you."

"Will you marry me, Thea, and spend the rest of your life with me?"

"Yes, James, I will."

Smiling, she looked into his eyes. There were no words of love spoken, but when James caught her face in his hands, then bent to seal her promise with a kiss, his embrace branded Thea in a way that made her soul sing with pleasure.

When he eventually raised his head, he smiled at her. "I think we shall deal very well together, Thea."

It was a sentiment she echoed wholeheartedly.

Of necessity the marriage took place quite quickly. The terms of James's pardon stated he had to be married within four months of his return to Scotland, or the pardon would become void. As he had been back for almost two when he asked Thea to marry him, there could be no long betrothal period. Both James and Grant MacLonan wanted the union celebrated and consummated well within the four-month period.

It was agreed that the wedding should take place three

weeks later, at the end of April. That was not very much time to organize a wedding, but Arabella understood the necessity, so she agreed and immediately set to work. The family threw themselves into the preparations, which seemed to take enormously more time than expected. Thea had hoped for more opportunities to be with James, but her days were filled with wedding plans, leaving her with little leisure time. It was in the evenings, at social gatherings, that they were able to meet. Then they were the center of attention, feted by well-wishers who saw the marriage as evidence of more positive relations between England and Scotland.

Even though Thea knew that James was marrying her because of her nationality and her political connections, she still found comments of this sort disturbing. She thrust the concerns aside, however, and continued on. Marriage would not change her life greatly. She would continue to live in Edinburgh, and for a few weeks after their marriage she and James would even remain in the Tilton household. There was time enough then to learn more of the man she had married.

The wedding was a sumptuous affair, with St. Giles Cathedral filled with guests. The bride wore a gown of silver tissue, while the groom was dressed in gold and white. The groom said his vows in a strong confident voice, while the bride spoke more quietly, but with no less certainty. When the ceremony was over, the guests left the old damp stone church for the cold rain outdoors. There was much laughter as people watched James and Thea depart, then sought out waiting sedan chairs to return to the Tilton house in comfort. There they were to feast the bride and groom and generally enjoy themselves.

Daylight flooded the large bedroom, shining through the broad opening in the bed curtains, as Thea raised heavy-lidded eyes. She yawned and rolled from her side onto her back, blinking the mists of sleep from her eyes. Her brain was telling her she must get up, that the sun had risen hours ago and that she was late. Her body countered with the objection she hadn't got enough sleep last night, and demanded she roll over and catch up on the rest she so badly needed.

Her eyelids drooped and she yawned again. Just a few more minutes, then she would get up. *Not if your husband visits you again.* Her lovely brown eyes snapped wide open at that thought, as the events of the previous day and night came alive. Her heart gave a leap, then began to thump, and she had to swallow hard to subdue a sudden onslaught of emotions.

Marriage. She looked around her bedroom; the fireplace in one corner, the large square sash windows, the dressing table, its surface covered by a fine linen cloth. There she had sat last night preparing for her new husband, anxiously peering into the square, guilt-framed mirror as she wondered if she appealed physically to him or not and whether he would be gentle when he bedded her.

This morning, everything about her room was the same, but she was not. Absently, she pushed away a stray strand of golden hair that was tickling her nose. A memory of James slowly loosening her thick hair from the braid she always twisted it into at night warmed her body with remembered heat. He had run his fingers through the rich, silken mass and murmured soft words in a language she couldn't understand.

Stretching his long form above her, he had tipped his head toward her neck while she lay stiff and cold beneath him, unsure what she should do. Ladies do not respond to a man's touch, she'd heard time and again, although her mother had always blushed when Thea had asked her if she agreed.

The sensation of James's teeth on the tender skin at the base of her neck had created a craving that was new to Thea, tantalizing her. She began to move, in ways that certainly wouldn't be considered unresponsive. She looked up at James and saw that a small, satisfied smile curled his lips. He said softly, "Does my touch please you, pretty one?"

Slowly, without thinking, she brought her fingers up to stroke along his ribs. He sucked in his breath and shuddered. She immediately dropped her hands.

"No, don't stop."

Very unsure of herself, Thea lifted her hands to his face. "What you are doing pleases me very much, but I am not sure how I should—or what I should—"

"Don't think, Thea. Let yourself be guided by me. I will not harm you, I promise you."

Her eyes searched his face, then slowly she nodded. His teeth nibbled her earlobe. Then the tip of his tongue stoked the same area and some of the stiffness melted out of her. James made a satisfied sound, and reached down to push the fine, virtually diaphanous bed gown from her shoulders with one hand. As she felt his fingers stroking lightly on her rib cage near her breast, she tensed automatically. Her eyes sought his, looking for reassurance. "James—"

"Trust me," he whispered. His hand closed over her breast and the thumb gently caressed the sensitive peak.

Thea arched upward, her body seeking more. But her mind resented the liberty he was taking, and with a small moan, she whispered, "I would, but..." as heat seared from her breast to her loins.

"You are lovely, Thea. You respond to me with the promise of such fire." His free hand tangled in her hair, tightening to hold her head still as he kissed her soundly on her still-parted lips. When his tongue invaded the warmth of her mouth she resisted, but he was stronger, and after a moment the strangeness of the sensation gave way to pleasure. Without conscious thought her body began to move beneath him.

He shifted to position himself more securely above her, and his mouth left hers. "That's better, lass. Easy now." His teeth began to nibble the delicate shell of her ear, making Thea moan as she again felt that hot flood of pure sensation.

As his hand stroked softly up her leg, pushing the filmy folds of her bed gown with it, he used the pressure of his knee to coax her thighs apart. Half lost in a mist of sensations she couldn't describe, Thea moved instinctively, stretching her legs wide to give him easier access.

When his lips found hers again and his weight descended

upon her, she was prepared. Her tongue met his, bold and shy at once, touching and caressing as his penetrated. At the same moment his body thrust into hers, ending her maidenhood and jerking her out of the hazy dream of sensation. Reality left her cold, sore, and invaded.

For a moment he did not move. Then his lips left hers to nibble at that sensitive spot on her neck, while one hand stroked and toyed with her breast. Thea lay stiffly, wishing she knew what she should do next, but unable to respond as she had but moments before.

Finally, after what seemed an eternity, he gratified his own pleasure, then withdrew. She sighed, relieved and edgy at the same time. He quickly rolled off her to sit on the edge of the bed, breathing heavily.

Thea watched him, wondering what he would do now. It was common in their class for a man to bed his wife, then retreat to his own room for the night. A room had been prepared in the Tilton household for just this occasion. No one would criticize James if he left her now. He had done his duty.

Taking a deep breath, he flung back his head, then turned back to lean over Thea. He smiled down at her, one hand stroking her smooth cheek. "Did I hurt you?"

His voice was low and a little rough. Thea heard the sound as concern and smiled back at him. "A trifle, no more."

He raised the bedclothes, pursing his lips at the blood on her thighs and on the sheets. "I am sorry, Thea." His finger traced the dark stains on her skin, making her shiver. "Next time it will be easier, I promise you."

A moment or two before, Thea would have been quite happy never to participate in a "next time." Now James's caress was tantalizing her with a promise she couldn't define.

His hand slid up her leg to her hip, the thumb stroking her skin in small, tantalizing circles as it went. Thea's eyes glazed, then drifted shut. They flew open when he dropped a feather-light kiss on her lips.

"It will be easier this time, I promise," he said.

She moistened her lips. "James, you don't have to, um…I mean—"

"Yes, I do."

His expression was reassuring, but there was a promise of something more. He bent to kiss her deeply again, and Thea's eyes drifted closed once more.

After that she was ruled only by sensation as he used his mouth and hands to caress her body until she burned with desires and demands. "James! James, stop teasing me. I can stand no more. Please, help me!"

He entered her quickly, and with a shudder her body accepted his. This time, though, their joining set her free to soar.

When he was certain her satisfaction was complete, he took his own, then eased from her. Drawing her close, he whispered, "Love between a man and a woman is no more complicated than what we just shared. Will you let me pleasure you again, sweet Thea?"

She sighed in a lazy, voluptuous way, then drawled, "I am at your service, sir," as she cast him a teasing look from beneath her lashes.

James laughed. "I think I married the only woman in Edinburgh who has the fire and sparkle to entertain me for the rest of my life."

"Then you are satisfied with your marriage, James?" She pressed her body closer to his and lifted her hand to stroke his cheek.

"How could I not be?" He nibbled the corner of her mouth. "My wife is beautiful, intelligent, and she turns to fire in my arms."

His words sent hope leaping in her heart. Though she searched his face, she could find no evidence that denied his words. She snuggled closer, resting her head on his shoulder. I am too." His arms tightened around her, strong but tender.

She had been right to marry James MacLonan, she thought lazily. Held close in his arms, she could almost persuade herself that James's feelings toward her would grow into something deeper and that their marriage, begun as a political alliance, might yet become a love match.

She'd fallen asleep quite suddenly after that, or so she thought now, looking at the daylight streaming in her window. James had been with her then, but he must have left sometime during the night. Vaguely, for no reason that her rational mind could determine, she was disappointed. Suppressing a sigh, she pulled herself up.

"Ah, you're awake."

She blinked as her husband opened the bed curtains wider. Happiness flooded her. He had stayed. "Yes, I'm awake."

He sat down on the edge of the bed. There was a gleam in his eyes that made Thea's heart thump. "I'll ring for the maid to bring you your chocolate. But first, let me look at you." With gentle hands he stroked her mass of thick golden hair from her face. Where his fingers touched, fire burned along Thea's skin.

"You are beautiful," he said, his eyes roving down to her breasts, which gleamed rose pink and white under the thin linen of her nightdress. He bent and kissed her.

Thea wet her lips. "James?" she whispered.

He looked up, his hand cupping her breast, his brow raised in a silent question.

"Will you...can you wait for a moment or two before you summon the maid?"

He eased in beside her. "I am at your command."

They both laughed until passion absorbed them.

Thea was still in bed, pillows plumped up behind her to support her back, her golden hair loose and tumbled, when her sister opened the door.

"Thea, I could wait no longer!" Isabelle announced as she peaked into the room. "Are you alone?" she added somewhat belatedly, glancing about. A half-finished cup of chocolate rested on the table beside the bed, and at that moment Thea's maid emerged from the dressing room. Satisfied that these clues were evidence that James was no longer with her sister, Isabelle skipped inside.

"Isabelle, do come in," Thea said with amusement as she

watched her sister plunk herself down onto the bed. "Was there an urgent reason for you to seek me out?"

"So much has happened, Thea. Of course I wanted to talk to you!"

The bright questioning, look in Isabelle's eyes told Thea that she wanted to have a sisterly heart-to-heart talk and would be satisfied with nothing less. With a faint smile, Thea dismissed her maid with a wave of her hand. "There now, Isabelle. We are alone and we have hours to talk. I claim a new bride's prerogative of lying about lazily on the morning after her wedding."

"What is he like, Thea?"

Thea thought about James and the way he had made love to her. She blushed. "He is careful, considerate, and gentle. I cannot complain about my new husband."

"Did you…enjoy it?"

Thea blushed even larder. "Yes."

Isabelle hooted in a most unladylike manner that would have caused her mother's wrath to descend upon her should Arabella have heard her. "Thea! I would not have thought it! You are embarrassed."

Now quite red, Thea said, "I am not."

Isabelle began to laugh, and so did Thea.

"Very well, it is true. I am embarrassed talking about James's lovemaking, but in truth, Isabelle, I cannot complain of my treatment. He did not leave me after he had bedded me, as some men would. Instead he stayed the night, and he was here when I awoke this morning. I found that…" She hesitated, searching for a way to describe the hazy emotions that were churning about inside her. "Touching and reassuring."

Isabelle caught Thea's hand in hers. "Thea, I'm so glad to hear you say that, especially since you will soon have only James to rely upon."

It took Thea a moment to absorb her sister's comment. Then, frowning, she said, "Isabelle, what are you talking about? True, James and I must find a residence of our own, but I will still have you and Mama and Papa to visit. And I will continue on my round of activities. I will not be immured alone in our house with James!"

Isabelle sat back. Confusion drew her brows together into a frown. "Thea, have you and James not discussed where you will be living?"

Thea, who had just taken a sip of chocolate, returned the cup to the saucer with a click and set it firmly on the table. She pinned her sister with a level stare. "Isabelle, what are you hinting at? That James has decided we will live in the Highlands he loves so well?"

Isabelle bit her lip. "Yes, but..."

Thea sat very still. Her body was burning with a fierce heat that had nothing to do with embarrassment. "Tell me exactly what it was that you heard." Her eyes blazed with a fiery glitter. "Do not leave anything out, Isabelle. Nothing!"

Isabelle began to pleat the blanket. "I overheard Mama and Papa talking, Thea, and I did not think. I assumed that you would already know."

"What did you hear?"

Isabelle bit her lip and looked down at the blanket. "Mama was angry and Papa was trying to placate her. He was being quite logical in that way he has, and Mama was infuriated, as she always is. He said that of course James would want to live at Glenmuir. And Mama asked him if he'd known this before the wedding. When he replied he sounded oh, I don't know, chastened, I think. He said that yes, he had assumed James would want to live in the Highlands, but he'd only found out for certain during the wedding celebrations."

"Glenmuir," Thea said softly, staring far off into the distance. "We would be alone there."

"But you said that James was considerate and kind, Thea," Isabelle reminded her encouragingly. "Surely, it would not be so bad."

Perhaps, perhaps not. Thea was a strong-minded woman who had been raised to accept sudden shifts in her family life. She had learned to adapt gracefully to these alterations, but she had always been surrounded by those she trusted and loved, which helped her deal with the emotional upheaval that accompanied major changes. This time she would have to build a relationship with James even as she adjusted to a new place to live. The prospect was daunting.

"James did not tell me of his plans," she said slowly, still staring past her sister as if she was not there.

"Perhaps he feared that you would refuse to marry him had you known."

Thea drew her gaze away from the imaginary Glenmuir, back to her sister. "Isabelle, we have lived in Scotland, what, three years?"

Isabelle nodded.

"During that time I have learned that Scots like women who are intelligent and outspoken, and who are equal partners in any marriage."

Isabelle laughed. "You have certainly blossomed, Thea. I am amazed at the topics you discuss with the gentlemen of our acquaintance."

"Yes," Thea said slowly. She swung her legs over the side of the bed. "I think James MacLonan spent too many years in France and wandering across the Continent. He has forgotten that Scottish wives expect their husbands to treat them with a respect."

Isabelle looked at her sister with some alarm. "Thea, what are you going to do?"

Thea walked over to her dressing table and surveyed herself in the glass. After a moment she picked up a brush and began to ease the tangles out of her long hair. "I am going to talk to my husband, Isabelle, and let him tell me himself that we will be going to Glenmuir. I wonder when he plans to let me in on the secret. The day before we are to leave Edinburgh? The morning we depart? Am I to be the last person in Edinburgh to learn that I will no longer be living here?"

Now thoroughly alarmed, Isabelle wailed, "Thea, I'm sorry! I should not have said anything!"

Thea dropped the brush and came back to the bed.

"Nonsense, Isabelle," she said, hugging her sister. "I would feel no end of a fool if I continued on in a fog of pleasure thinking James cared about me and was concerned about my happiness, while everyone else knew that I was nothing more than a pawn. Your news has opened my eyes, and I thank you for it."

"No! Thea, you're wrong. James does not see you as a pawn, I'm sure of it."

Thea sighed. She would give anything to go back to that pleasant haze she'd been in before Isabelle arrived. But that was not to be. "Isabelle, James and I must find our own way of dealing together. If he thinks he can leave me out of decisions that will affect both of us, then I'd best show him now that I will not allow it. You've helped me immeasurably. Now, I must get dressed. Will you ring for my maid?"

Isabelle did what her sister asked. "Thea, James is your husband. I did not think that husbands had to explain anything to their wives."

"They do not," Thea said softly. "At least, legally they do not. But here in Scotland, society is more open and women have greater expectations of how they should be treated by their husbands. That is one of the reasons I accepted James's proposal. I believed that he would follow the customs of his country. I did not want to be stuck in a marriage where my husband expected me to be subservient. A part of me would wither and die in that kind of relationship."

"Oh." Isabelle flopped down on the bed beside her sister. "But Thea, Papa does not consider Mama subservient."

"No, he does not. But Papa is not a typical gentleman of our class. Besides, Mama would never let him intimidate her. She simply would not accept it."

"And you are the same, Thea. You will not accept anything but the most open, honorable treatment from James."

Thea hugged her sister. "You are right, Isabelle." She was quiet for a moment. "Although I may have to fight him for it."

CHAPTER 7

Edinburgh had never been one of James's favorite places. During the '45 he had spent weeks here while the Prince gathered up his army. He had been surrounded by men who believed as passionately as he that the Pretender was the man to force the Hanovers from the throne and return the Stuarts to their rightful place as kings of England and Scotland. Those had been heady days, when anything had seemed possible, and the mood amongst the Pretender's people had been light and happy. Despite that, James had still felt the cold shadow of grim authority in the city. Then he had shaken the feeling off. Now he was so suffocated by the place and the people that he longed for the freedom of his Highland hills.

He lounged in the comfortable wing chair and stretched his toes toward the fire as he waited for his father. It had been a long road from that small hovel in France to his father's well-appointed house in Edinburgh, a road that had meandered through strange places and at times had seemed likely never to end. He leaned his head against the chair back. For the first time in many, many years he was able to relax. It was an unexpected luxury.

There was a click as the door to the parlor opened, then the light tap of his father's cane. James rose lithely to his feet. "Sir."

Grant MacLonan considered his son, then smiled. "Well,

Jamie, how do you find married life?"

James smiled lazily. "I can't complain, sir. Miss Tilton and I seem able to get on very well together."

"Mrs. MacLonan, laddie, don't forget that. Whatever her strengths or failings, she's your wife now and you're bound to honor her."

James raised a brow. "I realize that, sir."

Grant eyed him levelly. "Aye, I know you do. I fear, though, that you may not be as comfortable living in her father's lodgings."

"General and Lady Tilton have done all that is polite." He shrugged, then smiled a little ruefully. "I feel much as I did in France, when I was billeted on a family that wasn't quite sure they wanted to have me about, but who could not ask me to leave."

"Tilton is a decent man, Jamie. He'll do his best by you."

James's mouth twisted. "In a cold, dispassionate sort of way." He hesitated, then changed the subject. "Papa, the day is clear, although it's still cool. I thought I would go out and see about some horses. I wish to buy Miss...my wife a proper mount."

"I'll come with you, Jamie." Grant waved down the protests that rose to his son's lips. "I am not so feeble that I cannot search for good horseflesh with my son!"

James grinned, relieved to see that his father's spirit could not be crushed by the physical ailments that plagued him.

When they were outside, Grant refused to order a sedan chair to carry him. He said he wanted to talk to his son, and could not do so all closed up in a chair.

James was touched, but had no idea how to express the affection for his father that threatened to overwhelm him at that moment. He took a deep breath and changed the subject. "Did you send the letter I wrote to Gregor MacLonan, telling him that I would be at Glenmuir as soon as the roads were clear?"

Grant tossed him a look from beneath bushy brows. "Aye, I did. He'll be glad to see you. Gregor has been doing his best to bring Glenmuir back to prosperity, but the land was badly ravaged. The estate needs you there, Jamie. There is no way around it."

James looked at the tall buildings that crowded the edges of the narrow wynd. "I look forward to going," he said honestly.

"Aye." Grant nodded. He cast his son another of his shrewd, penetrating glances. "But how does your bride feel about it?"

There was a moment of telling silence. "She will be fine."

"She doesn't know?"

James reddened at his father's incredulous tone. He'd been planning to tell Thea that they would be living at Glenmuir ever since she had agreed to marry him, but somehow he had never quite gotten around to it. "It doesn't matter. Now that we are married she will go where I go." Even to his own ears his voice had the cold, hard edge he used when commanding his men on the field.

Grant shook his head. "Jamie! English she might be, but Theadora Tilton is a fine, spirited lass and as outspoken as any Scottish girl! She will not fall meekly into line, to please you or any man."

"She agreed to marry me."

Slowly Grant shook his head. He thumped his cane impatiently. "What has that to do with your mad idea of ordering her to leave Edinburgh for an estate deep in the mountains without so much as a warning, to say nothing of a discussion on the subject?"

James couldn't help the surprise in his voice. "Why would she think we would live in Edinburgh?"

"Why would she not? I live in Edinburgh, or London. Most of the Scottish lords spend their time in either city, retreating to their estates only when the Season has ended, just as the English aristocracy does."

"Why would I return to Scotland so that I could waste my time attending parties? I had enough of that on the Continent."

Grant sighed. "You're not listening, lad. What seems so clear to you and me is not necessarily evident to others, particularly your wife."

James mulled those comments over as they walked. Perhaps his father was right. Perhaps Thea would be upset about moving to Glenmuir. She would, after all, be leaving her family behind. But she was a soldier's daughter. She must be used to separations. Then, too, he'd made no secret of his desire to return to Scotland, and to him Scotland meant Glenmuir, the MacLonan home deep in the Highlands.

As they reached their destination he asked, "Do you truly think Thea will balk at the prospect of living at Glenmuir?"

Grant's mouth twisted into a rueful smile. "I can guarantee she will." He shot a shrewd glance at his son. "So, what do you mean to do?"

They went inside the sales pavilion, where James was able to forget his father's question while he concentrated on the attributes of a lively gray mare with pretty black markings and a black mane and tail. After he put the mare through her paces in an indoor ring, he decided that the animal would do very well for Thea. His father suggested he should look at a fine chestnut stallion for himself. James also liked the horse, and decided to purchase it as well. Both animals had the breeding, strength, and spirit that he liked.

When they were heading back Grant asked his question once again.

"Jamie, how do you intend to tell Theadora that she will soon be traveling to Glenmuir?"

James said reflectively, "It is all in the timing, I think. Thea has shown herself to be a woman who is too sensible to allow emotion to rule her for long. I will simply tell her at an appropriate moment, when she will be most receptive to the news."

Grant eyed his son consideringly, then his lips twitched. "You know the lady better than I do, Jamie, but I would think that you'll have a devil of a fight on your hands! Take my advice, be very careful in the way you handle this, very careful indeed."

James looked uneasily at his father. Grant seemed to have a very different view of Theadora Tilton MacLonan than he did. "She will be fine. Sir, let me get you a chair," he added as his father's steps slowed.

Grant thumped his cane irritably. "You'll have to, Jamie. I do not think I can make it up these hills." He shook his head gloomily. "To think that once I roamed Glenmuir's mountains as lithe as a wild creature, and now I haven't even the strength to walk up Edinburgh's slopes."

"We've walked far, Papa. It was a longer outing than I expected."

The chairmen that James had hailed arrived and lowered the sedan chair for Grant to climb into. When he was settled he looked out at his son, his eyes twinkling. "Best think about getting back to your wife then, Jamie. I'll see myself home from here."

James was smiling as he entered the parlor at the Tilton residence.

"Good afternoon, Sir Frederick, Lady Tilton," he said automatically, as he crossed the room to Thea. He caught his wife's hand and lifted it to his lips. "Mistress MacLonan, your servant."

She smiled up into his eyes with the same sweet, melting expression she'd used the night before. His loins tightened.

"Mr. MacLonan," she said, mimicking his formal usage, "it is my pleasure."

He trailed the kiss down to her fingertips, then deliberately took one into his mouth and nipped. Thea gasped, then blushed. James was as pleased as a schoolboy who had just done something naughty his parents wouldn't approve of.

Sir Frederick cleared his throat. James grinned and straightened, his eyes still locked with Thea's. Then he turned to listen to what the general was saying.

"Care for a glass of sherry, MacLonan? Fine vintage this. I can recommend it." Tilton waved a hand toward the decanter resting on a side table.

"Did you have a pleasant day, James?" Thea asked, her voice flowing like silk along his skin.

He turned to her and smiled. "I visited my father this morning, Thea. We went on an expedition to purchase horses."

Sir Frederick choked on his wine and coughed. "An enjoyable experience, I take it?"

James glanced at Tilton. When he looked back at Thea, he saw that she was now seated ramrod straight.

"Were you able to purchase the horses you wanted, James?" she asked.

James suddenly realized that his father was right. He was in for a fight and he hadn't been able to choose his time.

Cautiously, he said, "I was."

Arabella's voice broke into the spell that seemed to lock James and Thea together. "Frederick you promised me that you would look over the household accounts. The totals do not add up and I cannot find where I have gone wrong."

She smiled at her husband in a coaxing way that reminded James of the way Thea sometimes looked at him. His lips twitched as the general tossed off the last of his wine in a cavalier manner and lumbered to his feet.

"An excellent idea, m'dear. I'm always ready to help in household matters."

James watched them go out, amusement in his expression. "I do hope I did not chase your parents away, Thea."

Pink flags of color flared on Thea's cheeks. "I think my parents believed we should be alone for a time."

"Sensible people. Mistress MacLonan," he said softly, his eyes scrutinizing her expression, "would you care to take my arm?"

Thea didn't move. "Why?"

He raised his brows. "I wish you to come to the window. I have something I would like to show you."

She rose in one fluid, furious movement. "As you wish, sir."

Eyeing her warily, James took her arm and guided her to a

window. "Look outside. What do you see?"

"Pedestrians, horses pulling carriages. Oh, there is Olivia Ramsey and her husband. They must be going to a dinner party. Why else—"

"Not the traffic, Thea. Your gift!"

She frowned. "I can see nothing that resembles a gift. Perhaps it is too far away...."

He caught her head between his hands and turned it so that she looked in the direction he wanted her to. "There," he said softly. "Do you see it now?"

"The horse?"

Somewhat deflated by her reaction to his present, he snapped, "Yes!"

Thea looked more closely. "Though we are three stories up, the horse does appear to be a fine animal." She looked up at him, a smile on her lips, but not in her eyes.

James saw the fury simmering in her eyes and knew he was indeed in trouble. He said coaxingly, "I had hoped you would be more pleased with the gift than this."

She cocked her head, still smiling that empty social smile. "Have you already made plans how I might best make use of the animal?"

He sucked in his breath. She knew. He had no idea how she had learned that they would be living in Glenmuir, but as his father had predicted, she was very, very angry. "Why do you ask?"

Thea looked out the window again. Her tone was musing. "Although I have ridden much in the past, I rarely do so in Edinburgh. The streets are too narrow and there is no place for polite society to ride here, as there is in London. I did wonder if you had other plans."

Silently cursing whoever had forced his hand, James said coolly, "What do you think those plans might be?"

Turning away from the window, Thea went toward the hearth. There she prodded the fire with an iron poker, almost as if she would prefer to be poking him instead, James thought ruefully. "Since you force the issue, sir, I will tell you what you should have told me in the first place. Your plans, I believe, include leaving Edinburgh for some benighted spot in the mountains."

James suppressed his annoyance over her description of his beloved Glenmuir. "You don't approve of our removal to the Highlands."

Thea tossed down the poker, then swept him a graceful, mocking curtsy. "I go where my husband commands. It is not mine to approve or disapprove."

James said mildly, "You would do well to remember that, madam."

Rising to her full height, Thea's angry brown eyes challenged him. "When we've reached Glenmuir, Mr. MacLonan, do you intend to tell others all of those unimportant little details that a husband usually tells his wife? Will I be the last to know if you decide to visit one of your other properties, only finding out when you don't sit down to dinner with me?"

"That is unfair, Thea."

She made a little sound that seethed with frustration. "Was it fair of you to tell my parents that we would be living in Glenmuir before you told me?"

"So that is what this is all about," James breathed softly. He suspected that his father had decided that the Tilton family deserved to know that their daughter would not be living in Edinburgh, and so he'd mentioned the issue to General Tilton—in confidence, most likely, James thought cynically—Tilton had then told his wife, who had told Thea. The result was the righteous fury that was driving Thea now.

"I expected better of you, sir!"

"Thea, have done! I did not deliberately set out to slight you."

"But it happened!"

"Yes, it did."

Her eyes blazing, she hurried to the door in a rustle of silken skirts. There she paused, dramatically outlined in the opening. "We both know the reasons for our marriage, James

MacLonan. I do not expect affection from you, but I do expect respect. Next time you have an order to give which concerns me, pray consider informing me before any other."

"That sounds remarkably like a threat."

Thea opened her eyes in a wide, guileless expression. "Would I threaten my husband? I merely ask to be accorded the civilities any married woman is owed by her mate."

She was giving him fair warning that she would not allow herself to be treated as anything other than his equal. Very well, he was willing to accept that, but there were some matters in which he refused to concede his power over his wife. A slow lazy smile touched James's mouth as he caught Thea before she could fully enter the hallway. Gently he drew her back into the room. "I think," he said softly, touching her cheek, "I begin to understand you."

Though she did not struggle, she turned her face away, refusing to meet his eyes. He bent and kissed her lightly along her elegant jawline. She shuddered. He took advantage of the moment to slip his arm around her waist and draw her to him. "I promise you, Thea, you have my respect and more."

"James...the servants."

He shut the door and turned her face so that he could kiss her on the lips. "The servants are an excuse. Kiss me, Thea."

He had the great satisfaction of feeling his fierce, willful wife surrender to the pleasure of his touch.

Although it was nearly May, there was a bite in the gusty wind that whipped through Edinburgh's narrow streets. Sitting in the sedan chair carried by two stalwart bearers, wrapped up in a fur-lined cloak, Thea shivered. She thought about her husband, walking beside the chair, and wondered if he were as cold as she. Then she dismissed the idea with a certain amount of pouting disdain. James MacLonan could not be cold! After all, was he not the man demanding that they travel to his Highland estate as soon as possible, even though spring had hardly arrived?

She shivered again, not from the cold, as her thoughts

dwelt on the future. Although she did not know much about the Scottish Highlands, beyond the obvious—that the region was a vast tract of mountainous country and that it was home to the Jacobite sedition—she was not burdened with the prejudice against the area that many others in Edinburgh were.

Moreover, although Thea had lived the past several years in cities, first London and now Edinburgh, she had been born on her father's small estate in Kent and had spent most of her life there. Country life had no fears for her; indeed, in some ways she preferred it. Her concern now was not country life, but life amongst strangers.

She had hoped, no, she had assumed, that she would have some time to become acquainted with James here in Edinburgh where her family would be nearby to champion her and give her comfort should she need it. At Glenmuir she would be alone, forced to cope with whatever James thrust at her as best she could, with little or no support. Deep in her soul, the prospect terrified her.

Hence her defiance. Theadora Tilton was the daughter of an officer in the British Army. She had been raised not to show her fears no matter what the situation. *Leadership*, her father had said to her many times, *begins with strength. Show contempt for danger and you will give yourself and your men heart. Show fear and you will find yourself alone.* So Thea had learned not to cry when she was afraid. Instead, she laughed, taunting her fears rather than bowing down to them. Usually it worked, but there had been so many shifts and changes to face since she had met James MacLonan. She was weary in a way that went beyond physical fatigue.

Glenmuir. A pretty name. She considered it as she tried to imagine what the estate was like. Grant MacLonan was a wealthy man, so his home must be a very fine property indeed. She envisioned a large house, old-fashioned, for the MacLonan had lived on the estate for generations, but well kept, as befitted the principal residence of an aristocrat. Around it was a green park, with gently rolling acreage, including a small stream that lead into a picturesque lake. A romantic ruin, in the Classical style, was situated between the house and the lake. In her mental image, Glenmuir was a gentleman's property, well kept, well loved, and very safe. It was also remarkably like her father's estate in Kent.

Reassured, Thea sighed and laid her head back against the cushions. Her eyes closed.

On this evening, the party was a poetry reading at the home of one of Edinburgh's leading citizens. The reading was in full swing when Thea and James arrived. The hostess greeted them effusively and dragged Thea into the salon. James was given into the care of his host, and borne away to converse with the gentlemen or join a game of cards in progress.

In the salon, Thea stood quietly, listening without much attention to the young man spouting endless lines of uninspired poetry about the noble past of the great Scottish nation. Fanning herself idly, she scrutinized the crowd. The party was well attended. She noticed Olivia Ramsey in one corner, her daughters nowhere in sight. Olivia was glancing around as Thea was, clearly bored by the recital.

She caught sight of Thea and her gaze brightened. With a polite word here and a nod there, she made her way over to Thea's side. "My dear, how good to see you!"

Thea chuckled. "Is poetry not to your fancy, Mrs. Ramsey?"

"Of course I dote upon poetry, when it is done properly! But really! How is one expected to enjoy a full evening listening to men who should have better ways to occupy their time than writing and reading maudlin verses about the history of Scotland?"

Thea chuckled. "You may be listening to the birth pains of a great genius, Mrs. Ramsey."

"Stuff," retorted Olivia roundly.

"I fear that you are too practical to enjoy the artistic flights of fancy of your Scottish poets."

"I am also loyal to the Crown! Some of the poets tonight have verged on seditious in their writings!"

Sedition was a word loaded with meanings that went beyond what was happening in this room tonight. "Better that they verge on sedition than that they carry through," Thea murmured.

Olivia eyed her shrewdly. "Your husband has mellowed you, my dear. Perhaps you will have the same effect on him."

Surprised, Thea shot her a questioning glance.

"I simply meant that Mr. MacLonan, being a pardoned Jacobite, will always need the strength of your Whiggish views, Miss Til—Mrs. MacLonan!"

"My husband has left his Jacobite leanings behind him, ma'am," Thea said stiffly.

Olivia patted her on the arm. "Of course he has, my dear. And after a few seasons here in Edinburgh he will have forgotten all of those silly Highland ideas of his."

Thea turned her face away.

Olivia drew a quick breath. "Thea? He is remaining in Edinburgh, is he not?"

Thea waved her fan. With a great effort of will, she assumed that bright, bold expression that hid the fears that tormented her. *Strength!* How she needed some right now. "We repair to Glenmuir as soon as the roads are clear."

Frowning, Olivia scrutinized Thea's expression. "You will have much to prepare for between now and then."

Thea smiled and said with an enthusiasm she didn't feel, "Yes, I will have to begin immediately. The house has not been lived in since the Rising, so I intend to purchase linens, draperies, and some furnishings at the very least."

"At the very least," Olivia repeated.

It was Thea's turn to frown. "Mrs. Ramsey, you sound...oh, I don't know, ominous, perhaps. Is there something about Glenmuir that I should know?"

"Travel in this weather is bound to be uncomfortable."

Thea nodded, her brows raised. Olivia was stating the obvious.

"By the time you reach Glenmuir you will be exhausted."

By this time Thea knew that Olivia Ramsey had more to impart than a few self-evident observations.

Moving closer, Olivia caught Thea's hand and patted it affectionately. "Edinburgh can be a bleak place in the winter months and hot in the summer, but there is plenty of society to keep a person busy and everything is so close together that visiting isn't difficult. You would be much happier here than in a desolate place like Glenmuir."

All the fears that had been plaguing Thea since she had learned she and James would be living at Glenmuir surfaced dangerously. She firmed her jaw, but her voice shook a little.

"I know the trip to Glenmuir will be difficult, Mrs. Ramsey, and I am prepared for it. I believe Mr. MacLonan has written to his steward advising him that we will be arriving within a month and to have the house prepared for us. Once there, I am sure I will adapt quickly."

"Thea," Olivia said urgently, "you don't know what life in the Highlands is like! The people are savages! Barbarians!"

Thea had heard expressions of this sort before. Until she had met James MacLonan, she had believed them. Now she shook her head. "Mrs. Ramsey, how can I accept a statement of that nature? My husband is a Highlander and he is no barbarian!"

"James MacLonan is an aristocrat. The common people are different."

Doubt flickered through Thea's mind, but she kept her features calm and confident. "As it is true I have no experience of the ordinary people of the Highlands, I cannot disagree with you. But I see no reason to worry about the common people. They are not my concern."

"They will be," Olivia retorted grimly. "The Highlands are a harsh region, thinly populated. High mountains separate the valleys, making travel difficult. Thea, do you know what the name of your husband's estate means?"

Frowning, Thea shook her head.

"Glenmuir—wooded valley. Does that not tell you something of what you should expect when you reach your new home?"

Since she had been raised on her father's small estate in Kent, Thea's idea of country-living meant large manor houses staffed by dozens of servants, a regular round of social visits between the members of the gentry who lived in the vicinity, dances and parties that ended with overnight stays or late-night drives through the gentle countryside. She couldn't imagine an area where such things were not possible. Smiling tranquilly, she said, "You make the estate sound very pretty. Rolling hills surrounding a lush green forest—"

"Jutting mountains dominating a narrow valley choked with evergreens more like!" Olivia interrupted crisply.

Thea swallowed. Olivia Ramsey was well known for her dislike of the Highlands. Now she was simply showing her prejudice.

Olivia swept on, as unstoppable as a flooded river in the spring, and just as destructive. "The only people you'll find at Glenmuir are MacLonans, all clansmen of your husband's. There'll be no other gentry but yourselves, and if he chooses to remain there through the winter, you will be imprisoned in your valley after the snow closes the passes, and will go nowhere until the snow melts in the spring. Think of the loneliness, Thea. Of the harshness of the life you will have to endure."

Olivia's words destroyed what was left of Thea's fine bravado. She was barely able to whisper, "James has told me nothing of this."

Olivia squeezed her fingers gently. "Stay here in Edinburgh. If your husband wishes to retreat from the town for a space, you are welcome to use our estate."

"I don't know." Thea moistened dry lips. "I—I would have to ask James."

Olivia laughed, confident and assured. "Then the matter is settled. I did not think you would persist in this foolish notion once you were aware of the true situation. I will write our steward and tell him that you will be staying for some weeks during the spring and summer."

Cornered, Thea flashed, "Mrs. Ramsey, nothing is decided yet!"

"Nonsense! An intelligent woman can easily talk a man around to her way of thinking. Now, we have been gossiping here overlong. I see Judge Denholm across the room and I promised my husband that I would be polite to him, even though I find the man to be a dreadful Tory in his views."

"But—"

"Think positively, Thea," Olivia said breezily as she departed. "Your husband will follow your dictates once you have learned the best way to persuade him that what he wants is exactly what you want."

Very doubtful that she would have the least affect on her husband's decision to return to Glenmuir, Thea pushed Olivia's invitation from her thoughts. The woman's earlier comments about the Highlands were not so easily dismissed, however, and Thea's fears returned, stronger and more painful than before. She stared at the poet, who was just finishing his long, rambling verses, and forced a smile onto her lips as she clapped politely along with the rest of the company.

For the rest of the evening, no one, including her husband and family, had the least idea of the foreboding that tormented her.

When Olivia Ramsey returned home that evening, she stopped to dash off two quick notes before retiring to her bedchamber for the night. The first was to her steward at Ramsey House.

The second was addressed to one Gregor MacLonan, steward of Glenmuir.

CHAPTER 8

When they left the party that evening, Thea looked at her husband from the shadow of the hooded cloak she wore. "I feel the need to walk, James. Would you mind dismissing the chair for tonight?"

He raised a brow, but did as she requested. The journey back to the Tilton residence close to the Castle wasn't particularly far.

Their footsteps echoed on the cobbled streets as they walked. Thea took a deep breath. Then somewhat tentatively, she said, "I would know more about Glenmuir, James. Where is it? What is the house like? Who are our neighbors? I…I do not mean to pester you on the subject, but I have a thousand questions that are churning about inside of me."

They walked on. James was silent for a long time too long, Thea thought uneasily, remembering Olivia Ramsey's descriptions.

At last he said, "I have not been to Glenmuir for nearly five years. I left when Charles Edward Stuart raised the clans in '45, and although I was there briefly after the Battle of Falkirk, I have been gone ever since. All I can tell you is what the place was like in January of 1746."

"Then tell me what it was once like."

James glanced down at her and smiled. "Glenmuir," he began softly, "was a rich green valley where the people lived well. It is in the mountains, so the land was mainly used for grazing. Some crops were grown, enough to feed the people, but it was in the herds that Glenmuir was rich, that and the trees which were felled for sale."

"Who lives there?"

He raised his brows in surprise. "My clansmen, the MacLonans."

Ominously, Olivia Ramsey's words came back to Thea. "There are no other gently bred people there?"

James paused, then said carefully, "Thea, Highlanders are different from the English, or even the Lowland Scots. My clansmen are all free and equal and expect to be treated that way."

"But you are the laird—"

"No, I am not." He laughed. "My father is the MacLonan, the clan leader. He is the first among equals."

Thea bit her lip. She stared at the old stone buildings crowding High Street. Her experience was of cities and a well-stratified country life. The world James was describing was beyond her imaginings and so very threatening. "My home in Kent and the way of life there are very different," she said. "I fear I will not know how to cope in your Highland stronghold."

He patted her hand where it lay on his arm. Thea looked over to find him watching her with concern. "Glenmuir will be strange at first, but in time you will become familiar with all that goes on there. I know it will be difficult, but you will adapt."

Unspoken was his own experience as an exile. With a pang, Thea wondered how much hardship he had endured after he landed in France, certain that he must make a new life, that he would never be allowed to return to his homeland. In some ways, he understood her fears, but in others he did not, for he was obsessed with the need to return to Glenmuir.

Thea smiled and made the best of things. "Tell me about your home. What is Glenmuir Castle like?" She glanced at James in time to see a spasm of pain cross his face. Fear placed its icy print on her spine, and doubt brought her fears alive. She moistened her lips, then set her jaw as she waited what seemed to be a very long time before he answered her question.

"Glenmuir Castle was a place of winding corridors and drafty rooms. It was built of stone that caught the rays of the sun, so that it often seemed to glow golden, like a place of magic. But in the winter the rooms were cold, and the warmth never penetrated in the summer. It was a place of imagination and dreams, not everyday comforts."

"You used the past tense," Thea said, her voice rising dangerously. "It was, they were! Why?"

"I told you! I haven't been there for five years."

"There's more, isn't there?"

Goaded, he snapped, "You are right, there is more! Much more! I did use the past deliberately because Glenmuir Castle is gone! After the defeat at Culloden, the Duke of Cumberland decided to rid the Highlands of the clans. He burned and raped and murdered. But you knew of that, did you not, Miss Tilton?"

His anger cut through Thea's fears and drew her defiant temper to the surface. "MacLonan!" she countered fiercely. "Mrs. James MacLonan. Remember that, sir! And kindly remember as well that I was not in Scotland during the rebellion or the period directly afterward. Nor was anyone in my family."

A muscle flexed in James's jaw. They had turned into a narrow wynd. The Tilton residence was halfway down the short street. As they reached the steps, he bowed with elegant irony. "I shall endeavor to recall the fact, madam."

As he raised his hand to knock on the door, Thea asked softly, "Mr. MacLonan, if there is no castle at Glenmuir, where will we be living?"

He raised his brows and rapped sharply with the knocker. "My clansmen are building us a house, in honor of my return."

"A house?"

"A cottage actually."

The image of a two-room hovel leapt into her mind. "How large will this house or cottage be?"

"I don't know!" he retorted impatiently. "It will be the kind of house that is fit for the clan leader of the MacLonans and his family to live in."

"And what is that? How can you not know a detail such as the number of rooms in the house being constructed for you, on your lands?"

The door opened. The butler welcomed them home and announced that Sir Frederick and Lady Tilton had not yet returned. Neither James nor Thea acknowledged this useful bit of information.

"My father's steward wrote that a suitable house was being built by the clansmen," James said impatiently. "I did not inquire further because it would be an insult to do so."

Thea's doubts, born of her husband's poorly managed method of telling her that they would be living at Glenmuir, encouraged by Olivia Ramsey's carefully worded phrases, and nurtured by Thea's own experiences in Scotland, compacted in to an insurmountable barrier. "You did not wish to insult one of your clansmen, yet you were content to take your wife to live in a building which could be nothing more than a hovel! Your consideration for my feelings astounds me!"

The butler took their outer garments and hastened to leave them.

James glared at Thea. His eyes were an icy blue. "I am needed in Glenmuir."

"And I was needed to get you there," Thea retorted, her dark eyes blazing.

James bowed with an elegance that was decidedly French. "Just so, madam."

"Then be glad, sir, that I have given you the opportunity to return to your beloved burned-out ruin, for I will not be accompanying you!"

A muscle jumped in his jaw. "We leave for Glenmuir as

soon as the roads are passable."

"You leave!" Thea balled her hands into fists. "I do not intend to live in the crude cottage your clansmen are making for you. I shall stay here, in Edinburgh. You may visit me whenever the whim takes you."

He caught her shoulders in a tight grasp. "Then I will be visiting you very often indeed, wife, because you will be sleeping in my bed, beside me, at Glenmuir!"

"I will not!"

"Thea," he said grimly, "the people of Glenmuir need me—us. We cannot linger here in Edinburgh indulging in our own pleasure."

"Us!" She pulled away, anger once again sparking from her eyes. "If your barbaric Highlanders feel as you do, James MacLonan, they will not want an Englishwoman in their midst! What need have you of my presence in your desolate Highland hills? If you must go to Glenmuir, then allow me to remain here, in civilized society!"

There was nothing she could have said more calculated to inflame her husband's temper. "Never! You come with me to Glenmuir the day I get word the roads are clear."

They glared at each other for a long, tension-charged moment. Then Thea dropped her gaze submissively. There was nothing submissive in the deep curtsy she swept him, however. Indeed, there was more defiance in the act than dutiful obedience.

In her bedchamber, Thea rang for her maid with such force that the bellpull was almost ripped from the wall. Then she paced the room with all the fury of a trapped wildcat. When her maid mistook her annoyance for the impatience of a new bride to be ready for her husband's evening visit, Thea's temper almost snapped. She did not tell the maid that the last thing she expected was a visit from her husband, but it was true. After their argument tonight she was quite certain James would not be joining her.

In that she was wrong. She was curled up in her bed, the covers pulled up to her chin and her eyes firmly closed, though she was far from sleep, when the door quietly opened. Thea froze. If this was her mother or sister coming in to talk, she was in no mood for a cozy conversation tonight, and if it was James... He wouldn't consider lying with her tonight—would he?

He would.

She opened her eyes a crack, still pretending sleep. He stood beside the bed, holding a candle. He was wearing a blue velvet bed gown and nothing else. It was clear that he had not come to her chamber to continue their discussion.

"Open your eyes, Thea. I know you're awake."

Her eyes flew open. "I am very tired," she said, not moving.

A smile flickered across his set features and was gone. "Then you will soon be exhausted." He set the candle on the table beside the bed and shrugged off the velvet bed gown.

Thea's breath caught. She still hadn't gotten used to the intimacy that a physical union with a man brought, and she found herself looking as closely at James's muscular body as if she had never seen it before. Still, when he slipped in beside her, she stiffened.

He lay on his side, one arm bent to prop up his head, and looked at her soberly. "Do you wish you could deny me your bed?"

Thea swallowed. "What would you do if I did?"

His free hand wrapped around her waist, drawing her close, and his other hand tangled in her hair as he moved to kiss her slightly parted lips. "I will not be denied, Thea."

He was talking about more than whether or not she accepted his caresses tonight, but at that moment Thea didn't care. He was seducing her, there was no doubt about it, but she wanted to be seduced. She accepted his caresses and his passion, for her body was already warming with remembered pleasure. Desire, she discovered, was a very potent force.

In the aftermath, she sighed and curled against his warmth. She was sated and lazy, and did not feel like arguing with him again, but she did not want him to think that her physical submission was also a mental one.

"James…"

He rolled on his side with a little murmur and kissed her lingeringly. Then he smiled faintly and said, "I like the sound of my name on your lips."

Thea's mouth slowly curled into an answering smile. He looked as relaxed and contented as she felt, and she believed that his words were spoken from the heart. She stroked her fingers along his short, dark hair. "It still seems very strange. I am not used to being a wife yet."

He kissed her again, shifting her so that she was on her back. His kiss deepened. "Nor am I used to having a wife. You please me greatly, Thea."

He meant physically, for surely he could not want a wife who fought him on issues he considered trivial. Still, for those few pleasurable minutes, Thea allowed herself to believe that nothing could be that bad with this man by her side.

She was breathing heavily and her heart was pounding when he released her lips once again. "James—"

Laughing, he stroked his hand down her rib cage, teasing the side of her breast. Her nipple peaked. Thea groaned.

"Yes, my dear? Did you want to discuss something with me?"

"Yes," she managed to grit out before desire got the better of her and she gave up the attempt to talk so she could concentrate on the wonderful sensations created by his hands and mouth.

This time when her body arched beneath his, she cried out his name in fierce exaltation and heard him hiss, "Yes!" in triumph. His strokes quickened and he kissed her roughly, sending her cascading into a fiery climax that left her limp. She slept through the night, cradled in his arms, well content.

James was still asleep when Thea woke the next morning. Her thoughts were confused as she lay beside him, thinking of the pleasure he had given her and of the arbitrary way he had planned for their removal to Glenmuir. Try as she might, she could not understand how the same man could be both so gentle and so cold. Drawing away in an attempt to look into his face, to see if she could find the answers she sought, she woke him.

He smiled lazily. "Good morning, wife."

He looked smug and distinctly pleased with himself. Thea's dimple appeared as she tried not to laugh. "Good morning."

Brushing her thick, golden hair away from her face, his hand lingered for a moment. "What a pleasure it is to know that the woman sharing my bed is not only beautiful at night, but when she wakes in the morning."

The woman sharing my bed. The phrase, with all of the subtle implications they'd argued about last night, snapped Thea out of her pleasure-induced haze. She caught his hand to still the idle, seductive caress. "James, I need to talk to you."

He didn't move, beyond raising one questioning brow. "I am at your disposal, madam."

Now that the moment had come, Thea couldn't make the words come out. "James, I…"

Gently, he freed his hand, drawing it down to her shoulders. Feeling the tense muscles there, he kneaded her flesh. Thea felt a flash of pleasure and sighed, arching into his touch.

"You want to talk about our journey to Glenmuir." He smiled at her surprised expression. "You merely have to ask, my dear."

"James, will you not reconsider? You have admitted that you do not know what to expect at Glenmuir. Why must we both go into a situation where the living conditions may be impossible…"

"There are dozens of people who rely on Glenmuir for everything in their lives. As I told you last night, Thea, they need the support of the clan leader."

"They don't need me!"

"Yes, they do."

"James, I will come to Glenmuir eventually, but for now, until you know what the situation is, why not leave me here, where I will not be a burden to you."

James smiled. "Believe me, Thea, you are not a burden to me." He touched her cheek with his finger, then slowly ran the tip down her soft skin to her jawbone.

Her heart began to beat hard. "James…"

"I will not leave you here, Thea." He flipped onto his back and put his hands behind his head. "The people of Glenmuir need both of us."

"You said last night that the Duke of Cumberland's army had burned Glenmuir, then raped the women and stolen the livestock. How do you think those people of yours will feel when the wife you bring from Edinburgh is not a fine Scotswoman, but one of the hated English?"

He lay silently, staring up at the bed hangings, his mouth set in a compressed line. Finally, he said, "I have thought of that. Do you think I did not take it into consideration before I offered to marry you?"

The pain caused by his words was sharp and jagged. It tore at Thea with the savagery of a deliberate, personal attack. "Perhaps then, you should have discussed the matter with me so that we could have avoided this stupid, impossible situation!" When she began, her voice was low and throbbing, but as she spoke it rose, until she spat out the last three emphatic words.

James swung out of bed in one little movement. Then he turned to face her. She knew the thin linen of her nightdress did little to hide her body, for James stared hungrily at her for a moment, then said roughly, "The issue of our residence was discussed, by my father and your father. Your family was well aware that you would be living at Glenmuir after your marriage."

"But I was not!"

He put his hands on his hips. "That is immaterial."

"On the contrary, James MacLonan! I will not be disposed

of like some piece of unimportant furniture!" She leapt from the bed. "I make my own decisions and I choose not to go to Glenmuir with you!"

A muscle jumped in his jaw. "You are my wife and you will go."

He looked very dangerous standing there, his eyes blazing and every muscle in his body tensed for battle. Thea glared at him, hating him for seducing her into liking him enough so that she had agreed to marry him, and for seducing her with his physical magic so that she was responding to the promise in his body even as they fought over the most basic element in their marriage. She lifted her chin defiantly. "You are making a mistake, James. Do not force me to go to Glenmuir with you."

"I do not appreciate threats," he gritted, glaring at her.

Thea opened her eyes wide. "Do you find me threatening, James?"

He opened his mouth to say something, then thought the better of it. Instead, he spun on his heel and marched furiously from the room.

Thea watched him go as she stood straight and stiff, but more fearful of the future than ever. James was implacable. As the door slammed shut behind him, she slumped, her hair falling around her face in a thick, golden veil. Soon she would begin a journey into a forbidding land whose people were hostile to everything she knew and understood. She would have no friends, no one she could confide in, no one to care about her well-being. Yesterday she would have scoffed at this thought, believing James would easily fill the role of friend, as well as husband.

Now she knew differently. Slowly she straightened again, then tossed her head, shifting her thick mane away from her face. Very well. They were married. She knew her duty. Despite her taunts, she would follow him north to his savage stronghold. She would make love with him, she would bear his children, she would be the dutiful wife he wanted.

But she would not be a fool and lose her heart to a man who could never return her affection.

* * *

When James stormed out of Thea's room he had nothing more on his mind than putting some distance between himself and his wife before he lost complete control of his temper. He forgot to put on his night robe, and so strode into the hallway completely naked. There he practically knocked over Sir Frederick, who blinked and made a dismayed sound in his throat. The general was fully dressed, in the scarlet uniform coat and white breeches of the British infantry. The sight only added fuel to James's rage.

Seething with unexpressed anger, James felt no embarrassment as he stood naked in front of his father-by-marriage. He didn't bother to apologize for his appearance. Instead, he curtly ordered a hovering servant to summon his valet.

"Going out?" Sir Frederick asked, eyeing James warily.

"As soon as I am dressed," James retorted shortly.

"You seem rather—annoyed," Tilton said cautiously. "Is there a problem?"

James glared at him. Over the past few days he had begun to like General Sir Frederick Tilton, despite his prejudices against the man's profession and country, but right now he was in no mood to be pleasant to anyone in the Tilton family.

"Yes, there is a problem! Your daughter!"

Enlightenment and a certain male compassion dawned on Tilton's face. "Ah, Thea! Yes, she can be somewhat trying at times." He glanced down James's naked form. "What's she been up to now?"

"She refuses to travel to Glenmuir. She wants me to live here, in Edinburgh," James stated wrathfully.

Tilton nodded. "I thought she might have some difficulty with that."

James clamped his jaw shut to keep from observing that Tilton's remarks were of no use whatsoever. Fortunately his manservant arrived at that moment, so he was able to retreat into his room without coming to blows with his host.

However, as he slammed the door shut, he thought he heard Tilton chuckle. His simmering temper flared.

Once he was dressed, he knew he could not remain in the Tilton household where he was very likely to meet either Thea or her parents at any time. There was much that he needed to do before he left Edinburgh, so he decided to make use of the day rather than allow it to be devastated by the way it began.

A gusty wind whipped his cloak out behind him as he strode down the narrow wynd on which the Tilton residence was situated. He clutched at the worsted material, wrapping the long garment around his body. The day was cold and raw, with a hint of winter still in the air, although the precipitation that fell intermittently from the iron-gray sky was rain, not snow.

As he marched along the steep alley toward High Street, he cursed Edinburgh, the stink of human habitation that made walking a chore rather than a pleasant pastime, and the north wind that blew the fetid reek of the polluted North Loch into the city environs. Focusing on the disadvantages of life in Edinburgh allowed him to push his angry thoughts of Thea to the back of his mind, and walking, despite the odors that assailed his nostrils, helped dissipate the frustrated energy that plagued him.

The narrow wynd ended at High Street, the main thoroughfare of Edinburgh, which led from Holyrood Palace, along the spine of the ridge on which the city perched, to the Castle at its summit. James found his footsteps heading down the slope, away from the Castle, toward Holyrood Palace. At the gates he paused, looking into the gardens at the pretty structure built more than two centuries before.

Memories assaulted him. Of the evening when Neil introduced him to Charles Edward Stuart, of the charm of the man, and his interest in a younger son who came as one of many to join the Prince's cause. One of those people who possessed phenomenal memories, the Prince had been an expert at making every man believe he was valued for himself alone. In the glittering throng that surrounded the rebel leader, in which all the men dressed in their richest clothes, the Prince had stood out, regal, yet one of them. Wearing a fine tartan kilt and velvet jacket, with a tartan sash across his breast, and lace of the finest quality at his throat and wrists, he was the quintessential Highland warrior.

A fine memory to carry all these years, thought James cynically, his mood reflected in the cold sky and the wilted vegetation of the ornate gardens beyond the wrought iron gates. The Prince had been a master of illusion, putting on a fine performance for the faithful here in Edinburgh. An actor, a dreamer, a charmer of men, Charles Edward Stuart was all of these, but he was not a leader or a decision-maker, and that was what had defeated him in the end.

Impatient with himself, James turned away. Aimlessly walking, he entered a deserted alley. The past was gone. It was the present he must be concerned with now. And the present meant coming to terms with his wife and the life they would live together. The quarrel with Thea had been unfortunate, though perhaps necessary. He hadn't meant to be so harsh in his demand that she journey with him to Glenmuir, but he'd been surprised at her expectation that they would remain in Edinburgh and he'd reacted quickly, as was his nature, instinctively doing what he must to ensure the survival of himself and his men.

Thinking in terms of survival in relation to his argument with Thea brought James to an abrupt halt in the middle of the narrow street. Without consciously admitting it to himself, he'd already come to rely on her presence. Her merry laugh, her clear, intelligent view on issues and people, her steely refusal to be intimidated by situations that would make other women cringe and weep.

A rough voice, shouting for him to step aside, brought him back to an awareness of his surroundings with a start.

He moved quickly as two panting chairmen, carrying a fat merchant with several double chins and a hefty bulk, passed by. The interruption brought all of the dislike James felt for Edinburgh surging to the surface. It was a city of wealth and of local power and, as in all such places, the ruling class applied their power through a combination of right and coercion. Highlanders had never been welcome in this city, except for that one unreal period when Charles Edward Stuart forced the smug Lowlanders to bend to the power of his rebellious Highland army.

As the chair disappeared around the corner, James began to walk again, his thoughts returning more pleasantly to Thea and their more intimate moments together. Thinking back over the course of their argument, he began to feel a trifle happier. Theadora Tilton MacLonan was an independent, determined woman, but she responded to reason and she could be swayed given the right circumstances. Now all he had to do was convince her that her presence at Glenmuir was important to both him and his clansmen, but how was he to do that?

She responded to him physically, and in those moments when they were making love he believed, without conceit, that she would agree to follow him anywhere. At other times, she was less tractable. Was that the clue he needed?

As he walked, he considered the bright, charming woman he had married. What was important to Theadora Tilton MacLonan? In his mind he saw her again, mimicking fashionable dandies with good-natured mockery, laughing and smiling at him as they walked in Olivia Ramsey's garden, at the parties before their wedding, standing by his side and responding to the inevitable teasing with amusement and wit. Gradually he came to realize that talk itself was important to Thea. Discussion, communication, the use of words to express feelings. She liked to take a subject, turn it around, inspect it from all angles, then pull it apart, using words.

James groaned aloud. Giving Thea ultimatums that denied discussion did nothing but distress her, or worse, it made her angry. Then, once she was angry; she fought like the daughter of a soldier that she was.

Very well, if what she needed was discussion, he'd tell her what he planned and let her say her piece, before he went out and did what he'd intended to do in the first place. That should keep her happy, and it didn't seem to be too high a price to pay for an amenable wife.

Feeling very much better, he continued on his way, organizing his thoughts around what needed to be done to prepare for their departure from Edinburgh.

CHAPTER 9

Over the next week the Tilton household became a place of strong, leashed emotions as Thea spoke pleasantly to her husband on unimportant subjects, but bowed her head politely whenever he made a suggestion on their departure, or even mentioned Glenmuir. Try as he might, James could not get her to discuss the emotions simmering inside her. If he pressed her, she would smile and say that she was obeying his commands as he wished.

But James didn't wish for a wife who was dutiful and proper. He wanted Thea's clear observations, quiet courage, and bright, laughing charm. He wanted the woman who had stood in front of the Duchess of Argyll and championed him without a second thought. Frustration began to gnaw at him. He was doing everything he could to try to convince Thea that his intentions were good, but nothing seemed to work.

Tension in the household escalated, snaking along everyone's nerves, so that even Arabella, with her great store of patience born of raising her high-strung, independent children, snapped at the least provocation. Finally, at the end of that long week, Sir Frederick ordered each member of the family to cancel their activities for the evening. He wished to have a family conference.

He directed each member of his household to a chair, so that Thea sat beside James, with Arabella and Isabelle beside her. All of the chairs were set in a small semi-circle facing the fireplace, where Tilton stood erect and imposing, his hands linked behind his back. He was very much the general officer conducting a meeting of his staff and expecting attention and obedient willingness to carry out the dictates that emerged from the session.

James watched him with rather cynical amusement. He suspected that Tilton was about to issue a few orders to his errant daughter, and James wasn't sure whether he approved of the concept or not. He certainly didn't think it would work. In fact, he was quite sure that ordering Thea to gracefully accept her inevitable departure to Glenmuir would only inflame her temper more.

"I've been thinking," Tilton began, fixing each member of his family with the forceful glare that made his junior officers quake.

Although James raised his brows at this statement, no one else seemed particularly concerned by this information. Isabelle looked up and smiled, before once more bowing her head over the cushion cover she was embroidering, Thea smoothed the fine linen of the cloth she was sewing, and Lady Tilton murmured, "That's good, Frederick."

The general nodded, not at all put out by this tepid response. "The weather," he noted, "is becoming much warmer."

At that Thea did look at her father, then shot a quick glance at James, before once more staring at Sir Frederick. "What are you saying, Papa?"

"Seems to me that we'd all be wise to make plans."

"What kind of plans, Papa?"

Sir Frederick shot his daughter a shrewd and compassionate look. "Plans on how best to keep this family together once you are permanently settled at Glenmuir."

The expression on Thea's face as she looked over at James could only be described as hostile. "I go to Glenmuir under duress."

"Precisely!" Tilton said. He looked from his daughter to James. "Seems to me that you two young people need to remember that you will be spending a lifetime together, many years of it at

Glenmuir, I'll wager. You'd best learn to be friends."

Listening to Thea's father critique his marriage made James uncomfortable and not a little resentful. "I was not aware that friendship was required in a marriage," he said.

"Friendship is the basis of marriage," Sir Frederick stated.

"I can't say I agree with you," Arabella interjected in a thoughtful way. "Marriage is made up of many elements, each significant."

Sir Frederick glared at his spouse. "Respect and obedience are also important."

"Indeed," Arabella said, not in the least intimidated. "As are affection and liking."

"What has this to do with my going to Glenmuir?" Thea demanded, exasperated.

James leaned back in his chair and stretched out his legs. His opinion of General Tilton had changed radically since he had come to live in the man's house. Now, this unruly discussion was adding a new dimension to his view of his wife's family. There was amusement in James's voice as he said, "Nothing at all, my dear, but it does make for a somewhat spirited conversation, do you not think?"

Isabelle, who had abandoned her needlework, opened her eyes wide at this comment, and looked hurriedly at her father to see how he would take his new son-in-law's remark.

"Papa, I don't want to go to Glenmuir," Thea said, ignoring her husband's statement.

"Your father is well aware of that, Thea," Arabella said. "We are all well aware of that. You have been sulking about it for days."

"I don't sulk!"

James laughed.

Thea turned on him, outrage in her eyes. "I am not the moody one in this marriage, Mr. MacLonan. You have been polite and passionate in turn since we argued on this very subject."

James sat up straight. "*You* call *me* moody?"

Tilton cleared his throat.

"Yes!" snapped Thea. "I am straightforward and open and I am used to people with like natures…"

"We're getting into deep waters here," Tilton announced. "Thea, have a care what you say."

James was so outraged at Thea's description of his personality that he ignored the general's comment. "I am not moody!"

"How else would you describe a man who refuses to discuss problems, then pretends that they do not exist?"

"The decision was made. I didn't need to explain or discuss!"

Thea's eyes blazed. "I am your wife, not one of your soldiers! Your partner, not your subordinate! I wish to be part of the decision, not the victim of it!"

"Precisely," General Tilton interjected. He walked over so that he stood before the warring partners, forcing them to look up to him and remember to mind their manners. "In the earlier part of our discussion we considered what was important in a marriage."

James and Thea both glared at him. Isabelle sat wide-eyed, her mouth open in a small O of surprise.

"Now, it seems to me that you two are talking again, and that is good. Now what you must do is reflect on how to get yourselves back to the liking you had for each other before Thea learned that she was to live at Glenmuir."

"Do you not think this discussion should be private?" James drawled after a moment. His blue eyes were narrowed, hard and watchful.

Tilton frowned. "We are private. No servants here tonight. I told 'em not to bother us unless we rang."

"I think James means that he and Thea should talk over these issues without the rest of us listening," Arabella offered in a conversational tone.

"Perhaps James is right, Papa—" Thea began, looking at James uneasily.

"No," Tilton said quickly. "If we allow that, you'll just end up at each other's throats again. You've a temper on you,

Thea, and you tend to be stubborn when you set your mind to it." James grinned until Tilton thoughtfully turned to him. "And you, MacLonan, carry too many scars from old battles to be able to consider things dispassionately." His comment wiped the smile from James's face. Tilton nodded grimly. "No, you both need help until you've learned to deal with each other."

"What are you suggesting, Papa?"

"That we fight out this problem about moving to Glenmuir here and now, as a family, then you both live with what is decided."

"There is nothing to discuss," James said shortly. "I will be living at Glenmuir and Thea will live there with me."

"I will not!"

"You are my wife, Thea! You will live where I live and I choose Glenmuir!"

"Let her walk by your side, MacLonan," Sir Frederick said mildly. "You'd be surprised how much more useful a partner is than a subordinate."

"Thea, why don't you want to go to Glenmuir?" Isabelle asked innocently.

"A good question," James muttered.

Forced to put her objections into words, Thea hesitated. She looked around at her family. Her father's expression was encouraging, her mother's faintly amused. Isabelle looked concerned, but also quite delighted by the whole argument.

Most important of all, James was watching Thea with narrowed eyes and the predatory gaze of a hawk. She glared at him and took a deep breath. "I have heard that the Highlanders are dangerous, unpredictable, and warlike."

"Careful, madam!" James growled.

Thea didn't look at him. "And that they do not accept strangers in their midst. They are a most inhospitable people."

"Untrue!"

After James's outraged outburst, Tilton said mildly, "I did not fight in the rebellion, but I've policed this region for well on three years now and I cannot agree with your description, daughter. The people of the Highlands are proud, aye, that's true enough, and that can be dangerous at times, but they are no more unpredictable or warlike than many another race. As to inhospitable, I think you have been listening to Olivia Ramsey's tales. She's got a remarkable dislike of the Highlander, why I don't know—"

"She's Lowland bred," Arabella said. "The Lowland Scots have always feared the Highlanders. 'Tis a long tradition in this country. The rebellion has only added fuel to a fire already set."

"Mama…"

"I wish you had come to me with your fears earlier, Thea," Arabella continued mildly. "Is it true that Mrs. Ramsey has been putting these bleak ideas into your head?"

"She and others," Thea said in a small voice.

"Is there more than this nonsense?" James demanded.

Tilton shook his head. "Too early for a frontal attack, boy," he murmured. James glared at him.

"Yes, there is more!" Thea snapped. "You didn't tell me about the move, James, you told someone else, and that is how I learned of it."

"We've talked about that," James retorted.

"Yes, we have, but I wish to feel as if my contribution is of value! Having someone other than my husband tell me that I will be uprooted within weeks was more than infuriating." She paused, then added quietly, "It was upsetting."

James shot a look at his father-in-law, then said gently, "Thea, has it happened again?" At her puzzled expression, he explained more fully. "Have I made any arbitrary announcements? Or allowed you to learn of some important subject from someone else?"

"No, but…"

"And I will not."

"Excellent," said Tilton. "We are making progress. Now, Thea, have you any more difficulties about living at Glenmuir?"

"Yes," she whispered, biting her lip. "The location."

"I cannot move the valley!"

"No one expects you to!" Thea retorted, stung.

"What is it about the location that concerns you, Thea?" Arabella asked.

"I am told that it is deep in the mountains, that the roads are poor, making travel difficult, and that there is little polite company. Once we reach the estate we will have to remain there." Thea stared down at her skirt, rubbing her hands together as if to somehow gain reassurance. "Those few people who might consider visiting us will change their minds when they learn of the state of the roads and the distance involved."

James stared at her, his expression incredulous. "You fear loneliness!"

Thea looked up at him, nibbling her lower lip. She didn't confirm or deny his statement.

"You consider living in Glenmuir a form of exile."

At the amazement in his voice, Thea stiffened. "I suppose I do."

James slapped his hands on the arms of the chair in a gesture of frustration and stood up. Turning his back to Thea and her family, he stared at one of the paintings that adorned the wall, "Damn," he said softly, before he turned to her once more. "Of all people, I understand what it means to be an exile. Thea, you need not fear that will be so for you."

"Do you understand? I think not. Glenmuir is your home, one you have been away from for a number of years, and one you ache to return to. Your exile is over."

"And yours need never begin! Thea,"—he came over to her and took her hands—"just because we make our home at Glenmuir does not mean that we cannot visit Edinburgh—or London—occasionally!"

"And we shall visit Glenmuir, Thea," Isabelle added enthusiastically.

"I think it is time that we retire to our chambers, and leave these two to settle their problems on their own," Tilton said quietly to his wife and younger daughter. Arabella nodded and swept Isabelle out with her. As he passed, the general said quietly to James, "Now's the time for the frontal attack, my boy. Good luck."

Thea was very much aware of the silence when the door closed behind her family. Her eyes scanned those of her husband, seeking the truth there. "James, is that how you felt, angry and frustrated and—I don't know, helpless—when you found yourself forced to travel to France, fearing that you would never return to Scotland?"

He looked down at her hands. Slowly, reflectively, he turned them palm up, then caressed them gently with his thumbs. Finally, he looked up into her face. "I was not at Culloden. I was wounded at the Battle of Falkirk. By the time I was well enough to move about, Staverton and my brother, Neil, had concluded that the rebellion would never be anything more than that—the Prince was not the man to lead the Highlands into victory. They put me on a boat for France. I protested, but they refused to listen. Neil died at Culloden, Staverton fought, but escaped, and all the while I kicked my heels in France, not knowing what had happened, or the fate of my friends and family." He drew a deep breath. "I hated France, Thea. I hated the way the officers treated their men, like so many slaves, not the free men they were! I hated being an outsider, and a powerless one at that! And yet, I saw it as my fate, one I could never change."

He dropped her hands to catch hold of her shoulders. He kneaded them gently; then his hands slid upward to cup her face between his palms. "I would wish that fate on no one, Thea, but least of all on you!"

"James..." Thea placed her hands on his chest. As she looked up into his face, reading the sincerity there, her eyes began to fill with tears.

"Glenmuir is my home, Thea. I want it to be your home, too." His voice was soft, but rough with emotion.

She smiled, a little tremulously. "I will try, but I will need your help."

"I will give it with pleasure." He bent, touched her

forehead with his for a short minute, then slowly began to kiss her. The caress was tentative, almost questioning. Thea responded by relaxing against him, surrendering her loyalty and trust into his care. James recognized what she offered, and gathered her closer to him. The tentative element in the kiss deepened into tenderness, admitting without the use of words the very real affection that was creating a bond between them.

Thea's hands crept up to his shoulders as she pressed her body more closely to James's. Surrender became demand, and the passion that burned between them flared into life. James pulled his lips from hers to take a deep, searing breath. "Thea, be advised, I will come to your bed tonight."

"Is that a promise?" She rose up onto her tiptoes to nibble enticingly on his lower lip.

He groaned. "How can it be otherwise?"

This time it was Thea who began the kiss, and there was nothing gentle or tender about it.

They set out from Edinburgh on the afternoon of a fine warm day, with many false starts and tearful farewells to hold their leaving back from the early departure James had planned. The fine weather stayed with them for the first few days, but one morning they rose to find the sky darkened by huge black clouds. They were already in the coach and on the road when the drizzle began. By noon it had become a downpour. The land was rising, with rolling hills becoming steep rises, so that there hardly seemed a spot where it was level. At the steeper slopes Thea and James were forced to walk beside the carriage to relieve the horses, who strained to pull the heavy coach up the slippery roadway.

Thea was soaking wet and cold down to the marrow of her bones. The pelting rain seemed to be an unending downpour, rather than a squall that would soon be over. Once again, the coach came to a halt. Thea suppressed a sigh. She glanced down at the green velvet of her traveling gown, plucking wearily at its damp nap. On the last hill her cloak had ceased to hold out the rain, and her gown now felt clammy against her skin. Absorbed by the physical discomfort she refused to acknowledge, she didn't notice the concerned frown on James's face as he scrutinized her expression.

The driver appeared at the door beside Thea, pulling it open as he politely tipped the curled brim of his tricorn hat. A cascade of water sloshed into the coach, part of it further dampening Thea's gown.

"Watch that!" James snapped. Thea set her teeth over her own impatient criticism. They were all wet, cold, and tired. She would not complain over a trifle.

"Sorry, sir," said the driver, abashed. "We've come to another hill. You must climb out again."

James made an irritated noise in his throat. Thea shivered. "I'm afraid it's a long one," the man continued cheerfully. "We'll need your assistance with the coach, sir."

When Thea stepped out, she understood why the driver requested James's help. On a clear day after a stretch of fine weather the road would be difficult to ascend. On a gray, wet day like this one the steep grade made it nearly impossible. As Thea picked her way to the side of the roadway, the mud sucked at her boots and turned slippery under her feet. She paused, turning to watch the progress of the coach.

The driver was busy soothing the horses and preparing them for the task ahead. His outrider and James were behind the coach, intending to push the vehicle from the rear. Ordinarily, servants would have handled this sort of activity, but the old-fashioned carriage carrying the luggage, Thea's maid, and James's manservant, was lost somewhere behind them in the sheeting rain and heavy mist that obscured the horizon.

At a word from the driver, the horses strained at their traces, moving the coach bare inches. Frustrated, the lead horses whinnied and shook their heads. One even attempted to rear up onto its hind legs. The coach slid backward to the spot where it had rested a few minutes before. *They would take hours to reach the top of this hill,* Thea thought numbly after watching this scene. She turned and began to fight her own way up the rise.

Though she tried to walk on the grass that edged the road, she found her footing was even less secure there. After slipping several times and only just retaining her balance, she resigned herself to slogging through the mud.

She paused for a short rest after climbing steadily for a time. Panting in a most unladylike way from the exertion, she looked back at the coach. Even though she had not gone as far as she had expected, the carriage had made even less progress. She waited until the horses drew near, then continued on her slow climb up the hill.

Her gown and cloak were heavy with rain, throwing off her balance. Halfway up the hill her foot slid out from under her and she fell to her knees. Thrusting out her hands to save herself, she felt the mire squelch through her gloved fingers. Tears of frustration welled in her eyes as she knelt in the mud and slowly tried to wipe the muck from her hands.

She was surprised when she felt a hand on her shoulder and saw her husband crouch down beside her. His eyes scanned her face. "Are you all right?"

She smiled at him, too weary to do much more. "Yes, just filthy."

A flicker of relief showed in his expression. "When you didn't stand up I thought you had injured yourself."

At his concern she managed a faint smile. "I'm sorry, James. I didn't mean to worry you. For a moment I didn't think I could continue any further." Her dimple appeared as she gestured at the crest of the hill, still some distance away. "This wretched mountain makes me quite impatient! How presumptuous of it to continue on for such a distance! The next time we travel this way I shall expect—no, I shall demand—better weather."

Respect flickered in his eyes and he laughed softly. "Take my hand, Thea, and I'll escort you to the top. Together we can conquer this mountain."

"But what about the coach?" she asked as she took his outstretched hand. "They still need your help, don't they?"

"Presently," James replied, helping her to her feet. "Now, watch your step."

Thea sighed and abandoned her attempts to persuade him to follow the dutiful course. "I will admit, sir, that I feel easier with your support." They had begun to climb. She slipped, and would have fallen but for James's strong arm helping her. She flashed him a smile. "A perfect example to my argument."

He laughed and said, "I needed no persuasion, you know."

They slogged slowly through the muck and finally reached the summit, but it was barren of shelter. James was reluctant to leave Thea standing alone in the pelting rain, but she smiled and urged him to go back to the coach.

"The sooner it reaches me, the sooner we will be able to get out of this wet!" she said with a cheerful smile.

Reaching out, he tenderly brushed back several strands of wet hair that had escaped from the fashionable knot that bound her long hair. "I will return as quickly as I am able."

Thea nodded. Watching him slip and slide down the hill, she felt as if the only ray of light had gone out of her day.

Eventually, after much effort, the carriage made it up the hill and they clambered aboard once more, but Thea found that it provided little physical comfort as she sat in her cold, wet garments. She began to shiver uncontrollably.

James reached over to her, catching her waist and drawing her close to him. After untying the fastenings of her cloak, he pushed it from her shoulders, then wrapped her in his arms and cuddled her against his body. Even through her damp gown, Thea felt his warmth. With a weary sigh, she leaned her head on his shoulder and closed her eyes.

"We should reach our destination soon," James murmured gently. "It's a fine inn, run by a man named Chisholm. The rooms are clean and the beds well aired, and he has a cook who makes magic with the simplest of ingredients. You can rest there."

Snuggled against him, Thea smiled, closed her eyes, and savored the thought of a hot, well-cooked meal. It was a very appealing fantasy.

* * *

"You must be Mr. and Mrs. MacLonan. Welcome to my house! I'm Charles Chisholm, the innkeeper here."

Chisholm was a square, stocky man dressed in plain, well-made clothes. A smile of welcome creased his chubby features.

"You received my note?" James remarked, holding his hand to help Thea from the coach.

Thea stepped down, every inch of her aching from the travel difficulties they had encountered that day. While James spoke to the landlord, she looked around curiously. The large courtyard faced a two-story building that was made of gray stone as weathered as the hills that rolled away to the north of it. Like its owner, the establishment was prosperous and well kept. Ostlers were already at work, leading the carriage horses away to a corner of the large yard where the carriage would be parked for the night.

"Aye, I did, sir," Chisholm was saying, "and I've prepared the suite you requested."

"Good. We will be staying for three days instead of the two I'd originally intended. I trust that will not be a problem?"

"Not at all, sir!" the landlord said smoothly. "We are delighted to have your company for as long as you would like to stay with us. Now, sir and madam, if you would like to follow me, I'll show you to your rooms."

Thea plucked at the skirt of her traveling costume. The heavy velvet was wet and clung to her legs as she walked. She would be glad to change out of it.

They entered the inn through a wide, welcoming oak doorway, into a central hall warmed by a fire blazing in a deep hearth. The heat wrapped itself around Thea, making her cast a longing look at the hearth, but Chisholm was leading them to a square staircase at the rear of the hall that rose up to the second floor.

As they marched up the polished oak stairs, Thea whispered to James, "Three days, James? We will be staying here for three days?"

He looked down at her, a faint smile creasing his cheeks.

"Do my plans not meet with your approval, madam wife? Would you prefer to continue on our journey tomorrow?"

Thea laughed up at him. "Certainly not, sir! I am delighted to have a respite from coach travel." To her surprise, his smile died. "James? Is there something wrong?"

He began to shake his head. Then he changed his mind and said quietly, "Later, Thea."

The words were ominous. Thea's imagination immediately took flight.

CHAPTER 10

Chisholm cheerfully described the comforts his establishment offered as he ushered James and Thea down a long hallway to what he referred to as the "blue suite" because the cloth of the window coverings and bed hangings were a marine blue.

Thea was agreeably surprised by their accommodations, consisting of a private parlor and two good-sized bedrooms. These were joined by a connecting door and were furnished with old-fashioned walnut beds that shone with polish. At the end of each bed stood a chest, also of walnut and richly carved, providing storage. Two armchairs, square and sturdy, but with padded seats and backs, flanked the hearth.

"My best bedchambers, sir, and I hope you like them."

Spontaneously, Thea said, "Oh, they are lovely, Mr. Chisholm."

The innkeeper beamed, and James added dryly, "My wife does not exaggerate, Chisholm. These will be quite satisfactory."

The innkeeper left with the promise to send one of his maidservants to help Thea remove her wet clothes. "Although," she said, standing before the fire rubbing her hands together, "I'm not sure what good it will do as the carriage with our baggage hasn't arrived yet."

James wandered over to the window. "I expect them any time. I'm sure something can be arranged."

Thea frowned. Clearly he had something more than their present accommodations on his mind. After a moment, she joined him by the window. The view was spectacular. The countryside rolled away to the north, rising up to become mountains that were dark blue smudgy shadows in the distance.

He pointed to the dark, ominous shapes. "We are headed northwest, Thea, into those mountains. The road worsens from here, as do the accommodations. This is the last comfortable inn on our route."

Thea stared out at the looming shadows. The rain that had fallen throughout the day had finally stopped, but the clouds remained. The mountains looked enormous, framed against the threatening darkness of the clouds. Her stomach began to knot. "Thank you for the warning, James. I shall savor the small luxuries I find here all the more."

He turned to face her. Gently, he rubbed his thumbs along the dark circles beneath her eyes. "I want you to rest all you can, Thea. Once we leave the road here we'll have to continue on until we reach Glenmuir."

As she stared up into his vivid blue eyes, she thought she saw something more lurking there, another bit of bad news he didn't want to tell her. "You say that the road deteriorates. Will that hold us up?"

"It might." He hesitated then he added, "But we'll be riding from now on."

Thea turned to look out of the window at the rugged blue mountains. His hands fell away, and she found that she missed his touch. "But...but what of our baggage? All the goods I bought from Edinburgh? And my maid. I know she does not ride. In fact, I think she's afraid of horses."

"A sturdy cart can travel the route. My coachman knows the way. He will drive the cart. The servants will ride with him."

Thea continued to stare at those ominous, frightening mountains. "I suppose you have already made arrangements for riding horses?"

"Do you not remember the gray mare I purchased for you

in Edinburgh? I had her sent here to be fresh and ready for you when we arrived."

Thea had a sudden memory of the argument they had had the day he'd taken her to the window of her parents' house to show her the beautiful little mare. She turned to face him. "James, I—"

He interrupted, his voice emotionless. "Our route is through some rather desolate country. Villages are scarce. We may be forced to sleep wherever, we can find shelter."

She stared at him, trying to read between his words. "Please be more precise, James. I'd like to know what to expect."

He hesitated, then said carefully, "We may have to spend a night in the open or in a crofter's hut."

"Oh," she said blankly. Thea had never seen a crofter's hut, but the words conjured up frightening images that made her shiver. She lifted her brows haughtily. "Are there any other surprises I should know about, James?"

His eyes flashed and she braced herself for an argument. Then he said curtly, "No."

She relaxed, and her dimple quivered into life as she smiled up at him. "Thank you, James. I do not begrudge you the right to make the decisions, you know, but I do find it easier to cope with what is to come when I am prepared for it." Her smile died as she looked inward. "The unknown is always frightening."

Lowering his head, James brushed his lips gently over hers. "We have three days here. Let us enjoy them. We'll test the horses, go for walks, eat well, and sleep late. By the time we leave for Glenmuir we will both be well rested. That will make the journey easier to bear."

His caress made Thea's eyes brighten. She reached up to touch his cheek with her fingertips. The beginnings of a smile curled her lips. "I'd like that," she said huskily.

By the early afternoon of their second day at the inn the spring sun had warmed the air kept cool by the shadow of the mountains. Dressed in a royal blue riding costume, Thea waited on the doorstep of the inn as James disappeared into the stables to discover why the groom had not yet brought round their horses. She was feeling contented, relaxed, and at ease with her husband and the journey they were making together.

Closing her eyes, she lifted her face to the sun. There was a slight breeze, rich with the fragrant scents of spring flowers that grew in wild abundance on the moors behind the inn. The courtyard was quiet, dozing in the sunshine. A sense of peace wrapped itself securely around her. She wished she could stay here forever, dreaming in the beautiful weather, with no responsibilities beyond her own and her husband's pleasure.

With a little sigh, she opened her eyes. A wonderful dream, but quite impossible, for James would find no pleasure in idleness. His motives were powerful and overriding. What Thea wanted or needed would always take second place. She shrugged the thought away and stepped off the doorstep into the yard.

A moment later James rode through the arch that led to the stables. He was astride a big chestnut that pranced and tossed its head as it moved. A groom followed leading the beautifully marked gray that Thea remembered from that one brief glimpse in Edinburgh.

"Impatient to be on the move again, Thea? I thought you were thoroughly weary of travel."

A dimple appeared in her cheek as she smiled mischievously. "Indeed, sir, 'twas not impatience but curiosity that set me moving." She gazed admiringly at the two handsome horses. "I wished to see if the mounts you had chosen were sturdy beasts capable of enduring the mountain roads, or more lively animals."

James dismounted in one lithe movement. "And what have you decided?"

Thea laughed, stepped quickly over to the dapple gray mare, and stroked the animal's intelligent head. "Frankly, I did not think you would be satisfied with a mere 'sturdy beast' for the duration of our journey to Glenmuir."

His mouth quirked into a half-smile as he crossed the few feet that separated them. "The mare is a deceptive creature," he said deliberately. "Beautiful and gentle in appearance, mettlesome and hot to handle in temperament." He smiled, amusement deepening the blue of his eyes. Lightly, he touched Thea's cheek. "When I saw her in Edinburgh, I knew I could find no other horse better suited to you, my lovely wife."

Thea blushed as she caught his meaning. So James thought her high-spirited and temperamental, did he? That sounded like a criticism. Yet he'd also called her beautiful and gentle. Moreover, his eyes were amused as he spoke, not condemning. Could it be that her husband appreciated fire in a woman? The idea tantalized Thea.

They were standing very close to each other, so that she could feel his warm breath on her cheek. She smiled at him, lowering her eyes demurely, but peering out from under her lashes. Laughter tugged at James's lips and desire darkened his eyes.

Embolden by this response, Thea murmured provocatively, "I know no way to thank you for such a thoughtful gift, James. Perhaps later, when we return from our ride, we can discuss a suitable recompense."

He answered by tipping her chin up with one strong finger, then bending to cover her lips with his. His mouth was warm, gently caressing at first, then more demanding as his tongue teased her lips apart so he could deepen the kiss. Fire heated Thea's blood. Reaching up, she clutched his shoulders as her body melded itself with his.

It was not until James had lifted his head and her heartbeat had returned to normal that she remembered they were standing in the yard of a public inn, in full view of whoever cared to observe them. She smiled rather shakily and James, who was watching her with hungry eyes, said in a low husky voice, "Be assured I shall hold you to your promise when we return, madam, but now, would you care to try out your 'sturdy beast'?"

Thea laughed and nodded. As James threw her up into the sidesaddle, the gray curvetted daintily. Thea gathered up the reins and the mare tossed her head, then snorted.

James, now mounted on the chestnut, observed wryly, "She does not take to direct commands, but she is well trained and obedient. She will not buck or try to throw you."

He paused before adding softly, "She will, however, make life as difficult for you as she can, until you win her trust and confidence."

"I do not know if you are describing the horse or your wife," Thea retorted, shooting him a displeased look.

"Why, the horse, my dear," James replied with so much injured innocence in his tone that Thea had to laugh.

"Then I had best take your advice and do my utmost to gain Firefly's love. Shall we ride?"

"Firefly?"

Thea thrust up her chin defiantly. "A perfect name for the creature, I thought. Independent, lively, graceful, beautiful." A challenging smile curled her lips and sparkled in her dark eyes. "Impossible for a mere mortal to catch!" With that she dug her heels into the mare's side, urging her into a wild gallop. With a muttered oath, James followed suit, half his mind admiring Thea's horsemanship, the other half furious at her wayward action.

They rode through the countryside for hours. In between spirited gallops, their conversation was light, teasing, flirtatious. The afternoon became a chance to build on the shaky foundations that had been laid in Edinburgh. In those few short hours they acknowledged that the physical attraction they felt for each other could become something deeper and much more satisfying, if only they would allow it to grow.

That evening, after a substantial supper of roasted capon, Thea retired early to her room. Dismissing her maid as soon as she was changed, she pulled a chair close to the fire and settled down to wait for her husband to arrive. The promise of their afternoon made her certain that he would come to her this evening.

She spread her hands out to the blaze. As she leaned forward, the light of the fire delicately outlined the shape of her breasts through the fine lace and diaphanous linen of her bed gown. Fully aware of the picture she made, she didn't move as the communicating door to her husband's room opened, then quietly closed. She looked up and smiled, watching James's body tense as he gazed at her.

He was clothed only in his dressing gown of rich brocade. He crossed the room to her, walking with slow, deliberate steps, which Thea's pounding heart echoed. Reaching her, he perched on the arm of her chair, resting his forearm on the back, just at the level of her head. His robe fell open to expose one hard thigh. Thea found her gaze riveted to it. She licked her suddenly dry lips.

"Earlier today you wished to thank me for your gift," he said, bending to graze her temple with his lips. "I came to tell you that I require nothing more than your pleasure in my surprise, and that has been shown today."

She tilted her head to look up into his eyes, and discovered that their mouths were only inches apart. "You do not wish to discuss a recompense?"

He shook his head. He had taken off the fashionable wig he wore during the day. His dark hair was clipped short and he looked different, younger, or perhaps vulnerable, far from the determined, rather hard man he appeared to be on the surface.

"Then let me give you a present of my own," Thea murmured, reaching up to wind her arms around his neck and draw his head down.

"I cannot refuse such a delightful gift, so freely given," he murmured, his lips caressing hers as he wrapped his arms around her and drew her to her feet. The kiss deepened and Thea felt little flames of desire lick at her insides. She strained her body against his, wanting more.

James lifted his head to stare thoughtfully at his wife's passion-darkened eyes and full, trembling lips. Reaching up, he caught her hands and drew them from behind his head, then stepped back to gaze at all of her. She trembled, watching his eyes darken and his face harden with desire. She knew that beneath the soft covering of her gown, her breasts glowed milky white, their tips dark rosy peaks that begged to be kissed. When he bent, her breasts swelled with anticipation, but his caress was not for them. Instead he kissed the backs of her hands, then turned them to caress the soft skin on her palms.

Thea's breath rushed out in a long sigh. James looked up and grinned. Tugging gently, he led her over to the big bed, already turned down by Thea's diligent maid.

At the bed he kissed Thea again, this time with more intensity. His arms curled around her waist, then cradled her hips, pressing her against his lower body as his tongue entered the dark warmth of her mouth.

Thea could feel his arousal pressing against her loins, and the knowledge that he needed her as much as she did him, added fuel to the fire blazing inside of her. Their tongues tangled together, in delightful, tantalizing play, stoking fires already burning high.

He broke the kiss to brush the thin material of her nightdress off her shoulder. The soft caress of his hand was followed by the harder one of his teeth as he nibbled the tender skin. She sucked in her breath with a gasp, her feverish fingers delving beneath his robe to rake hungrily along his damp skin. James paused long enough to shake himself loose of his clothes, and to dispose of Thea's pretty but unnecessary gown. Then he lowered her to the bed and stretched his hard length on top of her.

Both were fraught with needs that had been growing all day, and their coupling was quick and intense. They lay afterward, James on his back, one arm outstretched to pillow Thea's head as she curled against his side.

"Your passion pleases me," he said, drawing Thea from her drowsy, half-dreaming state.

She blinked, trying to focus. He watched her lazily, from half-closed eyes, pride and satisfaction clearly written on his face. She had a ridiculous desire to giggle, something she did not think her husband would appreciate at this particular moment, so instead she smiled and snuggled closer.

"I had not expected to find that in a wife, particularly not an English wife."

Some of that passion, in a different form, leapt into life as Thea lifted herself up on her elbow with a sudden swift movement. Her luxuriant golden hair tumbled over her face in a cascade of untamed beauty. Impatiently, she pushed it away. "Did you think all Englishwomen were cold and unfeeling?" she demanded indignantly.

He grinned and tugged on her elbow, so that she fell back onto the bed and he was able to stretch himself above her. "Icy as a mountain stream and just as shallow," he said, agreeing with her, to her outrage. "And just like that mountain stream, they babble nonsense from morning until night, forcing a man to stop listening to save his sanity." He kissed her lips slowly. "But you, my dear Thea, are different. I like the sound of your voice and I find myself interested in the words you say."

Thea tried to ignore the enticing promise of his hand upon her breast. "I need you, James," she said huskily. "I need you each day we are together, and I will need you more when we reach Glenmuir."

For a moment his questing fingers stilled. "You surprise me, wife. I would not have expected you to admit to needing anyone, let alone your Jacobite husband."

Thea flashed him an annoyed look, then smiled prettily. "We all have our weaknesses, James. 'Tis only to you that I would make such a monstrous confession."

His frown made her grin, until he said softly, "Such an admission warrants a very special reward, and I have the night to deliver it."

"Promise?"

"Upon my honor, madam."

"I can ask no more than that." She sighed as his questing hands made her forget what they had been talking about.

Sensation was all she knew until she fell asleep much, much later.

* * *

The road along which the horses plodded was little more than a track, winding upward into bleak, desolate mountains. James had traveled this route many times, but with Thea beside him he considered the journey from a fresh viewpoint. He was now vividly aware of the boredom and physical exhaustion caused by the long hours in the saddle, riding along a path that was both dangerous and deceptively easy. He knew that there were places where the horses could run, making better time and adding some excitement to the ride, and he could pinpoint those spots where the scenery could be spectacular when the heather was in flower and the mountains loomed broodingly against a clear blue sky. But the miles to be covered ground away enthusiasm, so that the ride soon became an exercise in endurance.

The weather was once again a continuous drizzle, made more unpleasant by the wind. The track became too slippery to allow the horses to gallop, and the mountains rose stark and cold against the gray of the sky. To the distance was added the discomfort of the cold wind and their wet clothing.

Then, too, he was seeing things along the road that chilled him deep into his soul. There were scars that had not existed the last time he had traveled this route, scars that must have occurred as a result of the reprisals inflicted on Scotland after the rebellion. Anger simmered in him, anger against the English army, against the Hanovarian dynasty in London, and against the English race as a whole.

Around mid-afternoon they emerged from a mountain pass into the relative calm of the valley beyond. The buffeting wind didn't still completely, but it did die down a trifle. The rain continued to fall, but it no longer bit at their faces, making it unpleasant to be sure, but bearable. A thread of smoke appeared on the horizon, and James urged the chestnut forward. He wasn't sure who lived in the dwelling, but Thea needed rest. Her cheeks were flushed from the wind, but her lips were pale and pinched.

As they neared, James saw that the place was a narrow, single-story shack made of squared-off blocks of peat. James drew to a stop in front of it. Thea automatically did the same.

"James," she said huskily, "why do we stop here?"

He shot her a quick, all-encompassing glance. "You need rest Thea, and food. There is nowhere else."

She stared at the dwelling, the exhaustion in her expression tinged with amazement, and not a little distaste. James was about to explain some basic Highland customs when a fierce-looking man, clothed in rough woolen breeches, a tartan cloak wrapped around his torso, emerged from the doorway of the little hut. Thea's expression deepened to pure horror as her eyes were riveted on the glitter of steel beneath his covering. He was carrying a sword.

Ignoring Thea's dismay, James spoke to the man in Gaelic. At first the words came haltingly, for it had been years since he'd used the language, but he was pleased to see the man's face break into a smile as he offered them the hospitality of his house and gestured inside the croft.

James dismounted and came over to Firefly to help Thea from the horse. As his hands wrapped around her waist and he lifted her from the saddle, she demanded, "Why did you speak—what was it? French—to that man?"

"It was Gaelic, and I spoke it to prove to him that we aren't..." He began to say "English," but quickly altered the phrase. "To prove we aren't a danger to him."

Her feet touched the soggy ground, but Thea made no effort to move away from James's side. He looked down at her. She was staring at the croft and the huge Highlander. Intermittently, her body shook with shivers she couldn't quite contain. James wanted to get her into the hut and out of the rain. Thea had other ideas.

"You were about to say something else. What was it?"

Impatience added a bite to his voice. "Thea!"

"What was it, James? Please tell me!" Her voice had risen. James could hear the edge of fear in it.

Reluctantly, he said, "Highlanders are no longer allowed to wear the tartan or own weapons. This man has violated both laws. I wanted to assure him we would not turn him in to the authorities."

"Otherwise?"

"He'll protect his own, Thea," James explained grimly. "It's not in the nature of the Highlander to tamely submit to injustice."

She put her hand to her mouth in a frightened gesture. "And you want to stop here! How can you be sure we won't be murdered for our horses and the gold we carry?"

Until this moment James had stopped thinking of Thea as English, or as the daughter of an English general. Now, he remembered that she was both. "This man is offering us the hospitality of his house. He won't violate it by harming us, no matter who we are or how rude we happen to be!" With that he spun on his heel, too angry to say anything more. He led the two weary horses to the side of the hut, where he tethered them with the help of the fierce-looking Scot and fed them a small amount of grain to add to the meager grazing available. Then he turned back to Thea, who was standing where he'd left her, her back straight, her head high, and her gaze haughty.

He paused for a moment, watching her. He knew she was exhausted, cold, wet, and above all, frightened, but none of this showed in her expression or in her stance. She was every inch a powerful English lady, who would not be daunted by the experience she faced, no matter how difficult it was. A slow smile curled his lips, for he admired his wife's indomitable spirit.

Returning to Thea's side, he bowed gracefully and held out his arm. "Madam, will you join me inside?"

She shot him a look he couldn't define, then tentatively put her hand on his. He covered it in a reassuring way, then led her into the croft.

The interior was dark and smoky, lit only by the doorway and a fire burning brightly in a fire pit in the earthen floor. Over the fire hung a large black iron pot, bubbling with some sort of food. As James's eyes gradually adjusted to the gloom, he saw a woman, wearing a simple woolen dress, standing stiffly beside two little girls in one corner of the room—the crofter's family.

James politely introduced Thea and asked if there was any food. The woman came forward, smiling with warm sincerity.

"Our food is simple," she said in halting English, gesturing toward the fire. "Both you and your wife are welcome to whatever we have, and to sit beside our fire and try to dry yourselves."

A little of the tension that had been knotting itself in James's belly eased as Thea smiled and thanked the woman, then stepped gingerly to the blaze. Their hostess spoke sharply to the two little girls, and in a flurry of activity, they pulled a wooden bench close to the fire. Gratefully, Thea sank down on it, holding out her hands to the heat.

For the duration of their visit, through a meal of thick oatmeal porridge topped with last summer's honey, and slices of unleavened bread, James and the Highlander conversed in the musical cadences of Gaelic speech. James let the man talk, coaxing from him information on the changes caused by the rebellion. What the Scot told him was similar to other stories, but hearing it here, in the depths of the devastated region, chilled James as nothing had before. He began to fear what he would find at Glenmuir. How many would be dead or deported to the colonies? What devastation had been wrought by the marauding English armies? Would he find a crop of fair-haired babies as evidence of the depredations?

He glanced at Thea. For the most part, her golden hair was bound up in a knot and hidden beneath her hat, but a few rebellious strands had escaped and were curling around her face in the warmth of the fire. She was eating the tasteless, but filling, oatmeal with great concentration, as if she didn't like the food, but knew she had no option but to consume it. The color was returning to her face and her body was beginning to slump as her tension eased.

Thea was English, he thought. These strangers had treated her kindly, because she was with him, but he wondered now if his clansmen would accept her freely. He'd been so determined to get to Glenmuir that he had brushed aside the very real possibility that she would not be welcome.

The thought disturbed him. He knew what it was like to be an outsider, accepted under duress, never really wanted.

He would not force Thea into that sort of life. She deserved better.

CHAPTER 11

As Thea mounted Firefly, she shivered, but not with the cold. The people in the hut had seemed unaware she was not a Scot, as her husband was. How generous would they have been if they had discovered she was English, a member of the nation that made the laws they so blatantly flouted?

When she was in Edinburgh, she'd known she would be a stranger amongst the Scottish clansmen, but she'd never expected they would not speak her language. Already she felt isolated, walking a thin, dangerous line drawn by events and traditions she didn't understand. Here in the Highlands she was an intruder in a harsh, unforgiving world. How would she survive?

With the rain pelting down, Thea drew the hood of her cloak down over her eyes in a vain attempt to protect her face. She turned when her husband spoke. Although he didn't smile, there was a watchful care in his gaze as he looked at her.

"Ready?"

The word was simple, the question was not. Thea nodded, warmed far more than she had been in the little croft. As difficult as their journey was, no matter what the reception she received when she reached Glenmuir, James would be there. He kicked the big chestnut into motion, and Thea followed suit, urging Firefly to a little more speed so that she could ride beside her husband. This time when he looked over at her, he smiled, and Thea smiled back before she turned to face the road ahead.

The journey through the bleak mountains lasted four days. The weather, although it favored them enough to cease raining after the second day out, remained cool, the sky overcast. Thea's mood seesawed from hope to despair through those long days. At times she felt as if she was one of James's soldiers, on a forced march to fight a battle against an unseen enemy, for he drove them mercilessly, demanding extra speed even as she drooped wearily in the saddle. Yet at night he was gentle and tender, concerned over her well-being, insistent that she rest as much as possible.

There were no inns along their route, so they spent the nights in private homes, some more elaborate than others, all much finer than the humble croft. In this isolated area, where visitors brought news of the outside, James was welcomed with great pleasure, and the conversations he had with his hosts were wide-ranging and intense, while Thea's were shallow and strained. Used to being a part of discussions in Edinburgh, Thea saw this reserve as evidence that the Highlanders found her strange and alien, but were too polite to say so. The evenings fueled the fears that she was trying so very hard to ignore.

As the days passed, Thea's fears increased and her mood darkened, although she could sense a growing optimism in her husband. She could not forget that while she was blindly moving into the unknown, James was coming home to a way of life he had been willing to sacrifice everything to regain. And at those times when he bluntly ordered her to hurry up or mind where Firefly was putting her feet, when she wanted nothing more than to stop and rest, Thea wondered with aching regret if one of his sacrifices had been the loss of his freedom. For to return to his beloved Highlands he'd had to take a wife, an English wife. Although he made no reference to it, Thea could not forget.

On the fourth day their route led them steeply uphill into the thick, rolling mountains. After several days spent in the never-ending procession of steep rises and sharp, narrow valleys, Thea had a rough idea of their purpose. They were climbing toward a pass, a notch between two higher peaks that led into a valley beyond. They rode slowly, letting the horses pick their way along the broken track.

It was nearly dusk when James reined in, scanning the land ahead of them. Thea stopped beside him, happy for a chance to rest. He looked at her, suppressed excitement in his blue eyes. "Lonan Pass. We're almost home."

Thea caught her breath and smiled tremulously. "I'm glad." She leaned forward to stroke the mare. "Firefly is a lovely animal and a delight to ride, but my body aches. And we are both tired. She wants a rest as much as I do."

"I can't promise you much comfort, Thea." A muscle twitched in his jaw. "The house being prepared for us will be small and the furniture will be made in the valley. When the castle was burned after Culloden, all of the furnishings were destroyed as well. When my father knew that I would be returning to Scotland, he asked Gregor MacLonan to order what was necessary, but..."

Culloden. Thea shivered and peered down at the valley below. The battle had scarred this land in ways that would linger far too long. She drew herself up, facing what could not be changed. "Where is the village? I cannot see it." In the gray light she could distinguish little beyond the dark vegetation that lined the steep hillside.

"The glen is long and thin, shaped like a finger crooked at the final joint. The village,"—he hesitated—"and the castle are about a third of the way up the valley, beyond the point where it bends north." He put his heels to his horse's flanks. "Come. We still have some distance to travel and I fancy reaching our destination before dark."

As they picked their way down the slope Thea looked about her, curious at the first sight of her new home. There was a heavy, waiting stillness over the deserted land, as if nothing and no one lived there. The only sounds were the creaking of the saddle leather, the jingle of harness, and the muted thump of the horses' hooves on the ground. Irrational, primitive fear raised the hairs on the nape of Thea's neck. Ruthlessly, she fought down the errant emotion.

She had almost persuaded herself that the ominous quiet merely presaged a storm, when they came to what had once been a broad stand of trees. Now all that remained were twisted and blackened skeletons, some still upright, more charred stumps or blackened logs on the ground. The carnage had been the result of a fierce fire.

A glance at her husband's set face informed her that this devastation was recent, and unhappy intuition told her it was part of the havoc wreaked after Culloden. Uneasily, she moistened dry, nervous lips, then took heart from the new growth that was springing up over the dead layer. One day the tiny seedlings would be as large as the trees that had been burned. Eventually the scar would disappear. Glancing at James, she wondered if time would ever heal his anger and bitterness.

Gradually, they made their way up the valley, haunted by the unnatural quiet and the grim devastation. Thea decided she would be glad when they had passed through this section and rounded the bend into the populated portion of Glenmuir. She was unprepared for the sight that met her eyes when they did so.

A long, narrow lake, or loch, as the Scots would call it, extended most of the length of the valley. At the moment it was a forbidding gunmetal gray, its surface ruffled by the wind that had followed them throughout their journey. On the western shore loomed the Castle, and at the sight of it James roughly jerked his chestnut stallion to a halt. The animal snorted and tossed its fine head in annoyance. James didn't notice, for he was gazing with fixed concentration at what remained of Glenmuir Castle. Thea's grip on the reins slackened as she too stared ahead with fascinated horror. The mare obediently stopped beside the other horse, arching its dapple gray neck and playing with the bit.

The Castle was little more than a blackened shell of what it must have once been. A fortified manor house with corner towers and few windows, the structure had been built by a

MacLonan ancestor nearly two centuries before. Now the roof and living space inside had been destroyed, leaving only the stone shell reaching pointing fingers of decay into the sky.

Emotion swelled in Thea as she stared at the wreck of a once-proud house—anger at the wanton destruction, and fear of a future spent in this desolate place. Beneath was a reluctant but growing understanding of why one nation could hate another so wholeheartedly.

She looked over at James. He continued to study the ruin with a grim concentration that hurt to look at. Taking a deep breath, Thea said quietly, "James, do you know where the cottage is?"

For a moment he turned from his scrutiny of the damage done his childhood home. "No. Gregor MacLonan, the steward, has been notified we are coming. He will show us." With that curt statement, James went back to his bleak examination.

Thea looked around the empty countryside. She said doubtfully, "He may know we are coming, but does he know when?"

"Yes, of course he does! I sent a message before we were married giving him a rough calculation of when I expected to arrive. We're a few days later than I claimed, thanks to the poor weather, but nothing to signify."

Thea bit her lip as she looked around her. "If we are expected, wouldn't there be someone watching for us?"

That caught his attention. He took one last, lingering look at the Castle ruin, then urged his horse into motion and trotted off in the direction of the cluster of buildings that made up the small village of Glenmuir.

The wind was stronger now, biting through their enveloping cloaks. As they neared the habitations, Thea wondered if the entire place had been deserted.

Suddenly, their way was barred by a short, thickset man with a bushy beard and a shock of lank, dark hair. The chestnut snorted and tried to rise on its hind legs. James fought it down. The man waited until the horse was calm before saying in the rolling accent of the Highlands, "Are you looking for someone?" Shrewd gray eyes noted the wealth of their dress, and he added, "There's been no one at the castle for years. Not since..." Recognition suddenly halted his tongue. "Master James?"

"Indeed," James replied curtly. "I gather you did not expect me. My messenger must have met with an accident."

"We received your letter, sir, near two months ago. But we thought you'd changed your mind."

James's eyes bored into the other man's. "Explain yourself, Gregor MacLonan."

The steward stared calmly back. "We had a second letter, sir, saying you would be staying in Edinburgh." He glanced at Thea when she gasped. Her gray mare began to prance irritably. Gregor thoughtfully took hold of the bridle, ignoring the horse as it shook its head and snorted.

Frowning, James asked, "Who was the letter from, Gregor?"

"A Mrs. Ramsey. Said she was,"—he paused—"writing on the request of your lady wife."

"That's not true!" Thea declared.

Gregor continued. "We'd set about putting yon cottage in order for your arrival, but this Mrs. Ramsey sounded very sure of herself, so we halted work."

"What is the state of the cottage now?" James demanded.

He didn't look at Thea. She could hear the annoyance in his voice, but she was too tired and too dazed to try to do anything about it.

Choosing his words carefully, Gregor answered James's question. "You will have a roof over your head and a bed, sir, but little more, I fear."

It was fortunate Gregor was holding Firefly's bridle. The reins slipped through Thea's nerveless fingers as she listened to his damning words. All she could think of was that their cool welcome was the result of her conversation with Olivia Ramsey and so, in a way, her fault.

James glanced at her and, seeing something in her

expression, said abruptly, "That can be put to rights later. Thea!" His harsh tone pulled her up, forcing her to put aside the bitter recriminations that were gnawing at her. "Can you continue? Or would you prefer Gregor lead the horse?"

"I can manage, James!" she snapped, goaded by his rough tone.

"Good." Did she imagine it, or was there the faintest suggestion of satisfaction in his tone?

They began to move, Gregor striding beside the slowly walking chestnut. "You must know you are much needed here, sir." Gregor moved his head to indicate the surrounding area. "We still haven't recovered from the devastation which followed the Rising."

"How bad is it, Gregor?"

The man stroked his bearded chin. "You knew that many of the young men didn't come back? Well, we've lost many of the older ones, and the women, to sickness, hunger, and the pillaging of the accursed—" He glanced toward Thea, then quickly away. "There's a whole crop of light-haired bairns as well."

"What happened to the money my father sent? It should have helped alleviate some of the worst distress."

Gregor glanced at Thea again before he said carefully, "It did, sir, but it isn't wise to show too much prosperity these days. There are always those who demand to know where it came from and who won't believe a truthful answer."

James cast the steward a hard glance. "'We'll talk more of this later," he said curtly.

"Aye, Master James," Gregor replied easily. Evidently his evasive answer had not been shaped because he feared an accounting by the Master of Glenmuir. Thea was sure he had framed his response to avoid offending her. Unwittingly, his courtesy had reminded her once again that she was English and therefore someone to be wary of. With a lonely flash of insight, she guessed that this was the way her husband had felt during his years of exile: an outsider in a foreign land, acknowledged, but never accepted.

As they rode through the village, she was further

discomfited by the stares of the people who emerged from their small, neat houses. The people of Glenmuir took a moment to recognize their chief's son, come so unexpectedly among them, but when they did there were welcoming smiles and joyful greetings. They looked curiously at Thea, sizing her up without hostility, but also without warmth. She told herself that this reaction was typical of any small, isolated community with a stranger in its midst, but she couldn't shake the feeling that had she been Scots-born, her greeting would have been very different.

Gregor led them to a square cottage, built of stone plundered from the derelict castle. The harsh gray exterior looked solid, but unforgiving. Thea could only wish that the men of the MacLonan clan had chosen some other material from which to build the master's new dwelling.

The bearded Gregor opened the plain front door. "I beg your pardon for the size of the house, sir. We put it up quick when Mr. MacLonan informed us you had been pardoned. There were no rooms fit for occupation at the Castle. The English made sure of that!"

Thea knew that she had not been responsible for the devastation following the Rising. She had not burned Glenmuir Castle, or the woodlands that gave the long valley its name. But she could not shake the feeling that she personally was being blamed by the people of the MacLonan clan for the destruction that had changed their lives.

Refusing to acknowledge the veiled hostility around her, she swung her leg free of the saddle, then kicked her foot from the stirrup and slid to the ground unaided. Throwing the reins to Gregor with a haughty toss of her head, she ignored his last statement as she strode into the house.

Little light filtered through the small windows. "Is there a candle?" she called as she entered the main room.

Gregor replied, "Aye, lady. On the stairs."

She found a tinderbox beside the candle. After a few moments, flame flickered into life. She held the candle high as she strode from room to room, her emotions tightening until an impotent fury held her securely in its grasp. As she returned to the doorway, she saw that James had dismounted and was about to hand his reins to Gregor.

"Well, James," she said tightly. "Mr. MacLonan did not jest when he informed you all work had been stopped on the house. There is no furniture on the ground floor, the hearths are bare, and the place is as cold as a tomb!" Her voice quivered with emotion that threatened to overwhelm her. She closed her mouth tightly. If she said anything more, she would surely regret her words. Abruptly, she turned back inside.

James shot Gregor a sharp look. "The horses need to be stabled for the night. Also, a cart bearing our luggage and household goods comes behind us. My coachman knows the way, but in the dusk he might need assistance. Send a man to watch for him at the pass, will you, Gregor?"

While James gave his directions to the steward, Thea had lifted her voluminous riding skirt and climbed up the solid staircase to the upper floor. Unconsciously she noticed the staircase was graceful and well built, the boards of a light wood she couldn't identify, possibly a local pine. The elegance of the stairs made her realize that the people of Glenmuir had taken some care in the building of their master's house. Somehow the thought didn't give her any comfort. It was James they were honoring, not her.

Upstairs there were five good-sized rooms, the largest one being for the master, with a smaller room adjoining it. All were set around a square landing, and even in the dim light Thea was easily able to find her way around.

She had just entered the largest bedchamber when she heard James's steps on the floor below.

"Thea?" he called.

"Upstairs, James. In the largest bedchamber, on your right."

While he ran lightly up the stairs, she moved deeper into the room. Placing the candleholder on the mantel over the fieldstone fireplace, she waited for him. While she waited she surveyed the single piece of furniture in the house—the bed.

* * *

When James entered the doorway, she was standing by the hearth, her arms crossed over her breasts. Her face was impassive as she stared at the crude bed, the frame square and solid, but without the least adornment. He guessed that she was close to breaking down.

"Well, Gregor MacLonan is definitely a man of his word. This *is* the only piece of furniture in the house!" Her voice broke. "James, what are we going to do?"

"Tomorrow I'll arrange for some furniture to be built. What can't be constructed here can be ordered from Edinburgh."

"We just came from Edinburgh!" Her voice choked on a sob of exhaustion and disappointment. She went over to the bed, flopping down on the only available seat in the house. "Arrah!" she shrieked, jumping up. "The mattress is straw!" Leaning down, she disgustedly raised it to inspect the supports beneath. "Slats! 'Ods blood, James! Do you expect me to sleep on straw and slats for the rest of my life?"

"Thea," he growled warningly.

"No! I will not stop! Since we began this journey you have driven me mercilessly, James MacLonan, without a shred of consideration! Through the most appalling weather, on roads little better than quagmires, I didn't complain. I accepted, because you are my husband! When you insisted we must come to Glenmuir, I accepted! It is your right to decide where we will live and my duty to make a home for you wherever that might be. You have hardly spoken to me since we left the inn, and then only to criticize or condemn! Driving me onward when I felt I could go no further!"

He crossed the room in three strides. Grasping her shoulders, he said roughly, "Do you think I enjoyed watching you shiver in the saddle, exhaustion etched in every line of you? I organized our journey, Thea, so that you could rest each night in some comfort, in houses with feather beds and warm hearths and private guest rooms. Would you have preferred to take the journey in easy stages and spend your nights in the crofts you despise so much? Or out in the open, with no protection and the wet ground as your bed?"

"No." A sob caught in her throat. "James, did you really do that for me?"

Her eyes were huge and tears glittered in their depths. James sighed and pressed her head gently against his chest.

"Yes. I knew the journey would be arduous, Thea. If the weather had been better, the going wouldn't have been so difficult and the stages I planned wouldn't have seemed so long or exhausting. I do not mean to harm you, Thea, or bring you pain. But…"

She laughed thickly and sniffed. "I misunderstood. I was so sunk in my own fears I could not see the truth."

"Fears?"

"Since we left Edinburgh everything seemed to verify what Olivia Ramsey said. The people in the croft who spoke only Gaelic, the cool response I've had from everyone I meet. The desolation of the countryside. It all seems to fit."

James sighed again. "I was afraid of that." He squeezed her gently and kissed the top of her head. "Let's go downstairs and I'll see to lighting a fire. Then we can talk."

She sniffed again and nodded. Then she said hesitantly, "James? I'm sorry for being such a fool about this…"

"Hush." Putting a finger over her lips, he smiled, then lightly kissed her. "Come downstairs."

Smiling tremulously, she accepted the hand he held and allowed him to lead her down the stairs.

They were in a compact room in the back of the house, searching without success for fuel to build a fire, when they heard a woman's voice calling. James strode to the front, and there saw a round female figure carrying a large iron kettle and what appeared to be a loaf of bread. He immediately stepped forward to relieve her of the heavy pot. She sighed, dropped a small curtsy, and said, "Thank you, sir. I used to be able to carry a load such as that easily, but I'm getting old, I am. Now, sir, I'm Eileen MacLonan, Gregor's wife, do you remember me? When Gregor told me of your arrival I thought you might be hungry, so I've brought a stew, which only needs to be warmed."

As she spoke, Eileen peered past James into the gloomy interior of the house, obviously searching for something—or someone. James's expression relaxed into a smile. "That is very kind of you, Mrs. MacLonan, and yes, I do remember you, particularly the scones you used to bake for Neil and me when we snuck away from our tutor. My wife is in the room in the rear of the house. The kitchen, I think? Come along and meet her."

Eileen beamed. "I'd be proud to, sir."

Thea was standing awkwardly in the center of the room. She'd heard the conversation between Eileen and James, and the thought of meeting one of the cool people who had watched her earlier filled her with irrational panic. Drawing on every bit of self-confidence she possessed, she smiled as Eileen MacLonan entered the room behind James. "Hello, Mrs. MacLonan," she said carefully. "I heard you introduce yourself to my husband. Thank you for your thoughtfulness. You have no idea how long it seems since we last ate!"

"Aye, I can guess," replied Eileen, shrewdly sizing up her new mistress. In the dim light shed by the candle, Thea's features were strained with weariness, but in her dark eyes sparkled courage and pride. Eileen nodded to herself, apparently satisfied.

James watched with amusement as the two women assessed each other. When Eileen nodded, he knew Thea had made another conquest in the MacLonan clan. That pleased him. As his wife, she would always be given courteous treatment by his clansmen, but if they didn't respect her for herself, she would never be more than an outsider, suffered for her position. He didn't want that fate for Thea. He'd spent enough years as an exile to know the bitterness of never being accepted.

Eileen MacLonan's approval would ease Thea's adjustment to Highland life and speed her acceptance amongst the clansmen. A worry he'd refused to acknowledge eased from James's shoulders.

"If you'll tell me where the wood or peat has been stored, I'll make a fire, Mrs. MacLonan, to heat up the stew," he said.

Eileen put the loaf of bread she carried onto the hearth beside the pot of stew, which James had placed there. "Gregor will be bringing some in a moment." Her pale eyes flicked from lord to lady, a faint smile in their depths. "He's seen to the horses and sent young Donald to look out for the cart."

She gazed around the barren room, then said directly to Thea, woman to woman, "Men! If they aren't the most terrible creatures for giving up on things! When that last letter came, they up and stopped all work on the house. There was to be a table and chairs in this room, you know, and at least a bench and stools for the front room. I told them they'd best be prepared, and managed to get them to make yon bed. A sorry thing, is it not?" Without waiting for a reply, she continued. "We have a right fine carpenter in the village who was more than willing to make a proper bed for your homecoming. But when that letter came, why, the men canceled it quick. A crying shame, I say. It was a fine, handsome bed he was planning to build."

Shaking her head, she placed her hands on her hips. "I told my Gregor he'd best put some kind of bed in here, for if you did come you'd be wanting that first off. Give him his due, he listened to me, and there's not many men who will listen to a woman's good sense."

Thea blinked with amazement as this torrent of words washed over her. When Eileen had finished, she glanced at James, expecting him to be annoyed by the forthright speech. He was over by the fireplace, looking up the chimney to see if the damper was open or closed. Astounded, Thea realized that his lips were twitching with suppressed amusement. Dimly she began to realize that her own free-speaking ways must seem perfectly natural to a man raised in the same village with Eileen MacLonan.

Eileen's gaze had followed Thea's. Seeing her lord apparently concerned about the lack of a fire in the hearth, she shook her head with annoyance. "Where is the man! You need to rest before a warm fire, lady, after a journey like this.

I'd best go see what is keeping him."

After she had left through the kitchen door, Thea crossed to the fireplace. James emerged from his contemplation of the chimney, chuckling softly.

"Is she always like that?" she asked.

"Always," he agreed, amusement still in his voice.

The scent of the still-warm stew tickled Thea's senses, and she raised the lid to sniff deeply. "I'm so hungry I could eat this from the pot!"

James laughed. Taking the lid from her hand, he replaced it firmly. "Do that and you would forever wound Eileen MacLonan's sensibilities. Come away from the hearth before we both sink into temptation."

They settled against the adjacent wall, seated informally on the wooden floor, Thea cuddled warmly against James. She said apologetically, "It was very bad of Mrs. Ramsey to interfere the way she did. I hope you don't think she sent the letter at my suggestion?"

"Leave it, wife," he said gently. "Do you think I blame you?"

"I don't know, James! I do know I need to explain what happened in Edinburgh." She looked around the empty room. "We will need to be honest with each other if we are to cope with the coming days. Can we not begin now?"

He looked down into her serious features and agreed with a nod.

"Olivia told me that life in the Highlands would be too difficult, and before I knew it she had decided that if you wanted country living, we should stay at her house outside of Edinburgh. I did not think you would want that, but I did not want to offend her either, so I mumbled something polite about discussing the idea with you. She must have assumed you would agree and written her letter that very night. And so we arrived here without the comfortable surroundings we might have had."

"Speculating will change nothing. We're here now and must make the best of it." He hesitated, then added, "Thea, I was as disconcerted by our lack of welcome as you were. I wanted a warm house, filled with the smells of cooking and lit by dozens of candles, to be waiting for you when you arrived, but it was not to be. You have to admit that Eileen MacLonan makes up in human warmth what is lacking in physical comfort."

Thea laughed. "I have never met a woman who talks so quickly and without pause as Mrs. MacLonan. She's charming."

James grinned and said lazily, "She approved of you as well. Listen to her, Thea. She'll help you find your feet here at Glenmuir."

Thea glanced warily up at him. "I sensed an atmosphere of hostility toward me when we rode in, James. I am afraid I'll need more than Eileen's aid to win your people over."

Shifting so that his wife was seated in his lap, James said softly, "I know the bitterness that comes of being a stranger in a distant land. I will help you to learn Highland customs, and if you like I'll teach you a little Gaelic so you will never be excluded from a conversation."

Her lips parted temptingly and her eyes shone with gratitude. "James, I—"

Bending his head, he kissed her. "First lesson." He whispered a musical phrase against her lips. Giving herself over to the pleasure of his embrace, Thea decided he must be speaking Gaelic love words, hardly useful in her position as lady of the manor, but delightful while she lay in her husband's arms.

With James's promise ringing in her ears, she could almost believe he was happy with the bride who had been forced upon him. The fears she had been fighting since the night Olivia Ramsey had told her of the hardships of life in the Highlands slowly began to ease.

The coming months would indeed be difficult, but problems were made to be solved. Tomorrow she would have to begin the arduous task of making this chill little building a home. Tonight she would surrender herself into her husband's care, knowing, whether he said the words or not, that he sought only the best for her.

It was a beginning.

CHAPTER 12

Glenmuir,
August 1750

The dawn had not yet broken when Thea awoke. Slowly, she opened her eyes, aware of a deep contentment that she could not have imagined in those difficult weeks after she had married James MacLonan. She stretched lazily, then curled sensuously against her husband's side.

He was, she thought, two people. One was the public man—cool, decisive, and fair. This was the James MacLonan others turned to when they needed advice, or in times of trouble. They relied on him and trusted him to lead them to a place where life was better and at least a little bit easier.

But there was also the private man, the one Thea had come to know over the past five months. The man who had stolen her heart with his tender, thoughtful ways, whose eyes twinkled with amusement, and who smiled frequently, but didn't laugh enough. She had given her heart to the private James MacLonan, but she respected his dedication to his clansmen, and she was immensely proud of the work he had done to heal the scars still remaining from the rebellion.

Propping her head up on her hand, she looked at her husband. In repose, the tough inner strength in James MacLonan's features remained, but Thea had seen them blurred by desire and softened by tenderness as he made love to her. The thought of that made her sigh softly. The bedclothes had fallen away as he slept, and one broad, bare shoulder was tantalizingly close to her fingertips.

She reached over to stroke gently along his skin, enjoying the feeling of muscle and sinew beneath her hand. James made a soft sound of pleasure in his throat, then rolled onto his back. She waited for him to wake, but he slept on. Thea smiled faintly, a little disappointed, but she was happy just to watch him, to know that this was the private James MacLonan, her James, the man no one else ever saw. Alone with her, he relaxed completely, the only time he did so.

The past months had been difficult ones, for both of them. Thea had been faced with the problem of trying to adapt to Scottish life and customs, of proving her worth as an individual, and of learning a new language. None of these were easy tasks, but she knew that her success or failure in solving them would only affect one person, Theadora MacLonan.

James, on the other hand, had the onerous job of returning Glenmuir to its former prosperity and of leading his clansmen away from the bitterness that had consumed them since Culloden. As the son of the clan chief, in the absence of his father, he was also the source of law in this rugged Highland valley. He arbitrated disputes, dispensed justice, and directed the lives of his clansmen. The responsibilities were heavy ones, particularly for a conscientious man like James.

She trailed a finger down his jaw, tracing the line of bone from ear to chin. James smiled, but he slept on. Tenderness added a glow to Thea's features.

From the evening they had arrived at Glenmuir, when he'd listened quietly to Gregor's increasingly animated descriptions of the damage done to the Highlands since the battle of Culloden, he had weighed the information he was given, assessed it, then analyzed it. His responses, therefore, were based on information, not emotion. The people of Glenmuir, he'd said more than once, needed good sense and calm reasoning if they were to grow and prosper, not the heat of bitterness or fire of rebellion.

There were some who resented his point of view. Old men who'd lost a son in the Rising, or women whose husbands were dead or deported, clung to their bitterness like a shield to ward off further hurt. As she listened to him counseling the disaffected, helping them to see that further resistance to England was not only futile, but could cause even more destruction and suffering, Thea realized that whatever his personal opinions might be, James MacLonan's days as a rebel were over.

Pausing in her absentminded caress, she turned her thoughts inward, away from James, back over her own experiences since their arrival at Glenmuir.

She'd come here as an Englishwoman married to a Scot, but in a surprisingly short time she had begun to feel accepted in the valley. Now she saw herself as one of the people of Glenmuir, in the same way as the other MacLonans did. James, with the help of Eileen MacLonan and her daughter Morag, had taught Thea the customs of the Highlanders and what was expected of the clan leader's wife, but it was the people who had completed her adjustment to her new life, by making her welcome amongst them. On this August morning, Thea could admit that she was satisfied with the progress she'd made, even though she knew she had far to go.

There were those whose scars were deep and painful even now, and these were the most difficult for Thea to win over. People such as Maggie MacLonan of Ben Lonan. She lived on a plot of land some six miles from the village, beneath the looming mass of the tallest of the mountains that surrounded the valley. Once, according to James, her acreage had been prosperous. Ben Lonan Farm had boasted a dozen hardy Highland cattle, some sheep, and a rich harvest of foodstuffs. Then Maggie's husband, Dougal, had been convicted of treason after Culloden and condemned to being transported to the colonies. The party of English soldiers that had ravaged Glenmuir, burning MacLonan Castle and other houses, stealing livestock, and trampling the crops, had also taken Dougal MacLonan, after burning his house and brutally raping Maggie. She had been left abandoned and bleeding in the ruins of her life.

Thea felt deep compassion for Maggie MacLonan, for the woman had never recovered from her cruel treatment. Over the years, alone and despairing, Maggie hadn't been capable of returning Ben Lonan Farm to its former prosperity, and she lived a sort of half-life, refusing all offers of assistance and brooding over her fate. No matter how hard Thea tried, she could never get close to the woman. Their backgrounds were a solid wall between them, impossible to surmount.

Despite her lack of success with Maggie MacLonan and others like her, Thea's life at Glenmuir was happy, and far from lonely. She enjoyed the clanspeople, whom she now called friends, the duties she'd gladly assumed, and the status that being James's wife gave her in the small community.

Edinburgh and her life there were blurring memories that she didn't bother to keep fresh.

Eileen MacLonan's daughter, Morag, was now her assistant and housekeeper. Like her mother, Morag was shrewd, free-spoken, and a godsend for Thea. Morag knew who amongst the villagers was in need, whose respect was based on honest affection, and whose was just on the surface. Information like that was important for Thea to have. Due to the isolation of the region, Highland society was much more open than that of England or even of Edinburgh. The classes mixed readily together, and Thea had rapidly learned that a shrewd Highlander, of whatever rank, could be as good company as a wealthy and titled aristocrat.

James stirred in his sleep, catching her hand, then holding it close. Thea smiled faintly, then settled down beside him, her head pillowed on his chest. The sound of his heart beating slowly and regularly soothed her. She closed her eyes. Her thoughts drifted.

There would be much to do today. Mondays were always busy after the quiet of the Sabbath. After she and James had broken their fast, he was off to a meeting with his forester at the far end of the valley, while she met with Eileen and Morag for their weekly discussion on the status of the estate folk. Then she planned to work on the list of stores they would need for the winter months. After that, she'd wander over to see Isabel Graham, who'd been feeling poorly these last few days. At seventy years of age, Isabel had the right to her ailments, but she never complained. Thea found the old woman a font of wisdom and never begrudged the time she spent with her. Then she should...

In the midst of her catalogue of activities, sleep claimed her once more.

By the time Thea and James sat down for dinner, shortly after midday, the sun had erased the morning coolness and the temperature had risen to nearly eighty degrees. Though the heat impaired Thea's appetite, James tucked heartily into a selection of roast mutton, fresh trout, meat pie, salad, and buttered vegetables. A syllabub and cheeses made on the estate completed the meal.

As they ate, Thea and James talked in a companionable way about their activities that morning. Since their first days at Glenmuir they had used the quiet of the dinner hour to exchange views, plan activities, and focus on the development of the estate. Thea was certain that James had begun the practice to draw her into the life of Glenmuir and to help her get to know the people and their problems, but over the months it had become an opportunity for Thea to contribute to the redevelopment of Glenmuir. It had also proved to be an effective way to draw her closer to James, for she was better able to understand his concerns as well as the demands on his emotions and on his time.

On this beautiful August day, the major topic was the status of the reforestation project James had begun almost immediately after returning to Glenmuir.

"What did Logan say about the dying seedlings?" Thea asked as she cut a slice of lamb.

James shook his head gloomily. "He thinks some sort of vermin are eating the roots."

Thea frowned. The reforestation project was important to James. He was determined to heal the blackened scar of the once-beautiful woods that flanked Lonan Pass. He'd had the dead trees cleared away and had begun a program of replanting young, healthy trees in their place, speeding the process nature had already begun. The work had progressed well, but recently the forester had noted several of the transplanted seedlings dying for unexplained reasons, and he feared the rest might follow suit. "Vermin? What kind of vermin? Mice?" She shuddered delicately.

James raised one eyebrow, but his blue eyes danced with laughter. "Nothing quite so large, but I am sure you would find them equally offensive, my lady wife. He thinks it is some sort of beetle."

"Ugh! You are quite right James, I would not enjoy having to deal with such creatures. What is to be done?"

"Logan thinks he knows a way to get rid of them. For these trees, all we can do is apply his remedy and wait. We can also try replanting another type of tree, one that is better suited to the terrain and that doesn't have roots that are so very tasty to those little beetles. That might do the trick."

Thea wrinkled her nose. "Waiting does seem to be part of life up here, does it not? I went down the valley to see Isabel Graham this morning. She is mending nicely, but it has been a long time since she took to her bed suffering from chest pains."

James took a mouthful of wine, then gazed reflectively into his goblet. "Isabel Graham is a tough, indestructible old woman. Always has been," he said, then drank again.

"Tough she may be, but Isabel's pains were very real, James. You are not to mock them."

James looked at Thea over the top of his wine glass. This time the laughter in his eyes was mimicked by the twitching of his lips. "Yes, milady. As you say, milady."

Thea's eyes widened with indignation, then she laughed, "Fie, was I being dreadfully bossy?"

"Dreadfully," he agreed with a grin.

"Oh, dear. It is because I have come to respect Isabel, although I know not everyone can get along with her.

Perhaps I have picked up some of her traits. Eileen warned me that she is considered to be a terribly managing female."

"But she never did have your beauty or your charm, my dear. I do not think you are in any danger of being classed as the same type of woman as Isabel Graham."

Thea blushed. She couldn't help it. James's voice had softened and deepened as he spoke, and her heart had begun to beat faster as her body responded. "James..."

"Yes, Thea?" There was a small smile on his mouth while his eyes danced with wicked humor.

Thea cleared an obstruction in her throat. "Do you have any plans for the afternoon?"

There was a short, heavy silence during which their gazes locked, silently expressing more than their words ever would.

Slowly, James said, "I was to meet with Ian MacLonan to check on the progress of the rebuilding of the Castle."

"Ah. Then I shall not suggest you stay," Thea said lightly. Like the reforestation project, the rebuilding of the ruined Castle was part of James's plan to turn the people of Glenmuir's thoughts away from the bitterness of defeat and death and direct them instead to the future.

Pride stirred within her as she smiled at her husband. They rarely spoke of his time on the Continent, an exile with no prospect of return, but she knew James still felt the pain of those years keenly. Nevertheless, he refused to pass any lingering bitterness along to his clansmen. Thea respected him for that, for she knew how difficult it was to keep strong emotions, such as regret and anger, from tarnishing a person's outlook. She respected, too, his effort to ensure that he did not brand her with prejudices because of background.

As a husband, James MacLonan was not perfect, but she found it remarkably difficult to determine what exactly his flaws were.

Though the afternoon was still hot, the sun no longer burned as fiercely as it had around midday. Thea had abandoned the quiet seat on the sofa where she had been resting, and was standing before a large mirror in the hall, adjusting a wide-brimmed hat. She thought, with some amusement, that her appearance had changed drastically over the summer. Her gown, though of a fine-quality cloth, was muslin; not silk or satin. No hoops widened the skirt as fashion in London and Edinburgh demanded. Hoops were impractical in the confines of the small cottage, and her life was too busy anyway to be bothered with them.

Her fair complexion had taken on a soft glow from the hours she spent outdoors, either walking about the village or riding to outlying farms. Nevertheless, she had to be careful. Even though she'd acquired a light tan, her skin still tended to burn if she remained out in the sun too long without protection—especially her nose. That was why she was adjusting the hat at a saucy angle before she ventured out. Yesterday she hadn't been so cautious, as her pink cheeks and nose testified.

Outside the cottage she paused for a moment adjusting to the heat. A sound in the distance made her turn her head, her eyes searching for the cause. A rider was approaching, galloping hard. Thea frowned. As the horse drew closer, she was able to make out the color of the man's coat. It was red, laced with white, and it looked remarkably like the livery her parents had used since she was a child.

The rider slowed the horse as he neared Thea. She recognized him as one of her parents' servants. As she waited impatiently for him to reach the house, she began to smile.

When he identified her, he directed his horse toward her. When he reached her, he jumped down and bowed. "A letter for you, Miss Thea...er, Mrs. MacLonan. I am to wait for a reply."

Absently, Thea sent him off to stable his horse and then to get something to eat in the kitchen. She was looking at the writing on the letter he had given her. Not surprisingly, it was her father's hand. She held it lightly, half afraid of the words it contained.

She'd had letters from Edinburgh since coming up to

Glenmuir, but none had come by the hand of a galloping courier. That made her wonder if the contents of this missive might be more ominous than pleasurable.

She fingered the bold red seal embossed with her father's crest, then with a sudden resolution, snapped it open and scanned the words inside. What was written there made her smile. Then she bit her lip in consternation, but in her usual determined way, focused on the more positive part of the message.

Folding the paper, she looked toward the new "Castle," as the people of Glenmuir liked to call the gracious manor house James had designed. He was there now, overseeing the construction. With a smile that came from a growing excitement and a desire to share it, she hurried toward the building.

The new Castle was located a little distance from the village and the burnt-out ruin it was replacing. When the site was being chosen, James had said forcefully that he didn't want to look from the windows of his new home and be forever reminded of the past. Thea agreed with him. The gaunt ruins of the ancient Castle made her shiver each time she glanced in that direction; she knew she would never get used to the sight. The new manor was angled so the windows looked toward the tall mountains that dominated the far end of the valley and the busy village.

Thea's footsteps carried her along the now well-worn path from the village to the new mansion. As the building came into view, she studied it. Knowing the old Castle could not be recreated in its original form, James had worked with the architect to design a building that combined the best of both the prevailing European classicism and the ancient building style of the Highlands. Turrets, recalling the towers of the old ramparts, would flank a central doorway that in turn resembled the old gateway. Two wings, projecting to the rear, created a courtyard that would be filled with ornamental gardens. The whole design recalled the walls and forecourt of an ancient fortification, but now large windows would pit the walls to let the maximum amount of light into the interior.

Once the new house was finished, there would still be much work needed to complete the final effect. New furniture, carpets, china, and paintings, all the accoutrements necessary to a gentleman's style of living, would have to be bought in Edinburgh or London and transported here. When the Castle had been burned in '46, the destruction had been thorough. Furniture was reduced to firewood, priceless antiques wantonly destroyed, the fine bone china shattered to tiny shards, the gold and silver plate looted and carried off to points unknown as the profits of war. Everything would have to be replaced.

The work would not end there. A landscape designer would be hired to create the ornamental gardens where nature and man's work would be blended to make a pleasing vista of the parklands that surrounded the house. Though it would be years and endless hours of work before the house was finally completed, Thea didn't mind. She and James had been given the opportunity to create a heritage for their sons and grandsons to cherish and defend. They were building for the future, not looking to the past, and for that Thea would not begrudge any effort.

As she neared the house, she saw her husband emerge from the opening where the front door would eventually be. Her heart gave a little lurch of pleasure. The feeling was still new enough to surprise her each time it happened.

A stocky, muscular man followed James from the entryway—Ian MacLonan, the stonemason. A fine craftsman, James had said, but as thickly muscled between his ears as he was on his torso.

A naughty smile flickered across Thea's soft mouth as she remembered when James had said those words. It was one night, two weeks before. They were lying close together, his arm around her shoulders, her head on his chest, both spent in the aftermath of making love. James had just confided that he had hoped to have one wing of the manor house ready for them to move into before the winter, but he feared Ian, the stonemason, might slow the work and make that impossible. Once Ian grasped what was needed, he worked diligently and carefully, but making him understand took time and endless patience.

Thea remembered that she'd smiled with pleasure at her husband's words, but had told him she'd gladly remain in the cottage through the winter. The small building would be easy to heat, and she had come to like the atmosphere of closeness the compact rooms created. But James was adamant. This was a gift, he had said, his gift to her to thank her and to please her. After that, the house had taken on a special, personal meaning for Thea, and she took a proprietary interest in every part of the construction.

However, at the sight of James and Ian, she deliberately slowed her hasty steps to an amble. The two men were arguing, if the expressions flickering across Ian's face and the tension visible in the way James held his body were any indication. Whatever their disagreement, she wouldn't interfere.

The argument was still going on, and Ian looked to be getting the worst of it, when Thea drew close enough for Ian to catch sight of her. Relief flooded his features, for he was able to use her arrival as a means to escape. James was glaring at the stonemason's retreating back when Thea reached him.

She cocked her head, brushing the wide brim of her sun hat against her shoulder. "Is there a problem, James?"

A muscle jumped in his cheek, but he shrugged in a noncommittal way. "Not an insurmountable one. Ian miscalculated the amount of stone needed for the central archway because he misunderstood the drawings. It means another delay." He looked down at her and grinned, his irritation dispelled by the sight of her. "Have you suddenly decided to take care of your fair skin, my dear? Or is this a sop to propriety?"

Thea peered up at him, liking the way his shirt of fine linen emphasized the breadth of his shoulders, while his dark kilt and plain white stockings showed off his muscular calves. On his feet were brown leather shoes, with only the plainest of buckles. The first time she had seen him dressed in the traditional Highland garment she had been a little shocked, but now she found she rather liked the way the kilt swung about his legs.

"Well, sir," she said demurely, her dark eyes dancing, "last evening a certain gentleman of my acquaintance expressed decided criticisms of my bright cheeks, as he most unkindly described them."

"Churlish fellow," MacLonan commented, grinning.

Stifling an answering smile, Thea sighed in an exaggerated way. "Indeed he is, sir." She allowed the smile twitch at the corners of her mouth. "But I do like to please him, so that is why I wear this hat to keep the sun from my face."

Their gazes locked in wordless communication. "Damn it wife!" he muttered, "It's the middle of the afternoon!"

Her eyes brimming with mischief, Thea retorted, "Then, James, perhaps you will be good enough to show me the improvements which have been made to our new home since last I visited."

She put her hand on his arm. He tucked it securely in the crook of his as they began to stroll toward the house. "Wait until I get you alone tonight, Theadora MacLonan. You'll regret your sauciness!" he said in a voice pitched deliberately low so that it would not carry.

She smiled, shot him a look from the corners of her eyes, and said huskily, "I doubt that, James," then laughed again at his scandalized expression. Though he might make love to her in the privacy of their chamber with unbridled passion, when they were in public he treated her with the courteous respect he expected his clansmen to show toward her. Thea understood the need for this, but there were times when she couldn't resist teasing him a little.

As they stepped through the half-finished doorway, Thea said, "James, a letter arrived from Edinburgh by courier not fifteen minutes ago."

He looked over at her, a frown between his brows. "Good news, I hope."

She turned, a brimming smile on her face. "Yes, indeed! My father writes that he and my family will be coming for a visit, if that is all right." When James didn't say anything, she added more soberly, "He promises he will not wear his uniform, James. They would like to come to see Glenmuir before they return to London."

He stopped in the middle of the great entry hall. "London? Your family is leaving Edinburgh?"

"Yes, my father received orders that he is to assume a position at the Horse Guards." She hesitated a moment, then said softly, "Do you remember the party we gave, the night I took you to my father's study to talk?"

James smiled and his eyes warmed. "How can I forget? I almost didn't attend because of the reason the party was being given."

Thea dimpled. "My father's promotion was only an excuse, James."

"I know that now and I knew that then. That was why, in the end, I did go."

"I am glad you overcame your reservations." Their eyes met and held. James bent his head, almost as if he intended to kiss her, but at the last minute he drew away. Thea laughed. "Papa's promotion is the reason that he is to return to London. Apparently he is to have some sort of position in the government. The family leaves in September, but first they would like to see us." She added quietly, "And I would like to see them before they go away."

He grasped her shoulders. "Did you think I would refuse to allow your family to visit, Thea?" Gently, he stroked a stray strand of hair away from her face. "Even if your father came in full regimentals, I would still welcome him to my house, because he is your father."

"James," she said softly, "I know how your people feel about the English, particularly members of the military. I don't want to undo the progress you've made since your return."

He shook his head. "The work I've done has been reinforced by your efforts, Thea. Don't deny who you are, for no one else does." He grinned. "Besides, it will do the people of Glenmuir good to see that not all Englishmen are dangerous marauders to be feared. Send the courier back with a note to your family, saying that we both look forward to their visit."

Thea lightly touched his cheek in a tender gesture. More and more now, she felt that she and James were partners in the rebuilding of Glenmuir. Together they were reconstructing the valley for themselves, the family they would one day have, for the future. Life was very good.

She had no idea that on the Continent Prince Charles Edward Stuart, the Young Pretender, was indulging in a new game, one which would tear apart the careful world James and Thea were building, changing irrevocably the terms on which they lived and the ties which bound them.

CHAPTER 13

October 1750

"Summer's over," Morag said gloomily as she handed Thea a black beaver hat in the shape of a man's tricorn. "If you must go out today, my lady, you should wear this." She held up a fine woolen cloak, trimmed with fur.

Thea laughed at the sound of disapproval in the other woman's voice. "Morag, don't fuss! I shall be fine. I'm only riding over to Maggie MacLonan's farm to see if she is over that fever. It isn't as if I'm planning an excursion to Edinburgh!"

"You've more than yourself to think of now, my lady," Morag countered persistently. "You don't want to go and do too much, now, do you?"

Thea laughed again as she adjusted her hat. In the mirror her eyes met those of her servant's. "Morag, I'm perfectly healthy. In fact, I seem to have an unseemly amount of energy, once I get over the queasy stomach I have every morning."

"But my lady! 'Tis the heir you're carrying! If Master James knew that you were roaming the countryside while you were carrying his baby—"

"He'd wrap me in cotton wool and forbid me to lift so much as a finger. I know, Morag!"

Morag threw a cloak over Thea's shoulders. "You ought to

tell him, my lady."

Thea suppressed a smile. There were times when Morag could not be stopped. "I will, Morag. Tonight. Now that I'm sure I'm with child I know he'll be so happy."

As happy as I am, she thought silently. She reckoned that she and James had made the child sometime during her family's visit a month before. Somehow, that made the connection between her family, James, and Glenmuir all the stronger. Before the visit she had worried that her father would be treated with a bitter scorn by the MacLonan clansmen, but that had not happened. The people of Glenmuir had accepted him as their lady's father and treated him with courtesy and respect.

The visit had been wonderful for Thea, even though the timing had been caused by her father's reassignment to London. She had shown her mother and sister the designs for the new Castle, told them of the decorations she'd planned, and accepted her mother's suggestions for other improvements, while James took her father about the estate. What had been said between the two men Thea did not know, but to her great delight, she could see the relations between her father and her husband become easier and more open as the days passed.

When the visit ended, she'd wiped away a tear as she watched her family leave, but James had wrapped his arm around her shoulders and hugged her against him, easing a little of her loneliness. Then, as her family's beloved forms dwindled in to the distance, he'd whispered that next year they would visit London and spend some time with her family there. Thea had sniffed, buried her head in his shoulder, and cried softly. James hugged her closer, comforting her more effectively than he knew.

A week after their departure, Thea was beset by a gentle melancholy that was foreign to her nature. She told herself it was natural after being separated from loved ones, and with a great force of will continued about her business. Then the nausea started, followed by a break in her womanly cycle, and she realized she was with child. The sadness fled, replaced by euphoria. She wanted to dance and laugh and shout her condition to the world. Instead, she hugged the knowledge close and amused herself by choosing the perfect day on which to tell her husband.

Now she grinned at Morag. "Telling James he will soon be a father is for later, when we can be private. Right now I intend to ride over to Ben Lonan Farm and see how Maggie is faring."

Morag shook her head. "Maggie MacLonan won't thank you for your concern, lady."

"I know that, Morag." But winning Maggie over to her side had become a challenge Thea doggedly pursued. "I'd be a poor creature indeed if I allowed the bitterness of a much-wronged woman keep me from my duty."

Morag shook her head. "Are you sure this is necessary, lady? There are rumors of soldiers about, looking for—contraband."

Thea bit her lip, suddenly feeling apart from the others in the valley. On Morag's long, bony face was an expression of very real fear, which Thea knew she could never share because she was English and therefore protected from the danger, real or perceived, that the Highlanders faced. She said lightly, "The soldiers will not harm me, Morag, as you well know, and I must satisfy myself that Maggie can manage on her own. I should think poorly of myself if I allowed the chance of a patrol of soldiers to frighten me!"

"Still, lady, it would be best if you took one of the men with you. It is wise to be prepared."

"Morag, you let your imagination run away with you. No one will hurt me here on my own lands!" At the dubious expression on the Scotswoman's face, Thea suggested lightly, "I should be gone no longer than an hour and a half. You will know where I am and what I'm about. If it will relieve your mind, send one of the men after me if I have not returned in good time."

Morag nodded seriously. "Aye, lady, I'll do that."

As Thea left the house, she thought ruefully that Morag would indeed send out a search party if she were a fraction of a second over the time limit she'd set for herself. And James, when he discovered the reason for Morag's concern, would side completely with her. Thea chuckled to herself, not at all disconcerted by the scene she was creating in her mind. She had every intention of settling down and enjoying being cosseted by the man she loved and the people she'd come to feel respect and affection for. Tomorrow.

Firefly was already saddled and was being held by a groom outside the door. Thea patted the mare's neck and fed her a carrot.

"Looks like we're in for a bit of weather, lady," the groom said conversationally.

Thea looked up at the sky. A solid bank of gray clouds allowed no blue to show through and hid the tops of the mountains. A misty fog filled the crevices and softened distant edges. Thea shivered. "Do you think it's going to rain this afternoon, Fergus?"

He tossed her up into the saddle. "'Probably not, lady, but you canna be too careful. Mind the mare's footing if the weather turns bad."

As Firefly, full of oats and energy, curvetted and tugged at the bit, Thea glanced at the lowering sky. With a rather grim amusement she decided that if the threat of marauding soldiery couldn't keep her from doing her duty, then the mere possibility of bad weather would certainly not do so. She thanked Fergus and let the mare have her head.

As she rode, she passed a small croft. Smoke billowed from the chimney, cheering her immeasurably. If the weather became too bad she could always take shelter in one of the crofts. She had been in most of them over the past few months and was on respectful, if not friendly, terms with the occupants. It would cause more offense if she did not shelter in one than if she did.

Thea's destination was the northern end of the glen where the land began to rise toward the encircling mountains. Ben Lonan cottage was located on a moor beyond the first ridge of hills, hidden from the rest of the valley and dangerously isolated for someone like Maggie MacLonan, weakened by fever and living alone.

As the path steepened, Thea let the mare slow her pace, but when they topped the rise she urged Firefly into a canter across the open, relatively flat moorland. It wasn't long before Maggie's little house came into sight, nestled in the lee of the towering mountain, Ben Lonan.

Across the open ground, near the quick running stream that flowed beside the cottage, a dozen horses were clustered, their riders dismounted and standing in a rough circle. Their coats were a vivid scarlet, marking them as a patrol of English dragoons. Somehow there was a menace in the way the men were standing that alarmed Thea. She slowed Firefly to a trot as she considered what she should do.

Most likely the men were simply watering their horses in the stream, using the opportunity to rest a few minutes before they continued. On the other hand, they were dangerously near Maggie's croft and the woman, with her combative dislike of the English, might well say something to insult the dragoons, which could lead to unnecessary violence.

Thea wished James were here. As the clan chief, he had a right to know what government troops were doing in the area. And if the patrol was here because they suspected wrongdoing, then James and the officer in charge would have to work together to sort it out. She ought to go and find James, but if she did, Maggie, with her bitter, often acid tongue, might cause an incident that would escalate into something no one wanted.

Suppressing a twinge of fear, the natural result of being a woman alone confronting a large group of unknown men, Thea dug her heels into Firefly's side to urge the mare into a canter. But the closer she came to the cluster of horses, the more she wished she'd heeded Morag's warning and brought a companion with her.

Maggie MacLonan didn't hear the regular beat of a single horse's hooves for she was too terrified to notice anything but the cold, pale gray of the English officer's eyes and the icy touch of metal against her skin. In her mind she screamed the words *Don't hurt me!* over and over, but her throat had closed and her voice was a mere whimper of protest.

She had come out of the cottage to fetch water from the stream. Since her illness, every movement, every action took twice as much energy as it should, and she had to force herself to carry out even the smallest task. She'd plodded out of her door lugging the heavy wooden bucket, first in one hand, then the other. At each aching step she railed against the injustice that had taken her man and sent him to a far-off land from which he would never return. If Dougal had been here he'd be the one doing the heavy chores, not Maggie. He'd look after her, protect her, help her. Life would be so much more than this endless struggle to survive.

At the stream she had to stop and rest, her heart was pounding so, while her breath came in short, hard gasps. Only then did she hear the sound of hooves and see the troop of horsemen cantering toward her. Panic kept her immobile and a cold sweat of raw fear prickled her skin. Soldiers. English soldiers. The bucket fell from her hands with a thud.

An officer, dressed in a fine scarlet uniform, urged the troop toward her. The sound of his voice broke Maggie's paralyzed trance. Picking up her skirts she fled, heading for the treed hillside and the almost indiscernible paths she knew so well. But her debilitated condition and the precious seconds she had stood, unable to move, betrayed her. She was pursued and easily overtaken by two of the cavalrymen.

Casually they herded her back to the officer, who was sitting languidly on a big black stallion. He was a thin man of perhaps twenty-four or twenty-five years of age. Pale eyes under sandy brows watched her with dispassionate menace while his small, petulant mouth curved into a cruel, mocking smile.

A sharp blow on the side of her head drove Maggie to her knees and brought her thoughts abruptly back to the realities of the situation. A bullying voice shouted in her ear, "He asked you a question, and when Lieutenant Williams asks you a question, you answer! Understand, wench?"

Maggie looked up. All she could see was the massive shoulders of the horse and the black of the officer's boot. "Aye, sir," she whispered.

"Get her to her feet so I can hear her," Williams drawled. There was pleasure in his tone. He was enjoying the situation.

The soldier grasped Maggie's shoulder and pulled her up, tearing the seam of her dress in the process. The fabric fluttered down, exposing her thin, well-used shift that showed more than it hid. There were lascivious comments and a few guffaws from the watching troopers. Maggie hurriedly pulled her torn dress back together and defensively wrapped her arms against her breasts.

"Silence," shouted Williams. Quiet fell. Maggie felt a surge of relief that the lieutenant was able to control the rabble he commanded. Williams drew his sword, an elegant blade with a chased silver hilt, and flicked it under Maggie's chin. She gasped, then uttered a choked off sob of pure terror. The mocking smile on the Englishman's face widened.

"What are you doing?" Thea demanded in a loud, imperious voice. Her earlier hope that the group of horsemen had stopped at Maggie MacLonan's home for some benign purpose had fled as she neared the cottage and saw that Maggie was in the center of the ominous circle of men. A cold fear that the situation had gone too far for her to be able to take control of it made her wish, more than ever, that she had brought an escort with her today.

The officer looked up, but didn't remove his sword from Maggie's throat. "I am interrogating a witness," he said smoothly in the refined accent of southern England. His gaze traveled the length of Thea's body, taking note of the excellent cloth of her well-used riding costume, the expensive fur that trimmed her cloak, her patrician features, and her spirited mount. His head flicked to one side. One of his men moved surreptitiously. "Do I have the pleasure of conversing with the Lady of Glenmuir?"

"You do," Thea replied curtly. "You have the advantage of me, sir. What is your name and rank?"

He smiled cruelly, and bowed. As he moved, his sword scraped along Maggie's skin, leaving a long scratch. Blood oozed slowly from the mark. "Lieutenant Williams of His Majesty's Dragoons, at your service, ma'am."

"Lieutenant Williams!" Thea gasped, watching the blood dribble down Maggie's skin until it reached the thin stuff of her shift, where it left a bright red stain. "Take care! Sheathe your sword, if you please!"

"But I do not please."

As he spoke, Thea noticed that several of his men were standing unpleasantly close to her mare. Close enough to grab hold of the bridle, close enough to catch the stirrups and pull her off the horse. She raised her brows haughtily. "What are you doing on MacLonan lands?"

Williams's stallion moved and he allowed the sword to trail further down Maggie's shoulder. She flinched and tried to move away, but the trooper holding her forced her forward. The sword bit into flesh and she sobbed helplessly.

Anger flashed in Thea's eyes. *Who does this vicious junior officer think he is dealing with?* "My husband is the Master of Glenmuir. If you have some accusation to make about Maggie MacLonan, then you must bring it before him. Until then, release the woman and be on your way!"

Williams laughed. "I don't have to do anything, my fine lady. I've been ordered to patrol this area and make these barbarians aware that London rules here." His sneering smile showed sharp yellow teeth. "That includes enforcing the laws and searching out illegal contraband. I'm simply questioning this woman for information."

"I don't have information! I've been ill with fever. Please don't—"

Maggie cried out as the soldier holding her in place cuffed her on the side of the head. "You'll speak when you're spoken to, wench!"

"Well done, Brown," the lieutenant murmured silkily.

"Cease this pointless assault immediately, Lieutenant Williams." Thea looked hard at the dragoon holding Maggie's shoulders. She knew the man, and at her pointed stare he swallowed and looked down at the ground. Williams was new to her, but her father had told her that when he was transferred out, a number of other officers had also been reassigned, with new men coming in. Williams must be one of those. "You can see for yourself how isolated Maggie's farm is. Her husband was transported in '46 and she's been a recluse ever since! She knows nothing of what goes on in the valley."

"But you do, I'll warrant, Mrs. MacLonan."

Thea felt the hairs on the back of her neck rise with primitive fear. "There are no illegal activities in Glenmuir. My husband wouldn't countenance them."

Williams lowered his sword. Maggie closed her eyes and breathed deeply, her body trembling from the stress of the last few minutes. "No illegal activities at all, Mrs. MacLonan?" he repeated mockingly. "Your husband's word on it, I suppose."

"Yes!"

"The word of a Jacobite."

"The word of a gentleman," Thea countered furiously.

Williams smiled and relaxed in the saddle, the hand holding the reins resting lightly on the pommel. The big stallion pulled at the bit and stamped impatiently.

"A Jacobite hardly qualifies for the title of gentleman. A barbarian outlaw is what your husband is, Mrs. MacLonan. A lying rebel who cannot be trusted by any decent man."

"You impertinent jackanapes! I demand an apology immediately!"

The lieutenant's face twisted with rage. "Mind your tongue, woman," he snarled. "Or I shall make very certain you regret you ever learned to speak!"

The situation tottered on the edge of explosion. Williams was not the man to gracefully accept criticism from anyone, especially not a woman, and especially not in front of the men he commanded. Maggie, trembling and terrified, the sword still dangerously close to her body, unwittingly turned the situation in a new direction.

Her voice quivering with fear, she shrieked, "Tell him who you are, lady! Save us both! Please, tell him!"

Curiosity flickered in Williams's eyes, and the tension in his body eased away as if he felt he'd regained control of the situation. "How intriguing," he drawled in a perfect imitation of a supercilious society fop. "Yes, my lovely lady, do indeed tell me who you are."

Thea raised her brows haughtily. Her voice was icy with disdain. "She wishes me to inform you that I am English born and that my father is Sir Frederick Tilton, a general officer in the King's army, and recently in command of the troops stationed in Edinburgh." Though she kept her voice level, inwardly Thea was furious. Infected by her mistress's seething emotions, Firefly tossed her head and sidled nervously. "You cannot expect to insult me and get away with it!"

"Insult you, Mrs. MacLonan?" Williams nodded in her direction. One of the soldiers looked briefly at Thea, touched his cap, then grabbed her mare's bridle. A second stood by the mare's side and twitched the reins from Thea's hands. Williams laughed nastily. "You will allow my man to help you dismount, won't you, Mrs. MacLonan? That mare of yours seems a rather fidgety animal. Too spirited for your capabilities, I think. You're better off on the ground."

Thea looked down at the stony face of the soldier at her knee and bowed to the inevitable. After shooting a smoldering glance at Williams, she slipped off the mare, avoiding the soldier's raised hands, apparently outstretched to assist her. He was a stranger to her and she didn't like the appreciative gleam she could see deep in his eyes.

"An intelligent decision, ma'am," Williams said. Then he addressed the soldier holding the bridle. "Take the horse and tie it behind the house. You—see that the lady doesn't injure herself by getting involved in what she should not."

The dirty fingers of the nearby soldier's hand closed around Thea's arm above the elbow. Resisting a shudder, she faced Williams proudly. "You will regret this, sir."

He raised mocking brows. "Regret what, my fine lady? Having my man assist you in dismounting to ensure your safety?" He turned to the soldier holding the wilting Maggie. "Brown, I'm sure this woman can tell us any number of secrets if she's questioned properly. And remember, these are rebel lands. I want to be sure there's nothing afoot here that should not be."

"Don't touch her!" Thea ordered in a tone she'd heard her father use many times. It spoke of confidence and authority, but more importantly, it hid the fear that lurked very close to the surface.

The soldiers halted, instinctively responding to the command in Thea's voice. Firefly pulled at the reins held by one of the dragoons, reaching down to nibble at a tuft of grass. Maggie choked back a frightened sob.

Williams still lounged in the saddle, but his expression was impatient. "You're interfering in the interrogation of a rebel."

"Maggie is no rebel!"

"She's a Scot. They're all rebels at heart. Barbaric savages," Williams added for good measure.

"It is you who are the barbarian!"

"Take care, my fine English lady, lest you push me too far and I treat you like the Scots you so admire!"

"You wouldn't dare!"

Williams laughed nastily. "Would you care to put me to the test?"

"I am not without protectors!" Thea said hotly. "My husband will see to it you are punished for this day's work!"

"Whose word would be accepted regarding what happened here? A former Jacobite's? Or a loyal officer just doing his duty?"

"My word will be accepted. I told you..."

Williams raised sardonic brows. "The word of a turncoat? A traitor to her own kind? I think not, lady. I think not."

The color drained from Thea's face. Satisfied, Williams glanced at his men. In a voice that threatened violence if he wasn't immediately obeyed, he snarled, "You were given orders. Carry them out!"

There was a flurry of activity. The trooper holding Firefly jerked the mare's head up and pulled her into motion. His path led him past Williams, still relaxed on his horse, now watching with amusement as Maggie struggled against the soldier's hold. Her movements brought her near to his mount and he raised his sword to ward her off. Thea stared helplessly, her hands balled into fists of impotent anger.

The soldier leading Firefly was not used to a nervous horse that tried to rear, tossed its head, sidled, and generally did its best to resist the pull of the rein. As he led the mare past his lieutenant, the horse's hindquarters swung round as she danced with irritation. The big black stallion, catching the mare's scent, snorted and lunged with an instinct as old as time.

The movement caught Williams off guard. He teetered in the saddle, his balance lost. As the stallion bounded forward, the sword Williams had pointed insultingly toward Maggie pierced her flesh. She screamed and her knees buckled. Williams jerked hard on the reins, halting the stallion, then pulled his weapon free of Maggie's body. She collapsed into a heap on the ground.

In the silence that followed, the only sound was the beat of Firefly's hooves as she escaped from the limp grasp of the soldier leading her. No one moved or spoke as they all stared in blank horror at the wounded woman.

"Sergeant," Williams said at last. "Mount your men. We are moving out."

Thea dragged her appalled gaze away from Maggie's still form. "You're leaving? Just like that? You won't even carry her into her house? Or try to tend her injuries? Do you care if she's even alive?"

Williams rammed his blade into the scabbard. "I told you to mind your tongue, woman."

"You call the Scots savages, but I think it's a name you are better qualified to wear, Lieutenant! Your actions today are a stain on the honor of England. I hold you beneath contempt!"

The soldiers were mounted, the troop ready to depart. Williams spurred his horse into motion. As he passed, he leaned down and struck Thea squarely across the face with the back of his hand.

She fell to her knees, her ears ringing and her vision blurred. The tricorn hat she wore, a jauntily cocked imitation of a man's, flew from her head with the force of the blow and the pins holding her mane of thick golden hair were loosened. It fell in a bright cascade over her shoulders as the riders disappeared into the mist.

Emotions began to replace the numbing shock as the sound of the last hoofbeats faded away. Hatred flooded Thea first, then rage that a vicious, overbearing underling should dare to act as Williams had done. If the lieutenant had been beside Thea at that moment and she'd had a weapon in her hands, she would have killed him and smiled while she did so. But Williams was long gone and Thea's rage burnt itself out in helpless frustration, leaving desolation and despair in its charred ruins.

A pitiful moan from Maggie drew Thea out of her own troubles and back to the need to act. Shakily, she rose to her feet and went over to the other woman, then knelt down beside her.

"Maggie? Maggie, did you call? How can I help you?"

Maggie didn't reply. With fumbling fingers, Thea ripped a strip of cloth from her petticoat to bind the wound the sword had left in Maggie's chest. Then she undid the clasp of her cloak and, swinging the garment from her shoulders, draped it over Maggie's inert body. The garment hid Maggie's torn and bloodied clothes, but it couldn't hide the pallor of Maggie's face. Thea bit her lip. There must be something she could do to ease the woman's pain.

Looking around, she spotted the bucket Maggie had carried from the cottage. She began to rise, intending to fetch water to bathe Maggie's forehead, but the woman opened her eyes and croaked, "Don't go."

Thea jumped, so unexpected was the sound of Maggie's voice in the heavy stillness. Once she'd regained her composure, she said gently, "Maggie, I'm only going over to the stream to get some water. I won't be but a moment."

Something flickered in the other woman's eyes; then her lids drooped closed and she turned her face away. Thea shivered, feeling shut out and frightened. Not liking the sensation, she hurried over to the stream. When she returned, she tore another piece of cloth from her petticoat, dipped the rag into the icy water, and began to bathe Maggie's face.

"Someone should be coming from the village soon," she said as she worked, but whether she was comforting herself or Maggie she wasn't sure. "They knew where I was going and how long I'd be."

"I thought you'd left," Maggie muttered thickly.

"No, I only went to get water. I won't leave you alone."

"They'll be back."

"W-who?"

"The soldiers." Maggie shut her eyes. "I thought if they knew you was one of them they'd go away."

"Those men were renegades. Outlaws," Thea stated forcefully. "They weren't typical British soldiers—"

Maggie laughed. "You still don't understand, do you, lady? The first time the soldiers came was after Culloden. We hadn't heard, then, about the battle. If we had, my Dougal would have taken to the hills like a sensible man. He'd done nothing. Nothing! He'd refused to fight for the Prince, said he had no quarrel with London. Master Neil tried to persuade him to go, but he was adamant and in the end he stayed here to look after his own."

Thea sat back on her heels, watching the other woman's face.

"When the soldiers came we told them Dougal was innocent, but they wouldn't believe us. They took him anyway, bound his wrists with chains, and laughed at his anger. Then they slaughtered our animals and burned our house. And if that didn't shame Dougal enough, they raped me in front of him, made him watch while they took their brutal pleasure of me. Then they dragged him away, helpless and humiliated."

Maggie's breath was coming in short, panting gasps, as if she was having trouble breathing, and there was an ominous rasp underlying the sound.

"Maggie, it won't happen again. Someone will be here soon…"

"I never saw him again," Maggie muttered, her words slurring one into the next. "He was sent to the colonies for a crime he didn't do. And I am alone."

Thea reached under the cloak to clutch Maggie's hand.

"Not alone, Maggie. Not any more."

The Scotswoman fixed her eyes on Thea's. There was an unnatural glitter in them that burned into Thea's heart. "You're not alone, lady. My man is gone. He cannot help me now. But yours can. Master James can avenge you."

"But I don't want vengeance!"

"Blood demands blood," Maggie muttered harshly. Her eyes glittered fiercely for a moment more. "You see to it, lady," she said. Then her voice stilled and her eyes drooped shut as she sank into unconsciousness.

Thea crouched beside her, more terrified than she'd been before. She clutched Maggie's limp hand, staring at her face, but seeing instead the contempt in the Lieutenant's icy gray eyes and the sneer on his mouth as he called her a traitor to her own kind.

She began to shiver from a cold deep within her bones.

"James," she whispered, as she huddled there dispiritedly. "James." She needed him now, needed to feel his arms around her, needed to hear his comforting voice telling her everything was all right. For a moment her mind escaped from the horror of what she'd witnessed as she thought of her husband and of the life they were building together. Then that lovely dream shattered as she realized how very fragile it was.

For she could no longer pretend that the soldiers were renegades working against the law. The Lieutenant and his men had been ordered to terrorize the Highlands. Their cruel treatment of Maggie had been deliberate, without provocation. And James MacLonan had not married Theadora Tilton for love. He hadn't married Thea, the person, at all. He'd married the daughter of Sir Frederick Tilton, English general, hereditary Whig. He'd married so that he would be able to return to his Highland home and to ensure that incidents like this one wouldn't happen.

"No," she groaned aloud, shutting her eyes tightly as she took the thought one step further. Why would James want to comfort her now that Williams had proven how useless her family's power really was? All she was to him was the physical proof of a bargain he'd been forced to make; one that had not served him well. One that had left him with an obligation that could prove disastrous.

Above all, James was a Highland Scot, a proud, passionate, determined man who would fight for what he believed was right, or for the honor of those who were his responsibility. She'd heard stories about the kind of revenge Highlanders wreaked on their enemies—raids and murder and violent bloodletting. If James tried something like that against the might of the English army, he would surely be crushed in the attempt.

What could she do to keep him from taking a risk that would destroy him? How could she convince him that what had happened on this desolate moor could be handled through proper legal channels? Why should he believe that the system was not flawed, when all of his experience proved otherwise? The questions tumbled through her thoughts and as each went unanswered her despair grew.

When a sound broke the stillness, she lifted her head, not sure what it was. The mist had rolled down from the mountain crags, and she could not see more than a few feet beyond where she crouched. The sound strengthened, becoming clearer. Terror plucked at her, for it was hoofbeats that she heard, still in the distance, but getting stronger. Hoofbeats heading toward her.

What if it was the odious lieutenant returning?

CHAPTER 14

For a shameful moment she contemplated flight. Then she squared her shoulders and tossed her head defiantly. She would not leave Maggie alone to face the marauders again.

As the hoofbeats drew closer, her heartbeat pounded unnaturally loud. But the horse that materialized out of the deepening mist was her husband's powerful chestnut, not Williams's black stallion. Relief poured through her.

James swung down from the horse. Striding over to her, he demanded curtly, "Thea! What happened? Are you all right?"

"Yes," she said shakily, "but Maggie's been hurt." She looked down at the woman's face as she spoke, and was surprised to see that her expression had lost the bitter pain of moments before. Now she appeared at peace with herself and the world around her.

James glanced down at Maggie and frowned. He touched her throat, searching for a pulse. Gently, he detached Maggie's hand from his wife's grasp. Thea stared at him in puzzlement. He drew a sharp breath as he saw the bruise marring her cheek, but he said gently, "Maggie's dead, Thea. Come away."

"But we were just talking," she said blankly. When James stood up and tugged her to her feet, she followed him blindly.

"Your horse came back to the village, riderless and in a

lather. What happened, Thea?"

Thea blinked. Desperately, she said, "It was an accident, James. They didn't mean to hurt Maggie!"

"They?"

Thea began to shiver. Automatically, James draped his cloak around her shoulders. "Soldiers. They wanted information about illegal activities in the area. Maggie wouldn't tell them. She couldn't tell them what she didn't know!"

James's mouth hardened and a muscle jumped in his jaw. "How did Maggie die?"

"The lieutenant stabbed her." The shock of Maggie's death was beginning to wear off. Thea glanced up at her husband's face for a brief moment. "His horse bolted and the sword…just…sank into her body."

James touched her bruised cheek. "And this? How did this happen?"

"It's nothing…" She faltered, terribly afraid that if James knew the lieutenant had struck her deliberately, he would head down that path of bloody vengeance Maggie had spoken of.

"Indeed?" he said gently. "Permit me to decide that, madam wife. Who struck you?"

"Williams, the officer in charge of the troop. I said he was beneath contempt." Her voice cracked in a sob. "His answer, as he rode away, was…was this!" She shoved her palms against her eyes in a futile effort to stem her tears.

"Thea, dear heart, don't cry." James reached out, capturing her hands and drawing her against him. His arms wrapped around her, holding her shaking body tightly against him.

Thea sobbed helplessly while he crooned soft, soothing words and stroked her hair. Finally, she said shakily, "James, they knew I was English. I told them so. I thought it would make them would go away and leave Maggie alone. Williams laughed and called me a traitor. A traitor because I'd married a Scot. I was angry, but I was so helpless! I jeered at him, but that did nothing but make the situation worse. He made me dismount and they took Firefly away and threatened poor Maggie if she didn't tell them what they wanted to know..."

James pressed her gently. "Finish the story, Thea. You must, for your sake and mine."

She glanced warily up at him, but the strength of his arms holding her protectively offered her safety while the concern in his eyes urged her to continue. "Everything happened so quickly. Williams's horse bolted and the sword he was holding on Maggie...it stabbed into her. She screamed and..." Thea buried her face in James's chest. His clothes muffled her last words. "She fell."

On that afternoon, with the nip of fall in the air and the promise of rain adding to the cold James MacLonan made a vow to himself.

He was filled with a burning rage more powerful than anything he had ever felt before. As he stared grimly over Thea's head, he could far too easily envision the scene she'd described. The terrified women, the bragging, boastful officer, the subtle menace of the obedient soldiers. Violence simmering below the surface, brought to life by circumstances pushed beyond control.

His wife had been subjected to the casual exhibition of brute power through crude violence. An exhibition that had forced his proud, innocent English wife to look deeply into the ugly underside of a system that was flawed in ways she had never been forced to acknowledge before.

For him, it was the final insult, coming after years of injury. James vowed to himself that Williams, the English lieutenant, would pay for the crimes he had committed this day.

One way or another.

On their way back to the village, the rain that had been threatening all morning began to fall, so only those who had seen Firefly trot back to her stable were about when their master cantered up to the cottage, his wife held securely before him on his big chestnut stallion. James dismounted swiftly and lifted Thea down, refusing offers of help with a silent shake of his head. Trembling, Thea buried her face in his shoulder as he carried her into the house.

Inside, he called for Morag, asking her to prepare a bath, before he set Thea on her feet. She stood, huddled and shivering, her eyes downcast. Gently, James took her chin and tilted it upwards. He winced at the sight of the discoloration on her cheek. Thea's lips trembled.

"Damn the man," James whispered under his breath.

Thea swallowed hard and bit her lip. She looked up, her eyes glittering with unshed tears. James swallowed a curse and drew her into his arms. Over Thea's head he saw Morag standing frozen on the stairs, a startled expression on her face.

"Is the mistress all right, sir?"

"My wife has had a bad shock and an accident, Morag. Is the bath ready yet?"

"The water is heating now, sir." Morag came slowly down the stairs as Thea sniffed and turned. Morag gasped.

Trembling, Thea buried her face in James's shoulder once again.

"Mistress Thea! What has happened to you?"

"Nothing. I'm all right, Morag," Thea mumbled into the depths of James's coat.

Morag frowned. James shot her a grim look, then said quietly, "You might as well know, Morag. It will be all over the village by nightfall. There has been a death."

"A death! But who?" As James stared grimly at her, realization dawned on Morag. "Maggie? Maggie MacLonan? How?"

Thea drew a great shuddering breath and pulled herself out of her husband's arms. "At the hands of an Englishman. An English dragoon, in fact. One of my father's men."

"Thea, your father no longer commands in Edinburgh. You know that," James said carefully.

"Does that matter?" Thea demanded in clipped tones,

refusing to look at either James or Morag. "When my father was reassigned to London, Colonel Harris was left in charge, so he was the one who sent out this patrol. He issued the orders to harass the Highlands. It's true that the Lieutenant and his men were under the Colonel's command, not my father's, but Colonel Harris served my father for three years! He is my father's man."

Morag looked from one to the other. "I don't understand…"

There was a short, uncomfortable silence. Then James said slowly, "I believe my wife is saying that she holds herself responsible for what happened to Maggie. Is that right, Thea?"

Thea's head snapped around. Her hands were clenched beneath the wet cloak. "Yes! Yes, it's true! Maggie is dead because of me!"

"Ach, Mistress Thea, don't be daft," Morag said prosaically, after a moment. "No one blames you for what the soldiers do. 'Tweren't your fault."

"You don't understand Morag." Thea's shoulders slumped, "You don't understand why James married me."

Morag threw back her head and laughed. "I've served the two of you for these six months past lady, so I have a fair idea what makes your marriage."

To Thea's complete astonishment, Morag winked at James. He laughed.

"Come upstairs, wife. I'll be your lady's maid while Morag prepares your bath. I think you need quiet and a chance to relax before anything more is said."

Listlessly, Thea allowed him to lead her up the stairs. Morag's reaction confused her, but she knew without a doubt that with the lieutenant's assault and Maggie's death she had failed her husband utterly. Morag might not understand, but Thea did—and so did James.

The next day she did not want to go out for she was sure that the people of Glenmuir would blame her for Maggie's

death. After all, she was English and it was the English who
had murdered Maggie. She slept late, reluctant to even leave
the safety of her bedchamber, but Morag was there,
chattering to her in a normal way about the household
routine, asking what she had planned that day, and making
sure that Thea's maid, Jenny, kept her questions to what
Thea wanted to wear. Thea found herself responding, tensely
at first, then in a more normal way. Before long, she was
dressed and heading down the stairs to partake of breakfast
with James, who had waited his meal for her. With James
she could not pretend that everything was normal, as she had
with Morag. They talked of Maggie's death, searching for the
reason that an English patrol would be on Glenmuir lands,
but could find no sensible answer.

As she finished the meal, Morag's mother, Eileen
MacLonan, presented herself with a request that Thea visit
one of the villagers who was with child and close to her
term. A visit from the mistress would do her good, Eileen
said, and James agreed.

Thea suspected that this was nothing more than a trumped-
up pretense to force her to leave the security of the cottage,
but she could find no way to refuse, short of admitting that
she was afraid of facing the hostility of the villagers. As
Thea had never been one to give in to fear, reluctantly, and
with considerable trepidation, she allowed a cloak to be
thrown over her shoulders before Eileen shepherded her out
of the house.

It was not until she felt a shaft of sunlight on her skin that
she stopped. Putting her hand up to cover the bruise on her
cheek, she turned to Eileen. "I've come out without my hat. I
must go back inside." She needed the broad brim of the
small crowned hat she usually wore to hide her face from the
eyes of the villagers.

Gently, Eileen took her hand and pulled it down.
"Nonsense, lady. Let your people see your pretty face."

Thea stood tensely, her muscles trembling slightly, as if
she was about to flee. "I need my hat, Eileen."

Eileen smiled at her. "You can go back for your hat if you

must, lady, of course you can, but this babe of Maureen's is kicking something fierce. I think he is ready to be born any time. Maureen is set upon a visit from you before that happens. I'd not wait too long before going to see her."

Thea frowned. "You think the baby could be born today?"

"Today, tomorrow, in the middle of the night." Eileen shrugged, a twinkle in her eyes. "Babies come in their own time, lady. They don't wait on our convenience."

"No, no, of course not." Thea stood irresolute. The fine trembling was gone, though, and the tension in her body had eased. "I...I suppose we should go to her cottage."

Eileen nodded approvingly. "Aye, lady, the sooner the better."

Thea moistened her lips. "I..." She put her hand over her livid cheek again, and again Eileen gently pulled it away.

She patted the back of Thea's hand comfortingly. "Walk with your head high, lady. You've nothing to be ashamed of."

Sighing, Thea said, "But I do, Eileen. I do."

"Why? Because you could do nothing against the might of armed and mounted men?"

"I should have been able to do something, Eileen! They were my own people! My father's men. They should have respected my demand that they leave."

"Aye, should have, but didn't." Sadly, Eileen shook her head. "What could you have done? You were a woman, alone and unarmed. Mistress MacLonan, yesterday you faced what we have all faced. No one in Glenmuir faults you for what you could not change."

You faced what we have all faced. The words were an indirect allusion to the reprisals that occurred after the Pretender's defeat. "Is that what it was like, Eileen? Feeling fury while you watch the soldiers destroy, knowing you are powerless to stop them, then hating yourself for what you could not do?"

"It was a sad time, lady," Eileen said heavily.

"How did you survive? How did you cope?"

Slowly, Eileen smiled. "We helped each other lady. We'd all been victims of the same outrage. When the troops left, we banded together and gave each other comfort. We shared the pain and it was easier to bear that way. Come, lady, come and see Maureen. Feel her baby kick within her. Talk to people, lady. You'll be cheered, I know you will."

Still somewhat reluctant, Thea went with Eileen. The short walk took an hour as people stopped her to ask what had happened and to voice their disgust and outrage. Though there were no maudlin expressions of sentiment, she realized with considerable amazement that the people of Glenmuir didn't connect her in any way with the English officer who had murdered Maggie. In fact, for them Thea was as much an innocent victim as Maggie had been. Amazingly, the incident had made Thea one of them, in a way she could never have expected.

That evening, with their supper over, Thea and James had retired to the small parlor. Thea was on one settee, holding an embroidery hoop that she was supposed to be working on, but her fingers were still and her eyes stared into the distance, not at the silk fabric in her hands. A touch on her shoulder and the sound of James's voice made her jump. "James! Did you say something to me? I must have been daydreaming!"

"You were far away," he agreed grimly. He hesitated briefly, then sat down beside her. "I leave for Edinburgh tomorrow."

She stared at him, suddenly panicked because he'd put into words what she'd desperately hoped would never happen. "Must you go, James?"

He touched her cheek. "Williams has to be punished, Thea."

She flinched, and he withdrew his hand immediately.

"James, is it really necessary?" She knew it was, of course, but she was haunted by fears of her husband being forced back into exile if he returned to Edinburgh and there demanded more than Colonel Harris, now in charge of the garrison, would be willing to concede. Once she would have scoffed at fears like hers, but now she had a different, frightened, perspective. She no longer trusted the government she had so long believed in. But here at Glenmuir James would be safe. She wanted him to stay. "Couldn't you send someone else to inform the authorities of Maggie's death?"

James stared at her incredulously. "You expect me to send someone else to protest the insult done my wife?"

"You are going to report Maggie's death." She faltered, her hand coming to cover her cheek fearfully.

James stood up and began to pace restlessly. "Yes. But I go mainly to seek redress for the wrongs done to my wife! Thea I thought you knew that!"

She reached out for him. "James, don't go because of me!"

Standing stock still, he demanded, "'Why?"

"Because I am alive and unharmed!"

"Unharmed?" James repeated softly. "Thea, that infernal cur struck you. He taunted you and called you insulting names. He bullied you and forced you to see what you should not have seen. He—"

"But I deserved it! James, I am not blameless in Maggie's death! I jeered at Williams, I insulted him! If I had done as I ought and minded my tongue..." Her voice caught on a sob.

Striding over to her, he grasped her hands and pulled her urgently to her feet. "Thea, listen to me. If Lieutenant Williams was a decent man, he would not have been threatening Maggie with his sword and using the proximity of his men to make her afraid."

"He was unstable," Thea said on a sigh. "I could see the malice in his eyes, in the way he acted."

"Thea, dear heart, doesn't that tell you something? No one person can do more than they are able. If they do their best, then they should have no regrets. You did all you could to protect Maggie. Don't torture yourself with what might have been, or what you should have done. Blame should only be laid on those who don't bother to try."

She swallowed threatened tears and said thickly, "That is why you are going to Edinburgh."

"Maggie's dead. But Williams must be punished for his crimes. He must be brought to justice."

She looked up into her husband's hard, implacable eyes. "James, promise me something."

"If it is within my power, I will."

A hammering on the door interrupted them. There was the sound of stamping boots. Then a deep male voice spoke to Morag, who had answered the knock. Thea frowned. James moved away, his attention focused on the sounds from the hallway. Thea listened to the voices. Surely the accent of the man's voice was not Scottish.

The door to the parlor opened and Morag said in a hesitant manner, "Lord Staverton."

There was a moment of surprised silence. Then James strode forward to shake his old friend's hand in greeting.

"Staverton! This is a pleasure, but I thought you were in London."

"Indeed I was, MacLonan." He bowed to Thea. "Good evening to you, Mrs. MacLonan. I trust I find you well?"

Thea avoided the question. "You must have been traveling all day, Lord Staverton. Morag, tell Cook that we have company and to prepare Lord Staverton a supper. Once you have done that, make up the guest chamber." Morag bobbed a curtsy and hurried off.

While Thea issued her orders, James went over to a sturdy side table where several decanters rested, as well as a set of crystal wine goblets Thea had brought from Edinburgh. He poured brandy into a glass and handed it to Staverton. Thea turned back and for the first time Staverton was able to see her full face. In the act of accepting the glass from James, he froze. Then, without comment, he looked sharply at James, a question in his eyes.

James said pleasantly, "Sit down, Staverton, and tell us what has driven you north at this time of year."

Flicking up his coattails, Staverton sat on a carved wooden

chair with a wicker seat and back, then he sighed and stretched his long legs out before him. For a moment he stared at the dark wine, watching the shading shift in the flicker of the firelight. He looked up at James and said mockingly, "What would my cronies in London think of me if they could see me as I am now—dirty, disheveled, slouching! Crimes the fashionable man must never commit!"

James laughed. "I am sure the fashionable man would never attempt a journey into our mountains if he did not have something more to him than the stuffing of his coat."

The viscount sipped his wine and seemed to consider this. "Perhaps. But does the fashionable man want to be anything more than that? An interesting question, don't you think?"

"Have you been traveling long?" Thea asked tensely. The pointlessness of this conversation was irritating her already raw nerves. Lord Staverton would not have traveled to Glenmuir without warning, when the summer weather was worsening into winter and the days were rapidly growing shorter, unless he had a very good reason to do so. A need to discuss the philosophy of the fashionable man simply was not it.

Staverton tossed off the brandy in his glass. James poured him another. "Over a sennight, Mrs. MacLonan. I made good time from London to Stirling, but once I got into these endless mountains, I lost my way more times than I care to remember. There were moments when I thought I'd leave my bones among the crags and heather. Not," he added thoughtfully, "a pleasant prospect."

"You did not stop in Edinburgh and engage a guide?" James asked, surprised.

A grimace touched Staverton's features. "No. I didn't want to waste the time. That was a mistake, but I thought I remembered the way."

Thea frowned. "You've been here before?"

Staverton nodded absently. "Yes. I stayed here for several weeks in '46 when James was injured..." He broke off, looking from James to Thea.

Thea drew a sharp, annoyed breath. "I see." She noticed

Morag hovering at the door, and raised her brows in query.

The young Scot announced that Lord Staverton's supper was served and his room was ready for him at any time. Thea nodded. She returned to her place on the settee and picked up her embroidery once more. "James, are you going to join Lord Staverton? I think I will remain here. I pray you will excuse me, Lord Staverton."

"Thea, come with us."

Staverton looked sharply at James. The expression in his eyes said that he found his old friend's behavior very strange.

Thea shook her head. "I am sure you and Lord Staverton have much to discuss, James. When you are ready, you can rejoin me here. I will be waiting."

"I don't want to leave you on your own."

"Then I will ask Morag to sit with me. But that is no more necessary than your staying is. James," she said softly, "go."

After a moment he did. When they were alone in the dining room, Staverton dropped his pose of indolent society buck. "What the devil has been going on up here, MacLonan?"

"It's a long story. I'll tell you later. First I want to know what has brought you here all the way from London."

Staverton helped himself to a slice of cold roasted venison. "The Pretender. The Pretender brought me north."

"Bonnie Prince Charlie? Why? When Thea's family visited in August, General Tilton told me that he was dead."

A small, bitter smile quirked Staverton's mouth, then was gone. "Ah, but is he?"

A frown settled on James's forehead, but he remained silent, waiting for Staverton to finish.

The viscount watched the shimmering wine as he moved the crystal goblet delicately between his hands. Then he transferred his gaze to James and said very deliberately, "I too, heard that the Prince was dead. The rumor was all over town, as you say. But when I saw the Prince in London a month ago, he certainty looked very healthy for a dead man."

"The Prince was in London? Why? What was he doing?"

"Going to parties, touring the city, terrifying his former adherents with his audacity, converting."

James raised a brow. "Changing his faith? He became a member of the Church of England?" When Staverton nodded, James said, "The man is mad."

"Quite possibly," Staverton agreed.

James thought for a minute. Staverton politely tucked into his dinner and let James mull over his thoughts in silence. Finally James slapped the table and said, "Staverton, Thea must join us before we discuss this further."

"Do you trust her, MacLonan?"

"With my life," James said as he stood up.

"The way alliances mature never ceases to amaze me," Staverton observed as James vanished through the doorway.

Thea was still protesting when the couple returned. "Listen to Staverton," James said firmly. "His news is the clue we need to understand what happened here."

She frowned. "How could that be?"

"It is not completely clear to me, but...Staverton, tell us both what happened in London, all of the details this time."

"The Prince landed in England on September fourteenth. A few days later he was in London, meeting with his former supporters."

Thea's eyes widened and her hand crept up to touch the spot where Williams had struck her. "Is another rebellion planned?"

"Not amongst the Englishmen who once supported his cause," the viscount said grimly. "May I explain more fully, ma'am?"

Thea nodded.

"I spoke to him one time and heard a great deal more from others. I saw him at a card party. My hostess was once a supporter of the Jacobite cause and I had debated whether or not I should attend that evening, but I decided to go. I'd been there for about an hour when there was a bit of a stir. I looked up. Charles Edward Stuart had just entered the room. He'd gained weight since I'd last seen him and he looked older, but it was he. I tried to avoid him, but eventually we were introduced. He called himself Chevalier Douglas and laughed when he used the name, as if all of this was some great joke." Staverton's mouth twisted. "My heart was pounding so hard that I thought I was going to be ill. I expected a detachment of soldiers to charge through the door at any moment to arrest us all. But nothing happened. The Prince played cards and enjoyed himself as if he hadn't a care in the world. I can't say that I was infected with the same heedless pleasure."

"Is that the worst of it?" James demanded as Staverton stared gloomily at his glass of wine.

"No. There's more." Staverton sighed. "The Prince was observed at the Tower, apparently examining its defenses." James made a rude sound in his throat, and Staverton grinned. "He was also seen in other parts of London. He was apparently taking in the sights."

"I fail to see how this could affect us," Thea said a little stiffly.

Both men sobered. Staverton said, "Because, ma'am, the Prince also arranged a meeting with many of his old adherents. Then afterwards he very publicly abandoned his Roman Catholic faith to join the Church of England."

Thea uttered a soft sound and touched her cheek. James said grimly, "Did you go to the meeting, Staverton?"

"I was invited, but I did not go. I've been working hard, pretending to be a harmless fashionable fop who is of no danger to the government. My father is young and healthy and will live for many years yet, but when he dies I want to inherit his estates and his title in my turn. I finished with the Pretender after Culloden. My days as a rebel are over."

"So you do not know what was discussed."

Staverton shook his head.

"Is the Prince still in London?"

"That's the worst of it. No one knows. He's disappeared."

Aghast, James and Thea both stared at Staverton.

"He's disappeared? How can that be?" Thea whispered.

"He has a habit of doing it," Staverton said grimly. "Several years ago he was living in France, on the bounty of King Louis. Then the war between France and England ended and the Prince was asked to leave France. He refused. Louis sent a detachment of soldiers to escort him to the border, but the Prince went to ground and disappeared. He turned up in Avignon a short while later, but was asked to leave there. Once again he disappeared. He's spent years popping up here or there, then disappearing again. No one in Europe knows where he will turn up next."

James said grimly, "And the last time he was seen was in London."

"He could be anywhere now," Staverton said glumly.

It was Thea who said what they were all thinking. "He could be here in the Highlands."

The viscount nodded. "That is why I came north, to warn James not to become involved if the Prince approaches him. The Stuart cause is finished in England. Another attempt at rebellion would destroy Scotland."

Suddenly things made sense to Thea. She looked at her husband. "James, the lieutenant. He knew whose land he was on. His violence was deliberate—a warning of how the army would respond to any future risings!"

"What lieutenant?" Staverton demanded. "Was it he who put that bruise on your cheek, Mrs. MacLonan?"

"Worse than that, my lord! He murdered a woman in front of me." She looked from the viscount to her husband. "We could not understand why the patrol should seize a harmless woman to question her on activities she knew nothing about. Now you tell us the Pretender is loose somewhere in Britain! Lord Staverton, is it possible that the government knew the Prince was in England and while they were sure of his whereabouts they let him play out whatever game he planned?"

Staverton's eyes took on a distant look as he thought. Finally, he said grimly, "The Prince wandered around London making no effort to hide himself. Oh, he used a false name, as I said, but his face is easily recognizable. In fact, there have been plaster busts of him on sale for some time. Not a bad likeness either."

"The government must have allowed him his freedom for a reason. Why?" James asked.

"I've been a fool." Staverton stiffened. "It wasn't the Prince they wanted, but his supporters! Damn, I've probably been watched for weeks and not known it. By seeking you out, MacLonan, I've done the very thing they hoped."

James shook his head. "No. No, Staverton, I think you're wrong. The murder happened before you reached Glenmuir. I was only pardoned a year ago—I am as well known to be a Jacobite supporter as you are. No, I think the dragoons were sent to observe the Highlands, to watch for any signs of disturbance."

"Then the murder was an accident?" Thea saw again the sneering face of the lieutenant, felt her horse pirouette beneath her, knew the subtle menace of massed, armed men. "Could it be? Was Williams supposed to do nothing unless it was necessary?"

James watched her through narrowed eyes. "You said you identified yourself to him."

"I did. He called me a traitor... But that fits! He was ordered to watch, not interfere, but he did interfere and he overstepped his bounds! That was why he rushed away without making any attempt to help an injured woman!"

"Yes," James said, "it is possible. If Williams has acted in the same way in other parts as he did here at Glenmuir, that could be enough to inflame the Highlands and provide the Prince with the spark he needs to raise the clans again."

There was silence when James finished.

"Williams is a damned menace," Staverton said finally.

"I want Williams stopped." James touched Thea's cheek gently, tenderly. "I want him punished for what he did to my wife and I want him hanged for the murder of my clanswoman. I must go to Edinburgh, now, before his actions can be brushed away as part of a necessary action to control the Highlands."

"I'll go with you, MacLonan," the viscount said promptly. "You have my help in any way you need."

"And I will go too."

James cupped her cheek in his palm. "No, Thea. The journey is too long and the weather may well turn nasty. You must stay here."

Thea faced him defiantly. "You married me for my family connections, James MacLonan. Though my father no longer commands in Edinburgh, I am still his daughter and I have many friends there. My family has long supported the Hanovers and the Whig party. If there is any gossip that you are involved in another attempt at rebellion, then my presence by your side will go a long way to correcting that misconception. Now, James, if we are agreed, I have much to do before we leave."

CHAPTER 15

Edinburgh was bleak and windy when the party from Glenmuir arrived less than a sennight later. The weather had been kind to them in the mountains, but rain began to fall once they reached the more traveled road, soaking them all, for James had not had an opportunity to arrange to have a coach meet them. They rode quickly, rapidly outdistancing the cart that carried their servants and baggage. When Edinburgh finally came into sight, Thea was wet and very tired, though the morning sickness that had plagued her before the incident with Lieutenant Williams had disappeared. That in itself led her thoughts into dark concern. What if her ordeal had caused her to lose the baby? Her exhausted mind fretted over that, building a question into a fact, even though she had no evidence to justify it. Now it was impossible for her to tell James about her pregnancy, another grim reminder of the insidious power Lieutenant Williams wielded.

Grant MacLonan was out when they arrived, but the butler welcomed James warmly and invited them all in with the promise of a hot meal and a place to change their clothes immediately. Thea had included a gown in the baggage that was carried by a packhorse, and so she had warm, dry clothing to change into.

She was sitting by the fire with James, sipping a much-needed cup of tea, when a fuss was heard in the hallway.

Grant MacLonan, leaning heavily on his cane, limped into the room. He frowned at the sight of his son and daughter-in-law.

"Jamie! Theadora! So it is true, you are here!"

James stood up and nodded as he went over to take his father's hand and help him over to one of the wing chairs placed before the fire.

"Pray do not misunderstand, Jamie, but why have you come? I did not expect to see you until next spring, if then. Your last letter made no mention of returning to Edinburgh for the winter."

"'We are not here for the winter, sir."

"I see." Grant lowered himself carefully into the chair. When he was comfortable, he tapped his cane on the floor, then put it aside. "Would you care to tell me why you are here?"

"Perhaps we should wait until Lord Staverton joins us."

Grant shot James a sharp look. "Staverton's here, is he? Very well. I'll hold on to my curiosity, even though I don't like it.'" He looked past James to Thea and smiled. "My dear, I have not had the opportunity to greet you properly. Welcome to my home. I hope you did not find the journey too tiring?"

Thea smiled in return, but as she spoke she carefully kept her face in profile. "It was exhausting, sir. I was glad to reach Edinburgh and even more grateful for the warm welcome your staff gave us upon our arrival."

"Good," Grant said, responding to Thea's comment about his servants. He turned to James. "Was it necessary to bring Theadora on so urgent a journey, Jamie? Could she not have remained at Glenmuir?"

"No!" The word burst from Thea with far more emphasis than she intended. "No," she added more quietly. "No, Mr. MacLonan, I came despite James's reservations. In this instance, my place is beside him, whether or not the journey was a hard one."

His brows raised, Grant looked at his son. "My curiosity is definitely piqued. I do hope Lord Staverton will not be much longer."

"Do I hear my name spoken?" Staverton sauntered into the room. His coat was a golden damask, his breeches a rich royal blue. Nestled in the luxuriant fall of lace at his throat was a glittering sapphire pin in a gold setting, and on his gleaming black shoes were diamond buckles. He had even applied a patch to his cheek. He look the very picture of a London fop.

Grant turned in his chair. Briefly, he scanned the exotic finery that Staverton wore. "You did not have to make a show of your disguise for us, my lord. Everyone in this room knows you are far from being a fashionable fribble."

"I deemed it wise to continue as I mean to go on," Staverton drawled as he looked over at James, who was standing tensely before the fire. Like Thea, he was dressed in practical clothes, although his dark cloth suit was beautifully cut and fit his tall, muscular form perfectly. Staverton glanced back at Grant. "Edinburgh must see me as a lightweight. It is imperative."

Grant sighed. "I fear what I am going to hear will not be to my liking. Close the door, Jamie, so we may be private." When that was done, he said quietly, "Very well. Let us begin." He looked from Staverton to James and then to Thea. They all stared back, or at each other, reluctance clearly etched on their features.

Finally, James said, "There was an incident at Glenmuir. It is that which has brought us to Edinburgh, but there was more to it than we knew when the matter occurred. Staverton brought the information from London and it is not good."

"Then let us begin with Lord Staverton's news."

James nodded and looked at Staverton, who took snuff reflectively, then whisked the residue away with a casual flick of his wrist. "As you may have guessed, MacLonan, my news is of the Prince."

"I suspected as much," Grant growled. He paused a moment, frowning. "But wait! I had heard that he was dead. It was all over Edinburgh in August. Are you telling me now that he is alive?"

Staverton nodded very slowly.

Grant made a disgusted sound in his throat. "Very well then, what the devil is the infernal wastrel up to now?"

"He was making a show of himself in London, visiting the Tower and going to parties."

"What? Is the man daft?"

Staverton abandoned his foppish pretense as he leaned forward, his expression serious. "I suspect so. Since the war ended you have probably heard the rumors of his disappearances on the Continent. This is more of the same. I think he enjoys tweaking the noses of government officials, and it must be very satisfying to imagine King George and the Whigs squirming."

"But there is a thirty-thousand pound reward for his capture!"

"Which no one tried to get."

"Tried. You use the past tense, Staverton."

James broke in. "That is because the Prince has gone to ground again. He disappeared from London as suddenly as he appeared."

"No one knows where he is now," Staverton added with careful emphasis.

Grant closed his eyes briefly. "Dear God," he said softly. Then he looked at each man in turn. "This is a disaster."

"I fear so," James said heavily. He looked over at Thea. "There is more."

"No doubt," Grant said tartly. "The Prince has a way of embroiling my family in his mad schemes, much to our detriment. Tell me what it is."

James went over to Thea. He crouched before her chair so their eyes were level. She read his silent question and nodded. Carefully, she put her cup on the small table beside her chair, then composed her hands in her lap. "The next part of the story is mine, Mr. MacLonan," she began, somewhat hesitantly.

As she moved, Grant was able to see her bruised cheek for the first time. His eyes widened, then narrowed dangerously, but he smiled gently as he leaned forward. "Take your time, lass, and pray do not stand on ceremony. You are my son's wife and so the daughter of my heart. Call me Grant, or Father, as you choose."

Thea smiled. "Thank you, Mr.—Grant." She glanced at James, who nodded to her encouragingly, before she took a deep breath. "Almost a fortnight ago I surprised a patrol of dragoons. They had stopped at the croft of Maggie MacLonan to interrogate her. I protested, but the officer, a Lieutenant Williams, continued. There were hot words and then a scuffle. At the end of it the officer stabbed Maggie and struck me." Her hands were clenched tightly together. She looked down as James gently unclasped them, so he could hold them comfortingly in his. She smiled at him, and he raised her hands to his lips to kiss the knuckles. She sighed and went on. "James found me at Maggie's croft. She was dead by then and the soldiers gone. We could not understand why they had come onto Glenmuir land until Lord Staverton arrived with his story of Prince Charles Edward Stuart and the visit to London."

James took over the telling then, but he did not move from where he knelt beside his wife, or release her hands. "Because of Staverton's information, we assume that the visit by the patrol had something to do with the Prince's activities in London and perhaps with his sudden disappearance. Thea plans to write to her father to ask him to find out more, and I will visit Harris to see what he intends to do about this intrusion onto my property and the murder of one of my people." Gently, he touched Thea's cheek. "Then I shall demand satisfaction for the injury done to my wife."

"James, no!"

The protest was Thea's, and it was the only one. Grant was nodding bleakly, while Staverton had wandered over to the fireplace, which he leaned against lazily, once more the picture of a self-indulgent gentleman.

"James has no choice, Mrs. MacLonan," he said gently. "Williams must be brought to account for his crimes."

"For Maggie's murder, of course!" There was an edge of

panic in Thea's tone.

James squeezed her hands. Gently, he said, "With any luck, Harris will be as shocked by his subordinate's action as we are and he will support me in my demands that Williams be punished."

Thea was shaking her head. "James, you must not depend on Colonel Harris's goodwill. He can be a very petty man when he wishes. Before you and I married, he was quite particular in his attentions to me. I made it clear to him that I did not wish to marry him, but he believed it was because I had chosen you, not because I did not care for him. He may be difficult, simply out of spite."

"An unfortunate complication," Staverton drawled from his place by the fire.

James glanced at him, then looked back at Thea. "Harris has his duty. Despite his feelings towards me, he will be on our side in this instance, for Williams had no cause to strike you, Thea."

Rather desperately, she looked over at Grant. "Mr. MacLonan—Grant! Can you not talk some sense into your son? James must lodge his complaint about Maggie, of course he must! But my injury was slight. The bruise is almost gone…"

"But the scar on your heart remains," James interjected. He looked at her grimly. "Do not ask me to keep from avenging the injury done to you, for I could not."

"I fear for you," Thea said in a low voice. Her eyes searched his face. She turned her hand in his so that she was clasping it strongly. "There is danger here, I feel it! I would not have anything happen to you, James MacLonan."

He smiled at her. "Nothing will happen, my dearest wife. I promise you."

Thea smiled tremulously, "I must believe you, James, but promise me that you will take precautions. If Colonel Harris seems to be reluctant, or if he is hostile, will you contact Brendon Ramsey?" She slipped her hand free and put her finger on his lips when she saw a refusal forming there.

"Though he made his fortune as a merchant trader, he is

trained as a lawyer and well established in this community. Moreover, he is known to support the Hanovers. He can help you, James."

James raised a brow. "As his wife did?"

"What's this?" Grant demanded.

Thea laughed. "Mrs. Ramsey did her best to overset the beginning of our marriage, but it was only from care for me that she acted. James, Mr. Ramsey has been a good friend to my father. He will help you!"

"Listen to your wife, Jamie. Brendon Ramsey has money and influence and she is correct, he does know the law. Moreover, if he speaks on your behalf, no one will believe his words are tainted by support of the Prince."

Pushed on two sides, James conceded. "Very well, if I need to, I will seek the support of Mr. Ramsey. But Thea, you are worrying over nothing. You will see."

Thea smiled mistily. She raised her hand to cup James's cheek. "I do not want to lose you," she whispered.

He caught her hand and turned it so he could kiss the palm. "That will not happen. I promise you."

He thought of those words as he walked up High Street. The broad thoroughfare could not be dwarfed by the tall buildings of the town, but it was packed with pedestrians, chairmen, horses, and hawkers. The barrage of noise on the street, together with the smell of stale human sweat and animal odors, was reassuringly normal as he neared the Castle, the massive fortress that had dominated High Street and the city of Edinburgh for centuries.

The Castle was an impregnable bastion perched upon a barren rock outcropping. It brooded morosely over the city and was, for James, a mute reminder of the folly that had pushed him into war and the bitterness of a long exile.

In the early months of the '45, when the Prince had established his headquarters in Edinburgh, the Castle had remained in English hands even though the Prince and his supporters controlled the rest of the city. At the time, James had joined the Pretender in scoffing at the necessity of capturing the Castle, but he knew now that failing to secure the Castle had shown up one of the Scottish army's weaknesses—siege work.

As James passed through the massive gates, he reflected with wry amusement that siege work was hardly a Highlander's specialty. They were raiders, fierce fighters in the heat of battle, men who preferred a short, sharp clash to a long, dull siege. Although his experiences in France had tempered him, James knew he was true to his race. He wanted to deal with Williams swiftly, in a face-to-face encounter that would bring him the satisfaction he craved. He did not want to wait while unknown officials, safely out of sight somewhere, decided the lieutenant's fate.

As the walls of the citadel closed in around him, as if to trap him there, James suffered a brief moment of panic. Taking a deep breath, he told himself he was allowing his imagination to run wild. Nevertheless, he hoped the interview with Colonel Harris would not take long.

That hope was dashed when he was kept kicking his heels in the waiting room for half an hour before Harris consented to see him. The thought that he was being deliberately shown his place didn't auger well for the outcome of his mission.

When James was ushered into Harris's office, he found the colonel bent over his desk, writing. Harris looked up briefly, acknowledging James with a nod and a faint wave of his hand toward a chair. The ensign who served as his clerk faded discreetly from the room, leaving James to watch the colonel work.

A contemptuous amusement washed over James at the colonel's obvious ploy. He'd had plenty of experience with self-important underlings during his years in Europe, and he'd learned to deal with them on their own level. So, he ignored Harris and wandered lazily over to the tiny window that was the sole source of natural light in the room. That put him behind Harris, far enough away that he could not be accused of looking over the man's shoulder, but close enough to annoy. After glancing out, he paused for a moment to watch Harris, whose back was stiff and straight, before he sauntered back to the sole available chair. Placed directly in front of the desk, it was of a sturdy construction, with a high, slatted back and a flat wooden seat.

James sat in a leisurely way, flicked back the exquisite lace at his wrists to reach into one captious pocket then withdrew a miniature snuffbox and indulged in a pinch of snuff. He had dressed carefully for this meeting, choosing clothes that had been made in Edinburgh, not on the Continent, and that were of the finest quality cloth. The colors were sober, however, befitting the somber nature of the mission he was on. He was examining the artistry of the snuffbox, exquisitely painted with scenes from Roman antiquity, when Harris lowered his pen.

"Please forgive me. An urgent dispatch."

James looked up from his scrutiny of the snuffbox and raised an eyebrow. "Of course, Colonel. Pray continue. Far be it from me to interrupt so vital a communication."

"No need," Harris replied heartily. "The matter has been concluded. Though I do thank you for your understanding." They smiled at each other, two dogs circling warily, each searching for an opening from which to attack. The silence grew and lengthened.

James took snuff again and hoped he wouldn't sneeze. His silence forced Harris to make the initial move.

"May I ask on what matter you require my assistance?"

James regarded the Englishman thoughtfully. Was it possible that Harris was not aware of Williams's actions? A good officer would ensure that he knew exactly what his subordinates were doing, but James had no idea just how competent Harris was. He'd been introduced to the man when he was in Edinburgh, but he had done his best to avoid the colonel. English Dragoons were not his favorite social companions. Thea believed Harris was bitter and resented her refusal to accept his suit, making him dangerous. Looking at him now, James wondered if she was correct.

Very well, he thought, *if Colonel Harris wants games, then two can play.* "I am informed that you command the dragoons who patrol the Highlands now that General Tilton, my wife's father, has returned to London. Is that correct?"

Harris stiffened at the reference to Thea's marriage, but he nodded, his expression cautious.

"Then, sir, I am here to lodge a complaint against one of your officers."

The caution deepened to wariness. "A complaint, MacLonan? Nothing too serious, I hope?"

"How would you rate murder of a crofter and assault on a gentlewoman, Harris?"

For a moment Harris sat in frozen silence. Then he said carefully, "I take it that this incident occurred on your estate, MacLonan?" When James nodded, he said briskly, "Would you be so kind as to give me the particulars of the case?"

Disbelief made James hesitate. Harris was giving every indication that he was ignorant of the matter, something James found very difficult to accept. Still, he knew he had to play along if he was to discover what position Harris intended to take. As succinctly as he could, he described the incident at Maggie's cottage.

"The accusations you make against Lieutenant Williams are indeed serious, sir. However, I cannot act on them until I have discussed the matter with the officer himself."

James raised his brow. "Williams did not report on his activities in the Highlands?" His tone was heavy with sardonic disbelief.

Goaded, Harris retorted sharply, "He reported, yes. Information such as you have given me was not included, however."

"Understandably." James hung on to his temper, which was beginning to fray.

"Perhaps, perhaps not."

James stood quickly, in one lithe movement that brought him close to Harris's desk, as annoyance surged into fury, barely controlled. Planting his palms on the wooden surface of the desk he leaned forward, his eyes blazing, his expression hard. Harris arched backward, then had to look up into James's eyes.

"Lieutenant Williams is an insufferable cur," James said deliberately. "A coward and a bully who preys on those weaker than he for his sport. When my wife chanced upon his vicious little game, he thought he saw another victim. But you know Mrs. MacLonan well, Harris. I'm sure that you realize she would never submit to the threats of a villain like Williams. She has the courage of a lion and she does not take kindly to being bullied. She fought back, Harris, in an effort to save my clanswoman from further harm, even though she had only words as a weapon. That enraged your good lieutenant, and he threatened her with the same violence he was using against the poor crofter."

James stopped to draw breath. Harris didn't move. He stared silently into James's hard features, his own expression blank.

"And after Williams had stabbed Maggie MacLonan, in front of my wife's very eyes," James continued in the same soft, deadly, even tones, "he had the effrontery to strike her on the face with the back of his hand simply because she asked him to stay a moment and have his men carry his injured victim into her croft. Then he rode away, uncaring of the havoc he'd left behind."

There was a long, heavy silence when James finished speaking. Finally, Harris pushed back his chair, using the moment to shift his gaze guiltily. "I…I didn't know."

Contempt lashed through James. Either Harris had heard that Williams had been to Glenmuir, but not the details of the incident, or his officer hadn't bothered to recount his actions at all. More and more, James was beginning to believe that Colonel Harris was a man raised beyond his capabilities. As much as he would prefer not to, James had to give Harris the benefit of the doubt.

"I want justice done," James said, then paused a moment before adding, "When may I return to hear of your plans for Lieutenant Williams?"

"Well, I shall have to speak to him first."

"I guessed as much. How long does it take for a colonel to

summon a lowly lieutenant to his office?"

Harris glanced away evasively. "Williams had some leave coming to him. I believe he has already left Edinburgh. He will be gone for some weeks. Two months," he added for good measure.

Two months was a long time. By then it would be December and the passes into the Highlands would be closed. James did not want to have to choose between seeking satisfaction from Lieutenant Williams or returning to Glenmuir for the winter and allowing Harris the opportunity to arrange a new posting for his errant lieutenant.

"Where was he going?" James demanded briskly.

"Ah, going?"

"Yes, you said Williams had left the city. For where? His home? London? Where?"

"Well, ah, I don't, ah, know."

James leaned forward once again. "Listen to me, Harris. Wherever Williams has gone, I shall find him. If you would like to hear his side of the story, I suggest you locate him first. I will allow you two days to seek him out. When I return I want to know exactly how you intend to punish him."

With that, he turned on his heel and strode out of the room, leaving Colonel Harris sitting limply behind his desk.

"I lost my temper," James said grimly to the group assembled in Grant MacLonan's drawing room.

At this statement, his father made a sound of disapproval in his throat, Staverton raised his brows and smiled faintly, and Thea gnawed her bottom lip.

"Harris is sure to use that against you, MacLonan," Brendon Ramsey said. A new addition to the small circle, Ramsey's heavyset build and square, fleshy face gave mute evidence of his prosperity, while the excellent cut and expensive cloth of his dark suit made a quiet statement of his standing in Edinburgh.

"I know that," James said impatiently. He kicked at one of

the logs in the big fireplace. Sparks flew upwards.

Thea began to gnaw her lip in earnest. The nausea that had all but disappeared since the incident at Maggie's had retuned full force the previous morning. Only this time it plagued her all day. As she thought about her husband's meeting with Harris and the dangers it could bring down upon them, her stomach knotted. She swallowed and drew a deep breath. How she wished Morag had come to Edinburgh with them! She needed someone to confide in, and she could not burden James with her problems, for she had already given him far too many.

Staverton, who was holding a stemmed glass of brandy in his hand, gazed thoughtfully into the dark depths of the liquid, then said almost idly, "Men like Harris respond well to orders, Ramsey. He's used to doing what he is told."

"Colonel Harris can be a spiteful man," Thea said, remembering the cruelty in his expression the day he had told her James MacLonan was a pardoned Jacobite. "It would not be wise to underestimate him."

"I agree with Theadora," Grant MacLonan said. "Harris is in a difficult position. Almost certainly he's had word that the Prince has disappeared. He does not want to ignite the Highlands with an incident like the one at Glenmuir, but he cannot allow any show of weakness. He may consider bringing Williams to justice to be just that."

"Damnation!" James muttered, slapping the mantel with the palm of his hand. "Of all the wretched tangles!"

"Aye," Brendon Ramsey said slowly, "that it is, but like all tangles, it can be unwound with a little patience and some thought." He rubbed his prominent chin with his forefinger. "Let's consider Colonel Harris. What do we know about him?"

"He was posted here by London," Thea offered. "My father didn't ask for him as his second in command."

Brendon nodded, his gray eyes narrowed. "Anything else?"

"He's a man with an itch for money," Grant said. He smiled faintly at the surprise on the faces of his audience. "When I was looking for a way to bring James home, I tried every avenue I could think of. Harris was only one of many who took my money and made me promises he could not keep."

"You bribed Harris?" James demanded, indignation warring with shock in his expression.

Grant raised one brow. "Only reluctantly, when Sir Frederick Tilton proved to be unapproachable."

"So that's how he knew!" Thea said softly, almost to herself.

James heard, however. "Knew what? Was it Harris who told you I was a returned rebel?"

Thea looked at her husband squarely. "Yes, it was. I wondered at the time if my father had told Colonel Harris in confidence, or if he had made it common knowledge amongst the officers. I am glad he did not."

"Gentlemen, Mrs. MacLonan." Brendon nodded at each of them. "We digress. Shall we return to the issue at hand? Good," he said when they had fallen silent. "Now then, I, too, have some knowledge of Colonel Harris that pertains to his background."

"Investigated him on a legal matter, did you, Ramsey?" Staverton remarked with lazy effrontery.

Brendon Ramsey sat very still, his hands steepled before him, his broad features expressionless. Nonetheless, the atmosphere in the room was charged with tension until he said politely, "I find it useful to know all I can about the men who are assigned to the military government in this city. I know, for instance, that Colonel Harris did not buy his own commission. In fact, he barely scraped up enough funds to buy his captaincy. The rank he holds today was purchased for him by the grateful father of a young subaltern whom he saved from capture and possible death while on campaign in Europe. Harris is very much aware that he would not be a colonel had he been required to buy the rank himself. Perhaps that is why he is reluctant to press charges against Lieutenant Williams."

His words caught the attention of each and every one of them. "You've lost me, Ramsey," James said curtly. "What has Williams to do with Harris's rank?"

"Williams is a member of a wealthy and powerful family. He has cousins and uncles throughout the military. He was posted here in August. Scotland is considered to be a relatively safe posting, because the Highlands have been stable for so many years, although there is that remote possibility of danger. Williams was clamoring to be sent to America, apparently, something his parents viewed with considerable alarm, so they compromised with a request for Edinburgh."

"How do you know all of this?" Staverton demanded incredulously.

"Sir Frederick Tilton told me much of it. I discovered the rest myself."

"Why would Tilton confide so much in you?" Grant MacLonan asked.

"Williams arrived shortly before Sir Frederick was posted to London. Tilton loathed the man and had concerns about leaving him here in Scotland with Harris as his commanding officer."

"How right Papa was!"

Ramsey nodded. "Yes, unfortunately so. I fear that Harris, with his background of allowing himself to be rewarded by men of wealth and power, is not the man to force the issue with Lieutenant Williams."

"Then what do we do?" Staverton asked.

James shot him a quick, fierce look. "*We* do nothing! If Harris refuses to act, *I* will bring Williams to justice myself."

"What do you mean to do?" Grant asked uneasily.

"Challenge the lieutenant to a duel," James replied quietly.

"No, James you must not!"

"I cannot allow him to go free. Not after what he did to you, Thea. Not after he killed Maggie."

Lord Staverton bowed. "You will need a second, MacLonan. I am at your disposal."

"Jamie, stop being so hotheaded!" Grant stifled a curse as he pushed himself awkwardly to his feet. "Damn these old bones," he muttered. He walked slowly over to his son, then stood before him, straight and just an inch or two shorter. "I brought you home, James MacLonan, to see to Glenmuir, not to lose your freedom in a duel with an English officer!" He looked from James to Staverton, then back to James. "Are both of you mad? This is just the excuse the authorities need to send you into exile again."

Thea groaned. "No!"

"Not necessarily," Brendon interjected. He smiled wryly at the expressions on the faces that turned his way. Grant MacLonan's was fierce, his blue eyes snapping beneath heavy brows; Thea's desperate and afraid; Staverton's wary behind a mask of casual boredom; and James's surprised, but hopeful. "Pray do not misunderstand me. I do not approve of dueling, but in this case I fear it may be the only way to bring Williams to account for his actions. And I agree with Grant MacLonan. A duel in which James, a former rebel, with Staverton, another former Jacobite, as his second, challenged an English officer would only lead to disaster, no matter how correctly it was managed. But if James were represented by someone in good standing with the government, what could be done? Although duels are officially illegal, if all of the rules that surround the contest are carried out properly, there is nothing that can be done, provided one opponent does not kill the other."

"Are you offering your services, Ramsey?" James said slowly.

Brendon bowed. "I am."

Thea leapt up from her chair and hastened to where James was standing. She grasped her husband's arm and tugged. "No! James, listen to me! This isn't necessary. Please, please do not rush into anything."

"Knew it was a mistake allowing Mrs. MacLonan into this discussion," Staverton observed to no one in particular.

Thea rounded on him. "I am the only sensible one amongst you! I know Colonel Harris! He hates James, because of me. He will use a duel against James, no matter who James has as his second, and no matter what the outcome of the duel."

She turned back to her husband. "James, I've already written my father, telling him what happened and asking him to do whatever possible to bring Williams to justice. Give him time to make arrangements in London. Please, James."

Grant MacLonan moved away, leaving James to detach his arm from Thea's grip and take her elbow to lead her over to a corner of the room where they could be private. "Thea, I cannot stand idle and wait for your father to sort everything out. I cannot. I must deal with Williams myself. Do you understand?"

"No. James, all I understand is that you are taking risks that may drive you away from me! Please do not. Stop this mad discussion now, before words become actions and it is all too late."

He dropped her elbow and stood back a step. "Thea, I am sorry, but I cannot."

Her hand crept up to her cheek in a vulnerable movement that expressed more than mere words. She turned away moments before James took a step toward her.

Grant MacLonan cleared his throat. "Perhaps this plan will be unnecessary. Harris may be willing to deal with Williams."

"Quite possibly," Brendon Ramsey agreed heartily. "For all his faults, the man is honest. He will do what is right."

Staverton sipped his brandy and said nothing.

It was his amused, cynical gaze that Thea caught when she looked up, and the message she read there was very clear. The men were closing ranks against her, reassuring her so that she would no longer worry, while her husband did his best to get himself killed or exiled once again. Annoyance came to her rescue, pushing aside illness and fear. She glared at each man in turn. "I will not be patronized by any of you. You will not convince me that Colonel Harris will do what is right and proper, because I know the man better than any of you. Nor will you convince me that James will be able to survive a duel unscathed."

Colonel Harris would rub his hands with glee when he discovered that James had challenged Williams to a duel.

Thea was as certain of that as she was that no matter how hard she argued, she would be unable to keep James from challenging the lieutenant.

She tilted her head up so that she could look her husband in the eye and said the most difficult words she had ever forced herself to say. "I married you, James MacLonan, for better or worse, and you married me, sir, so that my English connections would lend you respectability. Therefore, my dear husband, I will continue to petition my father, but I promise to stand by your side whatever befalls you. You have my support."

At her words, the grim expression on James's face eased into a tender smile, a rich reward that Thea cherished. She reached out to him and he responded, catching her hands and drawing her close to him.

"Nothing will go wrong," he said in a soft voice.

Drawing on a strength she didn't know she possessed, Thea smiled. "I know, James."

She didn't believe a word of it.

CHAPTER 16

"MacLonan. Come in and sit down," Harris said, smiling a welcome as he stood and came round his desk to usher James into his austere little office.

James was instantly wary. Harris had no cause to like him and every reason to resent him. This show of goodwill sat ill upon the man. "May I take it that you have a positive answer for me?"

Harris appeared troubled, but he repeated in a friendly way, "Please, do sit down, MacLonan. Might as well be comfortable while we chat, eh?"

James glanced pointedly at the hard wooden chair and allowed a wry smile to quirk his lips. Harris cleared his throat and pretended not to notice as he returned to his own side of the desk. James settled onto the wooden chair, then observed the colonel through narrowed eyes.

"Two days isn't long enough to make a decision on a question of such magnitude as the one you raised," Harris said as he too sat down. There was a hint of nervousness in his hearty tone.

"Not good enough, Harris," James retorted crisply. "One of your men went beyond his orders." He paused for the space of a heartbeat before he added softly, "Or did he?"

Harris placed his hands flat upon the desk. "Explain that remark, if you please, sir!"

"The Highlands have been quiet for years now. Why the

sudden interest on the part of His Majesty's Army?"

His face an unreadable mask, Harris picked up a quill pen, then twirled it back and forth along his fingers. "Nothing sudden about it. We regularly send out patrols to check that the laws are not being contravened."

"If Williams was supposed to seek out illegal whiskey stills and rusted swords buried in the peat, why did he choose to question a woman on those matters? And when my wife suggested he come to me for information, why did he refuse?"

Harris smiled and shrugged. Throwing down the pen, he said, "Williams is young and enthusiastic, MacLonan! This was his first independent command and he was excited over the responsibility." Harris leaned forward, his smile inviting James to join him in his tolerance for the exuberance of youth. "Garrison duty is fine for an old soldier like me, but a young sprig like Williams hungers for glory and excitement."

"Then you admit Williams went beyond the acceptable limits of his orders?"

Harris sat up straight, annoyance expressed on his round face. "To some degree, yes."

"What are you going to do about it?"

Colonel Harris picked up the pen again. This time he flicked the quill through his fingers in a movement that reminded James of nothing so much as an annoyed cat, lashing its tail. "As I told you the other day, MacLonan, Lieutenant Williams is on leave at the moment. When he returns I will reprimand him, I assure you."

"Reprimand him?" James repeated incredulously. "Is that all the punishment he'll get? God's teeth, Harris! He murdered a woman. The man should be court-martialed!"

The pen whipped through Harris's fingers. "I cannot do that at this time."

James stood slowly, then walked over to the tiny window that lit the whitewashed room. He stood beside it, looking out, careful to keep his face in profile as he spoke, forcing his enemy to turn awkwardly in his chair. "Why, Colonel

Harris? Why is it impossible for you to court-martial one of your officers for cold-blooded murder and assult?"

"I…just can't. That's all."

James turned, his back to the light, his face in shadow. "By your own admission, you have an officer who is insubordinate, who murdered an innocent woman, and who taunted, then struck, a gentlewoman, and all you can say is that you can't punish him? Listen to yourself, Harris. Do you realize how weak and ineffectual you make yourself sound?"

Harris pushed his chair back and stood. "That's enough! I was commanded to send Williams out on that patrol. I knew there was some danger of his overstepping his orders, but it was a necessary evil for the greater benefit of all! I am sorry the woman was killed. I am sorry Mrs. MacLonan was injured. But at the moment I can do nothing! Williams cannot be brought to court-martial."

"So," James said softly, "Williams was not on a simple policing mission, looking for illegal stills as you claimed."

Harris glared at James, but neither confirmed nor denied his statement.

James pressed harder. Dangerous as it was, he wanted to hear the truth. He wanted an admission of what he already knew. "Was Williams sent to Glenmuir looking for rebels, Harris? One certain rebel who was seen in London, but who distressingly disappeared? A man who might decide to visit a former adherent in his Highland home? A prince once thought to be dead, Harris? Was that who Williams was seeking?"

Shock whitened Harris's features. Then he narrowed his eyes in shrewd speculation. "What do you know of the whereabouts of the Pretender?"

"Nothing, beyond what is generally known," James said contemptuously.

"I hesitate to contradict you, MacLonan," the colonel said with more confidence in his voice than he'd had for some time, "but the presence of Prince Charles Edward Stuart in London was hardly common knowledge."

James curled his lip in a sneer. "Is that what Whitehall is

telling you, Harris? No wonder you sent out a patrol with orders to intimidate and terrorize the Highlands."

"I did nothing of the sort!"

"A woman is dead and my wife assaulted by one of your officers!"

"You yourself admit the woman's death was accidental," Harris retorted belligerently. "Williams may have been at fault for thoughtlessness, but I will not ruin a man's career for a trivial incident..."

"Trivial!" James said savagely, stepping away from the window. "It seems that the law of what is right and wrong has blurred in His Hanoverian Majesty's Army! Very well then, Harris, I shall waste no more of your valuable time discussing this 'trivial incident' with you."

Harris stiffened. "What are you going to do?"

His brows raised haughtily, James surveyed the Englishman. "Williams is an officer and therefore, by definition, a gentleman. I shall settle my differences with him directly."

"Are you planning to challenge Lieutenant Williams to a duel?"

James curled his lip and looked down his nose in a supercilious way, a trick he'd learned in France and one he knew was guaranteed to annoy. "Dueling is illegal, Harris," he said gently. "And I am a law-abiding man."

"Go back to your Highland valley, MacLonan. Leave this to me."

James sauntered to the door, opened it, then turned back to the colonel. "What do you have to worry about, Harris? Lieutenant Williams is on leave at the moment, is he not?"

He watched the unspoken denial flicker on the other man's face. "Yes," he murmured dangerously, "I thought as much."

He closed the door quietly behind him, not at all dissatisfied with the way the interview had gone.

As James had expected, he soon received confirmation that Williams had not gone on leave. He began to plan how he would force the lieutenant into a duel. That particular feeling of excitement and reluctance that he always felt in the buildup to a battle began to take hold of him. Gradually, he pushed thoughts of everyday life to the back of his mind where they would not distract him. A man thinking about how much he would lose in death was sure to find himself on the brink of it. It was the man who focused on the moment who survived the battle.

There was one part of his life that was too big and too important to be easily forced from his thoughts, though. Before he challenged Williams, before he dueled with the man, he must ensure that Thea understood how his feelings for her had grown since their marriage. He had tried to tell her by actions, but now was a time for words.

He sought her out on the afternoon of the day he'd earmarked as the one when he would challenge Williams. She was seated in front of the fire in his father's drawing room, holding her belly with one hand and leaning her chin on her other. Her skin was pale. At the sight of her, he was immediately concerned. "Thea! Are you ill?"

She lifted her head in surprise at the sound of his voice. Then she smiled with real pleasure. "No, James, I'm—"

Relief flooded through him. "Good! Thea, I must talk to you."

He didn't understand why the blaze of pleasure in her eyes quickly burned itself out, or the closed expression that followed.

"What did you want to say to me, James?" She studied his features. "You look, oh, I don't know, elated somehow." Her eyes widened. "James, have you had word from Colonel Harris? Did he agree to punish Williams?"

"No."

She frowned as she searched his face again. Slowly, she said, "Then I do not understand. What is it you want to say to me?"

He pulled a chair up so that he could sit opposite her. Catching her hands, he stared down at her soft, slender fingers. They reminded him that Thea deserved better than the little cottage at Glenmuir, or the burden of a husband whose rebel past would never leave him. He looked up and said more abruptly than he'd intended, "Harris knows that I would rather be at Glenmuir than here in Edinburgh and that with the winter coming on the passes through the mountains will soon be closed. He realizes that I must see this incident resolved soon. That is why he claims Williams is on leave and why he tells me that he cannot find the man."

"Perhaps he cannot. James—"

"Thea, I've learned that Williams is here, in Edinburgh. If I can find him, Harris certainly can."

She turned her hands, so that she was able to clasp his fingers with hers. "James, I know Williams is guilty and I know that what he did was reprehensible, but I fear for your safety if you should take his punishment into your own hands."

"What would you have me do, Thea? Return to Glenmuir with nothing more from Harris than the promise that he will look into the matter?"

For a moment her expression said that she would like exactly that. Then she sighed heavily. "No, I know you could not do that, James. But I have written to my father. Can you not wait until he replies? It is possible that he will be able to order Harris to punish Williams."

James pulled his hands away and stood up. He stared into the fire. Part of him knew that Thea had a good point. Part of him wanted to agree with her, if only to make her happy. Another part wanted to avenge the wrong done to her, without the help of her father and despite the reservations he knew she felt. "Your father may not reply for weeks. He might not be able to make any arrangements in London. Or he might not be willing to help."

"Why would he not be willing to aid us in this matter?" Thea asked, frowning.

James turned to face her. "Like it or not, I am a Jacobite rebel, Thea, and all of this has come about because Prince Charles Edward Stuart decided to visit England to see if his former adherents would be willing to rise again. You father is a career officer. He may not want to acknowledge that he has allied his family with a rebel."

Thea stood slowly. Though her eyes flashed, her voice was cool as she said, "My father has far more honor than that, sir! You can be sure that when he agreed to our marriage, he thought over all the issues very carefully. Ours was not some mad, impetuous love match, James MacLonan." She hesitated, turning her face away.

James winced. What she said was true, up to a point. He had not married Theadora Tilton for love, and yet...

She looked back at him, lifting her chin proudly. "We were married for a purpose. And we married with the government's full knowledge of our match. My father has nothing to hide. Moreover, he has made a commitment to you and he will not abandon it on the mere supposition that you might be involved with the Pretender."

"Is that how you see our marriage, Thea?" When she raised her brows and continued to stare at him, her eyes cool and fierce, he said briskly, "So be it."

At that she frowned. "What do you mean?"

"Nothing and everything. Thea, I know how deeply you trust your father. I will bow to your judgment in the matter of his willingness to help us, but even if he is willing, I am not prepared to wait for someone else to do what I should be doing."

"And what is that? Challenging Lieutenant Williams? Surely you would find that petitioning the Scottish government to aid you would be a more effective use of your time. Men like Judge Denholm would be shocked to hear what Williams did. I am sure they would act on your behalf."

James grasped her shoulders. "Thea, in normal circumstances, I believe you are correct, but these are not normal circumstances. If the Pretender is loose somewhere in England and on his way to Scotland, then Harris has the right to ignore any demands the civil government might make. Denholm and the others know that. They may protest. They may demand that Williams be tried for his crimes, but if Harris doesn't want to do it, they cannot force him to act.

Only orders from London can do that."

"Orders my father can have issued!"

"Damn it, we've been through that!" He dropped her shoulders and stood back.

Thea shivered and sat down. "I know." There was silence for a time. Then she said, "We are at an impasse, are we not?"

"We are."

She crossed her hands over her breasts and hugged her shoulders protectively. "Nothing I have said will stop you from calling Williams out, will it?"

"No."

"If I told you that I could not bear to have you lost to me because you felt you must defend my honor, would you change your mind?"

He stood stiffly for a moment, then knelt beside her. Taking her hands, he said, "Thea, I do this for you. If we returned to Glenmuir without this issue being resolved, you would never feel comfortable there again. I want Glenmuir to be your home. I want you to be happy there."

"Glenmuir will never be my home without you, James, and I am dreadfully afraid that this duel will only bring you trouble. Please, please! Do not challenge the lieutenant."

"I must."

She shuddered. "When are you going to do it?"

"Soon. Before Harris does somehow spirit him out of Edinburgh."

She sighed and squeezed his fingers before she freed her hand to cup his cheek. "James, I will not retract my reservations, but as I promised before, I will do all I can to support you."

He turned her hand and kissed the palm. "Thank you, my love."

She drew her breath in audibly. "What did you say?"

Now was the moment to voice the words he'd planned to, but he could not. This evening he would challenge Williams, and within a few days he might be dead or in exile once again. He could not burden Thea with an admission that she did not want to hear. "A turn of phrase, nothing more," he said with a light smile.

Thea frowned, but then she nodded and smiled faintly. After a moment, she said, "Will you tell me when the duel is to take place?"

James raised his brows and laughed. "I fear that if I did so, I would find that my lovely wife is a determined observer."

Thea laughed too. "You are probably right."

"No, Thea, I will not tell you when it is to occur. I know that you would worry from the time I told you until the time I returned home. I don't want you to do that. You have worried enough."

Thea sighed and said softly, "I shall always worry about you, James."

It was a statement that he was to use as a talisman in the days and weeks to come.

The evening was well advanced when James groped his way down the dimly lit stairs that led to the tavern where he knew he would find Williams. It was a mean little place in the basement of one of the tall houses located on a narrow wynd just off High Street. Though it was dark, smoky, and rather dirty, the tables were always full with men from all classes.

Even though he knew he would stand out from the rest of the patrons, he had dressed in a sumptuous costume of velvet and silk, better suited for a fashionable party in Paris than for a public tavern in Edinburgh. He had considered wearing the full regalia of a Highland chief, but reluctantly, he had decided that he would frighten Williams off if he presented himself in a kilt and sporran. Whether Harris had warned him or not, Williams must know that James MacLonan would be looking for him. From what James had learned of the Englishman, the man delighted in taunting and deriding the Scots he met, but he always found a way to avoid defending his position. Instinct told James that he would have far more success in his challenge if he was dressed in the trappings of a fine gentleman and played upon Williams's expectations.

He stood for a moment in the shadows at the back of the taproom scanning the close-packed tables, looking for his quarry. Williams wasn't hard to find. As expected, his clothes immediately set him apart from the soberly dressed Scots. He was engaged in a heated debate with a middle-aged man all dressed in black. Beneath the fellow's old-fashioned, unpowdered wig, his long, narrow face was twisted with contemptuous ire as Williams adamantly expressed his opinion on some subject and waved his forefinger under the Scot's nose for good measure.

When he was seeking out information on the Englishman, James had discovered that Williams was well known in Edinburgh, although not for his better qualities. He was consumed by a hatred of the Scots that was so intense as to be irrational, and his favorite pastime was to visit the taverns where educated Scots met to do much of the commerce that made Edinburgh a wealthy city and to debate the great issues of the day. Williams would join a group, unasked, and deliberately taunt the worthy Scottish citizens. The man was thoroughly loathed, and demands that he be reposted outside of Scotland were beginning to be heard. James could easily see why.

He waited until the Scot had walked away from the table, his back stiff with contempt, before threading his way through the tables to where Williams sat. Conversations stilled, then rose again as he passed. Like Williams, he stood out from the regular patrons of the tavern, but that was all the better. He wanted to be noticed.

When he reached the table he sought, he stopped and said politely, "Lieutenant Williams?"

Williams looked him up and down, noting the suit of pale blue velvet, the coat braided on the lapels and cuffs with gold thread, and the gold satin waistcoat. Slowly, he nodded. Around them voices hushed as interested onlookers waited to see what this meeting was all about.

The readiness for battle that had been growing in James

peaked and steadied, locking his emotions in place to allow his mind to work even more rapidly than usual. He watched the lieutenant's gaze fix on the diamond solitaire nestled in the folds of fine lace at his neck. The gem winked in the flickering candlelight, and its exquisite cut fairly shrieked of wealth and refinement.

While Williams stared and considered, James examined the Englishman in his turn. This was the first time he had seen the man whose stupidity had caused Maggie MacLonan's death, and whose wanton use of his power had intimidated and harmed a woman James had come to respect and care for very deeply. He had not expected to find a man of strength, but he was surprised to see that Williams was thin, with little physical presence. He must have used his sword, his horse, and the troop of dragoons to enhance the authority he did not naturally have.

He was dressed in a coat of puce velvet with a white laced waistcoat and mustard velvet breeches, a combination that did little for his pale coloring. Moreover, the lace at his throat and wrists and the linen beneath were coarse and none too clean. The image James had created of the man altered subtly. Lieutenant Williams might be related to dozens of officers in the English army, but he was most likely from a poor cadet branch of these wealthy families. Without a doubt, in allying himself to this man Harris had erred.

In the middle of James's scrutiny, Williams gestured negligently to an empty chair. When James made no move to accept the offer of a seat, Williams demanded truculently, "Do I know you, sir?"

"We have some business together," James replied softly.

"Business, sir? I think not. I do not indulge in commerce." Williams managed to lace contempt into his voice. It went well with the sneer on his narrow lips.

James bared his teeth in a smile that was closer to a snarl. "You may wish you did before I am finished."

Williams frowned. Evidently he heard the threat in James's words, but could not understand the reason. "Tell me your name and state your business then, but be quick about it."

"My name, Lieutenant, is James MacLonan. Do you remember that name? It belongs to a woman you struck across the cheek. Do you remember a valley called Glenmuir? Or a simple clanswoman you terrorized, then murdered?" Williams stared at James, his expression frozen into a blank stare. "No? You remember none of these? Then perhaps I can help you regain your lost memory."

James picked up the wine glass resting on the table in front of Williams. He held the stem disdainfully between his forefinger and thumb as he allowed anger to build into rage that surged against his senses, demanding an outlet. Then, with a deft movement, he flicked his wrist and tossed the contents of the glass full in the face of the shocked Englishman. "You wanted to know my business, Williams? This is my business!"

The rich red claret drained slowly down the lieutenant's cheeks and dripped from the end of his sharp nose, but he made no effort to wipe it off. He sat immobile, horror clearly written on his features as he stared at the elegant man before him.

The whole room had fallen silent. Men craned their necks to watch the drama unfolding, and there was a murmur of support when James tossed the wine in the Englishman's face. Silence fell again as they all waited for Williams to respond.

Into the dire quiet Williams shouted, "The Devil! You can't be MacLonan! You're nowhere near the Highland brigand I expected."

There was a subdued murmur of disapproval.

James ignored the insult and said calmly, "Coward."

Williams reddened. "How dare you!"

"I dare," James informed him in a low voice that nonetheless carried to those around them. "I dare because I know the truth of you, Williams. You prefer to attack innocent women rather than fight a man armed as you are. And you're afraid to stand and face the consequences of the deeds you have done. Like the coward you are, you flee the scene of your misdeeds, then use the hint of family power to bully support from your commanding officer for an action no honorable man would condone."

There was a charged pause as Williams frantically glanced from side to side, looking for support, but finding none. Finally, he said disdainfully, "If I remember correctly, you are a Jacobite." His lip curled. "I don't deal with rebels!"

James smiled that dangerous smile again. "There are no rebels here, Williams, only honest Scots and a cowardly Englishman."

"Damn you! Name your second! You will regret this, MacLonan, but I will not. I'll enjoy feeling my blade slip through your ribs to your heart!"

As he pulled a card from his pocket, James laughed. "An unlikely occurrence, Lieutenant. You haven't the capability. Here is the name of my second." Deliberately, well aware of his listening audience, he added, "He is Brendon Ramsey, a man of some standing in this community. He will be waiting to be contacted."

James bowed infinitesimally and turned, raising a mocking brow at the rapt attention of the crowd before making his way through the close-set tables, well satisfied that Williams would not be able to find a way to squirm out of the duel. If he did, no one in Edinburgh would allow him to forget it.

The Forest of Drumselch was a large tract of land to the south of Edinburgh, a park ceded to the city by King David I in the twelfth century. Paths threaded through the clusters of trees, but otherwise the forest had been left in a natural state. The wildness of the area and the feeling of isolation the thick forest cover brought had made the place a favorite for duels and other private assignations.

Brendon Ramsey, acting as James MacLonan's second, had naturally suggested the forest as the site of the duel, and the English officer who served Lieutenant Williams in the same capacity had made no objections. He was newly posted to Edinburgh and his knowledge of the city—and of his brother officers—was extremely limited.

The precise location was a small meadow deep in the

woods reached by a series of winding trails, making it unlikely they would be disturbed. Brendon couldn't forget that dueling was an illegal activity, albeit one routinely practiced by the upper classes. Being a man of few illusions, Ramsey had decided that it would be wise to take particular care in the arrangements for this duel.

The duel was set for six in the morning a mere day after James extended his challenge. It had rained the night before, and the grass covering the hard ground was slippery. As Brendon Ramsey, James, and Lord Staverton waited in the quiet of the early morning, James tested the footing, advancing in a lunge, then stepping backward to parry as he warmed up.

The minutes ticked past with James concentrating on his fencing while Ramsey and Staverton watched silently. When a coach drew up, James placed the tip of his sword on the ground and waited. Though his stance was relaxed, the position he'd chosen sent the message of a man at one with his weapon, a formidable and intimidating image for his opponent to see when first stepping on to the field.

Unfortunately, it was not Williams, but the doctor hired to provide medical attention for the duelists, who stepped out of the carriage. A tall, thin man with a long narrow face on which his prominent nose, cheekbones, and chin contrasted with deep-set, almost sunken, eyes, he looked like nothing so much as a walking cadaver. He glanced nervously at James, bowed, announced he'd arrived, then told the driver to take him over to the edge of the clearing, well away from the action that was to occur.

James eyed the carriage with considerable cynicism, then shook his head and joined his seconds. "God's teeth! It's well past the hour. Where is Williams?"

CHAPTER 17

Lord Staverton took snuff with a contemptuous flick of his wrist. "Perhaps the good lieutenant is having difficulty mustering his pitiful store of courage."

Brendon fiddled with the fob chain on his watch. "I don't like this, MacLonan."

James turned to face him, his brows raised inquiringly. "Williams has a bad reputation," Brendon said. "There are even rumors that the man is a coward. I do not think he will show his face this morning, but if he does, we may find Colonel Harris attending as well."

James shot Ramsey a mocking look. "And if a troop of His Majesty's cavalry should happen upon us here in this fine meadow, what complaint would they have against us? We are but three gentlemen out for an early ride who have paused here a while to catch our breath and enjoy the morning sun."

"A fine conceit," Staverton said dryly. "What about the swords we brought with us? Hardly normal equipment for a morning's pleasure ride."

James grinned recklessly. "What! Cannot those same gentlemen enjoy some exercise and a little innocent swordplay in a secluded spot?"

Staverton grinned back. "There is the small detail of the doctor whose carriage waits on the edge of the clearing."

James raised one eyebrow. "Is that who he is? A doctor? I had no idea."

"Enough playacting, sirs!" Despite his admonition, Brendon was smiling. "Even if Williams does not appear, Harris may try to find a way to act against you."

Still buoyed up by reckless energy, James shrugged away Brendon's worries. "Harris does not concern me. I'll give Lieutenant Williams until the hour changes. Then, if he has not appeared, I shall challenge him again. This time I won't bother with seconds, or proper gentlemanly protocol. We'll have our duel then and there. And Williams will regret the cowardice that kept him from fulfilling his word of honor this morning."

"If you kill him in some back-alley brawl you'll be charged with murder," Brendon said quietly. "You will be hung."

"If I'm caught," James retorted coolly.

"If you are not, you'll have to leave Scotland. You will be an exile for the rest of your life."

"Then we'd best hope the good lieutenant values his honor more than I think he does and shows his face here this morning," James said, baring his teeth in a savage grin. "For I mean to make him pay for what he did to my wife. Now or later, I care not."

Brendon opened his mouth to argue, but Staverton held up his hand for silence. "Listen! Do you hear that?"

Brendon frowned. "What?"

"Hoofbeats," James said with satisfaction. "We shall soon see if the Englishman has the courage to face me."

The tattoo of trotting horses grew steadily louder until a figure emerged from the trees, then a second. Lieutenant Williams had arrived.

As they came closer, James kept his gaze trained on them, but he said quietly to his companions, "Williams is the thin fellow on the black. The other young man is his second?"

Ramsey nodded. "One Ensign Shorney."

Williams was closer now, near enough for James to once again take note of the sneer that seemed to permanently adorn the lieutenant's mouth and the nervous shifting of his gaze from place to place. "The good lieutenant isn't so self-assured without his troop behind him to enforce his orders and protect him from the results of his depraved temperament."

Williams drew his horse to a stop a few yards from where James and his party were standing. There was a heavy silence while the two combatants measured each other. It was Lieutenant Williams who flinched first. With a vicious slap of the reins and a sharp jab on the bit, he directed his mount to a spot a safe distance from James.

Satisfaction curled James's lips. He turned and said mockingly to the others, "The battle is half won already."

"Don't underestimate the enemy, MacLonan."

James glanced at Brendon, that dangerous half-smile still on his lips. "Wise advice, Ramsey. Thank you."

The Lowlander nodded and went to make the preliminary arrangements with the nervous Ensign Shorney.

Staverton and James observed Lieutenant Williams, who was shrugging out of his coat and pretending not to be listening to what the seconds were saying. "A fine, upstanding-looking fellow," Staverton remarked contemptuously. "Watch him, MacLonan. He will not stay within the rules."

"The only rule men like Williams acknowledge is the one that advises anything is acceptable provided you do not get caught."

"All the more reason to keep your guard up."

"I intend to win this duel, Staverton," James said quietly. "And I plan to do it in a way no one can fault."

The fighting began with polite salutes as each gentleman acknowledged the other. They had hardly been made when Williams lunged wildly. James parried the stroke, but backed away, careful of his footing on the slippery grass. His strategy was to take measure of his opponent's abilities before he planned his own offense. He was quietly impressed with the training Williams had received, for the man knew how to handle a sword, although he did not seem to have the sense to use his skills wisely.

Williams's sword whistled close. James met it with his own blade, and for a moment the two men were locked together, their bodies inches from each other, their gazes dueling as surely as their swords were. Each was panting slightly, and beads of sweat stood out on their brows.

"My colonel ordered me not to attend this meeting," Williams said. Even though his words came out on little gasps of air, there was a sneer in his voice.

"You disobeyed a direct order?" Like Williams, James was breathing heavily, but his wind was sounder, without the telltale gasping of the other man's.

"When Harris discovers I've dispatched another verminous Highland rebel, he'll give me a captaincy for my disobedience," Williams sneered boastfully.

A feral grin curled James's mouth. "*Another* rebel, Englishman? When did you have the courage to meet a man face-to-face in battle? I'm willing to wager that it was while you were dreaming, or in your cups."

A shriek of rage issued from the lieutenant's throat. "Damn you! I'll make you pay for that remark!"

As James laughed tauntingly, the blades slid apart and Williams attacked even more ferociously than before. And as before, James slowly gave ground, allowing the lieutenant, as well as all of those watching, to believe he was outmatched by his opponent.

Williams was puffing badly now, and sweat rolled down his forehead and into his eyes. His blade slashed out, knocking James's sword aside. Then he lunged for James's exposed heart. But James pivoted to one side. The lieutenant lost his footing on the slippery grass and went down on his knees, his sword falling from his fingers as he instinctively threw out his hands to protect himself. He was vulnerable, open to any thrust James might choose to make.

On the ground, Williams shook, waiting for his fate. James flicked his blade beneath the Englishman's nose, not touching him, forcing him to raise his bowed head and look into his opponent's eyes.

"Get up!" James snarled. "I'll not dispatch you like the cur you are. You'll die like a man, Williams, on your feet, with your sword in your hands. I won't allow you to tarnish my honor the way your contemptible nature has destroyed your own!"

"Pink me now and have done with it," Williams urged desperately.

It was the coward's way out, a last attempt to deflect his fate. In the rules of the duel the first man to draw blood, no matter how slight the scratch, could be declared the winner.

"Get up," James repeated contemptuously, holding his blade well away from the lieutenant. He had no intention of allowing Williams to leave the field with nothing more than a minor cut. He wanted the man punished. He would not end the duel until it had been done.

As Williams crouched on the ground, cravenly awaiting his fate, James's gaze flickered idly around the meadow. He noted the impatient look on Ramsey's face, the disapproving one on the surgeon's and the painfully embarrassed one on Ensign Shorney's. His eyes traveled on, to the spot where the horses were tethered. His chestnut stallion was standing alert, his ears pricked and nostrils wide as he sniffed the wind.

With the warning unwittingly given by his mount, James checked the edges of the meadow more closely. His gaze caught a slight movement in the trees some distance away.

There was a flash of scarlet, too big to be a bird. Instantly, his mind made the connection—Harris.

He turned his attention back to Lieutenant Williams. "My patience grows thin, Englishman," he said grimly. "Get up or face the indignity of being called coward."

"Do you think I'm afraid of the lies a couple of northern barbarians might spread about me?" Williams taunted, "If you won't pink me and have done with it, I'll walk from this field uninjured and tell the world I was the victor! Ensign Shorney will back me up, should any chose to listen to the vile rumors put about by a defeated rebel!"

"Turn your head, Williams," James said softly, dangerously. "See the movement in those trees? That is your colonel and a squad of men with him. He can see you cringing at my feet, sniveling and whining for your life. Do you think he'll allow you—or anyone else—to forget it? You are doomed, Englishman. Stand up and meet your fate."

Panic flickered in the lieutenant's eyes as he looked past James and observed that telltale flash of red. "Damn you!" he hissed, stumbling to his feet.

"En garde," James retorted coldly, raising his sword. Shakily, Williams lifted his blade in a salute and they began again, this time with James as the aggressor. He drove Williams hard, continually forcing him to parry, lunge, and thrust.

The lieutenant responded jerkily at first, then more confidently, but he was panting heavily and beads of sweat were dripping down his brow. When an opening seemed to appear in James's defenses, a rasping sound that was meant to be a laugh broke from William's throat. He moved forward quickly. His blade bit through cloth and skin to meet bone.

James hardly noticed the scratch Williams's sword made as the tip scrapped across his chest. He had toyed with his victim, pushing him ever harder with the taunting promise of possible victory, allowing him to believe he would eventually win. And he'd waited until the man was at the last extremity, until his arms and legs were leaden with exhaustion, before he sprang his trap. Even as the lieutenant's sword was cutting through his shirt to scratch his skin, James was sliding his blade between his opponent's ribs at a point just below his heart.

The delighted expression on Williams's face turned to surprise as he looked down and saw the sword buried in his body. With an abrupt movement, James pulled his blade free. Williams crumpled and fell.

Events moved very quickly after that. Harris and his troop exploded from the trees, surprising everyone but James. The surgeon, to his credit, ignored them as he hurried over to see to his patient. Ensign Shorney looked aghast, Brendon thunderous, and Staverton resigned. James picked up the lieutenant's fallen weapon, added it to his own, and sauntered over to the spot where his seconds stood.

Negligently, he tossed the fragile dueling swords into the case. While he had toyed with Williams, he had made his plan. Standing and fighting a squad of soldiers wasn't included in it.

He reached for his coat, which was neatly folded beside the case. "Ramsey, Staverton!" he said, pitching his voice low.

Brendon gritted his teeth. "Where did they come from?"

"Edinburgh. Williams apparently boasted to Harris that I had challenged him. How or why the colonel found the place, I don't care. I am quite sure, though, that he is here to arrest me."

Brendon rubbed his chin. "Did you kill Williams?"

James snorted. "Not cleanly. I wanted him to suffer a bit before he passed from this life. No, I wounded him in the lungs. If he survives I'll be surprised."

"You gave the fellow every chance to prove himself," Staverton muttered. "Surely…"

"It matters not!" James retorted savagely. "I don't intend to stay in order to discover whether or not the English judicial system can be impartial."

"MacLonan!" Harris bellowed over the sound of hooves striking the earth. "Consider yourself under arrest, sir!"

James turned and flicked the lace that adorned his sleeves free of the cuffs of his coat. Then he saluted Colonel Harris with an insolent gesture. "Walk with me, Ramsey," he muttered out of the corner of his mouth. "I'll not bide here and wait for my fate to be sealed."

"This is against my better judgment," Brendon said, but he did join James as he sauntered casually toward his mount.

"If you run for it now, you'll never stop! I'm a witness to the whole, man! You conducted yourself properly from the beginning. No jury would convict you, should the unfortunate Williams die!"

They'd reached the horses. "I do not intend to find out,

Ramsey!" James vaulted lithely into the saddle of the chestnut stallion. His heels raked the animal's side. Leaping into a gallop, it flew across the meadow.

"Good luck," Brendon muttered to the retreating figure.

James knew that his one chance of escape was to reach one of the paths that led deep into the forest. His mount was a fine animal, bred for speed and endurance, while the horses the troopers rode were heavy, sturdy beasts without the stallion's swiftness and agility. He crouched over the horse's withers, urging the animal to even greater speed.

Evidently, Colonel Harris knew as well as James that his dragoons would never catch the flying chestnut. Instead of giving chase, he ordered his men to fire on their escaping quarry. Shots rang out as the musket barrels belched thick black smoke. Little tufts of grass rose in the air as the balls fell harmlessly beside, beyond, behind James. Harris cursed his men and ordered them to fire again. At will, this time, as soon as their weapons had been reloaded.

The opening at edge of the meadow was in sight. Another dozen strides and the stallion would reach the protection of the trees. Then James would surely be free, his escape made good. He knew, of course, that he would have to flee Scotland again, forever this time. Deliberately causing a man's death, especially an officer's, would never be pardoned. But at least he wouldn't end his days in an English jail waiting to be hung on an English gallows.

The muskets barked again, and this time they found their mark. The stallion screamed and faltered as a musket ball bit into the powerful muscles in his hindquarters. Gallantly, the horse continued on when James urged it forward with heels and hands. But its stride wavered.

James glanced over his shoulder, saw the gaping wound on his animal's hindquarter. The dragoons, seeing their quarry falter, were galloping across the field, closing rapidly.

With the trees heartbreakingly close, James pulled the laboring stallion up and waited for Harris and his men to arrive.

"That was stupid, MacLonan," Harris said, reaching James.

Raising his brows contemptuously, James countered, "Was it, Harris? Perhaps I have no reason to respect English justice."

The colonel's jaw tightened. "You are under arrest, James MacLonan, for the attempted murder of Lieutenant Williams, an officer in King George's Army." He made a gesture to one of his men. "Seize him and tie his hands behind his back. I don't want him to escape again."

As they roughly bound James, Ramsey and Staverton hurried over to the little group.

"What the devil are you doing, Harris?" Brendon demanded, huffing slightly.

"I am placing this man under arrest."

"Lord Staverton and I were MacLonan's seconds, Colonel Harris, and I can testify that the duel was conducted with perfect propriety. If you must charge MacLonan, then release him into my care. I will ensure he remains in Edinburgh to stand his trial."

Harris flicked a glance at Staverton, then said politely, "I fear that is impossible, Mr. Ramsey, since you've already done your best to aid him to escape." He turned to his men. "Prepare to move out."

Brendon tried again, rather desperate now. "You know, Colonel, that the moment MacLonan is brought before a magistrate he will be released."

"This man has assaulted a King's Officer. He will be lodged in the Tolbooth until he can be brought to trial."

"The Tolbooth! Harris, don't be absurd! The Tolbooth is a pesthole that has been a blight on Edinburgh for years," Brendon protested. "You can't send him there!"

James, who had been listening silently to this exchange, curled his lips in a disdainful show of bravado. He knew his fate was sealed as surely as if the trial had already taken place. "Staverton!" All three men turned to look at him. James ignored the other two. "I've left a letter for my wife amongst my baggage. Ask my father to give it to her when they've hanged me. But not before."

* * *

Thea slept late that morning. As had become her custom, she drank a cup of tea and ate a slice of dry toast before rising to help tame the nausea that always returned when she awoke. Cradling the teacup in her hands, she closed her eyes, enjoying the warmth and feeling a contented lassitude that had carried over from the night before.

The previous evening she had been preoccupied, worrying about James dueling with Williams, regretting the argument they'd had the day before, wondering if she should have told him of the baby, and all the while fighting the nausea that was constantly with her now.

At least she could do something about the nausea for she had found that relaxing in a hot tub eased her physical distress, at least for a time, and she had begun to indulge in a nightly bath before retiring. Last evening she had been later than usual, for she had spent too much time sitting in the parlor, fretting over what she could not change, before retiring to her bedchamber. Then too, she had waited for James; for he had gone out and she had hoped to see him before she went up for the night. But James did not return, and finally she gave in to fatigue and sickness and retreated to her chamber and the luxury of a hot bath.

The water had turned her skin pink when she dipped her toe in to test it. Thea firmly placed her foot, then the rest of her, into the tub. The warmth surrounded her, soothing her ills immediately. She sighed and closed her eyes.

That was how James had found her a quarter of an hour later. She was lying with her head thrown back, exposing the creamy line of her slender neck. Slowly, she opened her eyes when he said her name, and smiled with welcoming pleasure.

He was standing just inside her doorway, watching her. "I just came in. You left a message with the butler that you wanted to speak to me."

"I had hoped to see you before I went to sleep tonight."

At that, he smiled and advanced toward her. "I am at your service, madam wife."

He was dressed in the opulent costume of a Highland chief, a dark velvet jacket, tartan sash, finely woven kilt, and jeweled sporran. There were diamonds in the lace at his throat and in the buckles on his shoes. His wig was powdered snowy white and the lace at his wrists and throat was exquisitely made.

The clothes were a defiant gesture in a town where Highlanders were not always welcomed. "You challenged Williams tonight," she said.

He shook his head. "No, not tonight."

Though he denied her statement, Thea could see a glitter of elation in his eyes that worried her.

He knelt by the tub, caught a stray lock of her golden hair, then wrapped it around one finger. "You are very beautiful," he said huskily.

Under his caressing gaze, she began to breath quickly, the rise and fall of her chest displaying a tantalizing glimpse of her breasts where they rose above the water. She blushed. "If you will ring for the maid I will dress as quickly as possible, then we can talk."

He grinned at her, a carefree, fly-away grin that knotted Thea's stomach with sexual tension. "Why do you need a maid, my lady wife, when I am already here?"

Slowly, Thea rose from the tub, water sliding off her in sensual rivulets. She was very much aware of her husband's eyes upon her and of the picture she made for him. "Would you dry me, please?" She wondered if he could see the pulse pounding in her throat, or if he noticed that her nipples had puckered with anticipation.

"With pleasure," he said huskily, picking up a linen towel, but he kissed her first.

A long minute later, Thea pulled away. A little breathlessly she said, "James, stop! I'm leaving marks on your beautiful coat—"

He released her long enough to remove his velvet jacket and the damask waistcoat beneath and toss both onto the floor. Then he caught her close again and kissed her, more thoroughly than before.

Thea responded to his passion. She kissed him hungrily, stepping out of the tub so that she could move closer to him. James lifted her, cradling her gently in his arms as he took her over to the bed. He dropped little nibbling kisses on the side of her mouth, teasing and tempting her. When he placed her on the bed, Thea caught his shoulders to draw him down with her.

He kicked off his shoes, then settled beside her. She looked up at him, smiling. "When you come to me, all I can see is you, James MacLonan. You make me forget all that concerns me."

Touching her lips with the tip of his finger, he traced their shape. Thea's tongue crept out and caressed his finger. James bent, and they kissed with tenderness and hunger. Fumbling slightly, she slid her hands beneath the kilt to stroke his hard thigh. James deepened his kiss, demanding more. Thea sighed and pressed herself close.

The linen of his shirt was very fine. Thea ran her fingers over it, then pushed it up so that she could stroke his skin. He pulled his mouth away, breathing heavily. Taking her hands, he kissed first one and then the other, before he slipped from the bed to completely remove his kilt and stockings. He tugged his neckcloth free and tossed it on the floor with the rest, then pulled the fine linen skirt over his head and dropped it, too.

For a moment he stood watching her. She knelt on the bed, her breasts high, the nipples peaked proudly, and reached for him. He came to her gladly.

They kissed again, then he eased her onto her back. "I had no idea," he murmured, tasting her ear, "that when I wed I would find a woman as passionate and loving as you, Thea MacLonan."

She arched against him. "My fire is for you alone, James."

"I know, but I am greedy, Thea." He entered her slowly, teasingly. "I want all of you. I want your fire. I want your passion. I want your heart."

She had closed her eyes as pleasure washed over her, but at that she opened them to look into his. She smiled. "You have what you desire, James. It is yours. I gave it to you freely, long ago."

His thrusts quickened. She cried out his name and he kissed her hard. Then she was melting as she felt her husband reach his own release. He held her in his arms, stroking her hair, and for a time she felt free of all the cares that beset her. In the midst of their passion, she had accepted that she had truly fallen in love with her husband.

She hadn't loved him when she married him. She had liked him, she had desired him, she had respected him, but she hadn't loved him. It was when they lived together, and she learned more of him, that she had fallen in love with him, despite her promise to herself that she would never do so. But tonight, when he'd asked her to give him her heart, she had realized that she had already offered it to him, without ever putting the emotion into words. It was only now, with the future in doubt, that she was able to admit her love for him.

James slept, and eventually Thea did as well, although her worries and concerns tarnished her dreams. He woke her sometime in the night, and made love to her again, swiftly, but with no lessening of his passionate demand. She responded, and when they had done, he murmured, "My wife, my sweet wife. I cannot imagine a love any greater than my love for you. Your passion inspires me."

Surprised out of her lazy haze, Thea looked at him questioningly. He smiled and kissed her, then stretched on his back and settled her so that her head was on his shoulder and his arm wrapped around her. She fell asleep listening to the steady beating of his heart.

When she woke, he was gone.

Aware that she had slept late, she finished her tea and dry toast, then dressed and went downstairs.

She found Grant MacLonan in the parlor. He was preoccupied when she entered, but smiled brightly at her and engaged her in light, mindless conversation that centered around subjects like the weather. Until Grant had talked to her about wind changes, rain, and the possibility of snow,

Thea had no idea that anyone could spend fifteen minutes discussing such a trivial subject when important, life-changing events were quite possibly occurring at that very moment.

Finally, she said impatiently, "Grant, was the duel this morning?"

He looked guilty, but nonetheless tried to avoid admitting anything. "A duel? My dear, what in the heavens are you talking about?"

Thea pursed her lips. Her expression was mildly chastening. "My dear Grant, would you have me believe that my husband has lied to me? James mentioned to me that he planned to challenge Lieutenant Williams. I expected the duel to take place quite soon. Was it this morning?"

Grant shot her a dubious look that almost made Thea laugh. Duels were the prerogative of men. Women were not supposed to discuss such bloodthirsty sport, even if they were aware that one was occurring. Clearly, Grant MacLonan was not prepared for his daughter-by-marriage to bring up the subject.

"I did not know that James mentioned he had found Williams and challenged him."

"James knows that I would prefer the lieutenant to be punished by the authorities, but he also knows that I support him in all things."

Grant thought that over, and apparently decided that he might as well confide in Thea.

"It was this morning, at six of the clock."

"Six!" Thea thought about the previous night, and realized that after the second time James made love to her, he must have risen from their bed to leave for the duel. The thought frightened her and warmed her at the same time. She glanced at the ormolu clock that adorned a pedestal table against one wall. "But it is now ten o'clock. The men should have returned long since."

Grant shook his head. "I do not like this delay. I fear that something has gone wrong—"

The sound of voices interrupted him. He frowned.

"What is it?" Thea heard her voice, pitched higher than normal, expressing the fear she refused to acknowledge.

Grant stood slowly, pushing himself up by the arm of the chair. "Ramsey," he said curtly, turning to face the doorway.

Brendon Ramsey marched heavily into the room with Lord Staverton prowling behind him, looking as put out as a stalking cat that had just lost its prey. Thea's fears instantly flared into full-blown terror.

"'Where is James?" she demanded shrilly, leaping to her feet.

The men looked at each other, a conspiracy of silence clearly their intention.

Thea stamped her foot in an unusual exhibition of temper. "Do not shut me out, gentlemen! James is my husband and whether you like it or not, I may be able to help if he is in trouble."

Brendon sighed heavily. "'Tis trouble he is in, Thea. Harris has arrested him and thrown him into the Tolbooth Prison."

Thea knew about the Tolbooth. She'd lived in Edinburgh for three years, and had found the old prison a much more brooding presence over the city than the famed Castle. The tales of the place were fearsome, but most of the residents of Edinburgh didn't worry overmuch about the prison, for it was rarely used nowadays. As she thought of James locked in the Tolbooth, her legs suddenly gave out and she sank into a chair.

It was Grant who spoke. "Why was he put into the Tolbooth?"

"For the attempted murder of Lieutenant Williams," Staverton said flatly.

"Is Williams likely to die?" Grant demanded.

Staverton shrugged. "The surgeon had great hopes that he would recover, but Harris refused to accept the diagnosis."

"A magistrate will soon release James, or see that he is housed elsewhere," Grant said optimistically.

"James is not to be brought before a magistrate," Brendon

said bleakly. "Harris is calling this a military case, as it is one of his officers who is injured."

Grant's blue eyes flashed. "But the injury occurred as the result of a duel!"

"Harris refuses to accept that it is a civil matter." Brendon shrugged. "We have been arguing about it for the past hour. Nothing I could say would move him."

"Of course it would not," Thea said. She was staring into the fire, hearing the men's words, but seeing James locked in a dark, dirty cell. "Harris has found his opportunity to humiliate James for stealing me from him."

"There is more to it than that," Staverton said.

Thea looked up. "I know that. Harris would never dare to imprison James unless he felt that the orders he'd received from London would provide him with a good excuse. But I do not doubt that he enjoyed being able to lock my husband away in some dank cell for a time."

"He did look rather pleased with himself," Staverton muttered. He cocked a brow. "What do you think, Ramsey, can we use his motives to force him to allow James to be released into your custody?"

Brendon rubbed his chin. Then with a sigh, he shook his head. "If it had been you who James walked with to his horse, I might have been able to arrange it, but Harris will only say that I am not to be trusted—"

Grant interjected, "Why would Harris not trust you, Ramsey? You've a fine standing in the community."

"Because young James used me as a cover when he decided to try to escape. I went along to try to talk him out of it, but to no avail. Harris's men fired on him and—"

"They shot at James? Is he all right?"

"Yes, dear child, he is," Brendon said gently, coming over to clasp Thea's hand. "He has a slight scratch from the duel, but that is all."

"He is injured?"

Brendon patted her hand reassuringly. "The surgeon cleaned the wound before James left the field. He pronounced it a mere scratch and nothing to worry about."

Jerking her hand away, Thea put it to her cheek. "Nevertheless, James cannot be allowed to stay in prison! Mr. Ramsey, Grant, you must do something!"

"As I said, I could not get James released into my custody, and when I suggested he be released into his father's care, Harris had the effrontery to laugh! He said there was nobody in Edinburgh untouched by Grant MacLonan's money or my connections whom he would turn James over to."

"The conceit of the man!" Grant said fiercely. "Does he think that someone like Judge Denholm could be corrupted by money or influence?"

Brendon shrugged.

Staverton said grimly, "Harris is using excuses. He wants James locked up in prison, well away from the danger of meeting up with the Pretender. James is a man with a grievance, a legitimate grievance. If the Prince were able to win him over, together they could set the Highlands aflame once more."

"You are wrong, Staverton," Grant said softly. "The Highlands will never rise again."

Staverton held his hands out. "I do not disagree, MacLonan. But I am not Colonel Harris, an incompetent officer sitting on top of what he thinks might be an explosive situation. He's worried, so he is using every power he possesses to make sure that he is safe."

"Despite what both of you think I believe that it is worth our while to make use of what influence we possess and to try to enlist the aid of members of the government," Grant said, his expression bleak.

"It can't hurt, although I doubt it will do any good. Harris is adamant."

"There is one person Colonel Harris would have to agree to turn James over to," Thea said slowly.

Brendon looked skeptical. "I doubt it, my dear. I do not like to dash your hopes, but I fear there is no one."

Thea smiled thinly. "Yes, there is. My father."

It was Staverton who broke the silence that followed. He laughed. "God's teeth, we are all fools! Mrs. MacLonan is right. Harris could not refuse to release James into the custody of General Sir Frederick Tilton. My congratulations, ma'am. Your suggestion is brilliant."

Brendon rubbed his chin. "There is a drawback. Tilton is in London. It will be days before a messenger gets to him, and an equal amount of time before he can present himself here to take custody of James."

"Then I had better write to him immediately," Thea said, standing up decisively. "I want James out of prison as soon as possible. Gentlemen, I will leave you to your plotting."

CHAPTER 18

A fortnight passed. Thea fretted, worried about James, and dreamed of their reunion. The messenger who had carried her letter down to London returned with a short note from Lady Tilton, decrying the infamy of what had happened and advising Thea that her father would be in Edinburgh as quickly as he could manage. Lord Staverton visited to tell Thea and Grant that he was returning to London to see what he could do there. Thea urged him to visit her father and add his requests to hers. With a curt nod, the viscount agreed to do so and departed.

But General Sir Frederick Tilton did not arrive, and Thea was soon desperate. She knew that the cell James was housed in was a horrible place, for Brendon Ramsey had managed to visit him and had returned to Grant's house looking grim. This made Thea worry about the wound James had received during the duel, whether it was healing properly and if James was in any pain from it. She guessed that he must be imagining the worst, that he was a pawn in a chess game played by a mad prince and a ruthless government determined to stay in power. For James, the outcome would not matter, for pawns rarely survived to the end of the game.

Thea did her best to try to let James know that he had not been abandoned by his friends and family. Every day since his incarceration she had made up a picnic basket full of his favorite foods, then walked over to the prison, where she delivered the basket into the hands of a warder, along with a few coins, and the request that it be given to her husband.

When she first started this, Grant MacLonan protested that the Tolbooth was no place for a lady to go. Thea's reply was painfully simple. The Tolbooth was no place for a gentleman to be incarcerated. Grant had bowed his head, then with a sigh, suggested that she send one of the footmen with the basket. Thea was tempted, but she could not allow herself to give in. James was in the filthy prison because of her. The least she could do was to bring his meals to him herself.

After the surgeon brought the good news that Williams was recovering nicely and would soon be on his feet, Grant MacLonan and Brendon Ramsey renewed their efforts to have James freed by working through political and legal channels, but neither found any success. While the Pretender was loose, his location unknown, the English garrison in Scotland was on the alert. Colonel Harris had every right to imprison anyone he thought might be a danger.

Thea had begun to believe that nothing could be done to save James when she received a note suggesting that she should visit St. Giles Cathedral on High Street on a certain day at the hour of one in the afternoon. She read the note several times, and with each reading she remained perplexed. The paper was unsigned and the wafer sealing it had no stamp identifying the sender. Why, she wondered, would someone send her such a communication?

Her curiosity thoroughly roused, she decided she would stop in at the church, which was near the Tolbooth prison, after she had delivered her basket of food to James. No one would be surprised that she took a moment to seek solace after visiting the prison.

On the appointed day she found a place near the front of the church, while she had the maid who accompanied her settle further back. The pews were empty now, but she remembered the day when she had stood at the altar and before a huge crowd of friends and well-wishers, made her wedding vows to James MacLonan. She closed her eyes as she knelt, fighting the fear that the happiness she had found with James would be short-lived, then prayed for her husband's safety. After a time the hallowed quiet of the church renewed her strength. Once again she could believe that there was hope for James. There was always hope. She would have faith in that.

She was so deeply immersed in her thoughts that the sound of a rough male whisper, directly behind her, made her jump.

"We should not be seen together, Mrs. MacLonan!"

"Lord Staverton! I thought you had gone to London."

"That is exactly what I hoped people would think."

"Then you never left Edinburgh?"

"No."

"What have you been doing then?" She shifted her body and moved her head so she could see behind her.

"Don't do that! It is very possible that you are being watched. I am sure I was before I pretended to leave Edinburgh. I don't want Harris to know I've contacted you."

"Why?"

"Before I answer that, tell me what has happened since I supposedly left?"

"Nothing, and everything. My father has not yet arrived from London. Mr. Ramsey and Grant have had no luck in persuading anyone in the government that James should be sent before a magistrate. They are all outraged, of course, but they have been told that the Pretender is loose and may be on his way to Scotland, so they are also terrified that he may try to raise the Highlands again. They will not make a move against Colonel Harris."

"Damned Whigs," Staverton muttered.

Footsteps sounded nearby, echoing upward into the vast, vaulted ceiling. Staverton's voice halted abruptly.

When the sound faded minutes later, Thea's heart was pounding and her throat had dried from sheer terror. Staverton's aura of secrecy and his contention that she was being spied upon brought her once again into her husband's world of rebellion and alienation. It was frightening. It was also exhausting. She doubted she would be able to live in it for very long.

After the danger had passed, Staverton's gruff whisper brought her attention back to him. "Let me quickly explain what it is I need of you! I wish to be gone from this place."

Thea nodded. Then, when Staverton did not speak, she whispered, "I am willing to listen, Lord Staverton."

"I have been able to arrange passage for James on a ship to France. I want to free him from the Tolbooth, but to do that I need your help."

Thea froze. "Escape?"

"Yes!" Staverton hissed. "I'd expected a little more enthusiasm from you, Mrs. MacLonan."

Thea thought of the anguish James would feel, separated from his beloved hills. "My husband would hate to live in exile."

"Better to live in exile than be dead because of a mad Prince and a foolish, revenge-filled government!"

Thea stared at the altar and the cross upon it. Should she help Staverton lead James back into a life of exile, or should she trust in the laws and political system of England to free her husband? Once she would have chosen without wasting a moment in thought. Now she could not decide.

Staverton's urgent voice forced the issue. "James is lodged in the Tolbooth prison, Mrs. MacLonan. The place is a fortress! I cannot free him without your help!"

"I understand, for I have been going there every day. There are guards at the gate, which is kept locked from the inside. What could I do?"

"I need to know details of the inside of the prison. How many guards there are, where James is being kept, if there is some weakness I can use to break him free. I cannot get in— I know, for I have already tried. But you can, Mrs. MacLonan, you can."

Thea thought about the prison and shivered. The mere thought of going inside it filled her with a heart-stopping panic. But James was there. He had no choice but to endure the horror of the Tolbooth prison. She thought about seeing him, soon, and a deep, comforting peace filled her. "When?"

"Tomorrow, when next you take James your basket of food, the guard will open the gate for you. Follow him. He will take you to James."

"Very well."

"And remember, notice everything!"

Thea nodded. "I will." She waited for more, but there was only silence. She risked a quick look around, but saw no one. The viscount had gone.

The Tolbooth was a large, looming structure of cold gray granite, imposing, grim, and ominous. In lamentably few places the thick stone walls were shot with tiny slits that must serve as windows.

As Thea stepped up to the massive gates, she shivered with nerves and a very real fear. Then she thought of James inside this enormous pile of stone, locked away from fresh air and the sun's light. The knowledge infuriated her and helped her to step quickly through the small inset door in the thick wooden gates that opened with a shriek of protest. Behind her, she heard her maid whimper. Thea turned and said coolly, "You may stay here, or you may accompany me. Do as you please."

The turnkey who opened the gate was a mean little man, with thick, wet lips, a large nose, and several days growth of beard. From the stench that emanated from him, it seemed that he evidently considered washing to be something others did. Small black eyes bored into Thea, then flicked over to her maid, a pretty girl who, until this point had been happy to be elevated to the position of personal maid. A lascivious leer split his cheeks. "She stays with you, lassie. Are you ready?"

His expression made Thea tremble deep in her bones, but she refused to allow her fears to show, hiding them behind a facade of cool hauteur.

"You will take me to my husband so that I can give him my basket of food myself," she said, looking down her nose at the warder.

He grinned at her, showing broken, blackened teeth. "Aye. It's been arranged. Come this way then lassie, and mind your step. This place ain't kept as clean as the likes of you expects."

The maid whispered urgently, "Is this really necessary, lady? I mean, the master must be getting his food, I'm sure he is."

"I wish to be certain."

"This be madness," the maid muttered, and pulled the hood of her cloak up around her head.

Thea lifted her head boldly, despite the atmosphere of decay and death that permeated the prison. Madness perhaps, but if so it was caused by Colonel Harris and the Pretender.

The only light in the closed hallway came from the oil lantern their guide held. It cast huge, lurking shadows on the dark stone walls. A disgusting stench filled the place, and as they went by an open refuse pit, Thea realized that the drains must no longer function.

They passed the common cells where pickpockets and sneak thieves were imprisoned with unfortunates whose only crime was indebtedness, then progressed toward the east wing, where the turnkey said James was being lodged. Thea forced thoughts of her own physical discomfort to the back of her mind as she concentrated on noting the route the warder was taking and looking for any possible flaws in the security that could be used to abet an escape.

How can James break free of this place? she thought desperately. The walls were thick blocks of stone with the only route in or out through this narrow corridor. The turnkey would have to be bribed, but would he risk the censure that would surely fall on him if it was discovered he had aided a prisoner to escape? Somehow, the prospect of this noisome little man as a fellow conspirator did not inspire Thea with confidence.

At length they arrived in the east wing. There were only three cells, one on top of the other. The stench intensified, and Thea's heart twisted as she imagined James constantly inundated by the foul odor.

The warder led them up a narrow stone staircase to the topmost room, then jerked his head toward the solid oak door.

"He's in there."

"Then open the door."

"Not so fast, my fine lady! There be rules."

"What rules?" Thea demanded indignantly. "Nothing was said of rules when this meeting was arranged."

The turnkey's small black eyes glittered in the light of the lamp. "Just the same, there's rules. You've ten minutes. No more. Then I lead you out of here. I'm taking enough chances without you wasting time." He pointed down the stairs, to the remaining cells. "See down there? Them cells ain't being used." Jerking his head in the direction of the upper cell, he concluded, "So I ain't got no excuse for being here if we're caught. See?"

"You have made your position clear," Thea said curtly. At the same time she abandoned any hope of using this creature in an attempt to free James. The turnkey was terrified of being caught by his superiors, though he tried to disguise the emotion by threats of his own. She added contemptuously, "If time is so precious, why don't you let us into the cell?"

"Ho, lady! Not the two of you. The lassie here stays with me!"

"She certainly does not!"

"Then we turn about and just head back the way we came! If I'm caught here I can always say I brought the bonnie lassie to this wing to bed her, it's so quiet like here." At Thea's gasp of disgust and the maid's shrill protest, he shrugged. "No one will wonder. It's a common enough price a wench pays to get in for a visit with her lover."

As her maid made an indignant sound in her throat, Thea glared at the turnkey. "If you are thinking of taking such a payment from my maid, then you may think again!" she informed him in a soft, albeit, dangerous voice. "If either of us is molested in any way, you will not be paid."

Feeling he had the upper hand, the warder leered, licking

his thick lips. "Might be pay enough."

Icy fear clutched at Thea's heart. While they were inside the Tolbooth, she and her maid were as much in this man's control as the prisoners were, and just as helpless. Unless she could think of a way of outsmarting him, he would surely rape them both. There was no physical threat she could successfully use against him. What then would suffice?

Money. Greed had caused him to agree to bring her here, conquering his terror of breaking the rules. *Appeal to his greed*, her racing thoughts told her. She prayed she had hit upon his main weakness.

Forcing faint amusement into her voice, she said, "You consider a tumble with my maid to be worth fifty pounds?"

The amount was probably more than the warder made in a year. The fellow dragged his gaze from the girl's shapely figure, and Thea saw that avarice gleamed hotly in his eyes. "Fifty pounds. That's what you said, lady. You remember it."

"You will be paid only if my maid and I leave this building unharmed. Now, unlock the door so we waste no more time arguing."

The guard grudgingly did as she ordered. Thea squeezed her maid's hand in a gesture of support then slipped into the cell. The door slammed closed behind her.

Inside, the tiny room was illuminated only by a thin shaft of light that penetrated through a slitted window set high in the wall. Through the gloom, Thea could see that the room was filthy. The walls were covered with a noisome sweat, the floors littered with foul-smelling straw. As she stood by the door, adjusting her eyes to the dim light, she heard a squeak and felt something scurry across her boot. Unintentionally she gasped, as she swallowed the scream she would normally have uttered.

"What the devil do you want?" demanded her husband irritably. His voice emanated from one corner of the room. Cautiously, Thea stepped in that direction.

"James?"

There was a shuffling sound from his corner. "Thea? Is that you? You'll have to come to me," he said grimly.

When she was close enough to see him, she halted abruptly and drew in her breath in a hiss of distress. James stood in the corner, his hands manacled together. A similar iron cuff bound one leg to a chain in the wall. "Oh, dear God!" she cried, her hands tightening on the basket she carried. "What have they done to you, my love!"

A wry smile quirked his lips. "Colonel Harris is determined that I shall not escape. He visited me personally to tell me that the conspiracies that my friends on the outside were hatching would not work. Then he watched while the chains were put on. He seemed to enjoy the entertainment."

"When was that?" Thea whispered. She was desperately afraid that her visit here had been the cause of James's discomfort.

James looked toward the thin shaft of light and thought for a moment. "A few days ago, I suppose. It is rather hard to estimate the passage of time in this place. Apparently, Staverton had managed to find a ship that claimed to be willing to carry me to France. In a drunken evening the master talked a little too freely, and so Harris came to be informed of Staverton's activities. A pity," James added in a musing tone. "At this time I would find a voyage to France quite pleasant, even if I do not return."

"You would be an exile again."

"True, but it matters not." He shrugged and raised his hands. "I am going nowhere now." His expression hardened when Thea inadvertently lifted her hand to her cheek in distress. "Thea, what foolish whim has brought you here?"

"Whim! James, this is no whim!"

"No?" he retorted mockingly. "What else but a whim would bring a fine English lady such as you into this hellhole?"

Love brought me, Thea thought unhappily. *A desire to make you a little less unconformable. A mad scheme to help free you from this place.*

Her eyes filled with tears, blurring the sight of him. Yet his image was burned into her soul. His clothes were ragged. The fine linen shirt was encrusted with his blood and his creamy silk waistcoat was dirty and torn. His dark coat hung loosely on his tall frame, telling her that he had lost weight.

The beginnings of a beard covered his cheeks, and he had discarded his wig. His short, dark hair was matted against his head, and his eyes burned with a fierce, angry fire. In appearance he was a far different man from the one she had lain with some two weeks before.

She went over to his corner and held out the basket. "I am not a fine English lady, not anymore. I am the wife of a Scottish Highlander. I came to this place to bring you food and to see what kind of conditions you are being held in."

He hesitated a moment, then took the basket with a nod.

"I admit that the food will not come amiss. The swill they feed me here is not even fit for the pigs."

Thea made a tutting sound. "I thought you looked awfully thin. I have been sending baskets like this one ever since you were put in this awful place. I suppose none has ever gotten to you."

"Not one," James said around a mouthful of fresh bread. He closed his eyes and sighed. "Thank you, Thea, for this little taste of heaven."

She smiled tremulously. The sight of him so moved by a mouthful of bread brought his plight clearly to the fore. "It isn't much, James. I wish it were more." She moved closer, reaching for him.

"Don't come too close, Thea," he said quickly. "I'm verminous."

Looking ruefully down at the hem of her gown where it dragged on the dirty straw, she laughed. "I fear I shall have to burn my gown after I leave this wretched place. I doubt I am immune from the problem." She hesitated, then added softly, "So it does not matter how close I come." She reached up to touch his bearded cheek. He flinched as if she had struck him, and jerked away. His chains rattled loudly in the quiet. Thea's hand fell to her side.

After a moment, he said roughly, "Thea, I wish you had not come."

"I had to," she whispered.

He dropped the loaf back into the basket, apparently having eaten his fill. Then he leaned back against the wet, noisome wall, a brooding expression on his face as he watched her. "Have you any news? For the most part, they tell me nothing in here. Oh, that is not quite true. Harris very kindly informed me that Williams still lingers, but is not expected to last."

"Well, Colonel Harris lied to you! The surgeon announced days ago that the lieutenant is recovering rapidly. He will not die from his wound and Colonel Harris knows it!"

"Well, that's something," James remarked calmly, apparently not much caring.

His apathy cut Thea to her core. He could not have stated his disillusionment more clearly in words "James, do not give up hope! Your father and Mr. Ramsey have been working hard to convince the civil authorities that your incarceration here is wrong."

"But they have not succeeded, have they, Thea?"

She shook her head wordlessly. She could hear the bitterness in his voice, and she knew she had no means of countering it.

"No, and they will not as long as the Pretender cannot be found," James went on. "Oh, heads will be shaken and sympathy will be given, but it is in no one's interest to free me, dangerous rebel that I am. They'll hang me if the Pretender turns up in the Highlands, and if he appears safe and away in Europe, they'll transport me to one of the colonies as they did to so many after Culloden. I'll be used as an example to any man who might consider following the Stuarts again."

"I don't believe that will be your fate, James."

His eyes burned. He said mockingly, "Even after all that has happened, you still have faith in English justice?"

She winced, then whispered, "How can I do anything else? I must believe in something—"

His voice roughened, then hardened. "Believe in this, wife.

It is because of your fine English justice that I am here, and for one excuse or another, I will not leave this prison a free man."

"Do not give up hope, James! I've written to my father, asking for his help. Your father and Mr. Ramsey are agreed that if my father demands that you be released into his custody, even Harris cannot refuse."

"Released into the custody of an English general? Damn you, woman, what were you thinking of?"

Thea shook her head. "What is the matter, James? I don't understand why you would dislike the arrangement."

"I am a Highland Scot, Thea, a Jacobite! Tilton is an Englishman, an English Whig. The two can never exist comfortably together."

His words bit hard into the dream Thea had long cherished, the dream that her husband would fall in love with her as surely as she had fallen in love with him. What of his tender words the night before the duel? His voice rang in her ears and she felt dizzy. She put her hand out, seeking support and found the cold, hard iron manacle on his wrist.

The shock of that sensation roused her from her aching, bitter anguish. She stepped back, avoiding James's reaching hand, and shook out her skirts. "Nonetheless, husband, if my father sees fit to arrange your release you will accept it, for you will be given no choice. Just as you had no choice but to marry an Englishwoman."

A small smile twisted his lips. "My beautiful Thea," he said softly, almost on a sigh. "Do you know you are magnificent when you are angry? Even in this poor light I can see the sparks flying from your eyes."

She tossed her head, still angry at him, but knowing her time with him was almost over. There was something she must tell him, whether he wanted to hear the words or not, and she could not be sure when she would see him again.

"I came here, James MacLonan, because I love you. I do not expect you to feel the same for me, but understand this, I will do anything in my power to free you. You may not like my methods, but I will not allow that to change what I must do!"

The door edged open and a shaft of harsh yellow light pieced the dimness. "Time's up and I've given you more than I meant," the turnkey said as he poked his ill-featured head through the doorway. He leered grotesquely. "But the lass here is a mighty fine piece—"

"If you've harmed her," Thea shouted, relieved to have someone to vent her temper on, "I'll personally carve you into little pieces!"

The guard jerked back. "Nay, I was only making a wee jest. The lass is fine. She's the same as she came in."

Thea caught up her skirts and swept regally toward her victim. "She had better be! For I mean what I say!" The guard cringed, nodding understanding as she strode past him.

As the door slammed, Thea thought she heard a low masculine chuckle, but the sound was so quiet she could have imagined it.

That afternoon she was in the parlor when Grant MacLonan arrived home. He was accompanied by Brendon Ramsey. Without preamble, Thea said, "I've been to see James."

Neither man looked surprised. By now they were both used to her daily visits to the prison. Thea tried again. "Did either of you know that Lord Staverton has been trying to arrange passage to France for James?"

This time Ramsey did look surprised, but the expression on Grant's face gave him away. He said slowly, "Why do you ask, daughter?"

"Because his attempts have put James in chains," Thea said, and surprised herself by bursting into tears.

MacLonan approached her and patted her shoulder awkwardly. "There, there, Thea. Don't cry. It will be all right."

She sniffed and dabbed at her eyes with a lace handkerchief. "Please tell Lord Staverton to stop what he is doing. The passage to France no longer exists and I could see no possible way of getting James out of the vile prison."

"You mean you really did visit James?" Ramsey demanded. "What on earth possessed you to do such a thing?"

"I told you, I was trying to find a way for James to escape from the Tolbooth so that he could make use of the passage Lord Staverton had arranged."

Brendon Ramsey muttered something under his breath, a rather uncomplimentary comment on women and Englishmen. "I have lived in Edinburgh all of my life. I visited James when he was first imprisoned. Did it never occur to either of you that I have seen the inside of the Tolbooth?"

At Thea's blank expression, he continued. "No, I can see that it did not. Had you thought to ask, I would have told you the place was a fortress and that it is quite impossible for someone to escape from it."

"I found that out, to my cost," Thea said bitterly. "Mr. Ramsey, Colonel Harris had chains put on James. Can you arrange to have them taken off?"

Ramsey tapped his fingers together. "I will do my best, Thea, but I can promise nothing."

Thea nodded. She put her hands on her belly, seeking comfort from the new life growing there. She must not give up hope.

"Thea," Grant said, drawing her eyes to him. "Judge Denholm has managed to force Harris to set a trial date. It is to be at the end of November, almost a month from now."

Excitement was followed by fear, as James's mocking words echoed in her mind. *Do you still believe in English justice, Thea?* Did she? Could she? "But that is good, isn't it?"

"There is more," Ramsey added heavily, and looked at Grant.

Thea looked at him too. His expression wasn't hopeful.

"Since Lieutenant Williams will definitely recover, Harris has agreed that should James be convicted, the punishment will be reduced to transportation to one of the colonies, not hanging."

Transportation! The bitter certainty of James's words came back to her, haunting her. *If he appears safe and away in Europe, they'll transport me to one of the colonies as they did so many after Culloden. I'll be used as an example to any man who might consider following the Stuarts again.*

Thea put her hands over her eyes and gave way to despair.

CHAPTER 19

The next morning the butler brought her a card as she was sipping tea at the breakfast table. She fingered the white pasteboard with a little frown. "Is Mrs. Ramsey still here?"

"She is waiting in the parlor, Mrs. MacLonan."

Thea looked at the card for a moment longer, then nodded her head. "I shall go to Mrs. Ramsey. Bring a pot of tea and a plate of Cook's delicious seed cakes, if you would, please."

The servant nodded and went away. Still holding the card with the elegant handwriting, Thea went to the parlor to greet her visitor.

Olivia Ramsey was standing by the fire, still wearing her hat, cloak, and gloves. She smiled when she saw the surprised expression on Thea's face. "I was not sure of my welcome, my dear, after you very nearly snubbed me in the street yesterday."

Thea could not remember the walk home from the Tolbooth. Her thoughts had been with James, there in the dank, filthy cell in which he was lodged. She bit her lip. "Surely not, Mrs. Ramsey. I would never do such a thing. I know you are a dear friend to my family!"

Olivia smiled thinly. "I am aware of your troubles, Thea, and so I did not assume your intention was purposeful, but I have heard others who are not so charitable."

"I had no idea," Thea murmured. With Brendon Ramsey so deeply involved in the efforts to help James, Thea did not want to insult his wife, so she hastened to help Olivia off with her cloak, then found her a place by the fire. Once the tea was delivered and poured, Thea said, "Mrs. Ramsey, pray do accept my apologies."

"Of course, Thea. Now, you will want to know the reason I am here."

Thea raised a brow. There was a decisiveness to Olivia's tone that she could not miss.

"As I am sure you have guessed, there has been much gossip about James's imprisonment. My husband and Mr. MacLonan have been talking to everyone of importance in this city, and their wives seem to have just as much information as they do."

Thea felt herself coloring. "And just what do they know?"

Olivia sipped her tea and eyed Thea consideringly. "They know that James has been imprisoned for dueling with Lieutenant Williams. They know that the lieutenant is expected to recover. They know that you have fallen desperately in love with your Highland lord and would do anything to free him, including a recent visit to the Tolbooth."

"Is that all?"

"They have not decided if you are a heroine or a hoyden for going to the Tolbooth. At the moment, opinion leans toward a heroine. And that is why I am here."

Thea shook her head. "I am thoroughly confused, Mrs. Ramsey."

Putting her cup down with a snap, Olivia said tartly, "Consider, Thea. Society has decided that you are to be congratulated, not censured, for bravely entering a horrid prison in order to ease your husband's suffering. Now is the moment for you to re-enter society. I am having a musical evening in three days. I want you to attend."

"Go to a party?" Thea said, aghast. "Mrs. Ramsey, the last thing I want to do now is spend an evening smiling and pretending to be happy!"

"Then you have not thought this through." She scanned

Thea thoughtfully. "My husband tells me that you have written your father, but he has not responded. Why did you write him?"

Thea blinked. "Why? Because I hoped that he would be able to help."

"In what way?"

"Why, he could use his influence, of course!"

"Yes! That is my point exactly. Your father has influence." She stopped for a heartbeat, then continued. "So do you."

Thea drooped. Shaking her head, she said, "No, I do not. That is what this is all about, Mrs. Ramsey. I had no power to help Maggie MacLonan, or to influence Lieutenant Williams. I could not stop James from coming to Edinburgh to challenge Williams and I could not keep Colonel Harris from chaining my husband like a common felon. I have not even been able to influence my father enough to cause him to consider aiding his son-by-marriage." Her voice wavered. "You are wrong, Mrs. Ramsey, I have no influence, or power."

There was silence after Thea finished. Then Olivia said gently, "Do not despair, Thea."

She sniffed. "How can I not? In a month James will be sent to trial. Colonel Harris is asking that he be transported to the colonies if he is found guilty. And he will be because the charge is assault with intent to kill, and that is exactly what happened."

"Nonsense. James participated in a duel that was conducted in a perfectly respectable way. It was not attempted murder." When Thea looked disbelieving, Olivia hurried on. "But that is neither here nor there. What is important is that you must assert yourself, Thea. Mr. Grant MacLonan is wealthy and can purchase influence, but he is a Highland Scot whose two sons followed the Pretender. My husband is a Whig and his influence is great amongst those who count in our society, but he too is a Scot. You, Thea, are not. You are English and your father is General Sir Frederick Tilton. Remember that!"

"How can I forget," Thea said bitterly, straightening all the same. "That is why James married me and look what good it has done him!"

"Than make it do some good, Thea. Come to my musical evening and let people know that Theadora Tilton married James MacLonan, but she is still a Tilton and she is still English and she is still a good Whig and..." Olivia paused and smiled dangerously. "She does not like the way her husband is being treated. You have more influence than you think, Thea, but you will never know how much until you use it."

Thea picked up a seed cake and began to nibble. "There is merit to what you say, but—Mrs. Ramsey, I have not been out in society since I returned to Edinburgh. I have nothing to wear."

Olivia sent Thea another of her shrewd assessing looks.

"You do seem to have gained some weight."

Thea blushed. The sickness that had plagued her was easing and she was beginning to notice changes in her body.

Evidently, they were visible to those observant enough to see them.

"Obviously," Olivia drawled, her gaze lingering at Thea's much fuller breasts and thickening waist, "marriage has been kind to you."

Thea blushed harder. "That wasn't exactly what I meant, Mrs. Ramsey. When we came down from Glenmuir I only packed morning dresses. I did not think that I would have need of any other, for I did not expect to remain in Edinburgh this long."

Olivia waved this away. "My dressmaker will fit you. I shall simply tell her that she must have a gown ready for you by Thursday or she will not be able to expect my custom to continue in the future. She is a sensible woman and she will do it."

"But—"

Olivia raised her brows. "Do you have another excuse? Something to do with the condition of your health, perhaps?"

Thea was not about to confide in Olivia Ramsey. James

had a right to know about his own child before half of Edinburgh heard, and Thea was quite sure that Olivia would not hesitate to use the information if she thought it might do some good, even if Thea had sworn her to secrecy. So she bowed gracefully to the inevitable. "I think a gown that used materials with bright, cheerful colors would be best, don't you?"

Olivia's eyes gleamed. "Silver tissue for the petticoat, I think, with blue, perhaps, for the overskirt. Yes, a blue the color of your husband's eyes. An excellent idea! You can point that out to people, Thea. The overskirt must be embroidered with silver thread. Should it be in a Scottish thistle, do you think?"

Thea nodded. Energy had begun to flood though her, driving away the depression that had sapped her strength since her meeting with James the day before. "Intertwined with an acorn and the leaves of an oak—an English oak."

Olivia clapped her hands together. "Excellent! Yes, Scotland and England entwined. It is perfect! Now, when should you arrive? Should you be there from the beginning? No, I do not think that will work. You should be late, Thea. Make an entrance. You know how to do that. Grant MacLonan must bring you. Together you will make people stop and look—force them to notice you. Hold your head high and show them you will not be daunted. They will be flocking about you before you know it."

Hope made Thea's eyes bright. "I believe you are right, Mrs. Ramsey." She hesitated, then added, "But what if you are wrong?"

Olivia smiled thinly. "Power withers and dies if it is not used, Thea. You must try. Now, let us put on our hats and cloaks and we will go to my dressmaker. She can work miracles, but not without a little assistance."

Thea's hand tightened on Grant MacLonan's arm as they paused in front of the door to the Ramsey residence. He patted her fingers reassuringly.

Thea took a deep breath. "I am ready," she said. "I hope

that Mrs. Ramsey was correct in her assumptions."

"What is the worst that can happen? That we are snubbed and Olivia Ramsey has to answer impertinent questions regarding her reasons for inviting a jailed man's wife to her party? I fear that would be more difficult for Olivia than for us."

Thea glanced at him, a little surprised by his words. His eyes were alight with mischief. In that moment he looked so very much like his son that Thea's heart twisted. Then she laughed. They were here to help James and for that cause she would risk anything. "Lead on, dear sir. We might as well discover what awaits us."

A burst of sound greeted them, for the party had been under way for well over an hour and people were chattering cheerfully over the music. Thea surrendered her cloak to the servant, revealing the gorgeous gown that Olivia Ramsey's dressmaker had spent most of the past seventy-two hours creating. The silver petticoat and cerulean blue overskirt were draped over the wide hoops that flared the skirt out, hiding Thea's thickening waist. The vibrant colors of the rustling satin were a rich compliment to Thea's fair skin and drew every eye to her when she and Grant were announced.

With her head high, she stood very straight and surveyed the crowd with slightly raised brows. Her glance was cool, almost, but not quite, haughty. In a bored way she snapped her fan open so that she could flick it casually as she surveyed the party-goers. Her gaze swept round, lingering here and then there as she deliberately made eye contact with only a few individuals. Conversation stilled as curiosity was piqued. After a moment she raised the fan to hide her mouth as she leaned toward Grant MacLonan.

"Has this gone on long enough?" she whispered.

In turn, he allowed his gaze to sweep the room, pausing occasionally. When he spotted the Duchess of Argyll he smiled and nodded. To those watching, unaware of what Thea had just said, it seemed that Thea had made a comment to Grant and he had been trying to verify it. Now he pointed to Olivia Ramsey and they moved toward her. Olivia, who had been lingering in the background, deliberately allowing Thea to be the center of attention, moved forward to meet them.

"My dear, you look lovely," she gushed loudly for all to hear. "One would never know that the government has taken it upon itself to persecute your family."

Thea was shocked by Olivia's direct tactics, and for the space of a heartbeat she was too surprised to think of anything to say. Then she rallied, smiled sweetly, and replied. "My dear Mrs. Ramsey, thank you for your kind words. I know that many Scots feel the English have treated them badly over the past few years, but I must believe that the system is sound. James has been imprisoned by a jealous man whose spiteful behavior has, unfortunately, been allowed because he has no one to rein him in."

"My dear!" Olivia said, apparently aghast. "Do you mean..." She deliberately let the question drift off as she noticed someone nearby avidly listening. "But I must introduce you to Mrs. Buchanan."

"I know Mrs. Buchannan!" said Thea brightly. "'Were you not Miss MacAuley last winter? I had not heard you were married. Tell me, how do you find your new status..." The conversation drifted into domestic issues. Thea would wait until Mrs. Buchannan, who was the daughter of a member of the Scottish Parliament, brought up the question of Colonel Harris before dropping her next little bit of slanderous gossip.

As the evening continued on, Thea laughed and chattered, flirting with the gentlemen, teasing them with her eyes, and making great play with her fan. Though no one would know it, her actions and those of Grant MacLonan and the Ramseys had been carefully thought out so that they would have a telling impact. Since the Prince's visit to England and his subsequent disappearance were not common knowledge, they'd decided that Colonel Harris could be used as a scapegoat for James's imprisonment. Thea would drop light, gossipy hints about his jealousy and envy of James all evening.

By the end Harris would be damned in society, and many would return to their homes convinced that James MacLonan was innocent of everything except winning the hand of the woman Harris desired.

After nearly three hours, Olivia whispered to Thea, "The evening is going perfectly. I do not think there is a woman here who does not see Colonel Harris as a great barbarian, while their men have begun to have grave misgivings about how the whole affair has been handled. You are doing very well, Thea."

Thea smiled prettily and gently plied her fan. To an observer she appeared to be having a pleasant conversation with her hostess. "How long must I continue, Mrs. Ramsey? I find this playacting quite exhausting!"

"Until the end of the evening, Thea. Oh, here is someone you must talk to. Judge Denholm, you know Mrs. MacLonan, I believe? Her father is General Sir Frederick Tilton."

The judge nodded and Thea dimpled at him. "Oh course I know Judge Denholm. My father had great respect for the judge's integrity when he was stationed here as the commander of the English forces in Scotland."

As the hour was late and the one thing Denholm was not known for was his sobriety, he had evidently drunk enough for his inhibitions to have worn off. A great Scottish patriot, but a man of the law, he had never approved of the Pretender's attempt to regain the throne by using Scottish levies. Now he looked down at Thea with a mocking expression. "I've had visits from Grant MacLonan and Brendon Ramsey, so I should not be surprised that you are adding your voice to their pleas for your husband's release."

Thea's temper flared, but she kept her smile intact. Although only her eyes darted fire, Denholm smiled as he drank from a crystal wine glass. He had scored a hit with his barb and he knew it. Thea dropped her lids and when she opened her eyes wide again, her expression was innocent. Denholm smiled more widely. He was evidently enjoying himself.

"Of course you received visits from my father-by-marriage and from Mr. Ramsey," Thea said sweetly, deciding that the best way to handle Denholm was to turn his barb to her own advantage. "You are the most respected member of the Scottish judiciary and you are known to be completely fair in all legal matters. You were Mr. MacLonan's and Mr. Ramsey's first choice when they were considering who might help them free James from his unfair imprisonment."

Denholm swirled the rich, dark liquid in his glass in a contemplative way. Brandy, Thea thought, catching a whiff as he raised the glass to drink.

He looked at her over the rim of the goblet. "Why is his treatment unfair?"

"If any other gentleman had participated in a duel that was respectably arranged, over the matter of an insult to his wife, he would have been freed with a reprimand and nothing more."

Denholm didn't agree or disagree. "Apparently there was some concern that the English officer would die."

"That was in the first few days! Lieutenant Williams is now well on his way to being a trial to some other poor woman. He is driving his nurse to distraction with his demands and will soon be able to report for duty. What does Colonel Harris do when he learns of this? He orders my husband chained! I ask you, Judge Denholm, is that the action of a dispassionate commander, or a man whose pride has been scarred because the woman he wished to marry chose another?"

Denholm straightened. He looked down at the thistle and the oak intertwined in rich silver thread and then shot Thea a considering look. "Tell me more of this."

Careful to keep her elation hidden, Thea shrugged with elaborate carelessness. "Did you not know that Colonel Harris had asked me to marry him, not once but several times? No? Oh, I had thought everyone knew, for he was quite serious in his attentions to me. I refused him, gently, of course, but firmly. He would not give up, however. Even so, when I first met James and my interest in him was very clear, Colonel Harris deliberately tried to drive us apart. He very nearly succeeded, but fortunately James and I discovered that we had much in common." She shrugged again, then said earnestly, "Judge Denholm, I fear that Colonel Harris has allowed his emotions to overrule his good sense. He is not a bad man, but he is a jealous one. I believe James is the target of that jealousy."

Denholm drank his wine again. "You've given me much to consider, Mrs. MacLonan. Why did neither Ramsey or Grant MacLonan think to mention this to me?"

Thea opened her eyes innocently wide. "They would have no knowledge of it, sir. I do not brag of the conquests I have made, or the offers of marriage that have been given to me! I only mention it to you now because I fear it may have a material influence on the way my husband is being treated."

"Aye, it may have at that," Denholm said. He shot Thea a sharp, considering look. "You know the Pretender is loose somewhere in England, do you not?"

"I do," Thea said promptly. "That is the excuse that Colonel Harris has used to imprison James, but it is only an excuse, Judge Denholm." Very deliberately, she smoothed the rich, blue satin, drawing Denholm's eyes as she brushed her hand over the symbolic silver embroidery of thistle and oak. "You know my circumstances, who my father is and what my politics are. I can assure you that my husband has finished with Prince Charles Edward Stuart. If the Prince should happen to return to the Highlands, he would receive no help from Glenmuir. When James MacLonan married me, he made a choice and it was not for the Pretender."

"Perhaps." Denholm raised the glass, drained what remained, then peered inside. "Empty again," he said in a rather bemused voice. "Don't know what happens to the stuff. Must go and get another. Mrs. MacLonan, it has been a pleasure talking to you this evening. I wish you the best success in your campaign to free your husband."

He bowed and moved away. Olivia hurried over to Thea and whispered, "How did it go? Was he persuaded?"

"I think so," Thea said with a sigh. "It is hard to tell."

"Judge Denholm is far enough into his cups that he would have been quite blunt. If he did not believe your argument he would have said so."

Thea grimaced. "If he is that drunk, I hope he remembers what I have said in the morning."

"Oh, he'll be fine," Olivia said, waving Thea's protest aside. "He conducts all of his trials with a bottle of wine on his bench, yet he never loses control. I should think that tonight is quite normal for him."

"I hope so," Thea said with a sigh, even though she was smiling. She waved her fan as she glanced about the room. "Whom should we target next?"

"We will let them come to us. You are the focus of attention tonight, Thea," Olivia said with considerable satisfaction. "Everyone wants to speak to you, and those who have done so already are receiving quite a bit of attention themselves. Now, we will help matters out, of course, by drifting in the right direction. Do you see the woman in purple?"

"Lady Huntley?"

"An excellent target, don't you think?"

Thea laughed and shot Olivia a mischievous look.

There was a little stir in the crowd. Voices hushed then began to talk again, more loudly. Olivia frowned and turned. "What on earth is going on? I—" She stopped abruptly. "Oh, my."

"What is it?" Thea glanced to where Olivia was looking, and her heart skipped a beat. Colonel Harris had just entered the room.

"This is entirely unexpected," Olivia said furiously. "Colonel Harris was not invited tonight. I do not know why he has come, but I shall ask him to leave!"

"You can't do that, Mrs. Ramsey."

"Why not?"

"Because people would think that I am afraid to speak to him." Thea's eyes hardened. "When I am not."

"A confrontation between the two of you is what concerns

me," Olivia said, waving her fan energetically. "Why is he here? Do you think he heard that you were coming? I made no secret of it. I told everyone I invited that I had convinced you to end your self-imposed solitude. He must have heard. He must guess that you would do your best to use your influence to free James. He...he is coming this way! Thea, are you prepared? I know you said you were, but—Colonel Harris what a surprise. I do not remember issuing you a card for tonight's party. I did not think you were interested in music."

"I am not," Harris said, his eyes on Thea. He bowed and reached for her hand.

Thea drew it away at the last moment, leaving him kissing nothing but empty air. "Colonel Harris," she drawled. "I will not say that it is a pleasure to see you again. I trust you understand why."

Harris's hard eyes darkened as his mouth tightened. "Have you forgotten your roots, Mrs. MacLonan?"

Thea raised her brows. "On the contrary, Colonel. I am very well aware of who I am and who my father is and the respect that each of us is due from the officers and men of King George's Army."

Harris drew himself up. "I don't believe that your father can complain of any disrespect, Mrs. MacLonan."

"I am sure my father, were he here, would disagree, Colonel Harris. I certainly do. You apparently have not been able to instill in your men an understanding of how they should handle themselves when out on patrol. I am the victim of that improper behavior and I know that were my father in command in Edinburgh, the officer in question would have been punished. It is a pity that it was my husband who was left to do just that when you failed in your responsibilities."

Harris colored. "Dueling is illegal."

Thea waved her fan. "So is striking a woman who did nothing more than criticize the behavior of a certain officer. Or causing the death of another who did nothing wrong, but made the mistake of remaining in her home when English soldiers happened to march by."

"Is this true?" said a woman's voice nearby. "Did Williams kill somebody?"

Thea turned to the woman, her expression drawn. She was not playacting now. She was back in the damp, gray coolness of that early October afternoon watching Maggie MacLonan babble hysterically as Williams teased her with the tip of his sword. "Yes," Thea said in a low, shaking voice, "it is true. The woman had done nothing to warrant the treatment Lieutenant Williams gave her. Nothing! He stabbed her with his sword, and when it was done he rode away, too much of a coward to even have his men carry her to her croft."

"Appalling! " someone said.

"And you did nothing to punish the fellow, Harris?" This was a man's voice, raised indignantly.

Harris shot Thea an angry look and tried to bluster his way out of the corner. "I intended to, but Williams was on leave and I had planned to wait until he returned. Unfortunately, MacLonan was impatient and he found Williams. The duel—"

"Was correct in all ways," Brendon Ramsey interjected. "I was MacLonan's second and I made sure that all of the proprieties were followed."

"Williams was badly wounded," Harris said somewhat desperately. Most of those attending the party were gathered around by now, listening intently. They were the cream of Scottish society, members of parliament, wealthy merchants, lawyers, patriots. There was a mood of growing indignation amongst them.

The night had progressed better than could have been expected. In a few more minutes the anger in the room would build to the point where James's release would be demanded, here and now. Then Harris would find it impossible to refuse.

Grant MacLonan shot a fierce look at Harris. "What you say may have been true at one time, Colonel Harris, but Williams is healing well now and will soon be able to report for duty. What will you do then?"

In the silence that followed Thea held her breath, her gaze fixed on the colonel's face. He was flushed, and there was a dangerous glitter in his cold eyes. She sensed that he wanted to strike out, and she could only pray that James would not be his victim.

When Harris didn't respond, a strong voice with a marked English accent said firmly, "Colonel Harris will do as he should have done when the complaint was brought to him. He will bind Lieutenant Williams over for court-martial. If Williams is convicted, he will be stripped of his rank and punished by His Majesty's Army."

Everyone turned around to look at the owner of the voice, who was at the back of the room, near the door. Harris whitened, but Thea clapped her hands together. "Papa!"

CHAPTER 20

Thea pushed her way through the crowd to her father, who opened his arms wide to catch her.

Olivia Ramsey followed. "Sir Frederick, what a pleasant surprise." She smiled wryly. "It seems the King's officers have decided that my little gathering tonight is one social event that cannot be missed!"

Thea moved out of her father's arms so that he could respond to his hostess. He bowed politely. "I am just now arrived in Edinburgh, Mrs. Ramsey. I hope you will overlook my effrontery in coming uninvited, but I went to my daughter's home and found that she and Grant MacLonan were here this evening, and I wanted to greet them as soon as I was able."

"Of course you are welcome, Sir Frederick! Do come and join us."

"I do not think that is possible, ma'am, but thank you. I have some dispatches for Colonel Harris that should be acted upon this evening." He patted his coat pocket. "Since I have had the good fortune to find Colonel Harris here, I will beg your indulgence and ask for a moment or two to make the Colonel aware of his new orders. Then I think I will oversee their implementation, just to make sure they are correctly carried out."

"Orders," Harris said with a gulp. His complexion was now pasty white and his expression strained. He was still standing where he had been when the general arrived, but he could see and hear all that was being said, for a path had been opened between the two groups.

"Orders, Harris," Tilton said easily, advancing toward him. "My daughter relayed the story of Williams's conduct to me. I was outraged, but I was forced to wait for proof that a certain gentleman had been located on the Continent before I came north."

"The Pretender has been seen in Europe?" Harris blurted out.

Tilton stopped within inches of his subordinate, sighed, and shook his head. "Yes, Harris, he has. Now you have no further reason to keep James MacLonan in the Tolbooth."

At that point, Judge Denholm decided to add a little spice to the proceedings. "But Harris claims that James MacLonan is in prison because he was involved in a duel in which a man was almost killed. That is what Harris told all of us who protested MacLonan's incarceration."

Tilton shot Harris a look that had withered many a junior officer. Harris's eyes shifted away warily. "Colonel Harris mishandled a delicate situation. Although he had orders to keep the Highlands quiet while the Pretender was in England—"

"Bonnie Prince Charlie was in England?" cried an agitated woman's voice. "When? What is to be done?"

"Nothing, dear lady, for the Pretender has retired to the Continent. Now that Britain is safe from his foolish whims, our army may stand down. Harris, you will see that James MacLonan is released immediately."

"Now? In the middle of the night?"

"Can you think of a better time? I cannot."

"Tomorrow morning," Harris suggested recovering a bit of his poise.

"You are a spiteful man!" Thea said. "You would be very happy if my husband had to spend another night in that awful place, wouldn't you? Well, I won't have it! James should be freed immediately."

"I agree," said a voice, and then another. Soon the whole room was clamoring for James's release, and it appeared that they all intended to go to the prison en masse to see that it was done. Harris was pushed, not too gently, toward the door with the crowd following behind.

Caught up in the general elation, Thea hesitated. She remembered the conditions under which James was being kept, the filth and the vermin. He would not want Edinburgh society to see him dirty and unkempt. She tugged on her father's arm. "Papa, you must stop them! James has been imprisoned for weeks. He will want a bath and a shave before he sees anybody."

"A few must go—Denholm, Ramsey, MacLonan, and some others, but you are right, Thea." Tilton paused, then said, "You must wait too, daughter. I know you want to see James, but wait until he is home before you greet him. Do not go to the prison. Allow him to keep his pride."

Thea smiled grimly. "I have already been there, Papa, and you are right. James was not happy about it. Very well, I will return to Grant's house and wait." She bit her lip. "It will not be easy."

The wind blew hard down Edinburgh's streets as James MacLonan stepped through the heavy oaken door of the Tolbooth prison. He stopped abruptly, cursing silently. The wind whipped his dirty coat and torn waistcoat and shirt, but he didn't care. It was no colder outside than in the dank stone cell he had languished in these past weeks. What made him stop was the crowd of people who all seemed to be speaking at once. Moreover, they all seemed to be speaking to him.

He looked over at Harris, who had accompanied the turnkey to the cell. Harris had awakened James from his usual dream-haunted sleep with a gruff announcement that he was free and could leave the prison. James had sat rubbing his eyes, wondering if he was really awake or if this was simply another wishful dream. But the key Harris produced had screeched in the rusty locks of the rough iron manacles that bound his wrists and ankle in a way that was particularly realistic, so when the colonel walked stiffly out of the cell, James had followed. He'd kept his distance from the Englishman, however, letting the wavering candlelight guide him through the dark, soulless halls until he found himself standing outside the door, a prisoner no more.

Now he wished he'd taken the time to find out what had happened so that he could have been prepared for this celebration. The members of the boisterous group of men were anxious to shake his hand and tell him how glad they were that he was no longer incarcerated in the Tolbooth and how someone would have to pay for this outrage. James thought that highly unlikely, but he kept his opinion to himself.

He found his father in the crowd looking tired, but smiling. The other gentlemen stepped aside as he strode over to his parent. Or he imagined he strode. Actually, he shuffled, cursing his weakened muscles, which wouldn't do anything his mind ordered them to. He was able to embrace his father though. That, at least, he could do.

"Now," he said, smiling, his voice rusty from lack of use. He cleared his throat and tried again. "Now, tell me what is this all about? How did you convince Harris to free me?"

Grant laughed. "I didn't, Jamie." He glanced to one side. "Your father-by-marriage is to be thanked for that."

James looked past Grant, to the red-coated man standing a little apart from the rest. He straightened painfully, drawing himself to his full height. "General Tilton," he said slowly, drawing out the man's name, trying to decide how he felt about being rescued by an Englishman.

Tilton nodded. "I would have been here sooner, MacLonan, but your Prince would not cooperate—"

"Not my Prince!"

Tilton smiled. "I'm glad to hear that, James, although it makes no difference now. The Pretender has returned to the Continent, where he is busy annoying the crowned heads of Europe and driving his father even deeper into despair with his antics. He's not our problem anymore."

"Was he ever?"

A rueful expression crossed the general's face. Then he shrugged. "There were those who thought he was. It seems our ambassadors to Europe's courts spend half their time tracking his whereabouts. The King's ministers here in Britain feel it is necessary to know what he is up to, even if they can't be sure where he is."

"So, General Tilton, the Prince turns up in Europe and you decide I can be released from prison. Am I supposed to thank you?"

"James..." his father growled.

"Here now," huffed Harris indignantly, "That is no way to speak to Sir Frederick—"

"Let the man talk," Judge Denholm said cheerfully. "He's a right to ask his questions. Not only that, but I'm interested, too. As I said before, Harris here had Mr. MacLonan put into the Tolbooth because he stabbed a man, not because he was suspected of being a Jacobite sympathizer." Denholm produced a flask from his pocket and took a drink. "In fact, that was the only way he could have done it. Sympathizing with an out-of-favor prince isn't a crime as far as I know. Following one in rebellion is, but sympathizing isn't."

Tilton said quietly, "Harris had orders to keep the Highlands secure while the Pretender was about his silly game of hide-and-seek. He was in command here and how he chose to keep Scotland quiet was at his discretion. Even if I had rushed north demanding your release, James, he had every right to refuse me. I needed the ultimate weapon—the whereabouts of Bonnie Prince Charlie—before I could be certain that my interference would do any good."

The military man in James couldn't fault Tilton's strategy. Don't waste limited resources on the futile storming of a heavily defended position. Wait until you have the weaponry to take it quickly and cleanly. James thought it was very possible that he would still be languishing in that dungeon now if the general hadn't used his good sense and waited. James only wished it hadn't taken Tilton quite so long.

Brendon Ramsey stirred uneasily. "You still haven't answered Denholm's question, Sir Frederick. He's right.

James was in prison because of the duel. Is he still being held over for trial?"

Tilton looked at Harris. "I suggest you answer that, Colonel."

Harris cleared his throat and looked at the sky. "As you know, Lieutenant Williams is returning to health. I recently had a long conversation with the lieutenant regarding his actions at Glenmuir. At that time, I learned that the complaint against the lieutenant was indeed a valid one. Taking that, and the testimony by Mr. Ramsey here about the way the duel was conducted, into consideration, I believe it is unnecessary to charge Mr. MacLonan with assault. He is free to go."

Judge Denholm made a sound between a snort and a laugh, then took another drink from his flask. James shook his head. It was an oddly unsettling conclusion to his stay in the Tolbooth.

He raised his face to the clear dark sky and felt the cold wind caress his skin. Images of Glenmuir stirred in his mind, images he had deliberately suppressed throughout his time in prison when he'd feared he would never be free to walk his beloved Highland hills again. Entwined with images of Glenmuir were visions of Thea laughing at hardship, cocking her head to one side as she flirted outrageously with him, gently encouraging his clansmen through one crisis or another, weeping because some troubles were beyond her ability to help. Thea, bruised and shaken by the run-in with Williams, her world rent apart because of one renegade officer. Thea, paling when he'd used the rough edge of his tongue on her when she visited him in prison.

He closed his eyes as shame washed over him. When the door had opened and Thea had walked into his tiny hell his heart had leapt at the sight of her. Then it had plummeted, for no better reason than his pride was hurting because she'd seen him dragged so low.

Opening his eyes, he focused on Tilton. "If the passes are still open, I intend to return to Glenmuir as soon as possible." His voice hardened. "Your daughter goes with me."

Tilton raised his brows. "Not my daughter, MacLonan. Your wife."

While the men went to the Tolbooth, Thea returned to Grant's house, where she had James's room aired, his bed warmed, a fire laid, and the bath set up before it, ready for him. She knew he would want to wash the Tolbooth filth from him as soon as possible, for she couldn't forget his comment about vermin. The cook was preparing a warming soup that would fill his stomach, but not overtax his system.

She was upstairs, fussing with the way his bedclothes had been folded down, when she heard a commotion at the front door. She rushed to the stairs and almost ran down them.

Her disappointment must have been visible when she saw it was only Grant MacLonan who had returned. He chuckled at her expression. "I came home in a chair, when Jamie decided to walk. He should be here soon, my dear."

Thea smiled a little shakily. "How is he, Grant?"

"Glad to be out and just as stubborn as ever." Again Grant chuckled as he dumped his cloak and hat into a waiting servant's arms. He rubbed his hands together. "'Tis a cold night out there. Is a fire laid in Jamie's room?"

"Of course. And a bath prepared, and his bed warmed."

Grant nodded. "Good. I'll send some brandy up. Come to think of it, perhaps I'll have a wee dram myself."

Thea laughed and Grant went off into the parlor. After she had told the servants to heat water for James's bath, she went upstairs again, this time to her room so she could check her gown and hair in the cheval mirror. Though she fussed with a few stray strands, there was little she could do to hide the lines of worry and fatigue on her face. She sighed, wishing James would see her again at her best. Then her spirit lightened. It didn't matter how she looked. James was free at last. That was what counted tonight.

She had reached the top of the stairs when the door opened once again. This time it was her father and her husband who entered. Thea's heart leapt. "James?"

He looked up at her, his face expressionless. "Thea."

Tilton looked from his daughter to his son-in-law, then leaned over and said something in James's ear that Thea couldn't hear. To Thea's complete surprise, James grinned, a ragged, lighthearted expression that eased the tension in his features. He looked up at Thea, the amusement still on his face. Tilton shot her a quick look too. Then he marched into the parlor and carefully shut the door behind him.

Swallowing hard, she started down the stairs. Now that the moment was here, she was suddenly frightened of the form this meeting would take. James watched her, saying nothing, helping her not at all. Nervously, she smoothed the blue silk of the evening gown she still wore. The fabric rustled as she moved, and the light from the chandelier hanging in the hallway flickered on the silver fabric and embroidery. She wondered if James had noticed the special significance of the intertwined thistle and oak then dismissed the idea. Though his eyes bored into her, she doubted he was noticing details such as the embroidery on her gown.

Two steps from the bottom she stopped. "I'm glad you are home, James."

He raised one dark brow. "Are you? I understand that you attended one of Olivia Ramsey's parties tonight."

Thea gasped. "I did, but—"

"Did you enjoy yourself, Thea?"

"I did not go to enjoy myself! I went to try to help free you!"

A smile flickered on his lips. "So I've been told."

Thea wasn't sure, but she thought that perhaps there was a hint of pleasure in her husband's voice. "James," she said firmly, as she descended to the bottom of the stairs, "I wanted nothing more than to have you freed from that dreadful place. I would have done anything to achieve that end. Anything."

Raising his brow again, he came toward her, then stopped a few feet away. "I am truly fortunate that anything was not necessary then."

Thea's temper flared and she took a step forward. James put out his hand. "Don't, Thea. I'm verminous."

In that instant, his words brought back memories of her visit to the Tolbooth. She paled, remembering his anger and her distress. James must have remembered, too, for he cursed and stepped back. "I must bathe, Thea, so I can—"

"Of course," she said brightly, stepping to one side so he could pass. "What am I thinking of! James, a bath has been prepared for you in your room. One of the servants will attend you. He has orders to burn your clothes."

"A wise move," James growled. He paused at the bottom of the stairs. "Thea, when I'm done, come up."

"I shall bring up some food for you," she promised.

"That's not what I mean. I—"

"You are tired. I understand."

James sighed. Amusement quirked his mouth again. "Stubborn woman."

Temper flared in Thea's eyes and she curtsied. The blue silk pooled about her, making the entwined thistle and oak stand out clearly. "Have your servant tell mine when you are ready. I will be in my chamber."

James laughed. "I see we truly are fashionably wed, sleeping in separate bedrooms and communicating through servants."

Thea whitened. She reached out her hand. "James…"

He shook his head. "Not now, Thea. Not yet."

Thea watched as he walked slowly up the stairs with the same careful deliberation that she had seen his father use. Realizing how weak he must be, she shook her head, angry at herself for forgetting that he was just now out of prison. He could not be expected to deal with her swings of emotion. Not now, not yet. Still, when he had disappeared into his room, she sank down on the bottom step and sobbed.

That was how Grant MacLonan and her father found her a few minutes later. The two men fussed over her with concern, then called her maid and told the servant to take Thea up to her room and put her to bed.

Thea allowed the girl to remove the gorgeous blue gown and clothe her in a simple linen bed gown and quilted wrapper. Then Thea settled before the fire while the powder was brushed out of her hair. As the girl chattered about how excited the servants were that young Mr. MacLonan was home again, Thea listened with only half her attention, for she was waiting for a knock on her door.

When it came, the servant was apologetic. "Mr. James is finished, lady, but..."

"But?" Thea coaxed, when the man stopped.

"Well, he's...he's gone to sleep, lady. After he'd stepped out of the bath I shaved him, and after I put away my razor, I turned and there he was, stretched out on the bed naked, lady. He hadn't even put on his nightshirt."

"Mr. MacLonan needs food more than sleep," she said briskly. "I've had some broth prepared for him. Go and bring a bowl up from the kitchens." She turned to the maidservant. "I have some ointment that is excellent for soothing wounds. Bring it, and some bandages, to Mr. James's chamber."

Thea swept out of the room with the two servants following. On reaching James's room, she had to smile, for she found her husband on his back, sprawled across the bed, using every possible inch of it for his comfort. When she sat down on the edge, he opened one eye and said drowsily, "Not now, Thea."

"I know," she replied softly. "James, your servant is bringing you some food. In the meantime, I want to check your wrists. I have some salve to put on them."

"No!"

"Yes." She signaled the maid that she could go, then examined the wounds. His skin was red and raw where the heavy iron bonds had chaffed it. She rubbed the ointment on gently, hating Harris, the Pretender, and Lieutenant Williams, then wrapped a clean bandage around the area. When she was done, she checked his ankles, eased them, then examined the new red scar across his chest, caused by Williams's sword. Even though it had healed in the poor conditions of the Tolbooth, the wound had mended cleanly.

She glanced at James's face. His eyes were closed and he was breathing deeply. She bent and lightly kissed the scar.

He stirred. "Thea…"

"James, I—"

The manservant flung open the door, then brought in a tray containing a bowl of broth. "I brought the soup, lady, but are you sure it is enough? Mr. MacLonan expressed a desire for meat before his bath and—"

"It is fine. You may leave it beside the bed."

When he had gone, Thea fluffed up the pillows and James pushed himself up. Leaning against the headboard, he eyed his wife with some amusement. "I did ask for meat, you know."

Thea colored. "James, I sent good food to you every day, though I believe you received little of it."

"Unfortunately, true. "

"Then your body will not be ready for a heavy meal. Eat the broth. Tomorrow you can have something more substantial."

"I hate broth," he observed.

"You also told me you didn't want me to tend your wounds, but I did." She held a spoon up to his mouth. "And you felt better afterward, did you not?"

He took the soup, letting her feed him as if he were a child. "I do not have the strength to fight you."

"Then do not."

"Or the desire," he added with a sigh. When he had finished, he slipped back down in the bed and let Thea fuss with his pillows and the covers.

When she was satisfied he would be comfortable, she straightened. "I should make you put on a nightshirt, but I will not. Sleep well, James. We can talk in the morning."

Rolling onto his side, he moved into the middle of the bed, then lifted the bedcovers. "Thea, stay with me. Come to bed."

She hesitated. "James, you need to rest."

"I am not an invalid!" He added more calmly, "I will sleep

much more soundly with you in my arms."

Still, she hesitated. He gave her a lighthearted grin and patted the sheets. Thea couldn't resist. She slipped into the bed and curled into his arms.

"I missed holding you like this," he said, drawing his hand down her side in a caress that was like ambrosia to Thea. "There were nights when I reached out for you, but you weren't there. I had nightmares that you had decided that life with a crude Highlander was more than you could bear and you had gone back to England."

"James—"

He put his finger over her lips. "Shhh. I want to finish, Thea. I want to finish because I want you to know how I feel, now and forever. When you came to the prison I was both overjoyed and furious. The sight of you was enough to give me the strength to endure whatever I had to, but I hated that you had seen me that way, chained like a mad dog and as filthy as a wallowing pig. I set out from Glenmuir to avenge you, and what did I do but cause you more grief."

She stroked his smooth cheek. Then she leaned forward and kissed him. "You did what Harris should have done," she said a long minute later. "You were a victim of the man's incompetence as much as I was of Williams's violence."

"Thea," he murmured, "I should not have said some of the things I did in the Tolbooth. Forgive me?"

A tear trickled down her cheek though she laughed shakily. "Tell me truly, James. Do you mind that you are married to an Englishwoman who is also a Whig?"

"When I saw your father standing outside the jail and discovered that he had been the one who was able to arrange my release, I realized that it is not race or political beliefs that make the strongest bonds, but love, respect, and blood. You have had my respect since we first traveled to Glenmuir, Thea, and sometime during the summer you also gained my love."

"And soon," she whispered, "our blood will be joined in the child we have made together."

James sat up. "What did you say?"

Thea looked up at him mischievously. "Are you surprised, James? Good, I had hoped you would be."

"Thea, you aren't teasing me? You are with child?"

She nodded, smiling and laughing.

"But that is marvelous! Tell me everything! When will he arrive? How long have you known? How do you feel?"

Still laughing, she pulled her husband back down. "I feel fine now. I did feel a little nauseous at first, but now that has passed and I am ravenous all the time." She hesitated, then said, "I was sure on the day that Williams killed Maggie MacLonan. I was going to tell you that evening. What happened to Maggie drove my own happy news from my head. Then afterward I wasn't thinking sensibly. There just never seemed to be a moment when the time was right."

He groaned and buried his head in the curve of her neck. "Oh, Thea. I was so obsessed with revenge that I forgot about you."

"I never thought you would be forced to spend more than three weeks in prison. Then, when Colonel Harris started talking about transportation, I feared that you would be exiled again, this time because of me. I could not bear that."

He did not reply immediately. Then he tangled his fingers in her hair and said huskily, "I would have taken you with me, Thea. If you were willing to go."

"I would follow you anywhere, James."

"Even back to Glenmuir with all of its painful memories?"

"Glenmuir is my home, James, but only because you are there."

"Do you mean a fine English lady like you would be willing to spend the rest of her life in a rough Highland castle?" He was joking, but there was still a question in his voice that needed an answer.

"Not an English lady, James, but the wife of a Highland chief and so a Scot by choice and proud of it."

He gathered her close. "You are my heart, Theadora Tilton MacLonan. Without you Glenmuir is as much a place of exile as France was. Stay with me always."

"Always, James. You have my word."

His eyes laughed at her. "The word of an Englishwoman?"

"The word of your wife who loves you beyond reason."

Drawing her close, he sealed her promise with a kiss that was itself a promise of a love that would grow and endure throughout their lives.

Turn the page for an

excerpt from

LOVER'S
KNOT

The Hearts of Rebellion Series
Book Two

Louise Clark

Excitement shivered through Alysa. This was a proposal of marriage, no matter how obliquely Philip had couched it. "I understand, Philip, of course I do! Papa has too many immediate problems to concern himself with my future."

Philip squeezed her hand, before gently removing his. "If he gave his permission for us to marry, Alysa, how would you feel?"

The excitement returned, stronger than before. Alysa laughed and cupped his face in her hands. "You have to ask?"

"Yes," he said seriously, but he was smiling at her jubilation.

"I did not think I would ever find a man who could move me as you do, Philip." Her eyes and voice had become as serious as his. Her hands remained warm on his face. "In many ways you are a mystery to me and yet I trust you implicitly. From the beginning you intrigued me, even when no one in my family was sure whether you were a Roundhead spy or a loyal Royalist—What is it?"

Philip's expression had tightened forbiddingly. He caught her wrists and pulled her hands away from his face. "You thought I was a Roundhead spy?"

Relief flooded over Alysa, drowning her momentary dismay. She told herself that it was good that they were finally having this conversation, for doubt had hovered between them for too long. "The question did come up from time to time. You must remember, Philip, that you were a stranger here. Old Sir Richard Hampton rarely spoke about his two nephews and no one had seen you in years. With the country in confusion after the death of Oliver Cromwell, those loyal to the king were hopeful that a rebellion would finally bring him home for good. We were very aware that we could not afford to have an agent of the Protectorate in our midst."

Grimly, Philip said, "What made you decide that I was what I appeared to be?"

"Time," Alysa said simply. "When you seemed attracted to me, I offered to encourage your advances so that I could get to know you better. Papa was reluctant at first, but eventually he agreed to my plan." The expression on Philip's face was still and dangerous. Alysa hurried on, determined to complete her confession and get the worst behind them. "As you courted me, I learned that you were a man of honor, as well as one I could respect. I told Papa that I did not believe that you would seek to harm our family, and I believed it, then and now."

She gazed up into his fathomless brown eyes, pledging him her trust and promising her love. His eyes searched her face, probing the depth of her honesty, but his own expression was unreadable. After a moment he pulled away to stare unseeing across the broad green lawns. "You shouldn't have done that, Alysa."

She touched him tentatively on the shoulder. "Are you telling me that you are not the Royalist brother, Philip? That my family should be wary of you? That you are the spy who has been plaguing West Easton?"

He drew a deep breath and let it out again forcefully. "No. I am not the spy who almost cost your brother his freedom. You must look to your own ranks for that. But I am not what you imagine me to be, Alysa. I am a simple soldier who has retired from active duty, nothing more. Do not make me into what I am not."

Her grip on his shoulder firmed and she turned him toward her. "What I see in you, Philip, I have not imagined. We are all more than we think we are or can be. I know that if the time came for you to make a decision, you would make the right one. I know it!"

Taking both her hands in his, Philip rubbed the soft skin with his thumb as he gazed deep into her eyes. The movement had a slow, seductive rhythm to it that hypnotized Alysa. "By whose definition of what is right?"

She smiled up at him, her eyes trusting. "By yours, dear sir. For I know that your definition and mine are the same."

LOVER'S KNOTT

available in print and ebook

THE
HEARTS OF REBELLION
SERIES

Pretender's Game
Lover's Knot
Dangerous Desires

Louise Clark is the author of both contemporary and historical romance novels. These two genres are combined in Fighting Fate, a time travel story set in contemporary Boston with an 18th century time traveler who comes forward into his future, and Ridgeway, a historical time travel that takes place in post-Civil War North America. Ridgeway is available as part of the seven book time travel boxed set, Swept Through Time. In 2014 she was a quarter finalist in the Amazon Breakthrough Novel Award contest.

In addition to working on new material, she is also republishing her out-of-print titles—Dangerous Desires, Lover's Knot and Pretender's Games—in e and print format. Louise holds a BA in History from Queen's University and a Master of Publishing degree from Simon Fraser University. Her books have been published in fifteen countries worldwide.

For more information please visit her at
www.louiseclarkauthor.com
www.facebook.com/LouiseClarkAuthor.

www.ingramcontent.com/pod-product-compliance
Lightning Source LLC
Chambersburg PA
CBHW020539020726
47494CB00006B/1836